Sweet Salt Air

Also by Barbara Delinsky

Escape

Not My Daughter

While My Sister Sleeps

The Secret Between Us

Family Tree

Flirting With Pete

The Woman Next Door

Coast Road

Three Wishes

For My Daughters

More Than Friends

Visit www.barbaradelinsky.com
for a complete list of titles.

Sweet Salt Air

BARBARA DELINSKY

St. Martin's Griffin ⚌ New York

SWEET SALT AIR. Copyright © 2013 by Barbara Delinsky. All rights reserved. Printed in the United States of America. For information, address St. Martin's Press, 175 Fifth Avenue, New York, N.Y. 10010.

www.stmartins.com

The Library of Congress has cataloged the hardcover edition as follows:

Delinsky, Barbara.
    Sweet salt air / Barbara Delinsky. — First edition.
        p. cm.
    ISBN 978-1-250-00703-2 (hardcover)
    ISBN 978-1-250-02038-3 (e-book)
    1. Female friendship—Fiction.   2. Secrets—Fiction.   3. Life change events—
Fiction.   I. Title.
    PS3554.E4427S94 2013b
    813'.54—dc23

                                                                              2013004041

ISBN 978-1-250-00705-6 (trade paperback)

St. Martin's Griffin books may be purchased for educational, business, or promotional use. For information on bulk purchases, please contact Macmillan Corporate and Premium Sales Department at 1-800-221-7945, extension 5442, or write specialmarkets@macmillan.com.

First St. Martin's Griffin Edition: June 2014

10 9 8 7 6 5 4 3 2 1

For Eve, a garden filled with magical flowers,
herbs, and a fawn

Sweet Salt Air

Prologue

CHARLOTTE EVANS WAS USED TO feeling grungy. As a freelancer, she traveled on a shoestring, getting stories other writers did not, precisely because she wasn't fussy about how she lived. In the last twelve months, she had survived dust while writing about elephant keepers in Kenya, ice while writing about the spirit bear of British Columbia, and flies while writing about a family of nomads in India.

She could certainly survive a *mizzling,* as the Irish called it, though the heavy mist seeped through everything—jeans, boots, even the thick fisherman's sweater she wore. The sweater was on loan from the woman under whose roof she was sleeping on this least populated of the three Aran Islands, and though Charlotte did have a fireplace in her bedroom, hot water was in short supply in the small stone cottage. She could have used a steamy shower, a thorough washing of her clothes, and a solid day of sun.

Her assignment was to write about the youngest generation of Inishmaan knitters, women who were adapting traditional patterns in breathtaking ways, and as with the pattern on her own sweater, she could now describe moss stitch, panel repeats, right and left twists, and cable designs. It was time to leave. She had to go home to put the story together and get it to *Vogue Knitting,* before heading to the Australian outback to do a piece on aborigine jewelry-making for *National Geographic,* a coup that one. Still, she stayed here.

Part of what kept her was the woman who owned the house, as warm and motherly as any she had ever met; part was the craft that permeated the place. No knitter herself, she could watch these women for hours. They were at peace with themselves and their world, enviable for Charlotte, who had no roots at all. So close to her age that they might have been schoolmates, they were trying to teach her to knit. She told herself this was cause enough to stay.

Bottom line, though, it was the island that kept her here. She had loved islands from the time she spent her first summer on one. She was eight at the time. Thirty-four now, she still felt the island aura—an isolation that made worries seem distant, a separation from the real world that lent itself to dreams.

Her eyes went to the horizon, or where the horizon would have been if the mist weren't so dense. *Thick o' fog* they called it in that other place, and it lent a sheen to her skin and a bulk to her hair here as it did there. She pulled those dark curls back now, fingers lost in the damp mass, and turned just enough on the scruffy cliff to face a few latitudinal degrees south.

There, on the far side of the Atlantic, would be Maine, but despite the shared ocean, her island and this one were worlds apart. Where Inishmaan was gray and brown, its fragile man-made soil supporting only the hardiest of low-growing plants, the fertile Quinnipeague invited tall pines in droves, not to mention vegetables, flowers, and improbable, irrepressible herbs. Lifting her head, eyes closed now, she breathed in the damp Irish air and the bit of wood smoke that drifted on the cold ocean wind. Quinnipeague smelled of wood smoke, too, since early mornings there could be chilly, even in summer. But the wood smoke would clear by noon, giving way to the smell of lavender, balsam, and grass. If the winds were from the west, there would be fry smells from the Chowder House; if from the south, the earthiness of the clam flats; if from the northeast, the purity of sweet salt air.

Oh yes, across the Atlantic would be Maine, she mused, as she opened her eyes and tried to penetrate that great distance through the fog, and this being April, she would think of it regardless of where she was. That was ingrained. Spring was when she started to plan her Quinnipeague summer.

Or used to. But no more. She had burned that bridge ten years ago with one stupid act. She couldn't go back, though she wished it sometimes. She missed the spirit of summer on Quinnipeague, so much more intense for being apart from the rest of the world. She missed Quinnie lobster rolls, which tasted better than lobster rolls anywhere else. Mostly, she missed Nicole, who had been as close as a sister to her once. She had never found another like her, though Lord knew she had searched.

Perhaps that was what staying on Inishmaan was about. The women here could be friends. They understood independence and self-sufficiency. Charlotte had felt such instant rapport with several that she sensed they would keep in touch.

Would? Maybe.

More likely not, the realist in Charlotte admitted. For all the writing she did for a living, she was a lousy correspondent. Within a day or two, she would leave Inishmaan behind and return to Brooklyn, and from there? In addition to Australia, she had go-aheads to do stories in Tuscany and Bordeaux, the appeal of the latter being the lure of Paris before and after. She had friends there—a writer, a ceramist, and a would-be fashion designer whose clothes were too bizarre for mass appeal but whose personal warmth was winning.

Would it be the same as Quinnipeague time? No.

But this was the life she had made.

Nicole Carlysle lived in blissful ignorance of the past. She had enough to handle in the present, though no one knew it, and that was the problem. No one knew. No one *could* know, which meant no outlet, no emotional support, no badly needed advice. Julian was adamant about silence, and, because she loved him, she gave in. *She* was his lifeline, he said, and what woman didn't want to hear that? But the strain was awful. She would have gone out of her mind if it hadn't been for the blog. Whether she was writing to tell her followers about a local cheesemaker, a new farm-to-table restaurant, or what to do with an exotic heirloom fruit that was organically produced and newly marketed, she spent hours each day scouring Philadelphia and the outlying towns for material. As spring took hold, the local offerings were growing.

On a different mission now, though, she sat in front of an iMac in Julian's study. There was no view of the Schuylkill from this room, as there was from most of their eighteenth-floor condo. There were no windows here at all, simply walls of mahogany shelves that held medical books Julian had either inherited from his father or collected before publications had gone digital. Nicole owned shelves here, too, though fewer in number. Hers were filled with the novels she couldn't part with, and books about entertaining that were both resource and inspiration.

Organized as she was, the papers to the left of the computer—jottings, printouts of fan comments, and endorsement requests from vendors—were neatly arranged. Her camera sat behind them, hooked to a USB port, and, in a ceramic bowl on the computer's right, lay the newly photographed subject of her upcoming blog: a head of purple cauliflower, still cupped by the veined green leaves within which it had grown. A leather sofa, with a matching side chair and ottoman, filled the room with the smell of lemon oil and age.

But that smell wasn't foremost in her mind as she read what she had already typed. "I go to farmers' markets all the time. Field-to-table is so my thing. But none of the herbs at any of them comes close to island herbs. Those herbs *make* Quinnie food—well, those herbs and freshness. Quinnipeague was growing organic and cooking local before farm-to-table was a movement, but, still, we think of the herbs first. I can't write about island cooking without talking about them, but I can't not talk about the people, either. That's where you come in, Charlotte. You've eaten Dorey Jewett's lobster stew and Mary Landry's clam fritters, and you always loved the fruit compote that Bonnie Stroud brought to the Fourth of July dinner each year. These people are all still around. Each has a story. I want to include some in the book, but I'm better at writing about food than people. You write about people. And you're so good at it, Charlotte. I google you all the time. Your name shows up in the best of the *best* travel magazines."

She paused, thinking about those pieces as she studied the mirror of her own eyes in the gloss of the screen. Just then, they were sea-green with worry, wondering what the chances were that her friend would accept. Charlotte was big-time professional, certainly used to having her own byline. She would have to split the billing here, and Nicole's advance wasn't all that much. If the book sold well, there would be more, but for now all she could offer was a small stipend, plus room and board in one of the nicest homes on the island—plus reading and talking and hanging out, all that they used to do before life got in the way.

She typed in the thoughts, rewording once, then again. Finally, tired of parsing, she added a blunt, "I need you, Charlotte. A Quinnie cookbook won't be the same without your input. I know you're busy, but my deadline is the fifteenth of August, so it's not the entire summer, and you'll get stories of your own out of this. It'll be worth your while. I promise."

Her eyes rose above the computer screen to find Julian in the open doorway, and she felt a visceral flicker of warmth. It was like that whenever he caught her unaware—had been since the first time she'd laid eyes on him in a Starbucks in Baltimore twelve years before. Back then, as a new environmental studies graduate of Middlebury, she was getting her feet wet writing publicity pieces for a state agriculture organization. Hoping to work during her afternoon break, she had set down her grande-caramel-frappuccino-with-whip on a table without noticing much of her surroundings, until she opened her laptop and became aware of an identical one, identically opened and angled on the table beside hers. Having made the same observation seconds before, Julian had an amused smile waiting.

He was a surgeon, in town from Philadelphia for a seminar at Johns Hopkins, and he had a quiet strength. That strength had been sorely tested in the last four years and yet, seeing him in the doorway of the study, she still felt the pull. He wasn't a tall man, but his bearing had always been regal. It was no less so now, though regular workouts helped with that. His hair had grayed in the last year or two, but even after a full day at the hospital, he was a good-looking forty-six. Tired, always tired now. But good-looking.

Wearing a smile, he approached. "Doing a write-up of last night?" he asked. They had eaten at a new restaurant with friends, a working night out for Nicole, who had insisted that everyone order different dishes and evaluate each while she took notes.

By the time she shook her head no, he was facing her with a hip on the desk by the keyboard. "The cookbook, then," he said as his smile grew, knowing. "You always get that look when you think of Quinni-peague."

"Peaceful?" she acknowledged. "It's April. Two more months, and we're there. You're still coming with me, aren't you?"

"I told you I would."

"Willingly? It's an escape, Jules," she urged, momentarily serious. "It may be only for a week, but we need this." She recaptured lighter thoughts. "Remember the first time you ever came? Tell the truth. You were dreading it."

His brown eyes laughed warmly. "What wasn't to dread? A godforsaken island in the middle of the Atlantic—"

"It's only eleven miles out."

"Same difference. If it didn't have a hospital, it wasn't on my radar screen."

"You thought there'd be dirt roads and nothing to do."

He gave a wry chuckle. Between lobstering, clamming, and sailing, then movie nights at the church and mornings at the café, not to mention dinners at home, in town, or at the homes of friends, Nicole had kept him busy.

"You loved it," she dared.

"I did," he admitted. "It was perfect. A world away." His eyes saddened. "And yes, baby, we need this." Taking her face in his hands, he kissed her, but there was sadness in that, too. Hoping to banish it for a few more seconds—especially in the wake of the *baby* that always turned her on—she was reaching up when he took her hands, pressed them to his lips, then smoothly slid behind her. With his arms braced on either side, cheek to her hair, he read the words on the screen. "Ahh," he said with a sigh. "Charlotte."

"Yes. I really want her on board."

He angled away only enough to meet her eyes. "You don't need her, Nicki. You can do the cookbook yourself."

"I know that," she said as she had more than once. "But she's an accomplished writer, and she has a history on Quinnipeague, too. Add her people pieces to my food ones, and the book's that much better."

"She hasn't stepped foot on the island in ten years," he said in the measured way that spoke of knowledge. Oh, he was knowledgeable—a pioneer in his field, always savvy on a personal vein.

But Nicole wasn't deterred. "How better to lure her back? Besides, if you're gone after a week, and Mom won't be there, I want Charlotte."

He was quiet. Nicole heard the argument even before he said, "She hasn't been the best friend. She called your dad her surrogate father, but she didn't even make it to the funeral."

"She was in Nepal. She couldn't possibly get back in time. She did call. She was as upset as we were."

"Has she called again since?" he asked, though they both knew the answer to that.

"We e-mail."

"Often? No. And you're the one who initiates it. Her replies are short."

"She's busy."

He touched her cheek. "You haven't seen each other in ten years. You have different lives now. If you want to lure her back to recapture what you once had, you may be in for a fall."

"I miss her." When his expression grew guarded, she insisted, "No, it is not about that. I promised you. I will not tell her." She grew pleading. "But it's like all the stars are aligned, Jules. There's the cookbook, and your being in North Carolina for the month, and Mom not wanting to go to Quinnipeague and needing someone to pack up the place—like I want to do it? That'll be bad enough, but being *alone* there while you're away? This is the last summer I'll ever have at the house, and Charlotte is part of what that place means to me."

He was quiet. "You don't even know where she is."

"No one does. She's always on the go. That's why I e-mail. She'll get it wherever. And yes, she always answers." He was right about the brevity of her replies, though. Charlotte never shared much of her life now. And yet, from the first mention of this project, Nicole had pictured her taking part in it. Oh yes, Charlotte knew Quinnipeague. But she also knew Nicole, and Nicole needed to see her. She and Julian were going through a rough patch, tender moments like this one—once commonplace—now further between. A month at Duke training in-coming doctors in the technique for which he was known would be a much-needed distraction for him. And for her? Charlotte could distract her. The memories were good; she and Nicole had always been in sync. If there was any fun to be had this summer, Charlotte was her one great hope.

Julian tucked a long strand of hair behind her ear. His expression was aching—and Nicole might have reached for him again if he hadn't cupped her head. "I just don't want you hurt," he said and kissed her forehead. Then he held her back. "Do you think she'll accept?"

Nicole smiled, confident in this at least. "Absolutely. I don't care how much time has passed. She loves Quinnipeague. The temptation will be too great to resist."

Chapter One

QUINNIPEAGUE LAY ELEVEN MILES FROM the mainland. With a year-round population of nearly three hundred, it was serviced by a daily mail boat that carried groceries and a handful of passengers, but no cars. Since Charlotte had one of those for the first time in her life, she proudly booked the ferry, boarding in Rockland on a Tuesday, which was one of only three days each week when its captain cruised past Vinalhaven to islands like Quinnipeague. Nicole had offered airfare to speed up the trip, but Charlotte flew everywhere else in life. This summer was to be different.

The car was an old Jeep Wrangler, bought from a friend of a friend for a fraction of its original cost. Giddy with excitement, she stashed the soft top in back, and, as the warm June air flowed freely through windows and roof, drove up from New York herself. She welcomed the time it would take. After a frantic two months of work to free herself up, she wanted to slow down, decompress, and maybe, just maybe figure out why she had agreed to a last summer on Quinnipeague. She had sworn she wouldn't return, had sworn off painful memories.

But there were good memories as well, all of which had flooded back as she read Nicole's e-mail in Ireland that day. She replied instantly, promising to phone as soon as she returned to New York. And she had. Literally. Right there in baggage claim while waiting for her duffel to come through.

Of course, she would come, she had told Nicole, only afterward doing the reasoning. For starters, there was Bob. She hadn't gone to his funeral because she hadn't had the courage to face even a dead Bob after letting him down—letting them *all* down—so badly. So she owed Nicole for the funeral, and owed her for the betrayal.

But obligation wasn't the only reason she had accepted the invitation. Relief was another; Nicole herself had suggested the collaboration. And nostalgia; Charlotte missed those carefree summers. And loneliness; she spent her life with people, but none were family as Nicole had once been.

And then there was the book. She had never worked on a book, had never actually collaborated on anything, though it sounded like a piece of cake, having someone else run the show. When she thought about the people she would interview, Cecily Cole came to mind first. Talk about compelling characters. Cecily *was* island cooking in many regards, since her herbs were what made the food special. She had to be the centerpiece of the book. Talking with her would be fun.

Charlotte could use a little fun, a little rest, a little make-believe— and Quinnipeague was the place for that. Even now, as the ferry passed in and out of fog, reality came and went. *You can't go home again,* Thomas Wolfe had written, and she prayed he was wrong. She expected some awkwardness; ten years and very different lives later, she and Nicole couldn't just pick up where they'd left off. Moreover, if Nicole knew of her betrayal, all bets were off.

But if Nicole knew, she wouldn't have asked Charlotte to come. Nicole Carlysle didn't have a devious bone in her body.

Leaning out from the side railing, she caught a breath. There it *was*—

But no, just an ocean mirage quickly swallowed by the fog.

After moving past empty benches, she held tightly to the front rail.

Anticipation had built since leaving New York, accelerating in leaps after New Haven, then Boston. By the time she passed Portland, impatience had her regretting the decision to drive, but that changed once she left the highway at Brunswick and started up the coast. Bath, Wiscasset, Damariscotta—she loved the names as much as the occasional view of boats, seaside homes, roadside stands. FULL BELLY CLAMS one sign read, but she resisted. Clams served on Quinnipeague were dug from the flats hours before cooking, and the batter, which was exquisitely light, held bits of parsley and thyme. Other fried clams couldn't compare.

The ferry rose on a swell, but plowed steadily on. Though the air was cool and the wind sharpened by bits of spray, she couldn't get herself to go inside. She had put on a sweater over her jeans when the ferry left Rockland, and while she had also tied back her hair, loose tendrils blew free. They whipped behind her now as she kept her eyes on the sea. Some called North Atlantic waters cold and forbidding, but she had seen others. Turquoise, emerald, teal—none moved her as gray-blue did. Seventeen summers here had made it a visceral thing.

Her camera. She needed to capture this.

But no. She didn't want anything coming between her eyes and that first sighting.

Having relived it dozens of times in the preceding weeks, she thought she was prepared, but the thrill when the island finally emerged from the mist was something else. One by one, as the fog thinned, the features she remembered sharpened: jagged outcroppings of rock, a corona of trees, the Chowder House perched on granite and flanked by twin roads that swung wide for a gentle descent from town to pier, like symmetrical stairways in an elegant home.

That said, there was nothing elegant about Quinnipeague, with its rutted paths and weathered docks. But Quinnipeague wasn't meant to be elegant. It was meant to be authentic. Shutters were practical things to be closed in the fiercest of winds, and, when open, hung crooked more often than not. Wood was gray, clusters of buoys tacked to the side of the fishing shed were bright despite their chipping paint, and the gulls that swooped in to perch on tall pilings always left their chalky mark.

Sailboats grew distinct from power ones as the ferry neared. There were fewer lobster boats than Charlotte remembered, fewer lobstermen she had read, though those who remained would be out pulling traps this Tuesday, hence moorings with only dinghies attached.

Her pulse sped when she saw a figure running down the pier, and in that instant, the bad of the past blew right back out to sea. She waved frantically. *"Nicki! I'm here—here, Nicki!"*

Like there were other people on the ferry. Like Nicole could possibly miss her. Like Nicole could even *hear* her over the thrum of the boat and the slap of waves on pilings. But Charlotte couldn't help herself. She was a child again, having traveled alone from Virginia with her heart in her mouth and here, finally, so relieved to have reached the right place. She was a teenager, a seasoned flier now from Texas, electrified by the sight of her best friend. She was a college student who had taken the bus up from New Haven to summer with a family that wanted to hear about her courses, her friends, her dreams.

For all the places she'd been in the ten years since that wedding summer, no one had ever been waiting for her.

In that moment, seeing Nicole bubbling with excitement on the pier, her own relief was so great that she forgave her the timidity, the docility, the sheer agreeableness that had made her such easy prey for betrayal—traits Charlotte had seized on over the years to forgive her own behavior.

But this was a new day. The hovering fog couldn't dull the reds and blues of the boats. Nor could the smell of seaweed overpower that of the Chowder House grill. Bobbing on her toes, she clutched her hands at her mouth to contain herself, while with agonizing precision and a grinding of gears, the ferry slowed and began to turn. She moved along the side to keep the pier front and center in her sight.

Beautiful Nicole. That hadn't changed. Always petite, she looked positively willowy standing there on the pier. Always stylish, she was even more so now in her skinny jeans and leather jacket. The wind whipped her scarf, which likely cost more than Charlotte's entire summer wardrobe—the latter being vintage L. L. Bean, emphasis on *vintage*, having traveled with Charlotte for years. Style had never been in her lexicon. The closest she came to it now were her flats, bought three years before at an open-air market in Paris.

Chug by chug, the ferry backed its snub stern to the end of the dock. The instant the captain released the chains and lowered the ramp, Charlotte was off and running. Throwing her arms around Nicole, she cried, "You are the best sight ever! You look amazing!"

"And *you*," Nicole cried back, clinging tightly. Her body shook. She was crying.

Charlotte might have cried, too, her throat was that tight. Ten years and such different lives, yet Nicole was as excited as she was. Grasping at everything that had been so right about their summers together, she just held on, swaying for another few seconds until Nicole laughed through her tears and drew back. Running her fingers under her eyes, she explored Charlotte's face. "You have not changed a bit," she declared in the voice Charlotte remembered—high, not quite childlike but close. "And I still love your hair."

"It's the same old mess, but I love yours. You *cut* it."

"Just last month, finally. I mean, I may still sound like I did when I was ten, but I wanted to *look* like an adult at least." Blond and straight, her hair had always fallen to midback. Cut now in a wedge, it was shaped neatly around her face in a way that gave focus to the green of her eyes, which were luminous with lingering tears and suddenly anxious. "Was the trip okay?"

"It was fine—"

"But it was long, and you're not used to driving—"

"Which was why I wanted to do it, and it was good, it really was— and for the record, Nicki, you always looked gorgeous, but this cut is very, very cool." By comparison, Charlotte might have felt unsophisticated, if she hadn't known that women paid big bucks for hair like hers, and as for her voice, which was neither high nor distinct, it got her where she needed to be.

Nicole was eyeing her shoes. "*Love* those. Paris?"

Charlotte grinned. "Absolutely."

"And your sweater? Not Paris, but fabulous. So *authentic*." Her voice grew urgent. "Where did you get it? I need one."

"Sorry, sweetie. It's a hand-me-down from a woman in Ireland."

"*So* perfect for this place. It's been a dismal, cloudy June. I should have warned you, but I was afraid you wouldn't come."

"I've survived dismal and cloudy before." She glanced up the hill. "The island looks just the same." Past the Chowder House were the general store left and the post office right, both buildings long and low so as not to tempt the wind. "Like nothing's changed."

"Little has. But we do have Wi-Fi at the house. Got it set up last week."

"For just us two?" she asked to be sure. Nicole had initially told her that Julian would be up with her the week before, but was planning to leave before Charlotte arrived. If he had decided to stay on, it would change the tenor of her visit, putting the fragility of her relationship with Nicole front and center.

But Nicole was all cool confidence. "Hey. We deserve it. Besides, if I don't keep blogging, people will lose interest and wander away, and then there won't be as many to hear me when I start pitching our book—which I feel a hundred percent better doing now that you've agreed to help. Thank you, Charlotte," she said earnestly. "I know you have more important things to do."

Charlotte might have insisted that this was as important a project as she'd done in a while, if a gruff call hadn't cut off the thought.

"Hellooo." The ferry captain shot a thumb at her Jeep. "Gonna get it off?"

"Oh." She laughed. "Sorry." Releasing Nicole, she ran back onto the ferry and slid behind the wheel. By the time she revved the engine, Nicole was in the passenger's seat, sliding a hand over the timeworn dashboard. "I am paying you for this."

Charlotte shot her a startled look and inched forward. "For this car? You are not."

"You wouldn't have bought it if it weren't for my book, and you won't take money for that."

"Because it's *your* book. I'm just along for the ride." She laughed at her own words. "Can you believe, this is the first car I've ever owned?" She eased it onto the dock. "Is it real or what?"

"*Totally* real," Nicole said, though momentarily wary. "Safe on the highway?"

"It got me here." Charlotte waved at the captain. "Thank you!" Still crawling along, she drove carefully off the pier. When she was on firm ground, she stopped, angled sideways in the seat, and addressed the first of the ghosts. "I'm sorry about your dad, Nicki. I wanted to be there. I just couldn't."

Seeming suddenly older, Nicole smiled sadly. "You were probably better off. There were people all over the place. I didn't have time to think."

"A heart attack?"

"Massive."

"No history of heart problems?"

"None."

"That's scary. How's Angie?" Nicole's mother. Charlotte had phoned her, too, and though Angie had said all the right words—*Yes, a tragedy, he loved you, too, you're a darling to call*—she had sounded distracted.

"Bad," Nicole confirmed. "They were so in love. And he loved Quinnipeague. His parents bought the house when he was little. He actually proposed to Mom here. They always said that if I'd been a boy, they'd have named me Quinn. She can't bear to come now. That's why she's selling. She can't even come to pack up. This place was so him."

"Woo-hoo," came a holler that instantly lifted the mood. "Look who's here!" A stocky woman, whose apron covered a T-shirt and shorts, was trotting down the stairs from the lower deck of the Chowder House. Dorey Jewett had taken over from her father midway through Charlotte's summers here and had brought the place up to par with the best of city restaurants. She had the gleaming skin of one who worked over steam, but the creases by her eyes, as much from smiling as from squinting over the harbor, suggested she was nearing sixty. "Missy here said you were coming, but just look at you. All grown up."

A lifelong Mainer, she talked the part. Loving that, Charlotte laughed. "I was twenty-four when I was here last, no child then."

"But *look* at you. That's some sweater!" The sheer ebullience of the woman made Charlotte laugh again. "And Missy? Well, I've seen her these last years, but I tell you, the two a' you put the rest of us to shame." Her brows went up. "You hungry? Chowder's hot."

Chowdah, Charlotte thought happily. It was late afternoon, and she was starved. But Nicole loved to cook, and Nicole was calling the shots.

Leaning across the stick shift, Nicole told Dorey, "To go, please, with corn bread and fiddleheads."

"You'll be taking the last a' those," Dorey confided. "I had a vendor try to convince me to shrink-wrap and freeze, but they're never the same. I only have 'em now because they're from up north"—*nauth*—"and the growing season was late this year. They'd have been gone a week ago, if business hadn't been slow, but the price a' gas is so high, and no one's out day-cruisin' anyways when the wind's so mean. Think you can tough out the chill?" she asked, seeming impervious to it herself with her bare arms and legs.

But Charlotte was still focused on hunger. "Maybe a couple of clams, too?"

"You got 'em. Drive up top. I'll bring 'em out."

Chapter Two

THE ISLAND WAS LONG AND narrow, undulating on the surface of the ocean like a kind and gentle cobra. Its broad head, which faced the mainland, was raised to support the center of town. Once a fishing village, its narrow streets remained home to a handful of lobstermen and clammers, though most of the property was now owned by the locals that serviced newer residents. The latter, whose homes descended along the neck, included artists, businessmen, and computer programmers, all drawn to the island for its peace.

Beyond the neck was the body of Quinnipeague, accessed by a single sinuous road that slithered past mud flats, sheltered beaches, and rock ledges. The dirt drives leading to summer homes were marked by mailboxes that, come July, would be nearly hidden by wild roses and geraniums.

Nicole's house was second to last, a full seven miles from the pier and two shy of the tip of the tail. Though less ostentatious than some of the newer homes that had been built since Charlotte had visited last, it was a grand white house, two stories high with a widow's walk, black shutters, wide porches, and arms skimming the ground on either side.

Those arms held guest rooms that had, on occasions like Nicole's wedding, slept twenty.

The main house was for family. Bedrooms here were on the second floor to optimize their view, while the first floor, originally broken by doorways and walls, had been reconfigured into two large rooms, one for eating, one for living. Both opened to a wide patio that led to the sea.

Whereas life in the kitchen revolved around a trestle table of pickled oak, the Great Room was furnished to take advantage of the fireplace, which was floor-to-ceiling native stone. This was where Charlotte and Nicole now ate, sitting side by side on the floor at a huge square coffee table. Nicole had insisted on setting beautiful places, arranging their food just so, and photographing it before they started, but the camera was set aside now and the napkins unfolded.

Those napkins picked up the colors of the sofas, throw pillows, and rugs—all vibrant blues and greens that were lush against the fog outside. The logs on the grate had caught; while the heat slowly built, the chowder picked up the slack. Nicole's jacket was gone, the scarf loosely looped on her silk shirt. Likewise, Charlotte had tossed her sweater aside.

Conversation was sparse, since Charlotte could do little but moan in delight at the food. At one point, after swallowing the juiciest clam belly she'd ever had, she laughed. "How can anything taste this good?"

Having dispensed with a spoon, her elegant friend was drinking the last of her chowder straight from the bowl. She finished, put it down, and wiped her mouth. "Dorey says the key to chowder is letting the ingredients cure in the pot for a day before dishing it up, which is counterintuitive since fried clams are best right after they're dug. Personally, I think it's the chives in the chowder." Pensive, she studied her empty bowl. "Or the bacon. Or the parsley." Her eyes rose. "Maybe it's just the butter. Since Dorey's chowder is Maine style, more milk than cream, the butter shines."

Charlotte took a simpler approach. "Maybe it's just that we haven't had Dorey's chowder in so long," she said, but Nicole gave a quick headshake.

"I had it two nights ago. I have it all summer long, and it's as good in August as it is in June."

"Then you still come for the whole summer?" Charlotte asked in surprise. She had always gotten an e-mail or two from Quinnipeague—quick little holiday greetings or thinking-of-you notes—but had assumed Nicole's visits shortened after the wedding. Julian certainly couldn't be gone from the hospital for three months.

"I actually do. I started coming up with the kids"—there were two from his first marriage—"because what else were preteens going to do in Philly, and this place was perfect for them. That kind of set the pattern. When they got older and had jobs at home, I kept coming. Julian comes weekends or sometimes for a week. Same with Kaylin and John. Mom and Dad like the company." She flinched. "Liked." Looking around, she said sadly, "It'll be hard not having this."

Charlotte squeezed her arm. The house was only one part, she knew. The rest was Bob. Every available space held photos taken here and so many included him, pictured at various stages of his life. It was more a celebration than a shrine, though she knew Nicole was mourning still.

They were silent for a bit, eating more slowly now. Having finished the chowder and clams, Charlotte ate the last of her fiddleheads. There had been summers when she had come too late to catch these before they leafed out into ferns, but once tasted, they were never forgotten.

Wiping her fingers on a moss-green napkin, she cradled her wineglass and rested against the skirt of the sofa. "I feel your dad here. He was a wonderful man. I'm not sure I'd have gone to college without his pushing it. I don't think I'd have had a career. I didn't have a clue what 'work ethic' meant." Bob Lilly was a lawyer, and though he had been adamant about spending summers on Quinnipeague, he was up at dawn every morning to study the packets delivered by the mail boat the previous day. In the last of Charlotte's years here, there were a fax machine, a computer, and e-mail—and always the phone. Bob insisted on satisfying his clients before he ever went out for a sail. Charlotte remembered times when they had waited for him to finish. In each instance, when he finally joined them, he shared the bare bones of the case so that they understood the urgency. "He set an example for me that I didn't see anywhere else."

Nicole was suddenly on her knees, reaching across the table to straighten the thick candle that stood in an even thicker glass pillar. When she was done, she settled back on the rug. "Your parents died too young."

Charlotte had freed up her hair when they came inside; now she gathered the mass in a single hand and pulled it away, needing clarity against the clutter of her parents' memory. Their lives had been an ongoing orgy of self-absorption and excess. She was a freshman at Yale when they died in a fiery car crash that they might have survived, had one or the other been less stoned.

She took a sip of wine, briefly reflecting on what might have been if they had lived longer. The reflection held little optimism. And she was a realist. "They were never role models, Nicki. I try to romanticize them sometimes—y'know, their being gone and all—but I keep coming back to the mess of their lives. They were married three times, including twice to each other, and in between there were affairs and divorces and bankruptcies. They could act a part, like that of respectable renters of the house beside yours in Baltimore, but it was superficial. I was thinking about this while I was driving up today. When my parents met yours, they had just been kicked out of their apartment in Virginia, which, of course, the rental agent didn't know because back then, there was no quick way to do background checks, and she had a high-end house that needed a short-term renter, and—voilà—in walked my folks. Your parents saw through them, but they kept up the charade. Why did they do that?"

"You."

"I'm serious."

"So am I. They loved our being together. They loved that you looked up to them. They saw your potential. Besides, your parents did great barbecue. I remember those ribs."

"Likely lifted from the gourmet section of the supermarket," Charlotte muttered. She was uncomfortable with praise. It put a spotlight on the guilt she was trying so hard to suppress.

"You're too harsh."

Releasing her hair, she let go of the turmoil of her parents' lives. "I guess. And even if they did steal the ribs, I met you in the deal, so it wasn't a horrible thing." She and Nicole had hit it off from the start, becoming inseparable during the year they were neighbors. After Charlotte moved away, there were overnights, though always at Nicole's house, and, of course, there were summers on Quinnipeague. "My parents would have been at a loss to find something for me to do. Your parents were a windfall when it came to that."

"But it worked both ways. My parents got me a sister at a time when my mom was still having miscarriages. I think your being here helped her accept that I would survive without a sibling. Besides, they trusted you more than they trusted some of the island girls." Eyes wide, she clamped her mouth shut against a smile that escaped anyway. "Remember Crystal? And *Brandy*?"

Charlotte laughed. "Bizarre Brandy. To this day, I've never seen so many piercings. What's she up to now?"

"She's a hairdresser on the mainland. Crystal's still here. She married Aaron Deegan, who lobsters with his dad. They have five kids."

"Five? Whoa. And Beth Malcolm? She was smart. I was always afraid you two would be friends, so you wouldn't need me here."

"Are you kidding? I was too shy to do much with her. I didn't mix with locals until you showed up. You were bolder than I was. You got me out. My parents loved that."

"Beth was a reader, too," Charlotte recalled, then thought. "What are you reading right now?"

"*Salt*. It's about—"

"Maine!" she broke in, delighted. "So am I! It was on sale at JFK when I flew in from Australia, and when I saw the island on the cover, how could I not buy it?"

"It's not our island—"

"No, but you can feel it, smell it, almost taste it. Are you loving it?"

Nicole grinned. "Loving it. Loving the setting, the characters, the magic."

Charlotte dittoed each point, which on one hand wasn't surprising. She and Nicole had always liked the same books. They used to spend hours on the beach, passing them back and forth while the surf pounded the shore.

On the other hand, ten years had passed. While Charlotte was building houses in post-earthquake San Salvador or post-tornado La Plata, Nicole had been decorating a plush Philadelphia home. While Charlotte was in remote towns writing about doctors, farmers, and artists, Nicole had been in Center City blogging about food. Granted, *Salt* was on every bestseller list. But that they would both be reading it right now was evidence of ways in which they were still the same.

"At first I thought the author was a woman," Nicole offered. "Chris Mauldin—it could go either way. There's no photo, and the bio is vague."

Charlotte had wondered it, too. The sex was powerful but exquisitely tender. She didn't know guys who made love that way—which was probably part of the wide appeal of the book. Chris Mauldin was serving up dream stuff to an audience that craved it. At least, Charlotte did. She wasn't sure about Nicole and certainly couldn't ask. "Well, if he was trying to hide being male, he's given up. I googled the name, and a 'he' came right up. Does anyone know his real identity?"

"Not on the forums. I swear that's part of the phenomenon. Think about it. He's self-published—"

"Only in e," Charlotte cautioned, sucking cornbread crumbs from her finger. "My hardcover copy has a big-time logo."

"Right, but *Salt* was an e-bestseller for weeks and weeks before he sold the print rights. Can you imagine his marketing genius? He knows how to work the Web and does it in total anonymity from wherever."

"Anonymity is part of what makes the success of the book such a phenomenon. It's the big tease. Here's this mystery guy serving up our dream, and we don't know who he is, where he lives, or what he looks like."

"Like it matters who he is?" Nicole asked. "He had me hooked on page one. I mean, what a great first line. *Every man wants love, if he can get past the fear of exposure.* We like him because he's honest. At least, I do." Scrambling up, she added a log to the fire. "I like him because he's willing to put himself out there and be vulnerable and maybe end up being hurt. Let me tell you, though, *I* would never hurt this man. I'd buy anything he writes—and I say that though I'm only halfway through *Salt.*"

Charlotte wasn't even that far. "Is he working on a second book?"

"I hope so, but he's being vague about that, too. One thing's for sure. He's blown away the competition. I'd love to do that with a book." She jumped up. "Stay. I'm getting dessert." She was off.

"Where am I supposed to *put* dessert?" Charlotte called after her. Nicole hadn't finished the fiddleheads or clams, but she was up and down, wearing off what little she'd eaten.

"You'll find room," came the voice from the kitchen, along with the open-and-shut of the refrigerator door. "I cannot have a guest here for take-in without adding something of myself to the meal." She returned with snifters of small, wild strawberries. "These are the first of the season. I picked them this morning."

"On the roadside?" Charlotte asked, tickled by a dozen memories. Nicole had always known how to spot the best patches, like her eyes could see the tiny red glow beneath the leaves from fifty feet away. She had been known to yell *Stop the car!* at odd times to fill either a bag or her hands.

"No. One of the families on the neck has wide open meadows loaded with fruit. They started a little pick-your-own business, with strawberries now and blueberries soon. They cultivate wildness, and they don't use herbicides. I go there as often as I can."

"These are *so* small," Charlotte marveled, though she knew they'd be packed with flavor. "It takes forever to pick a pint."

"It's about the process," Nicole said with a smile, seeming to relax just thinking about it.

So did Charlotte. And yes, she could find room. Slipping a berry into her mouth, she savored it, before returning to the interrupted discussion. "Maybe you will."

"Will what?"

"Blow away the competition. I read your blog, Nicki. You get hundreds of comments on every post—and on Facebook, how many friends?"

"Seventy thousand." This, said with quiet pride as she scooped up their chowder bowls and headed off again. "Cappuccino?"

"No, thanks. You are amazing, Nicki."

"The machine does it, not me."

"I meant your blog." She had taken a more traditional route herself, studying journalism at Yale, followed by a postgrad year at Columbia. It was all very safe—precisely why, needing to break the mold, she had signed on as a Web correspondent in Afghanistan, where danger was a constant. The deal was for six months. Back in the States, she poured herself into hands-on charity work while the nightmares receded. Writing was her therapy. Between pieces she did in Appalachia—or in communities struggling to rebuild after a hurricane or fire—and those from Afghanistan, she caught the eye of magazine editors, who signed on for the pieces she pitched.

It was a career trajectory that had been taken by scads of journalists before her. But Nicole—quiet, introverted Nicole—was breaking new ground. "How'd you do it? How'd you get so big?" she called.

There was silence from the kitchen, then a dry, "God works in wondrous ways."

"I want to know how it *happened*," Charlotte insisted. "Nicole, are you going to come in here and sit?"

She reappeared with a small ceramic creamer from which she topped the fruit in each snifter with something that looked far thicker than cream. "Sabayon, made with Dad's favorite Riesling," her high voice announced. "I forgot how much wine he'd stored here."

"Oh, yumm." Forget the strawberries; Charlotte tasted the sauce. "*Yummm.*" Of course, a mouthful of fruit *with* sauce would be even better.

She was about to dig in, when Nicole said a sharp, "Wait!" Up again, she grabbed her camera, arranged the snifters just so, and took several shots, before setting aside the camera. They were on the sofa now, the fire crackling around another new log. She didn't eat, simply sipped her cappuccino with her eyes on the hearth.

Charlotte sensed a melancholy. "Thinking of Bob?" Eating sauce made with his favorite wine would do it.

"And Jules." Nicole was suddenly teary. "He gave me the cappuccino machine a couple of summers ago. We have one just like it at home. He used to make cappuccino every morning and bring it to me in bed." Darting Charlotte an awkward glance, she added a quick, "He's too busy now."

Charlotte felt a twinge of envy. It wasn't about Julian. It was about loving and being loved in return. "You miss him."

"Yes." She gathered herself. "Hence my blog."

"Go on," Charlotte urged gently.

Sitting straighter, Nicole wet her lips. "Well, you know I like to cook. And entertain."

"*Martha Stewart Living.*" It had always been around the house. Even now, there had to be a dozen issues stacked on the coffee table. Granted, a second stack held copies of *New England Home, Summer Cottage,* and *Cooking Light,* but the *Living* pile was higher.

"My bible," Nicole admitted. "It still inspires me, but since I never have exactly the same ingredients she does for, say, a roast duck or bouillabaisse—or the same materials for a centerpiece—mine come out a little different. So Julian and I were having people for dinner a lot—doctors, hospital administrators, friends who'd bring friends—and afterward they'd ask for recipes, or menu suggestions, or how to arrange wildflowers in a vase, or where to buy grass-fed beef. After a while, I thought it'd be cool to have a place to post the information so that everyone could read it. Suddenly people I didn't know were e-mailing. They were picking up on organic and local and homegrown."

"It's a hot topic."

"I wasn't thinking about that when I started to blog, but by the time the site was built, most of my posts had to do with eating organic, buying organic, supporting local farms and markets, and identifying restaurants that did the same, because that's what people were asking about. I began tagging along with Julian when he traveled for work, so it wasn't just Philadelphia, but Seattle, Denver, and Chicago. And it was Quinnipeague. People here didn't give it a name, but they were living farm-to-table before farm-to-table was a movement. They didn't call their produce organic, but they let you know that they didn't use artificial pesticides and fertilizers, and you knew the result—all delicious and safe. Organic was ingrained in me. Majoring in environmental studies at Middlebury was a logical next step, but I swear I didn't put two and two together until I started blogging about Quinnipeague. It's amazing, Charlotte. Those blogs get the most responses. People love reading about local farms and hand-made goods and free-range chickens, and it's all about farm-to-table."

"Hence Nickitotable.com." Charlotte was still amazed. "How many people read you now? Say, a single post."

"Over time, maybe thirty thousand."

"And Twitter?"

"The same number."

Charlotte sat back. "That's *amazing*, Nicki. All from nothing in how long?"

"Six years. Mostly the last four." Pushing up, she was off for the kitchen again. "I have cookies."

"I'm *stuffed*," Charlotte cried, but the words of protest were barely out when Nicole returned with a dish of chocolate almond cookies.

"From the café." Settling back into the sofa, she retrieved her cappuccino.

Charlotte took a cookie, but didn't eat. "Did your dad know about the book?"

"He knew I was talking with a publisher. He'd have loved this." She frowned at her cup and said quietly, "I think about your parents, who weren't there for you. Then I think about Dad and me. To be so close to a parent—I was very lucky."

"You still are. You have Julian and his kids. You have Angie. They keep you anchored. I envy you that."

"You do not," Nicole scoffed with a small smile. "You love freedom. You love *adventure*. I'm the one who needs support." She stood, pausing as she reached for the fruit. "You've had enough, right?"

"For now." But before she could tell Nicole to sit and relax, Nicole was collecting utensils and plates. "Did you finish the Australia story?"

"I did." Gathering up wineglasses and napkins, Charlotte followed her into the kitchen. "Seriously. You have an incredible life. Freedom has its downside. There are times when I'd give anything for a real home. You—you have stability. I can't believe you and Julian have anniversary number ten coming up. Will you do something big to celebrate?"

"Maybe. What did you do about France?"

"Postponed. I'll go in the fall. But you need to do something for your tenth."

"We were in Paris two years ago," Nicole said as she loaded the dishwasher. "Julian delivered a paper there."

Julian Carlysle was cutting edge when it came to prenatal cardiac surgery. A brilliant surgeon, he had been a rising star at the time of his marriage to Nicole. Charlotte assumed Paris wasn't his only big-time venue. "How often do you two travel?"

"Every few months." Her green eyes lit. "Want to take a walk?"

"Where?"

"Wherever you want."

Having been in the car all day and just overeaten, Charlotte liked the idea. "The beach," was all she had to say.

Bundling up, they slipped out the sliders, crossed the stone patio, and went down two wide granite steps. Typical of the North Atlantic, the shore was rocky. The beach grass that sprouted between boulders was its only softening touch. Even the sand at the water's edge was hard packed and strewn with stones. But the ruggedness didn't detract from its lure. Here was nature in its raw beauty. The tide had ebbed, leaving behind swaths of seaweed. Drawn by its fishy smell, gulls squealed as they dove to peck marine life from the tangle.

Since it was still light, they walked toward the tail of the island. Sand and surf were rougher at this end, but invigorating. The breeze was steady, blowing hair, scarf, and grass. When Nicole looped an arm through Charlotte's, they walked as they had when they were kids—and for a time Charlotte was one again, on her own personal escape.

Then they passed the spot where she had been with Julian, and the escape turned dark. She had never retained the details of that hour. There had been too much wine, too much exhaustion, too much fog that night. There had also been subconscious baggage, at least on her part, though she didn't admit that for weeks. At the time, all she saw was a gigantic mistake. Julian had sworn her to silence the next morning, and she had readily agreed.

His life hadn't changed. He married Nicole a month later and had gone on with his career. For all she knew, he had convinced himself that nothing had ever happened.

She had tried to do it, too. There had been no love involved, no forethought. It was a gross error, a lapse in character, and while she might blame her parents for the example they set, she had no one to blame but herself. Julian had started it, but she had gone along.

Feeling ten years' worth of guilt now, she freed her arm under the pretense of scrambling over a cluster of rocks. When she returned to Nicole, she walked sideways. "So, how is the good doctor?"

"Fine," Nicole chirped. "Really busy."

"Still working long hours?"

"Uh-huh."

"Does that bother you?"

"He loves his work. What about you, Charlotte? Who do you date?"

"No one special. But you didn't answer my question. Do his hours bother you?"

"How can they?" Nicole returned. "He's in the prime of his career. He lectures, he sits on panels, and he's even on TV now, which is a total no-brainer since he's handsome and articulate. They call him when they're reporting on anything related to fetal surgery. He's their expert." Her fingers quoted the word.

"So he's in demand," Charlotte said and couldn't resist adding, "I'm glad. I was worried he'd have hung around here longer if I hadn't been coming." As tests went, it was subtle. His absence might be entirely innocent; any man would be wary of spending time alone with two women writing a cookbook. If Nicole knew about the sex, she hadn't let on in any of their earlier discussions.

Indeed, she seemed appalled now. "Oh no. He would have loved to see you, but he wants to be at Duke a week before the new doctors arrive, and he has to settle everything in Philly before he leaves."

"I'm amazed he can leave his own work for a whole month."

She waved a hand. "It's for teaching, which is honestly and truly, I mean, *really* his strength. Hold on." Having apparently felt a vibration, she dug the phone from her pocket, saw the screen, and picked up the call with a grin. "Hey. She did, got here just fine. What?" She covered her free ear. "I'm sorry, the ocean is pretty loud. Oh, wow, that's great. Beijing? You *should*. Uh, honey, we're just walking the beach. Can I call when we get back?" She listened for a minute, bowing her head at the end. "Oh," she murmured, walking faster, and said something Charlotte thought was *shit*, though Nicole didn't usually use that word. "Okay. I'll call. Love you."

Ending the call, she stuffed the phone back in her pocket, and, head still down, strode on.

Charlotte's legs were longer, but she had to hurry to catch up. "Everything okay?"

Nicole raised her head, eyes blank for a beat before refocusing. "He was invited to China. May have a conflict. It'll be okay." She didn't sound sure, but before Charlotte could ask, she glanced at the sky. "It's getting dark."

"Rain clouds?"

"Or dusk." She brightened. "Remember when we used to walk out here with the sun going down?"

"I do." Charlotte smiled. "We were taking a chance, going a little farther, a little farther, closer and closer to Cole land." She squinted, trying to penetrate the fog and spot the marker. "Cecily Cole is at the top of my list. I can't wait to talk with her."

Cecily's herbs grew in the garden of her home at Quinnipeague's outer tip, but to call her an herbalist was to understate her place in island lore. Her herbs were pure in flavor and powerful in use—and she knew how to use them, both gastronomically and medicinally. She had a way of appearing with remedies when they were needed most; this was the light side of Cecily Cole. But there was a dark side, or so island men claimed. They swore that when they suffered heartburn, it was one of Cecily's herbs punishing them for an alleged offense to their wives. A diminutive woman with silver hair that protected her back like a gossamer shawl, Cecily was alternately loved and feared.

"Oh Lord." Nicole was gaping at her. "You don't know. Cecily died five years ago."

Charlotte stopped walking. "Died? But she's key to cooking here. How can we do this book without her?"

"Her herbs are still around. Didn't the chowder and clams taste as good as ever?"

"Yes, but you can't talk about island food without talking about Cecily."

"We can still talk about her. We just can't talk *with* her. Not that we ever really could."

Charlotte remained stunned. As legendary as Cecily was, she had always been something of a mystery. She had come to the island at the age of twenty—or eighteen or twenty-two, depending on which version of the story you heard—after a disastrous love affair with an influential mainlander. Likewise depending on the storyteller, she had either chosen to leave the continental U.S. or been driven away, though it was generally agreed that she bought her house with a payoff from the affair. She had brought her plants with her, along with the seeds of legend, and lived quietly at her end of the island. Her interactions with islanders were limited to trips to the store for supplies and, increasingly, gifting herbs to those in need. Habitually distrustful, she did not welcome guests to her home. Rumor had it that she would put a curse on anyone who trespassed on her land.

But that was rumor, and in the interest of the cookbook, Charlotte had the perfect excuse to approach.

"I think we should go back," Nicole said.

Charlotte had done stories on some highly intimidating characters, not the least being a Native American on Martha's Vineyard, who claimed to be the descendent of Wampanoag medicine men and had a trail of miraculous doings to prove it.

Cecily Cole? She might have been an epic challenge, with the potential for information just as great.

But it was what it was. "She's dead," Charlotte said. "She can't do anything. I think we should go see if those herbs still grow."

"I wouldn't do that," Nicole warned. "Her son lives there now."

"I thought he was in jail."

"Not anymore. Come on. I'll race you back." She turned, facing home.

"Did he dig up the herbs, or are they still there?"

"I don't know."

"Someone must."

"Well, I'm not asking," Nicole said. "The last thing I need right now is more bad vibes."

Charlotte studied her face. The sky was indeed darkening, taking detail with it, but she could see tension. It seemed out of place on such an innocent face.

Likewise, the awkwardness with which Nicole waved a hand. "You know what I mean—Dad dropping dead, our selling the house."

"He would have loved your doing this book."

"I could have used his encouragement."

Charlotte slipped an arm around her waist. "You have me. I'll be right here until the book is done."

Nicole smiled. There may have been tears in her eyes, though it could have been the reflection of the ocean in the dim light. "I love you, y'know."

Charlotte hugged her. A moment later, exhilarated to be the object of something so rich, she dared Nicole with a look. They set off down the beach at a fast jog, trading the lead as they dodged obstacles in the sand. By the time they reached the house, they were out of breath and laughing.

Their movement on the beach steps set off floodlights from the patio all the way around to the kitchen door. Nicole stopped, sniffed. "Strange," she said and began walking toward the side garden, where a profusion of reds and pinks blurred at the edge of the beam. "I was out here this morning. The lavender was nowhere near being in bloom. It's been way too cold. But how could I not have smelled this?"

Charlotte hadn't smelled it earlier, either, but she couldn't miss it now. This lavender was in full bloom, its tall spikes clustered with purple flowers that looked too soft for the wind but apparently weren't, since they held their form well.

"My mind must have been somewhere else," Nicole said. "But this is *perfect*." Moments later, she had clippers and began handing sprigs to Charlotte, who was absorbing their smell to the point of stupor. Finally, Nicole stood, closed her eyes, and inhaled. "Ahhhh. Amazing." She took half of what Charlotte held and sang softly, "Those are for your pillowcase, these are for mine."

"Don't we have to dry them first?"

"And dilute the smell? Lavender has calming properties. I'll take it full strength, thanks."

Charlotte didn't need calming—or rather, didn't want it. She wanted to bask in the glow of hope. She was being given a second chance to prove she could be a loyal friend, which was more than she might have asked after living ten years and a huge secret apart. She had expected awkwardness, wariness, reticence—*something*. But her arrival on Quinnipeague had been as smooth as the ocean was not.

Besides, after leaving New York at dawn and driving for hours, she was exhausted. If the lavender sprigs did anything beyond making her smile, she had no idea. Minutes after her head hit the pillow, she had fallen into a sleep so deep that she heard nothing of the conversation coming from Nicole's room down the hall.

Chapter Three

NICOLE WAS A BUNDLE OF nerves. She had wanted to call Julian back sooner—hell, had wanted to talk with him there on the beach, but it was impossible with Charlotte along. And even when they were back at the house, what could she do? Sneak off to the bathroom to talk with him about life-and-death issues, then return to Charlotte like nothing was wrong?

"Hey," she said the instant he picked up, "I'm sorry. I thought she'd never go to bed. Tell me again what happened."

"My left leg went numb," he said quietly. "I was just getting up to leave at the end of a team meeting."

At the hospital, in clear view of doctors and nurses who knew him. *Nightmare.*

"I sat down again and picked up my cell, like I had a call, while everyone else left. The numbness let up after a few minutes, but my leg's never done that before."

"Maybe it just fell asleep," Nicole said hopefully. "That happens to me all the time, and if it went away—"

"It was numb, Nicki. Not asleep. Not trembling. Plain-out numb. That means this medication is not working."

"Maybe it just needs more time," she tried.

"It's been three months. It either works or it doesn't."

"Maybe the numbness is a side effect of the drug itself. You often have those."

"Numbness isn't a side effect. It's a symptom."

"But it'll pass." She had to believe that. He saw the best doctor, took the best drugs.

"New symptoms are not a good sign."

"Did you call Peter?" Peter Keppler was a neurologist. His office was in New York, where they could visit him without Julian's world knowing.

"He says it could be a fluke, but, cripes, this is getting scary."

Julian had multiple sclerosis. The MS diagnosis had come four years earlier, and though he felt near-constant fatigue, his symptoms, mostly blurred vision and tremors, remained intermittent and mild. Still, the diagnosis was devastating for a surgeon who was not only entering the prime of his career, but in a specialty where the tiniest wrong move of the scalpel could damage a fetus.

So, with the ink still wet on his diagnosis, he had stepped back from the work that he loved. When he scrubbed up now, it was to teach other surgeons the technique for which he was known. No one questioned this; it was a natural progression in a brilliant career. Nicole knew that, but it was little solace when she saw how much Julian missed not doing the work himself. Saving the lives of unborn children was heady stuff.

But there was no choice here. If he had continued to operate knowing he was impaired, he would have risked not only patients, but reputation and self-respect.

The key was controlling the disease, to which end he had tried every gold-standard treatment, but nothing had slowed the frequency of his symptoms. Adding to Nicole's own misery was his insistence on secrecy. Since no one at the hospital knew, she wasn't allowed to tell her friends, her personal physician, even her mother.

"Peter is the best, Jules," she said now. "There's always something else to try."

But he was discouraged. She could hear it in his murmur. "We're running out of options," he said, and he would know. An academic at heart, he had read every theory, every study, every paper there was to read on MS.

Nicole had married a positive guy. She didn't know what to do with this one. "I'm flying home tomorrow," she decided.

"No. You need to be there."

"I need to be with you."

"I need to be alone." He had said that before, and no matter how he tried to soften it, it hurt. "I love you, baby, but sometimes I'm so concerned about you that I can't think about what *I* need to do. Right now, I need you there doing your book." There was a meaningful pause. "You haven't told her, have you?"

"You made me promise not to," Nicole charged, releasing her frustration in this peripheral way. "Do you know how hard that is? I mean, talk about awkward. There were a dozen times when it would have been totally appropriate to share it—like when I realized I hadn't told her Cecily Cole was dead, which has major impact on this cookbook, but I must have been so preoccupied each time she and I talked that I hadn't said it. I mean, who's she going to tell, Jules? She doesn't know anyone you know. She can be trusted with a secret. Same with the kids." His son was eighteen, his daughter twenty-one. "It's been four years, and we see them a lot. Don't you think they'll be hurt when they finally find out?"

"So I should tell them now and have them terrified that I'm going to die—or worrying that *they'll* get it someday? There's no test to tell them that. What can they do?"

"Support you. Support *me*."

He didn't answer, simply said a despondent, "Well, I just wanted you to know about the leg."

"I want to *help*, Julian. What can I do?"

"There isn't much."

"You're my rock," she warned, only half kidding. His solidity was one of the first things she had loved about him. He knew what he wanted and made it happen.

"Rocks don't have tremors. They don't go numb in front of a roomful of colleagues."

"Being a rock is a state of mind. You're usually upbeat."

"So maybe I'm human," he snapped, but eased in the next breath. "Oh baby, I don't want to argue. I hate it when I get like this. It's just that I don't understand my body. I don't know why I react negatively to the best of the meds. Shortness of breath, high blood pressure, stiffness—so we change meds, or I take another pill, cut out salt, stretch more, add yoga. I can't operate. Barring a miracle cure, I won't ever operate again. So what's left? My self-image. I want to be *seen* as healthy, at least. But the longer this goes on, the greater my chances of being publicly exposed, and once that happens . . . *pfffffhhh*."

"You'll always be able to teach," Nicole said, though her eyes had filled with tears. "You can do research and write papers. Your mind is brilliant. That won't go away."

She must have said something right, because he seemed to regroup. "I know," he said. "I just feel weary sometimes." He took a breath. "Not the kind of future you expected, huh?"

No. It wasn't. She tried not to go there, but it was hard not to—hard not to google MS and read about its progression; hard not to think about Julian being there in not-such-a-long time. MS didn't kill. It disabled. Sometimes badly. And as his wife, she was totally helpless.

"Let me come home," she begged again. "You're all alone with this. At least I *know*."

"I don't want pity."

"I have *never* pitied you," she shot back. "That's such an unfair thing to say. But I could cook, do errands, pay bills—"

"Paying bills is *my* job. My income may be down, but I'm still the earner here. Don't rush me into a wheelchair, Nicole. I'm not debilitated yet."

"I didn't say—"

"You focus on your business, I'll focus on mine."

"That's not how a marriage is supposed to work."

He was silent for a time, then sighed. "Oh God. I didn't ask for this. I'm just trying to deal."

"So am I. I love you."

"Love can't cure tremors. Let me concentrate on what will, okay? Talk later. Bye."

"Later" was twenty minutes. Nicole had spent the time sitting on the bed, alternately rocking forward and back, side to side, trying to soothe the shakes inside and to think of something to do. When her cell rang, she jumped.

"I'm sorry," he said quietly. "I shouldn't take it out on you."

Her eyes filled again. "I'm just trying to help."

"I know. But this is the hardest thing I've ever faced. I grew up wanting to be a surgeon. I never wanted to be anything else." They had talked about this before. Each time he started, she let him vent. "My father is still operating, and he's sixty-eight. I know, I know. He's in orthopedics. It's not fetal. But it still requires a steady hand. Me, I was supposed to have another twenty years. I was supposed to discover newer forms of in-utero intervention. This was just supposed to be the start." He was silent. Then, "You there?"

"Yes."

"You're very quiet."

Nicole might have said that he had already made his mark with a breakthrough technique, which was more than most surgeons ever did—and as for his father, *he* would know that getting MS was not Julian's fault, but Julian refused to tell him, too, so he was without that support as well.

Right now, he was feeling self-pity. He had a right, she supposed.

"Nicole?"

"I don't know what you want me to say."

He sighed. "I guess there isn't much you can."

Lately, that was the state of their marriage, which was nearly as upsetting to Nicole as MS.

"My patients could teach me about dealing with illness," he murmured. "The frustration, the fear. I never knew. It's humbling."

Nicole knew about frustration and fear. For four years, her mantra had been *It's okay, something will work, there are new treatments all the time.* But it was starting to sound empty. She knew what the future could hold, and it wasn't the illness that terrified her most. She could deal with the illness. She just wasn't sure Julian could.

"Beijing will be great," she tried by way of encouragement. The invitation to speak there was a coup.

He was suddenly hesitant. "Should I be that far away if something goes wrong?"

Timidity was new. Not a good sign. "You're speaking at a hospital. Peter can get the name of an MS person there."

Julian was quiet. Then, "So, was it great seeing Charlotte?"

Nicole doubted his heart was in the question, but she welcomed the diversion. "It was. She's just the same. We still get along really well. We're both even reading the same book."

"Did you cook dinner for her?"

"I was going to, then Dorey met us at the ferry and started talking about chowder, and we couldn't resist. We brought it home and ate in front of the fire. Did you eat out?"

"No. I picked up chicken at Whole Foods. Is the weather still cool?"

"For sure. There?"

"Warm and humid."

"I wish you'd come up," Nicole said. In the old days, he would have eaten at restaurants with colleagues when she was gone, missing her enough to not want to eat home alone. Now he was hiding—not that she dared say that.

"I have to get ready for North Carolina."

"You could do that on Quinnipeague, then fly straight to North Carolina from here. Charlotte would love to see you."

"Nah. There's too much to wrap up here. Let me see if this numbness recurs."

"Will you let me know?"

"You won't be calling to check?"

She sensed he was teasing her, but she saw nothing funny in the question. "If I call, you'll jump on me for it, so I don't *dare,* but that doesn't mean I won't be thinking about you all the time."

"I thought the point of having Charlotte there was to think about something else."

"It is. But you're my husband, and everything in me is saying I should be in Philadelphia and *not* Quinnipeague, only you won't allow it, so will you do this for me, at least?"

"What if Charlotte's right there?"

"I'll say I can't talk."

He waited a beat. Finally, "Okay, baby. I'll call."

Nicole hung up the phone and cried. She did this a lot when Julian wasn't around, just lots of quiet, helpless, frightened tears. They always slowed in time, as they did now. She blew her nose and wiped her eyes. Then she spotted the lavender on the pillow. Lifting the sprigs, she held them to her nose. She breathed in once, then again.

Two sniffs wouldn't do it, of course, and the more she consciously tried to relax, the more she worried. Coming off the bed, she put on a robe and fluffy slippers, then, opening the door with care so that its creak wouldn't wake Charlotte, she crept down the stairs. In the kitchen, she made passionflower tea, turning the jar of loose leaves in her hand while a teaspoon's worth steeped in her mug. The tea was local, made from an herb that rarely grew in New England but did on Quinnipeague. A natural sedative, passionflower was another of Cecily Cole's gems.

The tea was still steeping when she decided she was hungry. On impulse, she took a jar of strawberry jam from the cupboard. It, too, was local, put up the fall before by one of the island women. Unscrewing the lid, she pried a layer of wax from the top and, taking a spoon, sampled it straight from the jar. She closed her eyes, isolating the sense of taste for the greatest enjoyment. Strawberries . . . and vanilla? Eyes popping open, she peered into the glass until she spotted the bean among the berries. A single bean. No surprise there. Vanilla beans came from a variety of orchid that had no business growing on Quinnipeague, but did. Not only was the flower a more vivid yellow than elsewhere, but the bean was potent.

After scooping out a glob of jam and adding crackers, she set the plate on the large oak table, but she didn't immediately sit. Distracted, she ran a hand over the pickled wood. She loved this table. If she and Julian had a bigger place, and she could take one piece of furniture, it would be this. Happy memories filled the chairs here, crowded in with hopes for three babies, maybe even four. As a lonely only, she had always wanted a big family, and Julian had been on board with that. But Nicole was only twenty-four when they married, and Kaylin and John, who lived with them part-time, were preteens. There was plenty to do before her own babies came, and when they finally started trying, instead of a pregnancy came Julian's diagnosis.

Her father was aching for grandkids. In his last years especially, he used to ask. *So, toots, any good news coming? Your mother and I would love to babysit.*

Bob hadn't known about Julian, either.

Her throat tightened. Determined not to cry again, she sank into the chair, opened her laptop, and logged on to Nickitotable.com. Blogging was her escape. It had struck her more than once that if Julian had not been diagnosed, she wouldn't have this site, this following, this book contract—and she would have been perfectly happy. Now, it was a godsend. What else would she do when she woke up in the middle of the night and couldn't sleep? Talking about what she did know was ten times better than imagining what she didn't, and she did know restaurants and farmers' markets, flower arrangements and menu planning. These were safe things. They were *happy* things.

Today, there were questions to answer from readers as well as ones from a woman named Sparrow, who had created her blogsite and now handled requests for everything from reviewing a new farm collaborative to submitting guest blogs. So sweet little Nicole, who had never aspired to work, had a staff. And businesses actually paid her to post ads. Initially, they'd been local to Philly, but increasingly they had a national reach. She was actually bringing in enough to net a profit. It wasn't as much as a book would bring in, but it made the blog self-sustaining, like the agro-elements she promoted.

Tonight, the readers' questions were easy—what different salad to serve with lasagna, how to store limes, suggestions for an anniversary party placecard. She suggested, in order, a beet salad, the refrigerator, and a Hershey's kiss with names on strips sticking out of the top. Yes, she wrote to Sparrow, she did want to advertise beef online but said a "no thanks" to the company selling frozen hors d'oeuvres. She knew the brand and didn't care for it. Money was money, but she did have standards.

Paying bills is my job, Julian had said. *My income may be down, but I'm still the earner here.* And if that changed? She shuddered to think. But it was one of the reasons she was doing this book. She wanted to be able to help.

Thinking of it made her hands tremble even without MS, and the irony of that?

Pulling up a blank screen, she began to type quickly, though it was a minute before her fingers stopped hitting wrong keys and found their way. "Charlotte arrived today, but we didn't even mention the cookbook. There's plenty of time for that. For now, it's about us. I've told you about Charlotte—Charlotte Evans?" She added a link to Charlotte's most recent piece. "She's the one who's collaborating with me on the cookbook. We've known each other since we were eight, which makes it so special to be working together. She's one of those friends you don't see for a long time and then pick up where you left off. Our lives are radically different—I'm married, she's not; I'm a homebody, she's always gone—but once she got here, we didn't stop talking.

We're even reading the same book—*Salt*. Have any of you guys read it yet?"

She described Charlotte's arrival and talked a little about Dorey, because the beauty of these summer blogs was to seed interest in the book. She had written about Quinnipeague many times in the past, though more out of love than ambition . . . not that ambition hurt now. "We brought dinner home from the pier, but I couldn't just plop it down on the coffee table by the fire. You know my mantra. It's all about the presentation, which is pretty easy if you keep the right materials on hand. Up here we do, because my mother loves pretty things, which is probably where I came by the trait. I used woven place mats that were a heathery blue. The dishes were a deeper blue. So were the napkins—and not paper ones, either. I like cloth. Linen, actually. I know you all hate to iron, but if you buy a whole bunch, and basket the dirty ones until you have enough to wash together, then hauling out the ironing board isn't so bad."

She reread the words, paused, dropped her hands to her lap. Julian loved cloth napkins. He loved lit candles and fresh flowers. His first wife had been a corporate type who was out several nights a week and, even when not, had no desire to cook. The second time around, he had wanted a homemaker. Old-fashioned? Maybe. But Nicole loved home-making. She loved playing backup to her husband. This was what her mother had done. It was all Nicole had ever seen, all she'd ever wanted.

The words on the screen blurred. Her mind jumped ahead to a future in which Julian would be unable to work, unable to travel, unhappy.

She blinked, took an unsteady breath, dragged her thoughts back to Charlotte, dinner, and presentation.

"What else?" she typed. "We have low stacks of books on the table, along with a grouping of hurricane lamps and votives. I didn't light them. It would have been overkill, with the fire going and the sun still up. But they were pretty just sitting there unlit. Take a look." Leaving the table, she retrieved her camera, connected it to the laptop, and inserted the pictures she'd taken of the table with its books, candles, and place settings. Refusing to be distracted again, she hurried on. "People usually pair white wine with seafood, but this being summer and our meal being mostly shellfish, the rules are loose. I found a fabulous Pinot Noir in the cellar."

She chatted about that for a bit, before posting several more pictures, these of food and wine, and she shared her recipe for sabayon sauce, right down to the Riesling. Then, pulling up a shot of Charlotte, she cropped to the head and sat back. Long, thick, wavy brown curls, a mouth that was too serious but had always been that way—Charlotte looked good. She did look older. But *good* older. Her skin wasn't heavily moisturized or made up. She had never been one for that, had never been able to afford it, and though Nicole guessed she could now, she apparently chose not to. And maybe she was right. She didn't seem to need it.

Nicole did. Lately, her eyes looked tired and her hair dull. There were times, worrying about Julian, when she felt ancient. So she went a shade lighter, bought new makeup, had a facial or a manicure—anything to give her a lift.

Charlotte was lucky. She didn't care if her nose burned in the sun or if the wind chapped her lips. And because she didn't care, neither ever happened. Nicole envied her the indifference, though it was easy to be indifferent when you had so little to lose. Nicole had a lot to lose—home, husband, lifestyle. Charlotte had never had any of that.

So is it harder to dream about what you don't have, than to live in fear of losing what you do?

She didn't know the answer. But she heard self-pity. And she had thought *Julian* had that?

Remorseful, she refocused on her screen. No, Charlotte didn't have a husband or kids. She didn't have time for them, what with chasing stories all over the world. By comparison, Quinnipeague was tame. Nicole was lucky she had agreed to come. She wanted to make it a nice time in spite of MS.

Which raised the issue of breakfast. French toast? Frittata?

Definitely frittata.

Leaving the table again, she transferred a small packet from freezer to fridge. It was salmon, home-smoked on the island and more delicious than any she had ever found elsewhere. Smoked salmon wasn't Cecily Cole's doing, but the dried basil and thyme she took from the herb rack were. Taking a vacuum-sealed package of sun-dried tomatoes from the cupboard, she set it on the counter beside the herbs. Frittata, hot biscuits, and fruit salad. With mimosas. And coffee. That sounded right. Eaten out on the deck maybe?

No, not on the deck, unless the prevailing winds turned suddenly warm.

They would eat here in the kitchen, with whatever flowers the morning produced. Surely more lavender. A woman could never have enough lavender—or daylilies or astilbe, neither of which should bloom this early, but both of which had looked further along than the lavender, yesterday morning, so you never knew.

Returning to the computer, she finished her blog post. Finally, entering "It's all about the setting" as the title, she signed it, dated it, and published it. She surfed for a while after that, checking her usual farm food Web sites for news, but there was little since she'd checked the day before. So, taking her copy of *Salt* from the counter, she settled in the Great Room with her tea and, in the wee hours, began to read.

Chapter Four

CHARLOTTE AWOKE TO THE SOUND of the surf, the smell of sweet biscuits, and a sense of peace. Some of that peace was from the lavender in her pillowcase, its scent a halo around her still, but she was convinced that what she felt went beyond that. Just as her coming here as a child had been crucial, so was this.

Redemption was part of it now. She could help make this cookbook special.

But there was more. This summer would be a turning point in her life. How else to explain the sense of rightness she felt?

True, it could be wishful thinking. She had felt rightness that February in Rio, when she was sent to do a piece on samba and ended up teaching girls in the slums how to write—and again that summer in Sweden with a guy she thought might be the one. Both trips had been great, but she had returned home alone, exactly the same.

Still, she knew that at this moment in time, she was supposed to be here.

Slipping from bed, she crossed to the window. The view from her room was of the rougher northeast stretch of beach that they had walked last night. As the morning fog shifted, the breakwater came and went. Likewise a fishing boat farther out. At least she thought it was a fishing boat, though it wasn't visible long enough to let her know for sure. Staring harder, she caught a glimpse of sails. No fishing boat then. In the next instant, though, the sails, too, were gone.

A ghost ship. That was an exciting thought. She could weave up a whole slew of imaginative stories around a ghost ship. Pressing her palm to the cool windowpane, she smiled. She was good at dreaming up stories, used to do it all the time. Imagination had been her escape when she was a child.

Here, reality was the escape. Choosing hot biscuits over a ghost ship, she layered a sweatshirt over her T-shirt and sleep shorts, pulled on a pair of wool socks, and followed the smell.

An hour later, she was stuffed. Frittata, hot biscuits, sliced kiwi and grapes, two mimosas, and endless coffee—Nicole kept plying her with more, refusing to let her move from her seat to either serve food or clean up. She was feeling pampered, but then, she always did when she came here. Nicole was mothering her the same way Angie used to. Back and forth between stove, sink, fridge, and coffeemaker—she didn't stop moving.

Nor did she stop talking. She mentioned the blog she'd just posted and the preliminary book cover her editor had sent, but these were only en route to discussing Charlotte's own work. She seemed to have read it all—humbling for Charlotte, who had spent the same years in ignorance of Nicole's life and wanted to hear about that, but Nicole wouldn't allow it.

Finally, when she was about to make one more trip to the sink, Charlotte caught her hand. "You're making me dizzy, Nicki. *Sit.*"

Nicole was quickly apologetic. "I'm sorry. I love doing this."

"The dishes can wait. I want to talk."

"We are talking."

"Not about what I want." She softened the words by jiggling her friend's hand. "I want to know about your life."

Nicole looked cornered. "My life? My life is great."

"So's mine. End of discussion." She stared in challenge.

Nicole stared back, then laughed. "You haven't changed. Same blunt Charlotte." When Charlotte continued to stare, she finally settled back into her chair. "What do you want to know?"

"Start with Kaylin and John," Charlotte said. "Are you guys close?"

Nicole's smile held affection. "Very. Julian and I share custody with Monica . . . well, shared, past tense, because they're both over eighteen now. Come fall, Kaylin will be a senior at Penn and John a sophomore at Haverford, but right up through high school, they were at our house all the time."

"House or condo?"

"Condo," she acknowledged. "We kept thinking we'd buy a house, but Kaylin loved playing Eloise in a high-rise, and Johnny loved running up and down the halls—and it was only ten minutes from Monica, who did have a house with a yard, and like I said, there were summers up here. Mom and Dad loved it. And the kids adored them. They've taken Dad's death hard."

Charlotte believed it. Bob was one of the warmest people on earth. Right from the start, he had considered Julian's children his grandchildren. But those two were supposed to have been a prelude to more. There had been lots of talk about that during the wedding summer.

So—yes, *same blunt Charlotte*—she asked, "Why haven't you had more kids?"

"Because we already had two to raise."

"You always talked about having your own."

"There's no rush. I know"—a dismissive wave—"I'm thirty-four, but that doesn't make any difference. All that talk about the biological clock? Sometimes I think it's a crock of you-know-what. Women today are having kids in their forties. *Lots* of women are. I know three doing it right now."

Her response was a bit too emphatic for Charlotte. "Is there a prob-lem?"

"Like fertility? No. We'll have kids. We're just taking our time."

"If Kaylin and John are both in college, and Julian is forty-six, what are you waiting for?"

"Charlotte. You're as bad as my mother!"

But Charlotte wasn't being put off. She needed to know that Nicole's marriage was okay. "He didn't change his mind about having more, did he?"

"Oh no," Nicole insisted. "He wants them as much as I do." She glanced at the window and brightened. "Sun's breaking through. Let's take coffee out to the patio." Before Charlotte could respond, she was heading for the mudroom. She returned carrying two parkas, and though her step remained light, her eyes had misted. "Mom's and Dad's. I was thinking I'd give them to the church. They'll know who can use them. You take Mom's." It was red. She held it out.

"I'm taller than you. Give me Bob's—"

But Nicole's arm was firmly around the larger blue one. "I need his," she said in a single fast breath.

Charlotte took the red one. Helping with the coffee, she carried mugs while Nicole grabbed biscotti. Minutes later, they were outside. The patio was a patchwork of granite slabs that had been quarried in Maine and set in an arcing pattern to mirror the shore. Two heavy wood chairs stood to the right of the beach steps, facing the sea. Closer to the house and more protected were the table on which they had so often eaten back then—glass on top, iron below—newly cleaned and surrounded by chairs.

Off to the side were a trio of lounges. They pulled two of these closer to the house, under a pergola whose vines would be overrun with peachy roses within the month.

Cupping her coffee for its warmth, Charlotte tucked her legs under her jacket and angled toward Nicole. "Are you happy?"

Nicole's eyes were bright over her mug. "Happy?"

"With Julian. With your marriage."

"Of course."

"Is he good to you?"

"He's an angel. Why do you ask?"

Charlotte wanted to believe that Julian loved her, that there was no pattern of infidelity, and that nothing about that one awful night lingered. "Just curious. You always had energy, but it feels nervous now."

"I've told you—lots on my mind . . . Dad, the house, the book."

"As long as it's not Julian. I want to know you're happy."

Nicole jumped up and, all but lost in Bob's parka, crossed the patio. "I *would* be happy if the gardener had done his job, but look at the mess here." She knelt at the creeping cypress that bordered the stone and began plucking brown tips from the lowest fronds. "They think we won't see these, but it isn't only about looks, it's about the health of the plant. If you want new growth, the old stuff has to go."

"Is George Mayes still doing your work?" Charlotte recalled him being a character, as likely to show up tipsy as not, but intent either way on talking the plants and shrubs through the toughest of times.

"George tries," Nicole said as she searched for anything dead she might have missed, "but he's in his eighties, so his son Liam does most of the work." Stuffing what she'd pruned in her pocket, she returned to the lounge. "Liam isn't as good, but they need the money, and it's not like there are dozens of landscapers on Quinnipeague to choose from, and then there's Rose." Wife of George, mother of Liam, Cheryl, and Kate, with however many grands, even great-grands by now. "Her slaw is still the best." She looked quickly around. "Where's my coffee?" Spotting it near the cypress, she scrambled up again. When she returned, she said, "I'm not sure if it's the celery seed or the dressing, but Rose is definitely on our list. Mayes Slaw is the perfect side."

Charlotte burrowed deeper into her parka. The memory brought a smile. "The best. And she made it for the whole town. I always imagined she had the grandkids lined up in a row, slicing cabbage at the counter like Santa's little elves."

Nicole laughed. It was a welcome sound. "Granddaughters. The boys'd be doing the physical stuff. They're a traditional family. Not all on Quinnipeague are. Wait'll you meet some of the new ones. We've gotten more diverse." Up again, she curved back toward the garden on the side of the house.

"What are you *doing*?" Charlotte called, perplexed by her constant up and down.

"Checking the flowers," Nicole called back. "Mom'll want to know if the sweet William is in bloom. That's the pink one. The lisianthus is ready to pop. It'll be a deeper purple than the lavender. Wait'll I tell her about *that*." She returned to the lounge. "By the way, I think it's mustard seed in that slaw."

"Is that an herb?"

"Mustard seed? No, it's a spice."

"What's the difference?"

"An herb comes from the leaves of a plant, a spice from the seeds," Nicole explained. "Some plants produce both, like cilantro and coriander. Salt is a mineral. We call it a spice, but it isn't."

"What's pepper?"

"A spice. A peppercorn is the seed from a pepper plant."

"Did Cecily Cole cultivate mustard plants?"

"Sure did."

Charlotte grinned. "Q.E.D."

Nicole laughed again. "That proves nothing. We don't know for sure what herbs Rose uses in her slaw."

"We'll ask. What we really need to do," Charlotte decided, "is to explore Cecily's gardens—you know, take pictures and all. She's the matriarch of island cooking."

"Tell that to her son."

"I will."

"He has a gun. He shoots gulls for sport."

Charlotte winced. "What does he have against gulls?"

"I don't know, but I'm not looking to find out. Cecily's plants are all over the island. We can get what we need from everyone else."

"But her garden is the source," Charlotte argued, as Nicole got up again. "Where are you going now?"

"I'm cold," came her little-girl voice. "I want to get dressed."

"Just grab a blanket from inside. It's gorgeous out here." She breathed in. "This air is amazing. Sweet."

"Charlotte, it's salt air, and there's no sun." She shot a hateful look at the clouds. "I honestly thought it was coming out, or I wouldn't have suggested this. Sun is cheerful. That's what I want. Actually," she called over her shoulder as she headed toward the house, "I think we should drive into town. It'd be good to let everyone know we're here."

Nicole had trouble sitting still. Charlotte couldn't shake the feeling that she was running from something and that the something was *her*. There were times when Nicole wouldn't look her in the eye, which meant maybe she did know about Julian and her, and was trying to move on.

Chastened, Charlotte got dressed. She offered to drive, but Nicole insisted on taking the old SUV that her parents kept at the house, giving her good reason for sadness. "Dad never worried about my driving here," she reminisced. "There's only one road, so you can't get lost, and you can't speed because it's bumpy."

"Do they ever repave?" Charlotte asked, jouncing now that she didn't have a steering wheel to hold.

"Not often. It's not a Quinnie priority. We're the spoiled ones. I was thinking I'd give this car to Eleanor Bailey, kind of as a thank-you. She was always bringing over crab cakes—remember those little minis? She knew Dad loved them."

"I loved them, too. That's another recipe we'll need."

Nicole was silent, staring out the windshield with both hands on the wheel, which would have been fine if her knuckles hadn't been white.

Charlotte touched her arm. "You okay?"

She nodded, cleared her throat, brought herself back. "Just thinking of Dad."

"As long as there's nothing else."

Nicole shot her a glance. "What else would there be?"

"Me," Charlotte dared say. "Are you sure you want me here to do this?"

Nicole looked stricken. "You don't want to be here. You have something better—"

"Better than *this*?" Charlotte cut in. "*Nothing* is better than this. Helping you with a book? I'm *honored*."

"Then don't say anything else," Nicole said gently. "We have the ingredients for an amazing team." More fiercely, she added, "And, please, don't even *think* of leaving." She drove on.

Paying penance. That was Charlotte's first thought in response. Her second was more poignant. "Maybe I bring back too many memories."

"Like, they won't come anyway? At least with you here, I have a shoulder to cry on."

"Promise you will?"

"Yes, but I'm fine. Really, I am."

And she was at first. They stopped at the post office, ostensibly to let the postmaster know that Charlotte might be getting mail, but since he did lobster bakes like no one else on Quinnipeague, and since he was a major conduit of island news, greeting him was good politics.

Then came the island library, which was connected to the hardware store, which the librarian owned with his wife, who made a great clam macaroni and cheese, hence a dual purpose there as well.

Neither visit was brief. Charlotte had forgotten how different island time was from time in the rest of the world. People weren't satisfied with a quick, "Hey, nice to see y'again." No matter what chore they were doing, they stopped to feed the wood stove and then stood there for the warmth, and you couldn't just walk away with them clearly in a gathering mood. They wanted to talk about Bob, of course, and Nicole graciously accepted their condolences. Since they had seen her over the years, though, it was Charlotte who was the novelty. They asked where she lived now, how long she had lived there, whether she had a husband or kids. When Nicole told them about her writing, they wanted to know how she came to doing it, whether flying bothered her, what Paris or Belize or Bali was like.

At times, it was a grilling. Take the hair salon. They stopped there because the owner was known for the quiches she brought to town breakfasts. When they arrived, the woman was in a cloud of scented styling mist as she finished with one client and started on another, and the questions came fast and furious. All three wanted to know *everything*.

Charlotte was beginning to weary of it, when they turned to Nicole. "And you, you're too thin. We'll fatten you up this summer. I didn't get to see your husband last week. Still curing the ills of the world, is he?"

"He is," Nicole said, slipping her elbow through Charlotte's and adding a singsongy, "We're off. We'll be back another time. Bye-bye." They were barely out the door when her elbow tightened and she muttered, "*Still curing the ills of the world? Is that supposed to be funny? It's disrespectful, is what it is. Why can't people keep their mouths shut, if they can't say something nice?*"

Charlotte was startled. "She thought it was." When Nicole didn't respond, she tried to smooth things over. "But hey, I'm glad we left. I'm usually the one asking the questions. It's hard being on the other end. I need a snack. Does the Café still have scones?"

Nicole was a minute settling. Then, she said, "Sure does."

"Are you game?"

"Sure am."

The Quinnie Café was as charming as Charlotte remembered. Relics of whaling days hung on dark-paneled walls, though the main attraction was the windows that looked out to the sea. Weather permitting, they would be open under awnings. This morning, though, it was all about the woodstove, whose dry scent flowed over armchairs, five round tables with chairs of a sturdy birch, and a counter with stools.

The tables looked new, as did the pendant lights that hung over each, but the biggest change since Charlotte had been here last was a profusion of outlets. Just then, two tables held people at laptops, newer Quinnies whom Nicole introduced as an op-ed writer for the *Times* and a computer programmer.

Since the Café was at the far end of the island store, hidden behind shelves of dog-eared magazines, jigsaw puzzles, and toys, those having coffee might not have been seen by those shopping for food if Bev Simone, who ran the store, hadn't spread the word, which she did—but only after following them in and updating Charlotte on ten years' worth of births, deaths, and marriages. "But Nicole and Julian, their wedding was the best," she concluded. "We still talk about it." She squeezed Nicole's shoulder. "Your daddy, God rest his soul, knew how to throw a bash. And such a handsome couple, you and the doctor. When'll he be back?"

"I'm not sure," Nicole said without blinking. "His schedule's tight. He's hoping maybe August."

"Hoping isn't good enough," Bev scolded.

Nicole's smile didn't budge. "It's the best he can do."

"He is one busy guy," Charlotte told Bev, who seemed mollified by that and, hearing a distant jangle, returned to the store. But she wasn't done. Since she viewed Nicole and Charlotte as celebrities—*writing a book, on us!*—she sent in one islander after the other to say hello.

So there were lots of questions in the Café, too, again aimed mostly at Charlotte, whom they hadn't seen in so long. Seeming happy to be left out, Nicole busied herself going back and forth in turn for scones, cappuccino, spoons for the cappuccino, knives to spread jam on the scones, and napkins.

Then came Beth Malcolm, the one who had worried Charlotte so many years before. She taught at the island school, which had just finished for the year, hence her being at the Café midday, midweek, and what she carried as she joined them was *Salt*.

"I must be the last person on Quinnipeague to read this," she remarked when Nicole and Charlotte exchanged a glance. "Have you read it?"

"Reading, present tense," Charlotte said.

"And you like it?"

"We do."

"Isn't it amazing?" she asked, then, seeming startled, abruptly turned to Nicole. "I saw Julian on TV. It was *so* awesome. I didn't recognize him at first. He was wearing a suit and looking so serious, but *good* serious, like you just knew he knew what he was talking about, and then there he was wearing shorts and a shirt here last week. The electrician—you know, the one who just did the wiring at your place—his wife had a baby in April and for a while before that they thought there was a problem with his heart, so everyone was talking about Julian and the miracles he does with preemies."

"Fetuses."

"We love it when he's here. When's he coming back?"

Nicole rolled her eyes toward Charlotte in a way that might have passed for indulgent if Charlotte hadn't known her so well. Here, it was pleading.

"Everyone's asking that," Charlotte told Beth, "and he's hoping for later in the summer, but he's swamped with work—"

"And besides," Nicole added in a high voice, "if he came back, he'd be on vacation. He wouldn't want people staring at him. He'd want privacy."

"Which," Charlotte quickly put in, because that high voice held an edge, "is the island specialty. How many kids are in the island school now?"

Distracted, Beth talked about that, then about her own two kids and her husband, whom she had met in college and brought back. He was a sculptor, creating masterpieces out of metal and struggling to be recognized, though after confessing the last, Beth said a contrite, "I promised him a sticky bun. Gotta go. Hey, we have a book group. You guys want to come?"

"Are you discussing *Salt*?" Charlotte asked with interest.

"Oh no, we all read that out of curiosity. But we're doing *Caleb's Crossing*. It's also about an island."

Charlotte had read it. "Maybe we will," she said and waved as Beth left. She would have asked if Nicole had read that one, too, if Nicole hadn't been looking in alarm at her scone. "What?"

"Currants," Nicole cried. "In these scones. *Not* grown here."

Charlotte was unsettled by what almost sounded like panic. Currants were no cause for that. Besides, the Nicole she had known was easy-going. Either she had changed, or something else was up, and it wasn't Bob. If she were thinking of Bob, she would be sad, not panicked.

They finished eating with little talk. Bev sent in another shopper, but the woman was innocuous and brief. As soon as she was gone, they slipped out themselves.

That was when they bumped into the publisher of the island weekly. He lit up when he saw them, though he quickly focused on Nicole. "I heard your good news. A book, huh?"

"Cookbook," Nicole corrected with a plastic smile. *Cornered* was the word that came to Charlotte's mind. She had thought it once yesterday, too.

"Good for you," the man said, "though I'm not surprised. Y'always had that little something special, right down to bringing that husband of yours to Quinnipeague. Say, I'd love to have a sit-down with the two of you to talk about your book—cookbook—and about his work. When's he comin' next? I'd do a story for the paper. This is front-page stuff. And hey, I'm sorry about Bob. He'll be missed."

Nicole nodded. She neither blinked nor stopped smiling.

The newspaperman barreled on. "He would have loved my doing a profile of the doctor and you—y'know, photo spread and all. Think Julian would agree to do it? Ahh, well of course he would. The paper's just for us Quinnies, and he loves it here." He reached for the door. "The wife needs elbows. She promised me lobster mac 'n' cheese, and I don't turn *that* down. If you want the best island recipes, you'll need that one. I'll tell her. She'll be excited about being in a book. So will you let me know when the doctor makes his plans? I'll come out to the house. That's worth profiling all on its own, but now we have you two stars in it. Book, TV—you're the power couple. Po-wer coup-le," he repeated, marking each syllable with a fist, before proceeding into the store.

Charlotte was thinking that it was true, when Nicole turned owl eyes on her. "I *remember* her lobster mac," she brayed, "and if she wants her dish in my book, she'll have to add something to it to make it different from every other mac 'n' cheese recipe out there today!" Charlotte drew her away from the store, but Nicole ranted on. "Power couple? *Power* couple? He doesn't know what he's *talking* about." She sounded frantic. "There are a gazillion cookbooks out there, I'm one of millions writing more, and Julian spends more time teaching than doing. *Power couple*? That is such a crock of *shit*."

Language, tone, look—all were so unexpected that Charlotte couldn't let it pass. Before she could ask, though, Nicole broke free and stormed off, away from the SUV and down the street.

"Where are you going?" Charlotte called.

Nicole stopped and looked around. Turning right, she headed for a cluster of rocks overlooking the pier. In summer, the rocks would hold visitors eating lunch, but on as cool a day as this, they were deserted. The only thing Charlotte could imagine was that she planned to jump.

She ran, catching Nicole's arm just shy of the rocks. "What is *wrong*?" she cried, frantic now herself.

Nicole's eyes were large, her face nearly as pale as her hair. "Nothing! Everything's fine!"

Charlotte shook her. "What *is* it, Nicki?"

Nicole put both hands to her head and pressed, her eyes suddenly confused.

"Please tell me," Charlotte begged gently.

"I can't." A whisper, pleading. "I can't."

"I'm here to help. I want to. It can't be that bad."

Nicole exploded. "MS *not that bad?*"

Charlotte gasped. "You?"

"*Julian!*"

The words echoed. Nicole looked around, thinking that someone else had said them, because if she was the one, it would be a betrayal of the worst kind.

But the only person in sight was Charlotte, who couldn't have known about this, and wouldn't have yelled it at her anyway, and Charlotte's face was blank.

Nicole felt a great sinking inside.

"He has what?" Charlotte whispered, cupping her shoulders.

She couldn't say it again. Julian hadn't wanted her to tell anyone, least of all Charlotte. Hadn't he specifically asked that last night? Now she'd gone and done it. She hadn't planned to, but that didn't matter.

He would be hurt, disappointed, *angry*. Their relationship had been rocky lately. This wouldn't help.

Thinking that she simply wouldn't tell him, which meant another secret to keep, she felt a great wave of despair and, sinking to her knees, burst into tears.

Chapter Five

CHARLOTTE WAS STUNNED. OF ALL the possibilities to explain what was going on, she hadn't imagined illness. The Julian she remembered was too active, too fit. He was too dedicated, too *famous*—which, of course, was an absurd thing to say. Famous people got sick all the time. Famous people *died* all the time.

Not that Julian would die. MS was doable. Charlotte knew this for fact. But it was chronic, and chronic illness changed lives.

Kneeling, she wrapped her arms around Nicole, but her friend didn't allow it for long. Pulling back, she said in a voice that was broken but urgent, her eyes a haunted green, "You can't tell anyone, Charlotte. Promise you won't?"

"I won't."

"Not a single person. If Julian finds out I told you, he'll divorce me."

"He will not. He loves you."

She pulled a tissue from her pocket. "I used to be so sure of that, but he's changed." She pressed the tissue to her nose. "He used to be open. He used to be easy-going and confident, and he's still that way with everyone but me. With me, all the worry comes out. I'm the only one who knows—other than you now."

Charlotte didn't understand. "You can't be the only one. His dad's a doctor." She remembered meeting the senior Dr. Carlysle at the wedding. While not as academic as Julian, he had been impressive in a quiet way.

"Not his dad, not his mom," Nicole said. "No one but his doctors, and they aren't even in Philadelphia—and I totally understand that his future depends on people *not* knowing, but do you know how hard this is for me?"

Charlotte struggled to imagine. She was self-sufficient, but Nicole? Nicole was more dependent, more *social*. To be under a gag order with friends? "How long have you known?"

She brushed the tears from her eyes. "Four years."

"*Years?* Omigod. Through everything with Bob? Angie must be devastated."

"Charlotte. *Listen* to me. Mom doesn't *know*."

"But she's your mother."

Nicole stared at her.

"He wouldn't let you tell your own mother?" Charlotte asked in dismay, then held up a hand. "I'm sorry. I shouldn't criticize him. I haven't walked in his shoes." She tried to take it in. "I thought . . . I thought maybe you guys were estranged, like he had an affair or something."

"Julian? Not Julian. He's totally loyal, but me? I didn't make it a *day* without blabbering."

"You shouldn't have waited even that long," Charlotte scolded. "You should have told me the second I got here." She was puzzled. "Four years, and no one could *see*?"

"That's the thing. You don't see fatigue, which is what he feels most of the time, and the other symptoms come and go. No one looking at him sees a problem." Her voice went higher. "But MS is progressive. He isn't responding to medication, so we know where he's headed. And sometimes I think I'm being totally selfish because his symptoms are still mild—but think of what he does. He's a surgeon who works on the smallest creatures, and if his hands start to shake at the wrong time, it's a disaster. He isn't operating now, he just teaches, and he's dying inside, and no one knows that or knows why. It's like he's leading two lives—one in public, where everything is normal, and one in hiding, where he's worried and angry." She stopped, eyes welling again. "I shouldn't have told you, but you and I always talked about everything, and now, here we are, with everyone asking when he'll be back." She caught a breath. "He made me promise not to tell you. Is this disloyalty, or is it not?"

There it was again, that word. Charlotte might have said a thing or two about Julian and disloyalty, if that hadn't been the last thing Nicole needed to hear, and she wanted to help, *needed* to help. So she gentled. "Not disloyalty, Nicki. Survival. You're human. You have feelings and needs. You're a saint for having kept this to yourself for so long." Tugging her down so that they were sitting with their backs to a boulder, she said, "Tell me everything."

Once started, Nicole couldn't stop. The cork had popped, and four years of agony poured out. In the telling, she relived it: being in their condo when Julian had first told her the results of his tests, being with him in New York when his doctor laid out a course of treatment and again, repeatedly, when one regimen was abandoned and another begun, living on the roller coaster of hope and disappointment, hope and discouragement—and through it all, long night after long night at her computer, reading way too much about MS.

Boats creaked at their moorings far below as the surf washed the pier, the fishing shed, the shore. Though the stone protected them from the brunt of the wind, the salt air still circled, mixing with wood smoke from every building in sight. It was soothing. More soothing, though, was the unburdening. Julian would be furious. But she *was* human. She had acceded to his needs for so long, but this was *her* need.

Charlotte didn't have answers. She just listened. She didn't call

Nicole spoiled and self-centered when she cried that it was unfair, that Julian had such a promising future and *why did this happen to us*. Nor did she sugarcoat things, like Nicole's mother would have done. Her questions were brief and to the point. And afterward? Charlotte drove back to the house—just took over, and that felt wonderful, too—while Nicole summed it up. "It's a juggling act. We need to find a treatment that slows the progression of the disease, but doesn't throw him into cardiac arrest in the process."

"Has that happened?"

"Not yet, but only because they watch him closely. With one drug, he had to sit there for six hours after the first dose, and then his heart slowed so much that they refused to give him a second dose. That's been the story. Some of the most promising treatments cause such a bad reaction in him that he has to stop. That cuts the options way down. If nothing works—*ever*—the whole thing is . . . omigod, so awful. When I think of where we could be in a few years, I go into an all-out panic, which would be so bad for Julian that I try not to think, but I can't escape it, y'know? He comes home, and he's down. He's thinking it's only a matter of time before the wrong thing happens at the wrong time. I mean, he's already removed himself from the OR, but no one's figured out why so he's still in demand. And there's *another* thing," she hurried on. "He likes being on TV or onstage doing symposiums in front of thousands of doctors. He likes being invited to London and Paris and Beijing. I mean, who wouldn't? It's totally flattering. But once they learn he's sick, they'll assume he's lost his edge and won't call."

"How bad are the flare-ups?"

"Not awful. They only last a day or two, so he cancels things in Philly, and we take the train to see his doctor in New York."

"Corticosteroids?" Charlotte asked.

Nicole was startled. "How did you know that?"

"I did a piece once on a small clinic in the English countryside—"

"I read it. It was about cancer."

"I know, but for a little while afterward, I dated one of the doctors there. His specialty up to then had been MS. It was a bad relationship, but I learned a lot. Corticosteroids are used to treat flare-ups."

"They help," Nicole confirmed, "but you can't take them forever. Julian has to find something that prevents flare-ups in the first place. The thing with MS is that what helps one person won't always help another. We hear success stories about a new medication, then either he has a bad reaction to it or it does nothing for his symptoms."

They were back at the house, on the patio again, sharing a single lounge like they did when they were eight, now sipping hot tea under a finally warming sun, when Charlotte asked, "What about yoga?"

Nicole studied her, relieved—*so* relieved—to be able to finally share all this and with someone in the know. "Your doctor must've really talked."

"Mostly about himself," Charlotte replied, only barely amused. "At least the MS part was interesting. He mentioned yoga as an alternative treatment."

"Not alternative for us. Complementary, like *with* meds, not without. Julian isn't taking chances. Same with diet. There are so few studies to prove that things like macrobiotics will help, so he's just careful about what he eats. He always has been. And he exercises. He runs, he works out." She understood Charlotte's surprised look. "Sure, he falls. He blames his sneakers or the treadmill or the *curb*. It terrifies me." She felt terror even in the telling, though it wasn't as jagged as usual. Isolation magnified things, but Charlotte knew now. She understood. "He goes for a run, and I wait for the police to show up at the door to tell me he fell and was hit by a car."

"You can't do that to yourself."

"How not to? I know that it's selfish of me, when we're so much better off than most—"

"Hold it, Nicki. Don't say that again." Charlotte turned to fully face her. "Pain is pain. You have a right to feel it. You didn't ask for this."

"But I'm not handling it well. I don't know what to *do*. Tell me, Charlotte. I want to help him, but I don't know how. He says I hover, but I hover because I want to help. Then I say the wrong things . . . *do* the wrong things. I really am a very small person."

Charlotte looked genuinely astonished. "Are you kidding? Another person would be paralyzed, but not you. Look what you've done in the last four years—helping Angie, mothering Kaylin and John, blogging well enough to win a book contract. Give yourself credit, Nicole."

But she had trouble doing that. She tried to hold it together when she was with Julian, but when she was not, she worried about everything. "The blog takes my mind off MS. Maybe he's right about my needing to get away. And he's been pushing for this book. He is totally supportive." She was intense now. "I need it to be a success, Charlotte. Oh, not for my name—I don't want recognition—but if the book sells, there could be others." She framed hopeful headlines in the air. " 'Nickitotable does Quinnipeague.' 'Nickitotable does Chicago or San Francisco, or New Orleans.' It's about . . ." Not fame. Not even distraction. "Security." The word popped out. Now she considered it. "I'm spoiled. I took it for granted that Julian would always have a job."

"He will."

"But he won't earn what he used to," she said, hearing the words aloud and feeling their impact. "I can't talk about this with him. He goes nuts when I try. But if nothing works and he gets really bad . . . I need a source of income, Charlotte. I mean, I know this is just a cookbook, and cookbooks don't sell a gazillion copies, but I need it to sell well." She felt a qualm. "Am I setting myself up for failure?"

Charlotte smiled. "What did your dad always say?"

"Aim high, hit high," Nicole reeled off. "But look what happened to Julian."

"Right. He aimed for a great practice and got it. He aimed for a close family and got it. I'd say he did pretty well."

"Okay. He got his dreams," Nicole conceded. "But what about *mine*? I had dreams, too."

She saw the exact moment when Charlotte got it—a certain tick in otherwise steady brown eyes. "That's why you haven't had a baby?" She seemed stricken. "He can't have sex?"

A week before, Nicole would have minded the bluntness, but not now. With everything out in the open, she was feeling so relieved that Charlotte could have said *anything* and she wouldn't have minded.

"Oh, he can. It's not that. The crazy thing is, we deliberately put off having kids. Kaylin and John needed attention, and I could give it, and they gave me back so much. Now, Julian's the problem. He's afraid he won't be able to pay for clothes and education—he's afraid he won't be able to physically *hold* a child—and I keep telling him it's okay, that we'll find a way to make it work, that people with MS have kids all the time, but he doesn't want to hear it."

"Is MS hereditary?" Charlotte asked.

"They don't know for sure. I mean, there's *so much* they don't know—like why women get it more than men . . . like whether there's a relation between MS and mono . . . like why there's more MS in the northern U.S. than down south. Julian's had every test in the book, and they have no idea why he got this. He won't tell his friends or his parents. And he won't tell Kaylin and John. He says there's nothing they can do. Maybe he's right." She was thinking about that, trying to move on, but something still rankled. "The power couple? Not quite. We may look happy and successful and powerful to the world, but inside we're not. Julian is sick, and I am a fraud."

"You are not a fraud."

"Writing a cookbook to fill a hole in my life? Pu-leeze."

"That's how half the world works, Nicole. You've always been passionate about organics, and the farm-to-table movement is right up your alley. What you're doing is called sublimating, and it can produce *the* best things."

Nicole let the words float around her, wanting so badly to believe. This was why she had brought Charlotte here. Feeling a swell of gratitude, she studied her friend as, cupping her tea, Charlotte studied the sea. She was somber, brooding even, and Nicole didn't question it, after everything she'd dumped on her. It was a lot to take in.

For her part, though, Nicole felt lighter than she had in months.

Impulsively, she gave Charlotte a hug. "I'm lucky to have you. Your coming here has saved my life."

"That's melodramatic."

"I'm serious. I'm glad I told you. I feel *so* much better. It's like . . . it's like the sea shadow moved," she said and felt her father's presence. "Dad talked about that, too. Remember? Directly under clouds, the black patches on the water where it's dark and freezing cold? Well, I just moved. I can still see the shadow, but it's warmer and brighter where I am now. Thank you, Charlotte. You're the best."

Chapter Six

Yoᴜ'ʀᴇ ᴛʜᴇ ʙᴇꜱᴛ, Nɪᴄᴏʟᴇ ʜᴀᴅ said. But Charlotte didn't think so. While she had been traveling around the world, picking and choosing assignments in a carefree, self-indulgent spree, her friend was at home going through hell. And if she'd known it, would she have hung around? Hanging around would have meant seeing Julian, and she wasn't sure he would have wanted that any more than she did.

Now that Nicole had confided in her, though, she shared the burden. Needing to know everything about MS—part refresher, part update—she spent the afternoon on the patio with her laptop. There was no fog now, and the only clouds were fluffy ones. The sun warmed her arms and legs, allowing her to unbundle, but the warmth didn't spread far inside. The advances in the five years since she'd broken up with Graham, her British doctor, were marked by new drugs, new theories, new trials. For every blog post touting a miraculous recovery, though, there was one claiming a hoax, and side effects were a recurrent issue.

Then came stem cell transplants, which had been niggling in the back of her mind. Graham had mentioned them as an MS treatment with future promise, and from what she read now, they were coming into their own. The process involved taking adult stem cells from bone marrow, tissue, or organs, and infusing them into the body to replace diseased cells with healthy ones. In the case of MS, a malfunction in the immune system caused damage to nerve coverings, disrupting the sending of electrical signals through the brain and spinal cord. This disruption was what caused MS symptoms. The aim of a transplant was to give the body fresh, new, healthy cells that could generate healthy nerve coverings.

Current thinking leaned toward autologous transplant, which entailed using a patient's own cells in the hope of minimizing the risk of rejection. Beyond that, embryonic stem cells held hope, though these cells carried a slew of political issues. Not so umbilical-cord stem cells, though from what she read, use of these remained experimental.

The whole thing was chilling. It took everything she had to hide her worry at dinner. But Nicole, in cookbook mode now, had recreated individual seafood potpies from a Chowder House recipe. She set places at the trestle table—bright orange place mats on the pickled oak, napkins in shell rings, and an aged Vouvray in unetched goblets—and again she insisted on photographing the whole thing before allowing Charlotte to eat.

"What do you think?" she finally asked after a period of pensive chewing. The absorbed look on her face said she was breaking down elements of texture and taste, pitting one ingredient against another, weighing their proportions against the whole.

This was the Nicole that Charlotte knew—the detail person, who remembered every subplot of every book she had read and could cite a reason why it worked for the whole. Charlotte, who usually moved on without looking back, had alternately loved and hated her for that.

It wasn't love or hate now, but admiration. Nicole wasn't moving on. She was simply pushing one thing aside to focus on another.

Inspired, Charlotte focused hard on the merits of the dish. "I like the lobster. And the crab. And I *love* the mussels. The shrimp feels . . ."

"Overdone," Nicole prompted.

"But this was frozen, right?" She certainly didn't want to imply that the shrimp had been miscooked, didn't want to even *hint* at criticism when Nicole was in escapist mode. *MS*? *Mind-boggling.*

Nicole chewed another mouthful. "Yes, frozen. Shrimping around here runs from December to April. They actually ended the season early this year because the catch was so big." She singled out another tiny shrimp and chewed. "Definitely tough. And there's already a crunch from the fennel, so I don't need anything this firm. Maybe I should use cod instead of shrimp?"

"That would work," Charlotte said thoughtfully. "But I do like this salad with it. And the bread."

The plan was to include menu suggestions with each recipe—what side would go with an entrée, what entrée would go with a side, what starter or sweet would complement each choice. Nickitotable.com was known for this. It was also known for presentation, which was why Nicole went to such pains to artfully lay out and photograph each meal. Of course, she didn't consider either a pain. She loved doing it.

Trying to follow her lead, Charlotte sat back now to look at the whole—a ramekin with a half-eaten pastry disc resting on what remained of a cream sauce chunky with seafood. Islanders didn't dilute their seafood dishes with dozens of sides, hence the simplicity of salad and bread. But there was an element of Cecily Cole in the cream sauce. "The parsley adds just enough green."

"And the ramekins add a chestnut brown," Nicole mused. "I got them at the island store a few years ago, and they weren't expensive. By the way, I'm making a resource list to put at the end of the book. Not everyone has access to our ingredients, and it's not like we can get fresh ones to them, but the island store ships ramekins, and since they're locally made—"

"By Oliver Weeks?" Charlotte cut in with an enthused grin. "Still? What a character. Big interview, there."

"The book has to focus on cooks."

"He makes implements for cooks."

"I don't know if my editor will go for Oliver Weeks."

"Then I'll interview him for me," Charlotte vowed. "I can sell a profile of him in a snap. Still here? Wow. Still single?"

"He's dating Alicia Dean."

Charlotte was appalled. "Alicia Dean? Bo-ring."

"You're only saying that because you thought Oliver was hot."

"He *was* hot." Growing cautious, she asked, "What's he like now?"

"Wrinkled."

"Really? He's not terribly old."

"Same age as Julian. Mid-forties."

Ten-plus years older than they were, which was one of the reasons Charlotte had never actively flirted with Oliver. Not that she'd flirted with Julian. Not that she'd ever thought Julian was hot. Not that she cared if Julian was wrinkled or gray now—other than as a bellwether of his health. To this day, she couldn't give what had happened between them any explanation remotely related to physical attraction. Loneliness? Perhaps. She had just broken up with yet another guy she thought might be the one, so she could add heartbreak to the list of excuses. Add wine and exhaustion, and the outcome was doomed.

"Alicia spent a couple of years on the mainland," Nicole said, "so there's a little more life to her now. She does PR for the Chamber of Commerce."

"The Chamber of Commerce," Charlotte droned. "Now there's an exciting organization, particularly since Quinnies hate tourists."

Nicole looked to be fighting a smile. "Day-trippers are okay. Dorey loves them." She pointed at the potpie. "She'll give me other Chowder House recipes, but I think this one's worth including. Potpie is an island staple."

And potpies on Quinnipeague weren't only for fish, Charlotte knew. She remembered ones that contained chicken, pork, and beef, though the latter was usually ground. "Shepherd's pie," she breathed in sudden euphoria. "Topped with mashed potato laced with horseradish descended from a plant in Cecily Cole's garden. Think her son still grows it?"

Nicole held up both hands and, in a very high voice, said, "Don't go there, Charlotte. You *know* the trouble I already have in my life."

"MS isn't trouble. It's worry."

But those hands covered her ears now. "I don't want to hear. We have to talk about the book." She left the table to grab a folder from the counter and, as she returned, pulled out two sheets of paper. Pushing the first to Charlotte, she said, "These are chapter headings, beginning with BRUNCH and ending with SWEETS. My editor thought there should be chapters for STARTERS and SALADS. I did add STARTERS, since they can be a whole meal if the portions are large, but salads are part of the menu plans, so they'll show up in different chapters. Besides, ten chapters feels right. See? I've already included POTPIE."

Charlotte also saw CHOWDER, FISH, FOWL, and FILETS, plus SIDES AND SNACKS. What she saw as she read, though, was Nicole in the kitchen, living and breathing food for the blog and the book. Charlotte wasn't much of a cook, but when she was home, she ate. When she was bored or tense, she ate. And there was Nicole—at home, certainly bored at times, definitely tense—wallowing in food but thin as ever. Nervous energy had to be nearly as good as gastric bypass.

"People of interest," Nicole said, putting the second sheet on top. "My editor doesn't know Quinnipeague, so I made this list myself. All of them are major players here."

Charlotte looked over the names, suddenly struck by how irrelevant these people were—how irrelevant the whole *project* was—compared to issues like illness and infidelity. And friendship. Friendship was definitely on the line here.

Misreading her expression, Nicole spoke in a rush. "You don't have to do these exact ones if you don't want. I just kind of went through the chapter headings and listed some of the people I'd want to ask for recipes, and then picked people from that list whom I thought were interesting, but if they don't interest you, they won't interest my readers, so that's a good litmus test. I mean, these are just suggestions."

"It's your book," Charlotte said, feeling like the *worst* kind of friend.

"But you're the writer."

"It's *your book*," she repeated, testier now. If Nicole had been more demanding of Julian, he would never have followed Charlotte to the beach. End of story. "You're the one who knows your audience, and you're the one who signed a contract. I don't know what your publisher wants. And I haven't been here in ten years, so I'm not the one to make executive decisions. Tell me who to interview, and I'll do the interview."

Nicole had recoiled.

Only then realizing how sharp her tone had been—and how old and one-sided her anger—she was immediately contrite. "I'm sorry. I'm probably tired."

"It's everything I told you this morning," Nicole wailed.

"No. It's cumulative. The last few months . . ." She let it go at the suggestion. *Of course* it was what Nicole had told her that morning. "But I really do want you to direct me in this, Nicki. You know what you're doing."

Nicole didn't look entirely convinced, but at least she didn't argue the point. Rather, as they finished eating, she went through her list, gaining confidence as she explained why she had chosen each islander on it.

Charlotte managed to express enthusiasm, though she had no idea how Nicole could so completely immerse herself in this. But then, Julian's MS wasn't news to her. She was used to smiling when things were dark. Charlotte had always thought of herself as the tougher of them. Not so just then.

They finished dinner and cleaned up, and still Charlotte was thinking about MS. She felt she had a lot of knowledge now with nowhere to go. What she wanted was to hear more about the different treatments Julian had tried. Four years wasn't a long enough time to run out of options. Some of the blog postings she read were from patients who had gone from one protocol to another over the course of twenty years.

But Nicole didn't raise the subject; she simply lit the fire as dusk fell, grabbed *Salt*, and curled up on the sofa. Since she was further ahead than Charlotte, she refused to discuss the book lest she spoil it, and the more Charlotte asked, the firmer Nicole's headshake.

Charlotte picked up her own copy, but not even *Salt* could keep her mind from going places she didn't want to be. For every three pages read, she had to reread two. Setting the book aside, she went to her room and returned with her knitting—though why she had brought it along, she didn't know. The women on Inishmaan had started her on what they claimed was the easiest of their sweaters, and she'd actually finished the back since then. Was it easy? No. Thinking that a smaller piece might be more manageable, she had started a sleeve. Did she know what she was doing? No. She studied the pattern, knit half a row, unknit the stitches, and tried again.

Eventually, she gave up and, sitting on the floor by the bookshelf, looked through picture albums. At one point, she got up to show Nicole a shot of the two of them, gawky and mismatched at thirteen, but Nicole held up a hand and shook her head *no* without taking her eyes from the page she was on.

Putting the album away, Charlotte returned to the sofa. *Salt* was the story of a fisherman, his dog, and a woman who had burst onto the scene unexpectedly, but with whom he was falling in love. Each of the characters had a vulnerability that tugged at her heart. But even love seemed irrelevant to her right now. So she concentrated on the writing style, which was clean and succinct but musical, ebbing and flowing as the ocean would do.

Thinking of the ocean made her crave air. Saving her place with the cover flap, she put the book aside and stood. "I need to move. Want to go for a walk?"

There were tears in Nicole's eyes when she looked up. "I can't leave now. I'm at a really good place." She swallowed. "And I want to call Julian. You go. I'll leave the door open."

Layering up with her humiliatingly perfect fisherman's sweater and a scarf, Charlotte went out the kitchen door. But she didn't head for the beach. She didn't want to pass the painful stretch that would make her think of Julian. She didn't want to think *at all*.

So she made for the road, where she would be able to walk faster, and headed west, toward town. A minute later, she made a U-turn. Town was safe, and safe was okay. If she wanted distraction, though, risk was better.

She walked at a clip back, past the Lilly mailbox and on, speeding up once her muscles warmed. Nervous energy? Oh yeah. She needed to get it all out—needed to *exhaust* herself if she hoped to sleep that night. And the fact of "that night" being only the second of her time here?

Leave, a tiny part of her begged. Julian sick, Nicole needy, Charlotte feeling responsibility—this was the kind of tension from which she had always run. She could easily claim a problem that demanded she return to New York or, better yet, to the site of one of her stories. She could be on the first ferry out, whenever that was.

But she kept walking. She couldn't leave. Totally aside from the fact that Nicole was counting on her, it was a matter of self-respect. And besides, she'd been looking forward to this last summer on Quinnipeague. She did love this place.

Not much to see now, though, she thought with a shiver as she gathered the mess of her hair and tucked it under her scarf. Darkness was dense this far from town. There were no cars here, no streetlights, no welcoming homes, and whatever glow had been cast from Nicole's house was gone. Trees rose on either side, sharing the narrow land flanking the road with strips of field, and beyond was the rocky shore, lost now in the murk.

But there was hope. As she walked, she saw proof of a moon behind clouds, etching their edges in silver and spraying more to the side. Those silver beams would hit the ocean in pale swaths, though she could only imagine it from here. But she did hear the surf rolling in, breaking on the rocks, rushing out.

When the pavement at the sides of the road grew cracked, she moved to the center. This end had always been neglected, a reminder that Cecily didn't invite islanders for tea. The fact that no repair work at all had been done said the son was the same.

Turn back, a tiny part of her begged. Nicole was right; they could get plenty on Cecily without coming here. But to see the gardens again, this time with purpose? How to resist?

She passed a string of birches with a ghostly sheen to their bark, but between the sound of the breeze in their leaves and, always, the surf, she was soothed. The gulls were down for the night, hence no screeching there, and if there were sounds of boats rocking at moorings, the harbor was too far away to hear.

There was only the rhythmic slap of her sneakers on the cracked asphalt—and then another tapping. Not a woodpecker, given the hour. Likely a night creature searching for food, more frightened of her than she was of it. There were deer on Quinnipeague. And raccoons. And woodchucks, possums, and moles.

The tapping came in bursts of three and four, with pauses between. At one point she stopped, thinking it might be a crick in her sneakers. When it quickly came again, though, she walked on. The closer she got to the Cole house, the louder it was.

The creaking of bones? Skeletons dancing? That was what island kids said, and back then, she and Nicole believed it, but that didn't keep them away. Bob and Angie had forbidden their coming here, so it was definitely something to do. Granted, Charlotte was the instigator, but Nicole wouldn't be left behind.

Feeling chilled now, she pulled the cuffs of her sweater over her hands as the Cole curve approached. That curve was a marker of sorts, as good as a gate. Once past it, you saw the house, and once you saw the house, you feared Cecily. As special as her herbs were and as healing as her brews, she could be punitive. Or so said the lore.

But what was lore, other than imaginative efforts to entertain? Cecily was dead, and Charlotte was curious. A look wouldn't hurt.

Slowing only a tad, she rounded the curve. The thud of her heart felt good. She was alive; she was having an adventure; she was breaking a rule, irreverent person that she was. The salt air held a tang here, though whether from the nearby pines or adrenaline, she didn't know.

Then, like a vision, Cecily's house rose up at the distant end of the drive. It was the same two-story frame it had always been, square and plain, with a cupola on top that housed bats, or so the kids used to say. But there were no bats in sight now, no ghostly sounds, nothing even remotely scary. A floodlight was trained on the upper windows, spraying unflattering light on an aging diva. And the sound she heard? A hammer wielded by a man on a ladder. He was repairing a shutter, which would have been a totally normal activity had it not been for the hour.

Wondering at that, she started down the long drive. The walking was easier here, the dirt more forgiving than broken pavement. An invitation after all? She fancied it was. The house looked sad. It needed a visitor, or so she reasoned as the trees gave way to gardens left and right where Cecily had grown her herbs. In the darkness, Charlotte couldn't see what grew here now, whether the low plants were herbs or flowers or weeds. She could smell something, though the blend was so complex that her untrained nose couldn't parse it. Unruly curls blew against her cheek; wanting a clear view, she held them back.

Cecily's garden. There was power here. She could feel it. But a man on a ladder in the nighttime? That was risky.

Her sneakers made little sound on the dirt as she timed her pace to the pound of the hammer. When he paused to fiddle with what looked to be a hinge, she heard a rustle in the garden beside her, clearly foraging creatures alerted by her movement.

Alerted in turn by that rustle, the man stopped pounding and looked back. He must have had night eyes; there was no light where she was. Without moving a muscle, though, he watched her approach.

Leo Cole. She was close enough to see that, astute enough to remember dark eyes, prominent cheekbones, and a square jaw. She remembered long straggly hair, though a watch cap hid whatever was there now. He wore a T-shirt and paint-spattered jeans. Tall and gangly then? Tall and solid now.

But thin-mouthed in disdain. Then and now.

"You're trespassin'," he said in a voice that was low and rough, its hint of Maine too small to soften it.

"What are you doing?" she asked, refusing to cower. She had met far more intimidating people in far less hospitable spots.

His eyes made a slow slide from her to the window and back. "What does it look like?"

"Repairing your house in the dark." She tucked her cuffed hands under her arms. "Is that so you won't see the broken windowpane over there, or do you just like being reckless?"

He stared at her for another minute. Then, holstering the hammer in his jeans, he climbed down the ladder, lifted a shutter, and, somewhat awkwardly, given its bulk, climbed back up. The shutter was wide, clearly functional rather than decorative. Though he carried it one-handed, he stopped twice on the way up to shift his grip. At the top, he braced it against the ladder's shelf while he adjusted his hands, then lined up hinges and pins.

He had one hinge attached but was having trouble with the second. She knew what this was about. She had worked with storm shutters. They were tricky to do alone.

Resting the shutter on the shelf again, he pulled the hammer from his waistband and adjusted the hinge with a few well-aimed blows. Then he tried the shutter again.

Watching him struggle, Charlotte remembered more about Leo Cole from her early days here. Not too bright, they said. Troubled. Stubborn. She had never known him personally; she was only there summers, and he ran with a different crowd. Actually, she corrected silently, he didn't run with a crowd. A lone wolf, he did damage all on his own, and it was serious stuff. The stories included stealing cars, forging checks, and deflowering sweet young things.

Her last summers on Quinnipeague, he was in state prison, serving time for selling pot. Rumor had it that Cecily was the one who grew it. The islanders always denied that, of course. They didn't want the feds threatening their cures.

Leo had been nabbed for selling it on the mainland. Did he still grow it? She couldn't smell it now, and she did know that smell.

Having returned the shutter to the shelf, he was readjusting the hinge.

"Want some help?" she called up. Wasn't this was about risk?

He snorted.

"Four hands, and you'd have that right up," she advised.

"Two hands'll do."

Charlotte looked past him toward the cupola. She didn't see any bats yet, didn't feel any ghosts. If Cecily's spirit was floating around, it hadn't cast a spell to keep Charlotte here. She remained because she was stubborn herself.

He was staring at her.

"I've done this before," she said.

"Uh-huh."

"I have. I've built houses."

"That so." He didn't believe her.

"Half a dozen in El Salvador after the big quake there, and at least as many when tornados hit in Maryland. I know how storm shutters work."

He continued to stare.

"All you need," she said, freeing a hand to hold back the hair that blew loose again, "is someone to steady it while you fit the pins in the hinges."

"Really. I didn't know that."

"Okay. So you did. But you could've had that hung and been down five minutes ago. Aren't you cold?" She was appreciating every thick inch of her sweater, while his arms were ropy and bare.

"I'm a man."

She waited for more. When nothing came, she said, "What does that have to do with anything?"

"Men run hot."

"Really." Refusing to be baited, she returned her hand to her armpit, shifted to a more comfortable stance, and smiled. "Great. I'll watch while you get that shutter hung. Maybe I can learn how you do it alone."

Apparently realizing he'd been one-upped, he grunted. "Fine. Since you know it all, here's your chance." He backed down, put the shutter on the ground against his leg, and gestured her toward the ladder.

"I'm not lugging that thing up," she warned.

"No, but if you climb the fuckin' ladder, I can hold the shutter while you to do the fitting. Assuming you can see. Your hair's a mess."

"Thanks," she said brightly and gripped the rail. Two ladders would have been better. She wasn't sure she liked the idea of climbing this one with him at her butt. She would be at his mercy. But she did have a point to prove.

So she began to climb, looking back every few rungs to see where he was. When she reached the top, she felt his shoulder against the back of her thighs. If she hadn't known better, she would have thought he was making sure she didn't fall.

But she did know better. Leo Cole had no use for women. If he was standing that close, he was toying with her.

She didn't like being toyed with—and, yes, her hair was in her eyes, but she wouldn't give him the satisfaction of pushing it back. Fortunately, she knew enough about hanging shutters to do it, hair and all. While he bore the weight of the wood, she easily lined up both pairs of hinges and pins, and that quickly it was done.

Nearly as quickly, he backed down the ladder. By the time she reached the ground, he was stowing the hammer in a toolbox. The instant she was off the last rung, he reached for the ladder.

"You're welcome," Charlotte said.

He shot her a scornful glance.

"I'm Charlotte Evans."

"I know." He looked up to reel in the top half of the ladder, which clicked and clanged as it doubled on itself. "You're doing a cookbook, and you want my mother's stuff. Forget it."

He didn't look like Cecily, she decided. He was too tall, too dark. According to what islanders said, Cecily's hair had been pure silver from the first day she set foot on Quinnipeague. Charlotte recalled it being long and flowing, the woman herself petite, almost spritelike. "I'm sorry about her death."

"Her gardens aren't public."

"How'd she die?"

When the ladder was fully compressed, he secured the extension and carried the whole thing around the corner. The clink faded into the rolling surf, or into a garage or a shed, though she didn't hear a door. He was empty-handed when he returned, walking past her to collect an assortment of tools from the ground near where the ladder had been.

Charlotte was thinking he had tuned her out, when he knelt by the toolbox not far from her feet and said, "She got sick."

Cecily. "With what?" When he didn't answer, Charlotte said, "She was a healer. Getting sick shouldn't have been a problem."

Angling away, he dug into a pocket.

"Did she die at home? Is she buried here?"

After dumping a handful of nails in the toolbox, he stood again, went to the pole that held the floodlight, and turned it off.

The darkness was a shock. But the moon was out now. As her eyes adjusted, she could see the gardens. Oh yes, something grew there, and it wasn't last year's crop. This was new growth, full-bodied and fresh. Several of the taller plants had even been staked.

With a rustle, a small, fat creature appeared from a row on the left, crossed the dirt drive, and waddled off down a row on the right. Charlotte might have asked about it if she hadn't suddenly spotted a deer. It was watching them from the edge of the trees, its pelt a tawny glow in the moonlight.

She took a breath. "How beautiful."

"You should see her fawn."

"Where?"

He hitched his chin toward the staked plants. "She leaves it while she goes looking for food."

"Why go anywhere, when she has a feast right here?"

"Oh, she won't eat any of this. She knows it's mine."

Charlotte looked at him, but if there was humor in his eyes, the night hid it. "Seriously?"

He didn't smile. "You need to leave. I have work to do."

"I'll say," she dared. "Your window's cracked, your drainpipes sag, and the shingles on your roof are lifting. Storm shutters are all well and good, but they won't keep rain from coming in the roof."

He straightened an arm, pointing back toward the road.

"But this was just getting fun," she protested.

He stared.

"Tell you what," she tried. *Aim high, hit high.* "Just say I can come back one day to see the gardens. One day. That's it. Then I'll disappear, and you'll never hear from me again."

"Sneakin' pictures with your iPhone, so the world knows what's here? No way." He hitched his chin toward the road. "You're gratin' on my nerves. Bear doesn't like that."

"Bear?"

"My dog."

"If you had a dog," she countered, "it'd have gone after the deer and her fawn and whatever that little fat thing was."

He snapped his fingers. From behind a bush by the house, a creature emerged that was large, black, and hulking. It plodded forward on huge paws, stopping several yards from Charlotte, and stared at her with what she could only call feral eyes.

She wasn't afraid of dogs. But she didn't like them. And this one? Not friendly. "O-kay," she said lightly and backed away. "I was just being neighborly."

The dog continued to stare. Its ears were alert, its jowls wet enough to reflect a sliver of moon.

After retreating a few more steps, making her intent clear as she put just that little distance between herself and Bear, she faced forward, chin up, and strode down the drive. She listened closely for the thud of paws or the jingle of a collar, but if the dog followed, it was silent.

She didn't look back until she was on the safe side of the Cole curve, and then it was only for a quick glance over her shoulder. She wasn't surprised to see the road deserted. Leo Cole didn't want her around, but she hadn't sensed untamed anger. Nor, in spite of the dog, had she sensed danger. Leo just wanted to be left alone.

She could do that. She had no interest in the man.

But those gardens . . . those gardens held her thoughts as she walked along the road. The promise of them was a drug, and she didn't mean dope. That smell she couldn't parse? It was fertility, healing, and hope all at once. She had to get back there, and not with an iPhone. She wanted to use her Nikon, ideally up close with a wide-angle lens, but with a zoom from afar and on the sly if need be. She could make those gardens come alive in print. She could capture that scent. Nicole's readers would love it.

So would Nicole. It was the least Charlotte could do.

Chapter Seven

CHARLOTTE DIDN'T TELL NICOLE THAT she'd been to the Cole place, simply because other things took precedence—namely, the arrival of summer. She knew it the instant she got out of bed Thursday, could see it in how the beach grass stood tall and hear it in the languid cry of the gulls. When she opened the window, she felt a special Quinnie warmth. This wasn't the sticky heat of the city, but rather a gentling of air that was balmy and sweet. It was also very possibly fleeting, she feared, having spent enough summers here to know how quickly the cold could return. Seizing the moment was key.

To that end, once they finished breakfast on the patio and felt the true warmth of that sun, she suggested the beach. Nicole looked at her, looked at the ocean, grinned conspiratorially, and rose.

An hour later, with no mention whatsoever of the cookbook, they were in the Wrangler, driving in the direction of town only enough to pass the clam flats and reach Okers Beach. Two other cars were already parked on the sandy berm by the path; had it been the weekend, there would have been more. Houses like Nicole's had their own beaches, but most were on the north side. Okers, being on the south and tucked into a Quinnie curve, offered calmer surf and softer sand. It also offered drive-bys from the Chowder House with sandwiches, chips, and drinks, though when Charlotte and Nicole arrived, lunch was still a ways off.

Dropping their bags, they set up low beach chairs, put on sunscreen, and reached for their copies of *Salt*.

"You'll finish today," Charlotte said, eyeing the small wad of pages Nicole had left.

Nicole grimaced. "I know. I'm trying to read slowly. I do not want this to end."

Charlotte, who was barely halfway through, wasn't rushing to finish either, and not for lack of interest. If she was bored, she wouldn't finish; she liked books to sweep her up, and if one didn't, it was gone. *Salt* offered contentment in a slow savoring, luxury in knowing there was more to read. "What is it about this book?" she asked. "It's not like the plot is unique. Man and dog are alone. A perfect woman comes for the summer. They try to make a go of it."

"You make it sound trite."

"But the way he writes, it isn't. That's my point. What is going on here that has us holding our breath?"

Nicole spread a hand on the page before her. "We love the hero. He's vulnerable. He really needs her. I mean, he's capable of living alone. He's done it for years. But his life is empty." She paused before adding a quiet, "We die for this. Every woman wants to be needed."

Even with the surf diluting it, Charlotte heard sadness. "Julian needs you."

"Does he? I mean, if he doesn't want me with him now, what does that say?"

"It says he doesn't know how to handle this any more than you do. It says he doesn't know what he's supposed to be doing."

Nicole stroked the book. "That's what we love about *Salt*. This guy knows what he wants. He's out on his lobster boat all day long, but he knows he wants to come home to this woman." Her voice melted. "She's his dream come true. Is that the sweetest?"

"They won't end up together," Charlotte warned.

"How do you know that?" Dismay, then accusation, "Charlotte Evans, you rat, you read the ending!"

"I didn't," Charlotte protested, laughing.

"You always used to, and it's just as bad now as it was then, because I *do* want them to be together." She swatted at Charlotte's arm. "You are a spoiler!"

Still laughing, Charlotte fended off another swat. "I have not read the ending. I swear. It's just that I understand this woman. She lives in Dallas. She's used to glitz and restaurants and shopping. How can she trade that for life on a small island?"

"Easy, if she loves him enough."

"You are such a romantic."

"And you aren't?"

"Of course I am," Charlotte conceded. "I love this book, too." She had a hopeful thought. "Tell me there's a twist coming that'll allow her to stay."

"I'm not telling," Nicole said and, lowering her sunglasses, began to read.

Thursday was the kind of day Charlotte had dreamed of when she agreed to come to Quinnipeague. They read, they walked the beach, they swam as much as the cold ocean water allowed. By the time the Chowder House van arrived, there were others on the beach. Nicole knew most as summer people, and while there were warm hellos, they kept to themselves.

Summer people were that way. Most were escaping busy lives and welcomed the hush. Locals were the ones who talked.

Today, there was just the smell of sunscreen and surf, hours without awareness of time, and when the sun was at its highest and warmest, crab cakes on buns, topped with Dorey's special tartar sauce. "Did you know," Nicole remarked, blotting her mouth with a napkin, "that the French were the ones who first popularized tartar sauce, which was named after the Tatars from Russia and the Ukraine, and that those early versions contained white wine vinegar and capers?"

Charlotte peeled back her bun. "I don't see capers."

"No. Dorey uses sweet pickle, parsley, and chive."

The Cecily Cole effect, Charlotte thought, but didn't say it aloud. Rather, they went back to eating, back to a serenity stroked by the tempo of the surf and undisturbed by talk of either the cookbook or Julian. The only tears were Nicole's when she finished reading *Salt*. And they were voluminous, punctuated by multiple *omigod*s and a hand pressed to her chest to steady her heart.

Still she refused to tell Charlotte how the story ended. Rather, after a dinner that night of pecan-crusted cod—a test, since it was one of the Chowder House's signature dishes, and Nicole wanted to be sure the recipe was right—she let Charlotte clean the kitchen while she dove into a new book. Charlotte, who liked to linger with characters when she was done with a book, was dismayed that Nicole could so quickly put all that emotion aside, but she claimed she needed to immerse herself in another to compensate for the loss. It was escapism at its finest—denial of *Salt*, denial of MS. True to her word, she was quickly absorbed.

So Charlotte went for a walk. There was no heading toward town this time. Right off, she went in the other direction. The night was mild and her step steady. She rationalized, telling herself that she'd been a slug all day—sitting, reading, *eating*—which was true. But she was also curious about what was happening at the house.

She walked in moonlight this time, enjoying the mild air, the sweet smells of nascent blooms. One day of warmth, and the shrubs lining the road added the scent of roses to that of sea salt all the way to the Cole curve, where the tang of pine sap took its place.

She slowed at the curve. She didn't hear anything tonight. And sure enough, when she went on, all was dark. She walked until she came abreast of the gardens, which, too, were more strongly scented than before. There were flowers here, not just herbs. She would stake her novice nose on it.

Stopping, she sat down right there in the middle of the drive. Far beyond trees, rocks, and the house, the surf rolled in, but its sound was muted enough by those objects not to hide that of small creatures on the move. A chipmunk darted across the drive, its tiny tail straight up. A frog jumped, croaked, jumped again, and disappeared into the plants with only the occasional diminishing croak.

Focusing on the woods, she let her eyes adjust to the shadows, separating one tree from the next and—ahhhh, there was the doe. Standing straight and still, it might have passed for a tree had Charlotte not known to look. It was watching her. She held her breath, wondering if it would accept her benignity—wondering, actually, if it would proceed to eat Leo Cole's goods now that he wasn't around to see. It didn't. In time, it simply turned and, without a sound, stepped gracefully into the pines.

Charlotte was thinking that she really wanted to look for the fawn, only that would likely bring the doe back, and this wasn't her land to disturb—when a dog barked. The sound was muffled; Bear was in the house. Anxious to get out and chase whoever trespassed?

Sitting in the dirt without moving, she waited for the front door to open. Alternately, her gaze skipped to the side of the house from which she half expected a hulking brute of a black dog to burst. What would she do if it did?

Run. Fast.

But there was no sign of Bear, either in that minute or the next twenty, which was how long she sat filling her lungs with Cole air. Its intricate blend of flowers and herbs, warm now and intense, was hypnotic. She half expected that her legs would refuse to move if she decided to leave.

But they didn't balk when she stood. They were rested and filled with energy—actually took her back to Nicole's house at a speed she would have marveled at had she been watching the time. Her mind, though, was filled with less honorable thoughts. She was wondering whether, if she returned another night, she might walk through that garden. She was wondering if the light of the moon would allow her to take pictures of the herbs there. She was *wondering* whether, if she was undetected then, too, she might *borrow* a few.

*   *   *

She might have shared the plan if Nicole had been in the kitchen when she returned, but she was asleep, and by the time Charlotte went downstairs Friday morning, the urgency had passed.

Nicole was late joining her. Carrying her laptop, she had apparently been working into the wee hours, not sleeping at all. After reading a tip in one of her favorite farm reports, she had researched and blogged about a new artichoke cultivar with a heart was so tender it could be eaten without being cooked. It was the kind of cutting-edge news she liked passing on to her readers, and having done that at length, she said, she had earned the right to play.

So they spent another warm day at the beach. There were more bodies on towels today; weekenders had arrived, delivered early by the ferry with a guttural noise that could be heard from the pier, and the beach was the go-to spot. Though there was no boisterousness, there were iPod docks and earbuds aplenty. There was also lots of talk, with Nicole in its midst. Many of those newly arrived were people she had known for years but hadn't seen since fall.

Watching her, Charlotte thought she looked better. She was in her element with people, and though there were questions about Bob and Julian, she handled them well. She even accepted a dinner invitation from friends of her parents, who had half a dozen others coming as well.

"They want you, too," Nicole informed her when she returned to their towels and stretched out again, but Charlotte shook her head no.

"Why not?"

"I'm not a dinner party kind of person."

"Are you kidding? You'd be the most interesting one in the room!"

"I hate small talk."

"You can do it."

"Oh, I can. I just don't want to."

Nicole must have sensed she was serious, because she said, "Then we'll go another time. You're my guest. I can't leave you home alone."

"Of course you can," Charlotte scolded. "You love the McKenzies. And besides, this breaks the ice for you. It's better to see some people now, than everyone all at once Sunday morning at brunch." Bailey's Brunch was an annual event, ostensibly to celebrate the summer solstice, though truly to welcome back seasonal Quinnies. Held at the church, it would be the first townwide gathering of the summer, and therefore an important one for Charlotte and Nicole to attend. "Besides, these are your people, not mine." She paused and said on a lighter note, "See the heads on the bluff?"

Nicole glanced up at the rocks that anchored the far end of the beach. The heads were attached to bodies of local teenage boys, for whom hours on that bluff each summer weekend was a rite of passage. "They're still at it."

"Obviously a different crew."

"For sure, but they do love taking it in. Warm bodies."

"Warm *female* bodies."

"And you in a one-piece suit. What happened to the bikinis you loved?"

"The French Riviera," Charlotte remarked, and at Nicole's curious frown, said, "Bikinis all over the place, looking great on some bodies and horrid on others, and the occasional one-piece suit looking so much better."

"But you have the body for a bikini."

Charlotte couldn't comment further. "Not like yours. You look amazing, Nicki. You absolutely have to go to the McKenzies' tonight. Trust me. You'll light up the party."

Nicole leaned close to be heard over the sounds of laughter and waves. Her eyes were a crystal-clear green. "Do you know how *glad* I am that you're here? Come? Please?"

But Charlotte shook her head and smiled. "After a day here with all these people? I'm socialized out. You go. I'll sleep."

* * *

She didn't sleep, of course. She planned to, but wasn't tired, and what she wanted, really, was to photograph herbs. Shouldering the Nikon, she walked down the road, familiar enough now with the terrain to move to the center even before the pavement worsened. She listened for hammering or barking but heard only the reverberating surf, and when she rounded the curve, there was nothing but moonlight on a dark house.

Flash would be a problem. Not only would it skew the true color of the plants, but a sudden glint, no matter now brief, might alert Leo Cole. So, no flash, just moonlight, which gave a silver glow to the plants and was actually charming. She had a steady hand. She also had enough experience taking pictures in the wild to know how to brace her body for greater stability.

By the time she thought this through, though, the smells had sunk in and were distilling her plans. Oddly mindless, she went to the same spot on the drive and sat down. *Take pictures,* ordered the tiny voice in her head. But she wasn't in the mood. *Borrow,* said the voice. But she didn't want to do that, either.

She felt lethargic.

No. Not lethargic.

Relaxed. Content. *Seduced.*

Legs folded, hands limp on her thighs, she dropped her head back, closed her eyes, and slowly inhaled. Basil? Mint? Cilantro? There were threads of each—but also of others far beyond her ability to name. And fertile earth. And sweet salt air. The moment was rich.

Then came breathing. She righted her head and opened her eyes. The road to the house was empty, but when she looked left down an aisle of staked plants, she saw the dog.

It came toward her on paws so large that she vetoed the idea of running. She wouldn't get far, and the damage of lunging jaws could be worse. So she held her breath while it approached and sniffed her face, her neck, her camera. Its nose was wet. She wanted to recoil, but didn't dare move.

"Caught," came a low voice from behind her. And still she didn't take her eyes off Bear.

"Call off your dog," she said through lips that barely moved.

"He doesn't like trespassers, either."

"I'm just sitting."

"On my land."

"Call off your dog and I'll leave."

He snapped his fingers—once, softly—and the dog lumbered past. Only then, with care, did Charlotte turn. Leo Cole was barefoot, bareheaded, bare armed and legged. Shorts and a tank, that was it. His face was shadowed, accentuating its hard lines, while the dog at his thigh watched her with distrust.

"Fancy camera," he said in that flat voice of his.

"It's part of my arm."

"Which you stand to lose if you lift it."

"No lifting. It's too dark. Call off the dog."

"If it's too dark, why'd you bring it?"

"There were flowers back on the road that were pretty in the moonlight."

"And I'm a leprechaun."

She might have snickered. He was way too tall and deep-voiced to be any kind of magical creature, and with a menacing dog, foaming at the mouth beside him? Well, maybe not foaming. But scary enough. Trying to stay calm, she took a slow breath.

"Were you meditating?" he asked.

"No." With movements measured enough not to alarm the dog, she rose. "I was . . . being. There's something about this air. It's like a drug."

"You with the FDA?"

"No. With the cookbook lady."

That was nearly as bad, to judge from the tightness of his mouth. "Yeah. Looking for pictures. And recipes. You won't get either, y'know."

"Why not?"

"Because I'll put out word that I don't want you to."

"Why will islanders listen to you?"

"Because I grow the herbs."

"I thought people here grew their own."

"I control the parent plants, and the parent plants control theirs."

Charlotte failed to make the connection. "Like, your plants decide whether their plants grow? That's imaginative."

He shrugged, clearly not caring what she thought.

"What's it to you anyway, our cookbook?" she asked.

"Publicity stinks." He moved aside in silent command, and made the smallest *scoot* with his thumb in case she missed the message.

She might have asked more—about Cecily, about the herbs, about what he did out here on the far tip of the island besides repairing his house in the dark—if it hadn't been for the dog, and while, looking down on it now, she didn't see any more viciousness there than last time, she wasn't taking chances. Leo didn't want her around. And Leo controlled the dog.

That said, she wasn't exactly sure how to get past them. Between him, the dog, and one narrow drive, there wasn't a whole lot of room. If she went to the left, she would be close to the dog. If she went to the right, she would be close to Leo.

She was trying to decide which was safer when, sounding vaguely amused, he asked, "Are you afraid of Bear?"

"I was bitten by a dog once." She saw no point in denial. As far as she was concerned, caution was a good thing when you didn't know the beast. "That one was supposed to be friendly. Yours looks anything but."

He touched the dog's head with the tips of his fingers, apparently another signal, because, seeming suddenly bored, the dog looked away.

Charlotte didn't trust that it wouldn't look back and lunge. Opting for the right side, she walked slowly past Leo and continued on down the drive.

* * *

"You what?" Nicole asked in disbelief. They were in the kitchen, topping off breakfast with seconds of coffee. Nicole had just given a blow-by-blow of dinner at the McKenzies'—good company, a pork tenderloin, from a local pig farm, that had been laced with rosemary and grilled and was surprisingly good, though pork wasn't her favorite meat, and a stunning centerpiece of wildflowers floating in a hollow gourd about which she had just blogged—and she wanted to know what Charlotte had done.

"I was at the Cole place."

"What do you mean, *at* the Cole place? Like walking around? Ringing the *bell*?"

"I don't think there's a bell," Charlotte said. She had her knees up, bare feet on the edge of her seat, hands cupping her mug. "The house is old and run-down. Leo was fixing a shutter. I gave him a hand."

"You what?"

"Helped him out."

"Leo *saw* you? Charlotte, you are not supposed to go there. If there's one thing Quinnies say, it's that. Leo is dangerous."

Charlotte remembered being up on that ladder Wednesday night. He might have easily tossed her off or touched her inappropriately, but he hadn't done either. He had steadied her until the job was done, then backed off. Granted, he was more annoyed last night, but hindsight cast a softer view on that as well. "I don't think he is. I've been there three times—"

"Three? *When?*"

Charlotte felt marginally guilty. "The last three nights. It's really no big thing, Nicki. That's just the direction I walk. The distance from here to there is just right."

"He's the island bad boy."

"Not a boy anymore."

"Which makes it worse. Three nights, and you didn't tell me? What else haven't you told me?"

Charlotte felt a stab of serious guilt. What to say to that? "He has a dog."

"He has a dog," Nicole repeated with a considering nod. "You hate dogs."

"Only because that Dalmatian bit me, but my father kicked it first, so it thought it was being attacked and went after the weakest thing in sight, that is, me. I've met some nice dogs."

"If this was Leo Cole's, it was not."

"You don't know that," Charlotte warned. "When it came at me, I felt threatened. But it didn't attack." She paused. "Have you ever seen Leo up close?"

"No. The day I got here, he was storming through the center of town. He was way down the street, but if looks could kill, I'd be dead."

Charlotte hadn't felt anything murderous. "He didn't seem so bad to me."

"What did he look like?"

She retrieved the image, considering it now as she hadn't before. "A man."

"Obviously."

"Fit."

"Muscular?"

"No. Just . . . fit. *Clean*," she added, though she wasn't sure why the word popped up—maybe because he had been anything but clean in the old days, so she had expected the opposite? His hands had been smudged while he worked on his roof. But she wouldn't have called him dirty.

"You must've seen more than I did," Nicole remarked. "Of course, you did. You were up close. Remember that long hair?"

"It's short now," Charlotte said. "Brown. Maybe with flecks of gray, though that could have been the moon. How old is he?"

"Four or five years older than us."

"So, late thirties. That fits."

"What was he wearing? When I saw him last week, he was dressed in black."

"The same last night, I think, though it might have been navy. He was wearing shorts."

"Oh boy," Nicole drawled. "Falling off his butt, I bet."

"Actually, no. They were nylon—long, like basketball shorts—and they hung at the right place."

"His waist."

"His hips." The shorts had been drapey in a modest way. "Slim hips. Ropy arms. What does he do, Nicki? I mean, he needs food, and for that, he needs money. I can't imagine Cecily left him much, so how does he get it?"

"He was a handyman for a while," Nicole said. "We never used him. He smelled."

Charlotte laughed. "Who said that?"

"Everyone."

"Well, he doesn't now. At least, I didn't smell anything."

"Not even the dog?"

"No. It didn't smell. It was short-haired."

"A pit bull."

"Uh-uh. Too big. He calls it Bear."

"That figures. He could be trouble, Charlotte," she advised. "He could charge you with trespassing. He could go to court to prevent us from mentioning Cecily in the book. He could sue my publisher for a cut in the profits."

"He won't do that."

"And if you really piss him off," Nicole went on, "he could get—I don't know—some kind of *injunction* to prevent us from printing any recipe that uses her herbs, which means the book is dead. Promise me you'll stay away from him, Charlotte."

"But there's a whole other side to this," Charlotte reasoned, thinking of the camera she hadn't yet mentioned. "What if I can get into his gardens?"

Nicole reached across the table and grabbed her hand. "There's nothing in those gardens that we can't get anywhere else."

"Yes, there is. There's—" *A photo op,* she might have said, but Nicole cut in.

"Herbs? There are herbs all over the island. We don't need any from Leo Cole. Promise you'll stay away?"

"There are roots."

"What—like parsnip, turnip, beet?"

"No," Charlotte said but stopped. The business about Leo's plants being parents that controlled their offspring was ridiculous—but she wouldn't put it past Nicole to buy it. At the very least, it would make her nervous. Besides, Charlotte wasn't sure if that was what she meant by roots. She wasn't sure what she meant. The word just popped out. Like clean.

"Promise, Charlotte?" Nicole begged. "Please? For me?"

Charlotte had nodded. It wasn't exactly a swear-on-the-Bible promise, which she would have had trouble making. But she couldn't go to the Cole place today, anyway. Weekends on Quinnipeague offered choices. Many involved food, others sport, yard sales, or entertainment. This weekend being the kickoff of the summer season—and Nicole being committed, for the sake of the cookbook, to being seen by as many Quinnies as possible—their day was filled.

They started at a library book sale, to which they brought bags of books culled from the shelves around the house. It was the first of the cleaning-out Nicole would have to do, but between the two of them, they worked with such speed and left so quickly, that the emotional impact was minimal.

From there, they hit a cookout on the pier—actually, a cookout on Susan Murray's forty-foot party boat. Susan was the CEO of a software company in Portland, which meant that, while she wasn't a full-time resident of Quinnipeague, she lived close enough to visit year-round. A born manager, she loved to party, but there wasn't an ounce of pretension about her. Her boat was an old pontoon, and the menu—Susan's standard—was hamburgers, hot dogs, and chips, with mounds of s'mores cookies. The cookies were a must for the book, as was Susan.

After lunch came softball on the school field. The school itself was small, limited to pre-K through five, with higher grades shuttled to the mainland, but the field was the largest open spread on the island. Two games were played simultaneously, with Nicole in one and Charlotte in the other, and there were cold drinks afterward.

Returning home sweaty, they went for a swim at the house and sat on the patio wrapped in towels until the shadows deepened, at which point they returned to town, grabbed salads at The Island Grill with six seasonals who happened to show up at the same time as they for dinner, followed by movie night at the church. This week's showing was *Titanic*, which everyone in the place had already seen, but the island ambience—the smell of hot popcorn bagged by the minister and his wife as quickly as their little machine could produce it, the whirr of fans in the cathedral ceiling, and the creak of old wooden chairs—added a special flavor.

The church was the go-to spot for every large island gathering. Saturday night was the movie, Sunday morning a service, and then, in a transformation that never failed to amaze Charlotte with its speed, came Bailey's Brunch.

The place was packed with islanders ranging from a ninety-year-old to a newborn, from weekend regulars to summer people to one-time guests. Charlotte and Nicole divided up here, too, working the crowd as much for the sake of the book as for fun. Charlotte had always been drawn to the less conventional of island residents, and though few of them were foodies and, hence subjects for the book, she remembered many and enjoyed catching up.

And, of course, there was food, which was set out on long tables where an hour before parishioners had filled rows of chairs. The presentation was nothing to write home about, with paper goods and plastic utensils in piles. And still, in all her travels Charlotte had never seen as appealing a spread. There were quiches of every variety, French toast casseroles, fish hash, and a curried fish that she adored, plus tuna mousse, salmon cakes, and crab fritters. There were chowders—no island event went without. There were cruelly delicious sticky buns, cranberry scones, and tuna muffins. There was the fruit compote that she loved, and chewy chocolate candies, each with an almond inside, individually wrapped and filling a bowl. She knew that the makings for those, not to mention the coffee beans behind the rich coffee in her cup, were from another part of the world. Nearly everything else, though, was locally caught or grown.

Charlotte mingled, catching up with people she hadn't seen in ten years. She booked interviews, often now alongside Nicole, who sampled every dish in an evaluative way, ever-so-subtly shaking her head or nodding to indicate which they wanted and which they did not.

They stayed even after the crowd thinned, enjoying themselves, which was a good thing. The enjoyment ended abruptly when Nicole's phone rang on the way home. It was Julian, apparently having been trying her for several hours, though Nicole couldn't have heard her phone over the voices at the church.

He was having trouble breathing. It was one of the more rare side effects of the drug he was on, and usually passed quickly. This time it hadn't. His doctor wanted to see him Monday morning. So rather than flying south, he was taking the train to New York. He suggested Nicole meet him there.

Charlotte drove her to the pier, where a boat was waiting to take her to Rockland. From there, she would taxi to Portland, then fly to New York. Though Nicole didn't tell her much beyond the basics, Charlotte felt the weight of worry. "You'll call me with updates?" she asked when she pulled Nicole's bag from the Jeep.

"It'll be hard. You're not supposed to know."

"But I do, so I'll be thinking of you the whole time. Text me. Or go down the hall and call."

"I'll try," Nicole said and gave her a hug.

*   *   *

Back at the house, Charlotte wandered. She tried not to let her imagination do the same, but it was hard not to think of what-ifs. *Salt* helped; the hero was rebuilding a boat, the process of which Charlotte found intriguing. But reading meant focusing in on words, and she was too antsy to do that for long.

So she knit for a while. It turned out that those incredibly good chocolate almond candies had been made by a newcomer to Quinnipeague who owned a yarn store in town. Charlotte planned to visit. That meant making progress on her sleeve, so that she didn't *totally* embarrass herself. Having finished the ribbed cuff, though, she was following the Aran pattern chart when she made a mistake. She ripped two painstaking rows, knit them again, and discovered she had dropped a stitch, which was now lost three rows back.

Frustrated, she set the knitting aside and went outside. She walked the beach. She swept the patio. Opening her laptop, she checked her friends' Facebook pages and looked at Twitter for the first time in days.

Dusk kept her waiting. But the minute it arrived, she was off.

Chapter Eight

LEO COLE WAS DOING SOMETHING different. The sound Charlotte heard as she approached was a sporadic clattering, like he was hurling something against metal. She couldn't tell what it was until she rounded the Cole curve and saw the floodlit slope of his roof. Two ladders stood there; near the top, a board stretched between them. Boots on the board, Leo was prying up shingles, tossing one after another into the Dumpster below.

She looked for the dog, didn't see it, and walked slowly forward. When she was close enough, she linked her hands behind her and watched for a while. Oh yeah, she had told him that his shingles were lifting. Watching him, though, she guessed he had known it. The way he went at the task spoke of experience. His movements were methodical and sure. From time to time, he grunted with the effort of removing a stubborn piece, but for the most part, he seemed untaxed.

In time, he stopped, pushed a forearm up his brow, hitched the claw tool to the next shingle in line, and reached for a bottle of water. That was when he spotted Charlotte, though if she hadn't been looking closely, she wouldn't have known. He didn't jump, didn't even fully turn, simply looked sideways as he drank. When he was done, he wiped his mouth with the back of his hand.

"Why am I not surprised," he muttered just loud enough for her to hear, then reached for the claw and continued his work.

She heard derision. But anger? Not really. "You knew about the roof problem."

"Yup. I ordered shingles a month ago."

"Why do you do this at night?"

He was silent. Then, "Why do you want to know?"

"Human interest." She shrugged. "Boredom."

He pried up several more shingles and tossed them back before saying, "Sun's down. Wind's down."

"When do you sleep?"

Another shingle fell. "When I'm tired."

"Studies show that the less sleep you get, the greater your chance of stroke."

"Studies get it backward," he countered. "Insomnia is caused by stress, which causes high blood pressure, which causes stroke. I'm not stressed."

She might have argued for the sake of argument, if he hadn't made total sense. So maybe he worked all night and slept all day. "You don't have a nine-to-five job?"

He worked on, finally said, "Nope."

"How do you pay for the shingles?"

He glanced down, sounding annoyed. "What's it to you?"

"Nothing. I'm just curious." Looking around, she spotted the toolbox. "If you have another roof ripper, I could help."

He snorted. "Dressed like that?"

"I'm not dressed any different from you." A tank top and shorts. His tank was chopped unevenly at the waist, the shorts as dark and drapey as always.

"You don't have boots."

No, but her sneakers were designed for traction. She turned one to show him the sole. When he simply went at another shingle, she said, "Seriously. I can help."

"You've done this, too?"

"I have."

He worked on for a bit. Then, "Nah. Only one claw." Moving to the right to reach a new spot, he said, "Want to make yourself useful, pick up the shingles that missed the Dumpster."

With the floodlight aimed at the roof, the ground was dark. Only when her eyes adjusted did she see what he meant.

But she didn't move. Climbing a ladder was one thing; groveling around on the ground with her arms and legs exposed was another. "Where's the dog?" she asked.

"In the bushes."

"Will he attack?"

"Not if you pick up the shingles and leave."

Trusting that he could control his dog, she collected an armful of shingles and dropped them in the Dumpster. After a second, then a third, she was done. Brushing off her hands, she called up, "What else can I do?"

"Get away from the Dumpster. Stay there, and you're gonna be hit."

"You wouldn't aim at me."

He barked out what might have been a laugh. "If my aim was perfect, you wouldn't'a had anything to pick up just now."

He had a point. Moving away from the Dumpster, she folded her arms on her chest and watched him work. He must have been trying harder, because every shingle went into the Dumpster, so there was nothing to do. After a bit, she sat.

"You said you'd leave," he charged.

"You said that. Not me." Her curiosity was far from satisfied, and the dog hadn't appeared. "What's it like being in jail?"

He shot her a look. But he didn't call the dog. "That's a dumb question. It *sucks*." He pried up several more shingles, tossed them down with greater force. One hit the ground, but he didn't seem to notice. "How'd you know I was in jail?"

"People talked about it back then," she said, standing, waiting. As soon as he tossed down the next shingle, she darted in for the one on the ground and tipped it into the Dumpster.

"You were here before?"

"Well, now you've hurt my feelings. I spent seventeen summers here. So I didn't make any impression?"

He stretched to reach higher shingles. "I don't remember much."

"High on Cecily's cures?"

Bracing the claw against the roof, he scowled down at her. "One of the reasons I work at night is because it's quiet. If you're gonna stay here, you have to shut up."

At least he wasn't harping on her leaving. This was progress. "I can shut up."

"Do it. Please." He moved farther right to work on a final swath of shingles. "And you're wrong. I wasn't high all the time. I was angry."

"Seriously," Charlotte mused. That scowl was what she remembered, but she didn't hear anger. "What did Cecily die of?"

He worked for a bit. She guessed he was ignoring her, but she had interviewed reluctant subjects before. She was about to lob up an easier question, when he said, "Pneumonia."

Pneumonia. That surprised Charlotte. Cecily would have known how to treat pneumonia. "I was thinking it had to be cancer."

"It was. She went to the hospital for that. While she was there, she got pneumonia."

Charlotte had heard similar stories, but it suddenly made Leo more human. "That's bad. I'm sorry."

"Not as sorry as I am," he said, grimacing against a stubborn shingle. "I was the one who dragged her to the hospital."

Since Quinnipeague had no hospital, that would have been on the mainland, and what Charlotte heard went beyond regret to guilt. Gently, she asked, "Is that why you hang around here, to keep up her house and garden?"

"Among other reasons."

"Like what?"

He looked down, annoyed again. "Don't you need to be somewhere?"

"Actually, no," though, sitting still, she was feeling a chill, so she unwound the sweatshirt from her waist. "Nicole's in New York. It's just me at the house." She looped the sweatshirt around her shoulders.

"Should you be telling me this?" he asked.

"Why not?"

"I'm dangerous."

"So they say," she remarked, because she was still alive now after, what, four visits?

"You know different?"

She smiled. "I know karate."

The movement of his cheek might have been a smile or a wince, though it was lost when he hung his head. After a minute, he straightened and took another drink of water. Then he climbed down the ladder.

Not trusting him, Charlotte stood. "Another few minutes, and you'll be done," she said, studying the small strip of remaining shingles. "What's next?"

He stood an arm's length away, seeming taller than he had the night before, when she'd passed him on the drive. "If you've done a roof, you know," he warned. The slightest pat of his thigh caused a rustle in the bushes.

Tar paper was next. But the dog was at his side now, so she put a smile on her face, turned, and sauntered off.

Karate might protect her from the man, but the dog? She didn't know which was more dangerous—or whether either was, certainly a thought there.

One thing was for sure, though. Both paled next to MS, which was what rose up in her mind the nearer she came to the house.

*   *   *

Nicole knew the drill. After landing at LaGuardia, she took a cab to the small hotel where they always stayed. It was an easy walk from the hospital, but this night even that seemed too far. Shortness of breath? A tight chest? Both were documented side effects of the meds Julian was on, but they were also classic symptoms of a heart attack. She suspected Peter Keppler had suggested he go straight to the ER in Philadelphia, but that he had refused.

Much as she told herself that, being a doctor, Julian would know the difference, she was terrified about what she would find.

Having already checked in, he had texted her the room number, so she pulled her roller bag straight to the elevator. Eight anxious floors up, she went down the hall and knocked softly. Praying he was still alive, she listened for sound. But he wasn't a heavy man, and, as it happened, he was barefoot. The relief she felt when the latch clicked and the door opened was intense.

He looked pale, but not blue. Though clearly tired, he stood straight.

Slipping into the room, she closed the door and wrapped her arms around his neck, relieved to be able to drink in everything that was Julian and strong. When he hugged her back, she imagined there was an element of clinging in it. He did need her. That was gratifying.

Finally drawing back, she studied his face. "How is it?"

"Better."

"But still there. Which one—tightness or short breath?"

"Both, but better. What did you tell Charlotte?" he asked, and she wanted to yell that Charlotte wasn't what mattered, *he* was.

But Julian, being Julian, was neurotic about secrecy, and if he was worried about Charlotte, she could help him with this at least. "I told her one of your colleagues died and I wanted to be with you at the funeral. I've gotten good at lying." Wasn't she doing it right then? Oh yes, she was good. If he had suspected she wasn't telling the truth, he would have pushed it.

But he simply asked, "Flight okay?"

"I guess. I wasn't really focused on it. I kept thinking I'd walk in here and—"

"Don't say it, baby."

"I know I know I know," she whispered, as much in contrition as anything else. "Were you sleeping?" Though he was still dressed, his hair was disheveled and his eyes heavy.

He shook his head, made the face that said he had been doing nothing worthwhile, which meant he was likely sprawled on the bed, staring at the ceiling, worrying about the same things she was and then some.

"Thanks for coming," he said.

And suddenly, out of the blue, she was livid. Growing up, the only child of adoring parents, she had been indulged on every level. She hadn't had to filter her thoughts back then, and though life experiences had taught her something of self-control, when she was upset—really upset—she still lost it.

That happened now. After a long day of travel, hours of worry, and months of strain, *thanks for coming* hit her wrong. "Where else would I *be*?" she cried. "You're my husband. I should have been in Philly with you. You take care of me, Julian. Would it be so awful if I took care of you once in a while?"

"There's nothing to do," he said, pulling away.

"There *is*," she said, telling herself that this wasn't the time, what with that lingering tightness in his chest, only this *was* the time. "You've cut yourself off from everyone who means something to you."

"Not true. I talked with my parents yesterday. I talk with friends all the time."

"But not about the truth, so it's all a show. And this, now? I'm your cover, Jules. We both know that if we're in the hospital tomorrow and you see a colleague, the idea is that I'm the patient—and that's fine, if it makes you feel better. But it doesn't make me feel better, because I'm your wife, and you're shutting me out, too. Is that all I am, your cover?"

He stared at her. *Ease up, you're making things worse, don't nag, don't hover.* She heard it all.

Turning away, he began unbuttoning his shirt. After that came his pants and his socks. It used to be that his boxers would follow, and that when he turned back to her, his need would be clear. MS affected the sexual response of some patients, but not Julian. He remained perfectly capable—*amazingly* capable. But it had been weeks since he had allowed himself to feel the need.

Granted, they couldn't make love with his chest tight, regardless of how he tried to minimize the problem.

Still, watching him undress, she couldn't help but remember the days when sex was a constant, when all he had to do was to call her *baby*—such a macho word for an academic guy—and the attraction flamed.

She felt the longing.

Leaving the boxers on tonight, though, he slipped into bed, snapped off the light on his side, and closed his eyes.

Peter Keppler was thorough. Nicole had always liked that about him. It meant hours of waiting for tests, but by the end of the day, he had enough data to make an informed decision. They were in his hospital office, which was little more than a glorified examining room, but Nicole wasn't complaining. Julian looked better, she thought. He always did when they were with Peter, like he could finally, fully let someone else take charge. And he had slept well, moving so that their bodies touched. She wasn't sure it was conscious, but she had cherished it nonetheless.

They were in separate chairs now, Nicole trying to be calm, while Peter reviewed the day's tests. The good news, he reported, was that Julian's heart would be fine, the bad was that the daily charts he kept at home in Philly confirmed that there was no improvement in the symptoms.

"We'll change the cocktail," Peter decided. "It's a small tweaking, but I don't like these side effects."

"Forget the side effects," Julian said in his informed way. "I'm worried about the efficacy of these drugs. After three months, there should have been improvement. These meds are the newest and best. If they're not working, I'm in trouble."

The neurologist made a sound that was halfway between a grunt and a laugh. "Doctors are the worst patients. They're always one step ahead."

"You bet," Julian said. "My hands are shaking as often as ever. And numbness? Sitting in a chair when it hits is bad enough, but what happens if I'm walking down the hall with colleagues?"

Peter studied him. "I wish I could operate and correct the problem with a scalpel like you do, but MS isn't that way. You're stable. One new symptom isn't much in the overall scheme."

Nicole agreed. Three months wasn't very long. The research she had done suggested that it often took far longer on a medication for the disease to get the message.

But Julian wasn't on that page. "One new symptom is one too many," he said. "I'm getting worse. This is my life, and it's heading in the wrong direction."

"You have MS," Peter reminded him. "For all we know, your symptoms would be worse without the treatments you've had." *Precisely,* Nicole thought, as the doctor went on. "I've worked with some patients for ten years before finding a path to remission. You and I, we've only been at it for four."

"The wrong direction," Julian repeated ominously.

Charlotte spent the morning sorting through a ragtag collection of cups in leftover colors and designs, mismatched plates, napkins, picnic tablecloths, and plastic cutlery. Nicole had waved a dismissive hand at the pantry in which these were kept; she far preferred the real stuff to paper and plastic, and had suggested a wholesale cleaning. Charlotte figured she could help with this, at least.

After filling two large bags, she drove them to the church. Though she kept her phone in her pocket, Nicole didn't call.

Having stowed her camera in the backseat, she continued on to the farm where Anna McDowell Cabot raised the chickens that produced eggs for so many island specialties. Anna was a rotund woman who waddled and clucked like her hens, but her clucking was informative.

A lifelong Quinnie, she knew as much about the island as anyone. She talked for hours about the ways in which the island had changed, and, with Charlotte's frequent rechanneling, how those changes had affected the food.

Having been the beneficiary of herbal remedies for acid reflux, she considered Cecily Cole a saint. But when Charlotte mentioned Leo, she grew cautious. "He's very private."

"A bad boy."

"Bad?" With a soft clucking, she considered. "Not so much bad, as misunderstood."

"By whom?"

"Everyone for a while. He was an unhappy child. Now, he just keeps to himself."

"What does he do for a living?"

"Oh"—a specious sigh—"a little of this, little of that," which told her nothing.

"He still grows Cecily's herbs," she tried.

"Leo does not." A wise smile here. "Those herbs grow themselves."

"Does he sell them?"

"I never heard that."

"Does he give them to people who need them, like Cecily used to do?"

"I guess."

"Does he trade them for food?"

Anna frowned. "Why the questions?"

Charlotte wasn't about to suggest there were personal reasons, when there was reason enough on a professional vein. "Cecily's been dead five years, but her herbs are going strong. We're assembling a cookbook. How can I not ask about the herbs?"

"You know what they say about curiosity and the cat," the hen-keeper clucked.

Charlotte certainly did. Curiosity killed it. Bob Lilly used to warn her about that, though he loved her questions and never once refused an answer. There was, of course, a rejoinder to the adage—*and satisfac-*

tion brought it back—but Charlotte let it go. Having taken pictures as they talked and walked, she was more than satisfied with the interview. While others on the list could talk about specifics, Anna provided an overview that would be crucial for the book.

Charlotte left the Cabot farm feeling a new enthusiasm. Wanting to share it with Nicole, she sent a quick text. When she didn't hear back, she grew uneasy and tried calling, but Nicole didn't pick up.

It wasn't until late afternoon, when they returned to their hotel to pack, that Nicole was able to call Charlotte. Texting wouldn't do it. She needed to hear a comforting voice. Julian was taking a shower—wanting to wash the patient from his body, he said. She stood in the farthest corner of the bedroom, hunched over the phone with her eyes on the bathroom door.

"It's me," she said in a low rush. "I can't talk long. If the shower goes off, I'm done. We're heading to LaGuardia for a flight to Chicago."

"Chicago?" Charlotte asked in alarm. "What happened to Raleigh-Durham?"

Thinking how glad she was to be able to share her frustration, Nicole murmured, "Postponed for a couple of days, and I'm not happy about Chicago, either. I mean, things were fine today. It wasn't a heart attack, just a problem with the meds. His doctor wants to alter the dosage and give it more time, but my husband is impatient. We're going to Chicago for a consult."

"Aren't there other specialists in New York?"

"Yes, but Julian knows who's doing what where, and this one's into different therapies."

"What kind of different therapies?" Charlotte asked with what sounded like rising alarm—but even that was calming for Nicole, who welcomed validation of her own worry.

"This particular doctor is into stem cell transplants." The words shimmied around in her belly. She pressed a steadying hand there. "Julian is willing to try something unproven, if there's a chance it'll work. This scares me to death, Charlotte, but he's getting desperate." The shower went off. Straightening, she spoke casually. "So Anna was good?"

"Desperate to do something radical?" came the voice at the other end, but before she could answer, Julian opened the bathroom door. Toweling off, he came into the bedroom, eyes questioning.

"Just letting Charlotte know I won't be back tonight," she explained.

Charlotte exhaled audibly. "Okay. Well, you got my text. Anna's a great resource."

"Did she give you her recipe for layered eggs?" Nicole asked lightly. "By the way, I don't know why she calls it layered eggs, since it's really about ham, zucchini, and mushroom, but she uses incredible herbs. Did she list those for you?"

"She did."

"Good. I'll do a test batch once I'm back." She relished the thought, and it had nothing to do with food. Immersing herself in even this tiny bit of work was a respite. "Did you and Melissa Parker agree on a time to talk?" she asked. Melissa provided baked goods for the Chowder House, the Island Grill, and the Quinnie Café. Not only was she a must profile, but Nicole had given Charlotte a dream list of Melissa's recipes for inclusion as well.

"Tomorrow," Charlotte said. "So you're flying out tonight?"

"We are." She reverted to alibi. "It's been tough on the family. I'll do some cooking and bring over a few meals."

"How long will you stay in Chicago?"

Now that he was off the offending drug and he knew he would live, Julian wouldn't stay more than a day. He wanted to get to Duke before anyone suspected something amiss. Besides, the consultation was strictly informational. He had even offered to go alone, but in that case, Nicole knew she would get an abridgement of the discussion and would forever worry about what she had missed.

She had a stake in this; she wanted to hear exactly what was said. "I'll fly up Wednesday," she told Charlotte. "Can you make it without me until then?"

Chapter Nine

CHARLOTTE HELD THE PHONE TO her belly for a long time after the call ended. Nicole wasn't the only one who was scared. When it came to experimental treatments for MS, stem cell transplants held great promise. But there were stem cells—and then there were *umbilical cord* stem cells. Umbilical cord cells came from the blood that remained in a baby's umbilical cord after it was cut, blood that was drained and whisked to a blood bank where it was frozen and stored for future need. The ethical issues surrounding embryonic stem cells didn't apply here. This was blood. There was no egg, no fertilization. A baby couldn't grow from it. But increasingly, in research labs and hospitals worldwide, stem cells taken from umbilical cord blood were being found to have properties for healing and regrowth in humans with different diseases.

Such were the facts. Nicole surely knew them.

But Charlotte knew something Nicole did not. She knew something *Julian* did not. If she had to tell what she knew, the damage might be catastrophic.

Dreading that, she sat on the beach for a while. The ocean air was warm, blowing her hair, skimming her skin. She watched a gull swoop into the shallows for a catch, then a pair of sandpipers flipping stones in search of crabs. The sea was eternal, she told herself. Life went on. Traumas came and went.

It was small solace.

Needing a dose of comfort, she drove to the Chowder House for a lobster roll and fries, drove home again, and returned to the beach, where she proceeded to devour every last crumb in the bag.

Did she feel better? No. If anything, she felt worse now, like a terrible *fat* friend.

She needed to walk, and not to Leo's. She needed to *really* walk. Heading for town, she moved as quickly as her stomach allowed, going faster as the lobster and fries settled, finally turning and running home. She wasn't a runner. She had always wanted to be, but her knees disagreed. No doubt, they would be screaming by morning.

The Jacuzzi in Angie and Bob's bedroom would help. Nicole would have insisted, as would Angie, which was why she couldn't do it. She was a traitor of the worst kind—betraying Nicole, betraying Angie and Bob, even betraying Julian.

She was a bad person. If Leo Cole was, too, they deserved each other, or so her thinking went as she scrunched her mutinous hair into a wad and set off for the island's tail. She was so absorbed in her own guilt that she didn't hear anything—not the roll of the surf, the hoot of an owl, or the slap of her own feet—until she reached the Cole curve and the sound of hammering registered.

He would be applying tar paper to the roof he had exposed the night before. She knew that even before she saw him at it. Moving steadily along makeshift scaffolding, he unrolled the paper left to right, and hammered nails at regular intervals to secure it.

She watched for a while unobserved. For a bad guy, he had nice legs. He also had a tight butt, though his shorts were loose enough so that the shape came and went.

"Can you hammer?" he finally called down.

Not unobserved at all. "Can I hammer," she murmured in wry affirmation.

He gestured toward the second ladder. When she reached the top, he picked up a new roll of tar paper, anchored it, handed her a hammer and a tin of nails, and let her at it.

Tar paper came in different weights. This one was of the heavier variety, which made sense given the climate. Until she had unrolled and secured a healthy swatch, it was awkward, but she refused to complain.

"Utility knife?" she asked when she reached the edge of the roof.

He walked it to her. Warm from his tool belt, it did the trick. She went back in the other direction, cutting again when she reached the paper he had laid. He touched her arm once to move her aside so that he could better work the edges together, but she was soon on her own again. When they finished one row, they climbed higher and started the next, then the next. In time, they reached the cupola, which was harder, closer. Their arms touched more than once, legs touched more than once, none of it unpleasant.

The air was still. He was right about the wind being down at night. Or maybe it was just this particular night, capping another long summer day. Even with her hair off her neck, it was heavy and hot. Not that she was alone. The floodlight picked up streaks of sweat on Leo's face and neck. He paused often to swipe at it with his arm.

"That's it," he finally said, taking a long look at what they'd done before collecting his things and backing down the ladder. As soon as Charlotte was on the ground, he lowered the ladders and carried them away. He returned with two bottled waters, handed her one, and drank the contents of the other in an unbroken series of gulps.

Charlotte was feeling better, like she had accomplished something, had earned her keep in an odd regard. She looked up at the roof. Still lit by the flood, it was dark and even. "That's good-quality tar paper," she said.

"What's the point of making the effort, if you don't do it right?"

She smiled. "I just read that in a book. The guy is building a boat and wants to use the best materials, which are taking forever to arrive, but he's adamant about waiting."

Leo was staring at her.

Puzzled, she stared back. "What?"

"You read that crap?"

"What crap?"

"*Salt.*"

She was amused. "What do you know about *Salt*?"

"It's all people are talking about."

"You read?"

He frowned. "Sometimes."

"But not *Salt*. Because it's crap. For the record," Charlotte remarked, feeling proprietary of the book, "I don't think it's crap. I think it's well written and tells a great story."

Leo stared for another minute, then said, "So does *Moby-Dick*. Lots of copies of that in the prison library."

"So they let you read there. That's not so bad."

He turned up his lip. "I also learned how to pick locks and hot-wire cars."

"I'll watch my Jeep. They used to say you stole money from the church box."

"They never caught me at it," he countered, not quite answering the question.

She shot a puzzled look at the house. "So how do you pay for repairs?"

"Embezzlement."

Charlotte didn't believe it for a minute. "Did you ever force a girl to have sex?"

"I never had to. They were willing."

"Did you ever make one pregnant?"

"I'm not that dumb," he muttered and, seeming to have had enough talk, walked back to the house to turn off the floodlight. Then, in long strides, he headed off through the herbs. As he walked, he pulled his shirt over his head.

"Where are you going?" she shouted as the moon glanced off his bare back.

"Swimming. Go home." He turned into the night woods and dissolved.

Charlotte wasn't about to go home. She wanted to see where Leo swam. If her calculations were correct, that path would lead to a stretch where the shoreline was rocky and forbidding. She and Nicole had never walked that far down the beach. Like broken pavement on the road, the message was KEEP OUT.

Now, though, she could approach it from a different direction. If Leo had cut through the woods, so could she.

She was about to do that when a rustling came from the bushes by the house. As the dog emerged, she held her breath. A black hulk in the moonlight, it looked first at her, then in the direction Leo had gone. She had no idea what its thought process was; she only knew that, after what seemed an inordinately long time, it set off after Leo. It walked slowly, plodding toward the woods. The word *gingerly* came to Charlotte's mind. As she watched, she didn't think the dog looked dangerous. She thought it looked old.

It hadn't gone after the doe or its fawn. It hadn't lunged at her. She had never seen it do anything but lumber along. Old. She couldn't rule it out.

Not that she was taking any chances. She waited until it was gone, then silently followed. Something sweet hovered in the garden, but her focus was beyond. There was definitely a path. Forest brush snapped under her sneakers, but the surf grew progressively louder. Then it appeared, reflecting the moon like a light at the end of the tunnel. Large boulders, small rocks, and flat little stones flanked a patch of wet sand. Had the tide been in, that sand wouldn't have been visible at all. Even now it was hard-packed. Leo's clothes were there, alongside his boots, kicked off and askew.

Hidden just inside the path, Charlotte searched the water. Moonlight bounced off the waves, which rolled gently in, but it was a minute before she was able to separate out a pair of arms. Pale white in the moonglow, they stroked steadily away from shore. A risky thing to do? She would think so. But he had to know what he was doing—had probably done this hundreds of other nights. He swam easily, rising and falling with the waves, seeming as comfortable in the water as he was on his roof.

Mesmerized by the rhythm of those arms, the turn of his head when he breathed, an occasional kick that broke the surface behind him, she barely breathed herself until something wet touched her leg. Startled, she whirled around. It was the dog, looking up at her with baleful eyes.

"It's okay," she whispered shakily. "It's okay. Good Bear. No harm."

Baleful? Or simply sad? In the rays of the moon that wove through the trees, she saw furrows on its brow, and patches of brown near its eyes and snout.

Heart pounding, she extended a hand. The dog sniffed it for a minute. It didn't growl, didn't bare its teeth or back away—it actually seemed to want something more. She put her fingertips to its head, much as Leo had done that first night. Its fur was short and coarse on the flat stretch between its ears, but those ears looked silky. Curious, she touched them.

The dog sat.

Charlotte's heart continued to pound, though no longer from fear. Now it was the pull of the moon, and before that the smell of temptation in the garden. She was hot. "I'm going for a swim," she whispered to the dog. "Okay?"

When Bear didn't move, Charlotte looked at the sea again. Leo's arms were distant, but they had reversed direction. He was heading in. If she planned to join him, it had to be now.

"Stay," she urged softly, and with only the quickest glance back to make sure the dog didn't follow, she hurried to the beach. The moon was bright, turning the ocean into a play of contrast, midnight and silver, dark and light, good and bad. This was her life. She had no business being here. She was playing with fire.

But that didn't stop her from stripping down to her underwear and running into the surf. The water was cold, taking her breath for an instant, but she didn't turn back. When she was thigh-high in it, she dove over an incoming swell and submerged in its wake. Surfacing a body length beyond, she gasped at the cold. Then, pausing only to locate Leo, she started to swim. Her body rose with each swell, working harder on the climb, but the effort warmed her. She stroked steadily until one ill-timed breath met the rolling surf. Just shy of swallowing a mouthful, she spit it out and, straightening, looked for Leo. She didn't have to look far. He had stopped swimming and was watching her. Dark head, dark eyes, wet face white, he was as much a contrast as the rest of the world.

Treading water, she remembered the warnings about Leo Cole. Just then, though, none seemed to matter. If Leo had done bad things, so had she. And danger? She had once dived off a cliff in Acapulco. It hadn't been pretty, and she wasn't about to repeat it, but she had survived and remembered the rush. Being in these waters with Leo couldn't be worse.

The surf brought him closer. She couldn't tell whether he helped it with his hands, since they were submerged, as were hers. Her hair had come loose and trailed behind her. Only her head and shoulders broke the surface as she kicked to keep herself afloat.

He stopped an arm's length away, staring at her with shadowed eyes. After a minute, he blew out a short breath. From the exertion of swimming? Not likely. It might have been a question: *What did I expect?* Or a warning: *You're pushing me.* Mostly, it felt like a bald statement: *We're in trouble.*

But wasn't that what she wanted? If there was a price to pay for this, what was one more price? And it wasn't just her. *We,* his expression said. This wasn't a one-way thing.

His leg tangled with hers. At the same time, he tethered her by the hair and brought her to his mouth. The loss of breath then was for real.

Part moon, part ocean, his kiss was like nothing she'd ever experienced. It was commanding, but not hurtful—thorough in the way she needed. By the time it was done, her arms were around his neck, her legs around his waist. The cold water should have depressed his need, but did not. The next wave brought a taunting undulation.

Breathing hard, he propelled them toward shore. They were barely in the shallows, their legs still washed by the surf, when he set her on the sand and levered up only enough to tug at her panties. She helped, but one leg was all they managed. Holding that leg, he looked at her, giving her one last chance. *Are you in or out?*

"In," she whispered, and he was. Head back, eyes closed, he held himself there for what seemed an eternity, before looking at her again. He seemed surprised. So was she. She hadn't been conscious of wanting him, hadn't drooled over his body while they worked or dreamt about it afterward. The way he fit into her now, though, satisfied something deep inside.

Wanting another kiss, she brought his face down, and the hunger was fierce on both sides. In time, she needed air, gasping at the power of what she felt. His thrusts went beyond the rhythm of the surf, creating sensations so strong that she cried out.

He went still. "Hurt?"

She laughed into a moan, moved her head no against the sand, and, crossing her ankles, pulled him deeper. It went on and on and on, both the lovemaking and the spasms at the end. Her body or his? She was too into it to know or care.

When he finally slipped to the side, she lay back, breathless and limp. Eyes closed, she refused to see anything around her. He stayed close, his abdomen to her hip and one leg over hers. She didn't fall asleep, though the sense of release was so great that she might have. She simply lay there for however long, totally drained.

Then she felt something. It was his hand, moving over her belly in a slow, tentative way that had nothing to do with sex—and in a flash, reality returned. Sitting up fast, she turned away and hugged her knees. When she looked back, he was on an elbow, frowning.

"You have a baby," he said.

She swallowed, shook her head no.

"Those are stretch marks," he stated.

She had always been careful to hide them. One-piece bathing suits were good for that. Same with silk camis. But she had never been so taken with sex as she'd been with Leo, and it was night. The dark should have kept her secrets.

Not that she had thought any of this out ahead of time. She had come to Leo's to be punished. But sex? *Punished?* He hadn't been a brute of a lover at all. Powerful, yes. But far from cruel, and that was as upsetting as the other. Sex with Leo had been . . . amazing. It wasn't supposed to be like that.

Frightened, she looked around for her clothes and quickly pulled them on. Leo was sitting up now, watching her, but he didn't speak, and as soon as she pushed her wet feet into her sneakers, she made for the path. She didn't pass the dog, barely heard the crunch of the forest floor or felt the sand matting her wet hair. When she came out into the garden, she hurried through the rows, down the drive, and onto the road. She didn't look back, *couldn't* look back. And when she reached Nicole's house, she closed the door and sank to the ground.

She had run to Leo's to escape a mess. Now she had created another.

There was only one thing to do. After showering away all signs of the night, she wrapped herself in a fleece blanket on the sofa downstairs and, picking up *Salt*, escaped into a world where love beat the odds.

At least, she thought it did. An hour later, though, she was worried. The lovers were perfect for each other, but they were rooted in such different worlds that only a sea change in one would keep them together. She didn't see it happening. The author had painted both in fine detail; she knew them well. They had overcome silence and secrets, and had changed in the deepest possible ways—but their differences remained huge. They simply couldn't change more and stay in character.

Unable to bear the suspense, she flipped through to the last pages, the ones Nicole had sobbed about. Minutes later, she slammed the book shut, buried it under a pillow in the corner of the sofa, and, heartsick, went to bed.

Chapter Ten

TUESDAY'S MEETING IN CHICAGO WAS tough from the start. Whereas Peter Keppler had an easy way about him, Mark Hammon was an academic. A slender, bespectacled man who wasn't prone to small talk, he studied Julian's file at length, turning from one page to the next, frowning, going back, removing his glasses to rub the bridge of his nose, glancing at Julian, replacing the glasses, returning to the file. When he finally spoke, he expressed serious reservations about Julian being a candidate for a stem cell transplant.

What little relief Nicole felt was offset by Julian's frustration. His face was tight with it.

"You're thinking that I've only been at this for four years," he argued, "but my reading says that stem cell treatment is the most promising when it's done in the early stage of a disease. I'm the perfect candidate."

Hammon didn't look convinced, though he considered it a while before saying, "You tend to have serious side effects. There are less risky things to try first."

"What we've tried hasn't worked." When Hammon named two

drugs that Julian hadn't tried, he only waved a dismissive hand. "The side effects of either one can be worse than the disease, and the promise of payoff isn't as good as with stem cells."

"Given your physiology and your history of reaction, an autologous transplant would be better."

"Using my own cells? With another patient, I might agree. But I've been on so many drugs that I doubt my own cells would be any good, and testing for that would only waste time. Time is the issue, Mark. If there's any chance of salvaging my career, I need to act now. I want to take a step that holds real promise. I know the risks."

Frowning, Hammon pushed at his glasses. "You know them? I've seen them. In some cases after we introduce cells, we can't control their growth, so tumors result. In other cases, the drugs we use to depress the immune system and avoid the rejection of transplanted cells turn out to be toxic. One of my early patients died from the chemo itself."

"What if we found a good match with donor cells?"

"Even then." But he stared at the file. "No mention here of tissue matches with family members."

Julian was silent.

"Parents? Children?" He asked, including Nicole in the discussion.

"They haven't been tested," she said, darting a nervous look at Julian, whose eyes warned her against saying more.

Hammon tipped his head; testing relatives would be a logical first step.

"What about umbilical cord stem cells?" Julian asked. "My kids were born before freezing cord blood was an option, but even if they were tested now, umbilical cord cells are the ones that hold the most hope. They don't require an exact match, and they carry regulatory T cells that can repair the damage and possibly even reverse the disease. That's from your own research."

"True. But using cord blood cells is even more experimental. In your case, there's still an excessive risk of rejection. Infusing those cells into your body could be lethal."

"I could go to Mexico," Julian dared.

Hammon didn't blink. "You're too smart for that."

"For *sure*," Nicole told Julian, horrified by the thought. Desperate for an alternative, she turned to the doctor. "What if Julian tried another standard therapy and it didn't work? If the disease begins to progress beyond what it is, would you consider donor stem cells?" She didn't want anything experimental, period, but if Julian was determined, later was better than now.

"I might, but the risk would remain." He was looking at Julian. "Stroke, pervasive infection, paralysis—any one of those could leave you worse off than you are. Your mind is good. You have years of productivity ahead, whether you're in the OR or not. Besides, I'm not the only one doing research. This is an emerging field. In six months or a year, we'll know more."

"He's right, Jules," Nicole begged. "Six months won't hurt."

Julian turned on her. "Six months could be *forever* for me. What part of this picture don't you see?" Dismissing her with a look, he faced Hammon again, but Nicole heard little of what they said. Nor did she speak. She had been silenced as surely as if she'd been slapped.

They were there for another thirty minutes. She managed to shake the doctor's hand when they left, but her stomach was in knots. Fear? Worry? There was also anger. She told herself that she had no right to feel it, that Julian was just trying to survive and she had only upset him more, but the arguments were empty. There was a whole other side to this that *he* didn't see. She couldn't seem to put that fact aside.

He took her elbow as they entered and left the elevator, and, as soon as they reached the street, drew her out of the stream of pedestrian traffic to the privacy of a granite wall. "What was *that* about?" he asked in a voice that was uncharacteristically emotional. "Was it necessary to embarrass me in front of a colleague?"

She might have pointed out that he had embarrassed her right back, if she hadn't been reeling from it still. "All I did was to say that the doctor had a point."

"You sided with him. That's not what I needed in there."

"You'd go to Mexico and have a procedure done in a no-name clinic? Jules, this isn't only about *you*."

He might as well not have heard. "Hell, Nicole, don't you *get* it? Experimental treatments are done at the insistence of the patient, and they can't express doubts the way you did. I've been there, baby. I know how it works. A doctor believes in his technique, but until he's done it a certain number of times, he can't know for sure if it'll work and, if so, on which patients. The first patients are always the ones who demand the procedure and are willing to take the risks. You sided with him. That was counterproductive."

"I'm frightened," she tried, wanting to diffuse the situation, much as she had wanted to do in the doctor's office, but it didn't work now, either.

"*You're* frightened?" Julian countered. "What about me? This is not a walk in the park. I know the risks, but the alternative is worse. You aren't the one who stands to lose everything!"

Turning abruptly, he set off at a rapid pace toward the hotel. She had to trot every few steps to keep up, but he was so lost in his snit that he neither noticed the occasional waver in his gait nor seemed to know she was there.

She was acutely aware of both, and while the first tugged at her heart, the second stoked her anger. His health wasn't the only thing at risk. It looked like their marriage was going right down the tubes. *And it wasn't her fault.* She was trying to understand what he felt, was trying to ease things for him. But she could do no right. He needed someone to blame, and she was it—like *she* had given him MS.

He wanted it to go away. Damn it, so did she. But it wasn't going to happen, and the longer he denied that, the more miserable he would be. Life didn't always go as planned. There were graceful ways of dealing with bad things that happened. What he was doing was only making it worse.

Back at the hotel, they packed and checked out, then took a cab to the airport. They didn't speak, other than to direct the cabbie to their individual airlines, Julian for a flight to Philadelphia, Nicole to Portland. She didn't offer to go home with him, and not simply for fear of rejection. Just then, she needed Charlotte more than Julian, therapy more than another fight.

Her drop-off came first. When the cab stopped at the curb, Julian reached for her hand and gave it a squeeze. She tried to smile, but couldn't. Oh yes, she feared for her marriage. But anger percolated, and, being a new emotion for her, she had little control. Scowling, she climbed out, took her bag from the cabbie, and set it on the curb. Then she ducked back in.

"For the record," she told Julian in a shaky voice, "you are dead wrong. I love you. You are my husband, my *life*. If I lose you, I *do* lose everything." Not trusting that she wouldn't burst into tears, she slammed the door, grabbed the handle of her bag, and wheeled away.

Charlotte felt every inch of her body that day, but she refused to think about Leo. It was easier with each passing hour and no call from Nicole. That gave her plenty to worry about. She had always been in charge of her life—as a child because her parents were emotionally absent, as an eighteen-year-old heading to college on full scholarship, as a pregnant twenty-four-year-old with a secret no one else in the whole world knew.

Now her future seemed to weigh on forces she couldn't control.

So she took refuge in ones she could. She spent hours that morning on Anna McDowell Cabot's interview, adding to what she had written the night before. After driving out to the farm to ask several follow-up questions—and still no word from Nicole—she met with Melissa Parker. Whereas Anna was in her seventies and had lived in Quinnipeague all her life, Melissa had married into it at thirty. Now forty, she was a pastry chef here. Since she had studied in New York prior to meeting her husband, she and Charlotte had an instant rapport. She worked out of her home, which boasted a spanking-new industrial kitchen. This was where they met.

Though Quinnies under thirty would make a beeline for Melissa's marble macadamia brownies, her specialty was an herbed brioche, a warm batch of which were on the counter when Charlotte arrived. Naturally, she didn't refuse a taste, but she didn't stop there. When Melissa raved about island sage, Charlotte sampled a sage croissant, then a roll laced with rosemary and basil, then a scone rich with thyme. Melissa felt that her skill had evolved since coming here, that Cecily's herbs had enhanced her baking in ways she couldn't begin to explain.

"Did you ever meet her?" Charlotte asked, wondering if she'd get a different perspective from someone who wasn't native to Quinnipeague.

"Several times. She was sweet. Reserved."

"Reserved, as in secretive?"

Melissa considered that. "More like private. I don't think she had any friends in the conventional sense. I couldn't grow her herbs. I tried, but they didn't take. It's too shady here. My soil doesn't drain well."

"You must have done something to upset Cecily," Charlotte said only half in jest. "Or Leo." She couldn't resist. "Do you know him?"

"No. He's happy staying out there at the house."

"That has to be isolating. He must come into town sometimes." Those roofing materials hadn't just risen from the sea.

"I'm sure he buys food at the store."

"Doesn't he have any friends?"

Melissa shrugged.

"Or *travel?*"

"Travel." She sputtered a wry laugh. "He doesn't even go to the mainland."

Charlotte was startled. *"Ever?"* she asked, wondering what kind of man could bear the solitude. Even year-rounders, who did mix with other islanders, made regular trips to the mainland. "Does he work for people around here?"

"He used to. I guess he still does. He's good with his hands."

Charlotte wasn't going *near* that one. "What does he do with Cecily's herbs?" she asked, because his garden was a treasure trove, and he didn't strike her as one to cook, himself.

"That's an interesting question," Melissa said, seemingly puzzled. "I don't really know. Maybe he sells them, but he isn't my source. I buy mine from Shari Bowen, whose soil does drain well and who needs the money. I think that's what Cecily planned."

Sensing that she couldn't push more on Leo without arousing suspicion, Charlotte simply nodded at the last. When it came to Cecily and the mystical, Melissa was preaching to the choir.

Her phone remained silent. As she left Melissa's, she checked it, saw four bars, shook it, waited and watched. Nothing.

Frustrated, she returned to the Wrangler. She was passing through town en route to the neck road, when she spotted a deep purple awning hanging off the porch of a small frame house. SKANE'S SKEINS, read orange script on the awning.

Thinking that a piece of chocolate almond candy would lift her spirits, Charlotte pulled in behind several other cars. The shop was the living room of the house, refitted with floor-to-ceiling bins that contained more yarn than she would have thought a lone island would warrant. That said, the yarn was nearly as yummy as Charlotte knew the candy to be.

Discipling herself on the latter, she browsed while other customers were helped, then introduced herself to the owner. A pear-shaped woman with bright red cheeks and hair, Isabel Skane had a pleasantly calm voice. Calm actually described the shop. Rainbow colors, softness, texture, low spa music—it was soothing. Charlotte browsed through the yarn, browsed through notebooks of patterns, put her favorites on a Wish List, and said she'd be back. Then, after helping herself to one candy from a bowl by the register, she popped it in her mouth, took a second to go, and returned to the Wrangler.

She was back at the house, typing up a rough outline of the material, when Nicole finally called.

Her voice was small. *"Omigod."*

Charlotte's pulse began to race. "What happened?"

"Oh, Charlotte." Defeat.

Charlotte was thinking that Julian had a heart attack after all, that he was hospitalized, in intensive care—when she heard background announcements, the likes of which she knew all too well. "Are you at the airport?"

"Yes." Nicole said in the same small voice. "He's at his gate, I'm at mine. Is that poetic?" she wailed softly. "What a nightmare."

"Tell me."

"Tomorrow. I don't have the strength right now." Coming from a woman who usually ran on at the mouth, the confession spoke volumes. "Would you believe, the flight's way late. There's bad weather just east of here, so nothing's landing." The PA system came on. She went quiet, then said a weary, "Finally. My plane's in range. But here's the problem, Charlotte. I won't get to Portland until ten, which means that I won't get to Rockland until midnight, so there's no way I can get to the island until morning."

"Where can you stay in Rockland?"

"There are some nice inns. I'll stay in one."

"Are you sure?"

"I don't have much choice, y'know?"

Charlotte would have gone to get her if she'd had a way of doing it, but boats that shuttled Quinnies to the mainland always did so in daylight. The occasional sunset cruise went out, but by the time darkness fell, every slip in the harbor was full.

She wanted details on that meeting with the doctor. Waiting was an agony, but it sounded like what Nicole had been through was worse. What to do to make things better?

Had she been a baker, she would have whipped up a batch of those marble macadamia brownies, and had them waiting. Since she didn't bake—and since marble macadamia brownies would be nothing new to foodie Nicole—she wrote up Melissa's interview and, after polishing Anna's, printed both out. Nicole would be pleased.

Placing the pages on the kitchen table beside a vase, which she would fill with fresh flowers the next morning, she took a breath, put her hands on her hips, and looked outside. Denial worked as long as you had something else to do, but she had just run out. It wasn't dark yet, but she couldn't wait a minute longer. She had to talk with Leo.

Chapter Eleven

FEELING AS MUCH URGENCY AS trepidation, she set off. The breeze crossing the road was stronger than it had been the past few nights, rustling the leaves in the trees, cooling her arms and legs. Uneasy, she glanced at the sky. Clouds were gathering in the west, likely from the storm system that had delayed Nicole's flight. The humidity was already up, and along with it, the volume of her hair. And then there was the thick sea smell.

Rethinking the walking plan, she returned to the house, changed into jeans, and took the Jeep. Minutes later, she parked just beyond the Cole curve.

If he worked on the roof tonight, he would be putting down plywood. But it wasn't night yet. And with a storm coming on? She wasn't sure he would work at all.

Rounding the curve, she saw the house in daylight. The shutter Leo had hung was straight, but others were not, and while the tar-papered roof was an unbroken expanse, the clapboard body needed a coat of paint. The poor thing was threadbare.

The foliage around it was another matter. Even in the overcast, she saw myriad shades of green, one more vibrant than the next.

When Charlotte had asked Leo where Cecily was buried, he hadn't answered. Now she half suspected that the ashes were sprinkled over these grounds, a fertilizer in perpetuity to chalk up to the Cecily mystique.

As Charlotte started down the drive, she studied the front windows for signs of life. Where she thought she remembered curtains from Cecily's time, now there were blinds, and though they were slatted open, she couldn't see much. She did smell the gardens, though, and stopped when a certain sweetness hit her. It whisked her back to the night before, when she had cut through on her way to the beach. Following her nose down that row now, she stopped at the end near the woods, where the shrubbery was nearly as tall as she was. No herbs here—these were small white flowers in bloom, their petals star-shaped, smooth to the touch and strong of scent. When she brought her fingers to her nose and inhaled, her insides quickened.

Frightened, she wiped her hands on her jeans. She didn't know what Cecily's message was, but it made her feel less in control. She had come here with a purpose, and it wasn't sex.

Backing away from the flowers, she continued down the drive. As she approached the house, the bushes moved, and Bear came out. A long-ingrained fear whispered, but it died down when he shuffled to her side, head up, eyes beseechful. He was a sweet old thing, nothing to fear.

The man was something else. She had no idea what to expect.

The house had no porch, just three steps and a landing. A tarnished knocker waited. Needing time to gather herself, perhaps to take courage from the scent of herbs, rising now over that of the small white flowers, she settled on the second step with her feet on the ground. Bear came and sat close beside her. Elbows on her knees, she touched the coarse hair between his ears and traced the furrows on his brow. He closed his eyes, seeming enraptured.

That ended abruptly when a whistle came from the back of the house. Ears perked, eyes worried, the dog looked toward the sound, then at Charlotte again.

"He's with me!" she called to Leo. She didn't look around until bootsteps approached, and even then she hesitated. Stretch marks were only part of it. There was also the sex.

But both were fact. She couldn't change them. Stoical, she raised her eyes.

For an alleged thug, he was clean-cut. Short hair helped. Likewise the shadow of a beard where scruff had been. And attractive? The same prominent cheekbones and firm jaw that had screamed *attitude* when he was younger were now just plain male. Same with his very adult body, which explained the physical side of what happened last night. The other side was what made her nervous.

He seemed unsure, though his face didn't betray much. It was all in his eyes. Seeing them for the first time in daylight, she realized they weren't black, but a very dark blue—and wary as they went from her to the dog.

"Figured it out, huh?" he said.

Charlotte stroked Bear's head. "How old is he?"

"I don't know. I got him from a shelter when I first got out of jail. The vet there guessed three."

That would have been ten years ago, making Bear thirteen. "What's the life span of a dog like this?"

"Nine to twelve. He's part Rottweiler, part mutt. Mutts live longer. I'm counting on that." He stood six feet away, staring at her with barely a blink. "So you know my secret. What's yours?"

It was all she could do not to look away, but she owed him this. Quietly, she said, "I did have a baby. I mean, I gave birth to it. But I gave it up."

"Why?"

"I wasn't married. The father was." Hearing it aloud, she felt rotten to the core—in recklessness and depravation, very much her parents' daughter, which she had never, ever wanted to be. That was one of several things that had haunted her these ten years.

"Why were you with a married guy?"

"He wasn't married at the time. He was engaged." She swallowed. "To my best friend."

She waited for judgment, but Leo remained expressionless. "Did you love him?"

"Lord, no. That's what was so *stupid*. It was once, and it was totally meaningless. We'd had too much to drink."

His eyes held hers. "We weren't drinking last night."

"Yeah, well"—she did look away then—"that's the other part of this that scares me."

"You were scared because I saw stretch marks?"

Something struck her then. "How did you know what they were?" she asked. He was so sure about it. Yet he didn't socialize. He wasn't married, wasn't a father. At least, he didn't have a wife or kids on Quinnipeague. Maybe elsewhere?

"I used to spend weekends on the bluff." Overlooking Okers Beach. "With binoculars."

With binoculars. "*That's* bad," Charlotte said. "They're still at it, y'know. We saw them last weekend. And yeah, some of the women weren't bothered that their stretch marks showed."

"But you were," he said, dragging her back to the subject at hand. She supposed it was good, if difficult on her end.

"I don't let them show," she admitted. "I don't tell people about this."

"You told me."

"I kind of had to, after what happened."

"It was just sex."

That hit her the wrong way. "It was *honest*. If you didn't see that, then I wasted my time worrying about it all night. Sex is sex, but that was something else. Don't ask me what, because I've been trying to figure it out, but that's the only word that comes up right now. Honest."

His expression did change then, mirroring her anger. His voice was low and hard. "Okay. Let's talk honest. Why are you here?"

His tone took her aback. "Today? Now?"

"No. Every night since last Wednesday."

"I didn't come Saturday," she said meekly.

"Why come at all?" he shot back. "Here you are, just perfect for me, knowing how to put on a roof, like you were recruited to seduce me. Is it the cookbook? The herbs?"

She sat straighter. "*Seduce* you. I didn't *plan* what happened. Did you *not* get the bottom line of what I said before? The last summer I was here I made a major mistake. Why would I want to make another?" She realized she'd said more than she should have, but the words were out. Honest? Oh yeah. She stared at him for another minute, then stood, bowed her head, pressed her brow. "This is not working. It's getting dark. I should go."

"Don't," he said quickly, with what she actually thought sounded like vulnerability. When she dared a look, his expression was guarded. "I just needed to know."

"Whether I'm using you?" she asked. "If that was true, would I be as obsessed as I am about what we did?" She reconsidered. "Maybe 'obsessed' is too strong. Troubled, is more like it. I don't do this, Leo. I don't travel around the world having affairs, and if you're worried you might have made me pregnant, don't. I protect myself. I've seen the downside of carelessness."

His voice was lower than ever. "A baby isn't a downside."

To her horror, her eyes filled with tears, but she couldn't stop either the tears or the words. "It is if you grow it for nine months and feel it move inside you, then watch it being born and hold it in your arms and love it even when it's covered with blood, and just when you're thinking you can't give it up, a nurse takes it away and you know you'll never see it ever again—" She stopped short. Folding her arms over her middle, she forced herself to calm.

He didn't speak for the longest time. "Sit," he finally said, adding a low, "Please."

She sat mainly because her legs wouldn't carry her far. They were limp, like they'd been pulled tight, stretched, and suddenly released.

Her whole body felt that way, no doubt from the run she'd taken earlier, though the emotional element now didn't help. She didn't usually talk about the baby—didn't *ever* talk about the baby. Truth be told, she didn't think about it much. The girl was with good parents. She was benefitting from the kind of life Charlotte couldn't begin to give her. All things considered, Charlotte had made the right decision.

Leo sat at the other end of the step, leaving a body's width between them. Bent forward, he had his elbows on his knees. His hands were linked, his eyes on the drive. "That was an eloquent argument."

Charlotte watched Bear. The dog was oddly soothing. "I didn't intend eloquence. Usually I have to work at it."

"You mean, your writing. I googled you. You've been doing this a while. Did you always want to be a writer?"

She was about to answer the question when she paused. "You googled me?" She eyed him askance. "You're connected out here?"

"Aren't you?"

"Yeah, but I don't live the life of a hermit in a house at the far end of the road."

"I'm not . . . entirely a hermit." He seemed uncomfortable. "I surf. I know what's going on." He sat back, elbows on the upper step, not quite nonchalant but as close as she'd seen him to it. "The pieces you write—how long do you edit?"

"Until it's right."

"How do you know when it is?"

"I just do. I guess that's part of the skill. I'm not the best writer in the world, but I'm a picky reader. When I reread a piece and feel like my subject has come alive, I'm done."

He considered that. Then his brow furrowed like Bear's. "Do you ever spend a long time on a piece and end up throwing it out?"

"Yes."

"Because an editor says it's bad?"

"Because I do."

"What if an editor asks you to do something you think is wrong?"

"Wrong?"

"Something that would compromise you as a writer. Has that ever happened?"

Charlotte didn't have to think long. "You mean, like the time an editor asked me to fabricate a piece?"

"Did you do it?"

She met his eyes over her shoulder. "No. She won't ever hire me again, but that's okay. There are other publications."

When he looked off down the drive again, she studied his profile. Though dusk softened its lines, they were surprisingly intelligent for a guy who wasn't supposed to be bright. And for a guy whose social skills should be primitive? Okay. So he surfed the Web. That certainly wouldn't make him a master of small talk. She had been with countless sophisticated people who couldn't think to ask her anything more than how many pieces she wrote in a year.

Leo Cole was a surprise. She had known that last night on the beach, when he had been worried he was hurting her. She had no idea who he was.

Seeming to gather himself, he looked at her. "What now?"

"What what?"

"Want to go back to the beach and screw?" There was a lift at the corner of his mouth that might have suggested a smile. Humor, too?

"No," she said, though not sternly.

"Why not?"

"First, because I don't like that word. Second, because both of us need to know I'm not easy. And third, because it's going to rain."

"No, it isn't. Not 'til morning."

"How do you know?"

"I have a weather station inside that gives me an hour-by-hour. It's never wrong."

She had expected something organic, like his knowing when a storm approached from the angle of the herbs. "A weather station. And a computer. To look at your house, you'd think there's nothing inside that didn't come from the last century. Tell me you have a sixty-two-inch flat screen."

He shook his head no, then glanced up at the roof. "It's getting dark. Want to help nail plywood to that tar paper?"

Charlotte wasn't about to refuse. Leo asking for her help was a first. Was he sly? Oh yeah. Four-by-eight sheets of plywood were nearly as bulky as the storm shutter had been. It was a perfect task for two.

Raising two ladders, they clamped on scaffolding and carried up the first of the sheets. Once it was there, he positioned it, then she held it straight while he secured it with a *pop-pop-pop* of the nail gun. Between them, they had a second and third sheet up in no time. She would have liked to use the gun, would have liked to feel a little power. But there was only one gun, and he didn't offer to share. She allowed him the machismo by way of thanks for making what might have been a nightmare of a discussion less painful.

They didn't talk. Charlotte was fine with that. Her day had been filled with internal chatter, and though the issues hadn't gone away, working with Leo was a respite.

They were nearly at the top of the roof when her phone vibrated. It was Nicole, texting to say that she'd landed in Portland. When Charlotte finished reading, she found Leo studying her.

"Who?" he asked.

"Nicole." She returned the phone to her pocket.

"Still in New York?"

"On her way here." She looked up to find his eyes on her mouth. He returned to work in the next breath, but her mind wandered. Even aside from recognizing stretch marks, he was a talented lover. She wondered where he normally satisfied himself.

"Do you have a girlfriend?" she asked.

"No." *Pow pow pow.* "Do you have a boyfriend?"

"No."

"Why not?"

"I travel too much."

"Where's home?" he asked.

"I have an apartment in New York."

"Was Nicole staying there?"

"No. She was with her husband. My place is in Brooklyn, and it's barely big enough for one. They can afford a hotel suite in Manhattan." For what it was worth, she reflected. Money certainly didn't buy happiness. She could still hear the misery in Nicole's voice.

They put up another two sheets before Charlotte had a thought. The hero of *Salt* cruised through the night sea to pick up his friend. Leo wasn't exactly a hero, but he did live on an island. He was physically adept, a heroic swimmer, and if he was macho enough to wield a nail gun with command, he had to know something about a cockpit.

"Can you drive a boat?"

He snorted.

Taking that for a yes, she said, "I need your help, Leo. She'll have to stay over in Rockland if we don't get her."

He seemed amused. "We?"

"I can't go alone. And you owe me."

"For what?"

"Helping with your roof. Do you have a boat—or one you can use? Oh." She remembered. "You don't go to the mainland."

"Who said that?" he asked, seeming offended.

Charlotte wasn't about to bring the Cole curse down on Melissa. "It doesn't matter."

"It sure as hell does." Letting the nail gun hang, he looked at her. It was only eye to eye—no mouth this time—but she felt it. Those dark blue eyes had depth, and what she saw there was pride. "I know how to get to the mainland. If I don't go, it isn't because I can't, but because I won't. I can get you there."

She wanted to believe. Getting Nicole back tonight would be the answer to a prayer. "How?"

"Magic carpet," he said with a quirk at the corner of his mouth. Then, "When'll she get to Rockland?"

"Midnight."

"What time's it now?" The only thing on his wrist was a spattering of hair where a watch might have been.

"Ten fifteen," she read from her own.

"Help me finish, then get your car and pick me up at the curve."

Having issued the order, he put nail gun to plywood, and the popping resumed.

Charlotte assumed he had his own car and wondered what kind, how old, and whether he was embarrassed to use it. Not that it mattered. She didn't have to go home for the Jeep. It was waiting on the road just beyond the curve.

Excited to be able to do this for Nicole, she texted that news, then helped Leo finish.

Once the ladders were stowed, Leo went around back with neither explanation nor invitation and came back shortly, wearing his watch cap and jeans. The jeans were old and fit him well. She spotted a bulge in the back pocket, likely a wallet, though she didn't see keys. As soon as he slid into the Jeep, he moved the seat back to make room for his legs.

Cool air whipped her hair as she drove. She might have worried about rain if she hadn't trusted Leo in some odd way. He knew the weather here as well as anyone, and he did have Cecily on his side.

That said, his arms were bare. *Men run hot,* he had said; still, she wondered if he would be cold once they hit the water. She was none too warm on land. As soon as she parked at the pier, she grabbed her fisherman's sweater from the backseat and pulled it on.

The harbor was deserted. Other than those few people cleaning up at the eateries, Quinnipeague was asleep.

"I'll meet you on the dock," Leo said and loped to the back of the Chowder House. With the slap of a screen door, he went inside, returning moments later with a takeout bag and a set of keys. "Dinner," he explained and, without commenting on the keys, led her to a slip on a side arm off the dock.

Charlotte had no idea whose boat they took, but it was relatively new and decidedly sturdy. With a minimum of effort, he untied the lines, backed out of the slip, and guided them away from the pier before gunning the motor and shooting them into the moonless ocean night. With the fading of Quinnipeague, she did feel a qualm. The boat's headlight bounced off the occasional patch of fog, but otherwise it sank like dead weight in the waves.

Standing beside him, she struggled to see a horizon. "How do you know where to *go*?" she finally called over the wind, clutching a hand-bar on the dash as the boat surged ahead.

"Done it before," he called back. "Nervous?"

"Yeah, I am. I can't see a thing."

He pressed a button, and the GPS came on. "We're here." He pointed. "Your friend is there."

Charlotte studied the screen. If it was accurate, they were headed right.

"Where's the bag?" he asked.

She pulled it from under the seat and opened it. Even diluted by the wind, the smell that rose from inside was unmistakable. "Little bits?" she asked in excitement. Little bits were one of Dorey Jewett's gems: small, sweet lobster knuckles that were sautéed in butter. There were no herbs involved, just enough of a Ritz-cracker coating to absorb the butter for ease of eating.

"Want some?"

Charlotte was sorely tempted. "Oh no. I had dinner."

"There's enough for two," he said and, taking a handful from the bag, popped one after the other in his mouth. He didn't exactly roll his eyes in ecstasy, but he looked content.

She watched, salivated, finally sighed and reached into the bag. He was right; there was plenty for two. Wondering if this was Leo's idea of a dinner date, she savored every bite. When they were gone, she crinkled up the bag, stowed it in a side pocket where it wouldn't blow away, and returned to Leo's side.

They didn't talk then. It seemed a wasted effort, what with the roar of the motor and the crash of the boat as it flew through the waves, but there was something exhilarating about standing beside Leo Cole with her hair flying back from her face. One thing was clear. He was as comfortable at the helm as he was on the roof of his house. He didn't seem bothered by the bite of the wind. Nor was he bothered by the darkness, either truly knowing his way or simply putting his faith in the screen on the dash.

In a surprisingly short time, the lights of Rockland appeared. Deftly, Leo slowed, turned, and let the waves carry the boat the last few feet to the dock where Nicole stood, a lone, frail figure with her luggage beside her and the woes of the world on her huddled shoulders.

Scrambling out, Charlotte wrapped her arms around her, and Nicole started to cry. She didn't speak, just sobbed softly for what seemed the longest time. Finally, she drew back, wiped her cheeks with the backs of her hands and looked around for her roller bag.

"He put it on the boat," Charlotte said gently, at which point Nicole looked closely at who the "he" was.

Her wet eyes widened. "Leo Cole?" she mouthed to Charlotte, and, with a look of alarm, whispered, "You *promised*."

But Charlotte was guiding her to the boat. "We'll talk about it tomorrow. Right now, you need to be home."

Chapter Twelve

CHARLOTTE SPENT MOST OF THE night in the Great Room, anxiously imagining every possible scenario, and distractions didn't work. She wanted to read but couldn't focus, wanted to write but couldn't create. Finally, picking up her knitting, she got the sleeve of her sweater back on track, only to realize three inches later that the cables weren't right. She studied the pattern, studied the cables, studied the pattern again—and pushed the whole thing aside in disgust.

Through it all, she was listening for Nicole, but the only sound she heard came at dawn in the form of wind-driven rain. It slapped the patio stones, bowed the beach grass, and whipped up the waves. It would be a good morning to talk, she thought, but when Nicole finally came downstairs, talk seemed the last thing she wanted. Her face was pale, her hair flat, and she reached for the coffee like she couldn't think beyond that.

"Did you sleep?" Charlotte asked once they both held steaming mugs.

Nicole was uncharacteristically quiet. "Barely."

"Can I get you something to eat?"

Smiling sadly, she shook her head and sipped her coffee.

Rain gusted against the windows, its earthy smell mixing with that of the dark brew in what would have been a soothing blend if Charlotte hadn't been so keyed up. "Was it really bad?"

A nod, another sip.

"How?" Charlotte asked.

Eyes on the mug, Nicole lifted it again. When she put it down this time, she sank deeper into the chair and finally looked up. "What's with Leo Cole?"

Charlotte would rather talk about Julian's condition, but Nicole clearly needed a warm-up. "I've been helping him, so he helped me. I have no idea whose boat it was, but he knew how to drive it."

"It was Hayden Perry's," Nicole said. "He and Dad used to talk boats all the time. I wonder if Hayden knew he took it."

"He must have. Leo got the keys from Dorey, who wouldn't give them to just anyone. Besides, twenty-two miles full-throttle in a boat like that, and the fuel gauge will be way down. He'd have to notice."

Nicole looked to be considering that. Frowning, she pulled Charlotte's interviews close, thumbed the first few pages, but didn't read. Her eyes rose. "Does this mean you owe Leo something?"

"No. It's the other way around. He owed me for helping with his roof."

"Will he give you access to Cecily's gardens?"

"I'm working on that," Charlotte promised. It was a major goal of hers. "The idea is to befriend him. I'm not sure he has many friends." Then again, she wouldn't have guessed that a prominent islander would loan his expensive boat to Leo Cole. "It's weird," she mused aloud. "There are times when I feel like the thug act is a show. He can be as well-spoken as you and me."

Nicole sighed. "Well-spoken didn't get me far yesterday." Her eyes filled with tears. "I think my marriage is in trouble. And I'm not the only one who thinks it. Kaylin called last night right after I landed in Portland. She had just talked with Julian, and she knows something's wrong. She said he sounded removed. That was the word she used—

removed. She asked me if he made a mistake in the OR and was being sued, or if the hospital was being sold and his department was going somewhere else. When I said no to those, she asked if we were getting divorced." Her expression turned stricken. "She actually asked that."

"She was just tossing out wild fears, Nicki. That doesn't mean she believes any of them."

"Why wouldn't she? The reality is that he divorced her mother, so he could divorce me. It's easier to do if you've done it once."

"You're nothing like Monica. You fill a gaping hole in Julian's life. He *loves* you."

"After what happened yesterday, I'm not so sure," Nicole said. The fact of her voice being so quiet—so *dull*—said something. "It's like he's pushing me away, too."

"Maybe he's trying to protect himself."

"From *me*?"

"Maybe he's building a wall, in case you leave him."

"Why would I leave him?"

"Because you're young and healthy, and you want a child."

Nicole sat up straight. "That is so wrong, Charlotte. I wouldn't leave him. I'd have gone to North Carolina with him in a heartbeat. I'd have done the book another time, and if my publisher bailed out, I'd have found another. He knows this. I told him more than once."

But Charlotte was into the psychology of Julian's situation. "Monica abandoned him. She chose her business over him. Maybe he fears that because he's sick, you'll choose a younger guy over him. Maybe"—she was thinking—"he's afraid your book will be such a success that you won't need him at all."

"I would *never* dump him for a career," Nicole argued, "and I would *especially* never dump him because he's sick. That's not how marriage works—at least, it isn't in my life—and if you think it does work that way, well, maybe that's why you aren't married yourself!" Silence hit. Seconds later came remorse. "I'm sorry, Charlotte." She grabbed her friend's hand and held it tightly. "I shouldn't have said that. It was mean."

Charlotte understood that she was upset. She was actually grateful to see spunk and fire, rather than pure sadness. And Nicole raised an interesting point. Quietly, she said, "I'm not married because I can't find the perfect guy."

"No guy's perfect."

"No, but if you don't think it at least at the start, you're sunk. Forget my parents' experience. Half the people I meet are divorced."

"And that terrifies you?"

"What terrifies me," Charlotte said in a measured way, speaking from the heart as she couldn't with anyone else, "is falling hard, getting hurt, and having to put my life back together again." The truth was, she had lousy taste in men, dating ones who turned out to be either chronic playboys, profoundly needy, or married. Maybe she went for the bad ones to keep from falling hard in the first place.

She had thought about this. She had analyzed it in depth. When you live alone, travel alone, exist solely on the outskirts of other people's lives, you do have time to wonder why what you want most in life is out of reach. You also have time to tell yourself that you don't want it at all, though whether you can ever be completely convinced is something else.

She sighed. "Not your worry, Nicki. Besides, I'm in agony waiting here. Tell me," she begged. "What happened yesterday?"

The diversion had helped. After taking another drink of coffee, Nicole sank back in her chair. "He agreed to try a different medication."

Charlotte breathed a sigh of relief. "Ahhh. That's good, isn't it?"

"I don't know." She was studying her coffee. "There's a new one that's supposed to work on the immune system to keep it from eroding the myelin that covers the nerves, because when the myelin erodes, the nerves don't communicate with the brain, which is what MS is all about." The words were rote; clearly, she had read the same description of MS hundreds of times since Julian's diagnosis.

Charlotte already knew what the disease was, though she let Nicole take her time.

"This new treatment means injections every day," she finished, raising her eyes. "No problem there. Julian's a doctor."

"What's the drawback?"

"Liver damage. He'll need constant monitoring. But he's willing to risk it. He's convinced he's just sitting around watching himself fail." She pushed an arm high on her forehead, baring resignation. "He's always been on the cutting edge of medicine, so he takes risk for granted. And he's made up his mind. He wants to try a stem cell transplant. He's only taking this other drug to show the doctor it won't work. I would put money on the fact that this minute, as we sit here talking, he's calling around to find a doctor who wants a guinea pig. He doesn't seem to care that the risk of rejection is worse for him, and he still refuses to tell his parents or his kids, any of whom might be a donor."

"He's talking about adult stem cells, then?"

"Actually not," Nicole breathed defeatedly. "He wants to use umbilical cord cells."

Charlotte was horrified. *"Now?"*

"He's tired of going from one drug to the next. He feels like he's wasting time. Bottom line? He wants it all: stop the symptoms and reverse the disease. UCB cells may do both."

"They don't know that for sure."

"Tell me about it," Nicole breathed. "When I talk about the risk, he says it's *his* life—only, it isn't just him." Ardent, she sat forward. "It's my life, too, but I don't think he gets that. He refuses to anticipate what the worst would mean to me. I might lose him. A transplant like this could leave him a vegetable."

Charlotte let a beat pass before saying a soft, "Or cured." She had a vested interest in what happened, and would much rather Julian not want to use UCB cells, but she had read enough about them to know the promise. She couldn't lie to Nicole about this.

"Yes," Nicole admitted, deflating again.

"How impatient is he?"

"Very. He'll look around until he finds someone who's willing to do it."

Charlotte felt a sinking inside. If Julian went ahead, she had a moral obligation to tell him about the baby. A better match could save his life. But then Nicole would know the truth.

Charlotte could make Julian promise not to tell. He could simply say that the doctor had found a good match in a cord blood bank. But that would be lying, nearly as wrong as what they'd done in the first place. "Have you talked with him today?"

"No. We texted. *You okay?* I wrote. *Fine,* he wrote back. That's it. *Fine.* He's removing himself from me, too. Like, who's left?"

Not me, Charlotte thought. She didn't want any part of Julian Carlysle, other than to save him for her best friend, who wouldn't be her best friend then, but was still for now. Desperate to preserve that, she reached for Nicole's cold hand. "Okay. Here's a plan. Text him often, but be brief, just a line or two to let him know you love him. Don't *let* him remove himself. Keep at him with lots of little thinking-of-you notes."

"And if he doesn't answer?" Nicole asked in a woeful voice.

Charlotte remembered that voice. It was a throwback to her childhood Nicole, who shied from the limelight and was socially unsure. That Nicole was long gone, replaced by the one her parents had trained to be confident and adept. Everything she had accomplished in the last four years, all under an ominous cloud, was proof of that.

She had a right to occasionally regress. But the answer was obvious. Charlotte didn't even have to say it, simply pointed at Nicole's laptop, the stove, and her own printouts.

Nicole craved sweets. Her list included peach pie, rhubarb pie, and pumpkin pie, all of which would be on hand the following week for the Fourth of July cookout on the bluff, so she knew Quinnie cooks would have their recipe cards nearby. In addition to pies, she wanted recipes for blueberry cobbler, apple crisp, molasses Indian pudding, Isobel Skane's chocolate almond candy, and, of course, Melissa Parker's marble macadamia brownies.

Since the book was her baby and she was the cook, gathering and testing recipes was her job. Some would have to be resized, but she had experience with this. Others wouldn't need testing at all, assuming she trusted the donor and had personally sampled the result. She needed signed releases for each recipe, which meant return visits once she either cooked or read through each for discrepancies, so she had double reason for starting today.

Immersing herself, she spent the morning in town. Oh yes, islanders talked, though mercifully now about themselves and their recipes, rather than about her—and she loved what they said. Realizing that she could add sidebars with tips from those not being profiled, she took careful notes, and though she returned to the house at midday with fewer cards than she'd hoped, one of them came with a quart of fresh blueberries, from which, following the donor's recipe, she made a bubbling cobbler.

Topped with yogurt, that was lunch.

She spent the afternoon typing up notes, answering readers' questions, and blogging about a new online source for organic cinnamon and nutmeg, either of which she could have used for testing the island recipe for Indian Pudding that afternoon. Both spices were produced from a tropical evergreen that, Cecily's miracles notwithstanding, did not grow on Quinnipeague, but since Indian pudding was a prized dessert here, Nicole refused to leave it out. Typically, Quinnie Indian Pudding called for cider molasses made from island apples. The recipe she had been given listed bottled molasses, which she supposed made sense, given its wider availability, though the taste wasn't quite the same. She made a mental note to ask Bev Simone about her supply of the real stuff.

Meanwhile, Charlotte interviewed Susan Murray, who was on Quinnipeague through the Fourth and was a good example of a part-timer drawn here for food and fun. She was flattered to hand over her recipe for s'mores cookies, which Nicole baked, and which they sampled along with the Indian Pudding that night.

*   *   *

Waking up Thursday morning to another dreary day and the sense of being physically stuffed, they focused on FISH. While Charlotte interviewed the postmaster about the origin, techniques, and ingredients for his best-in-Maine lobster bakes, Nicole set off to gather recipes for glazed salmon, baked pesto haddock, and cod crusted with marjoram, a minted savory unique to Quinnipeague, and sage.

She baked the crusted cod for dinner using fresh herbs from the island store and cod filleted that morning at the pier. Other than adjusting the amount of savory to compensate for a lack of mintiness off-island, Nicole thought the recipe was perfect and blogged as much before going to bed.

She also told Julian that. Since arriving in North Carolina, he had begun calling her each night before he went to bed, which she took to mean that her short texts were working, and though he sounded tired, they talked about work, not MS. He was pleased with what he was accomplishing. So was she. The month apart would be productive at least.

Work was a distraction for Charlotte as well. Even when Friday morning brought sun, she wasn't tempted to play. Totally aside from Leo, or from Julian and Nicole and umbilical cord stem cells, the amount of work to be done was daunting. The more she and Nicole talked, the larger the project loomed, and collecting raw material was only the start. Every profile had to be written, edited, and polished, with accompanying photos cropped and enhanced. Nicole would be the menu-planner, as Charlotte knew nothing about that, but since she was the professional writer, she would tie everything together. It was a lot to do in a brief period of time that might be made all the more brief if Nicole had to leave on a moment's notice to be with Julian again.

Today being the start of a long weekend, they addressed BRUNCH. Holiday weekenders would start arriving by noon, but islanders generally rose with the sun, which made seven in the morning doable. At least, that was the plan the evening before, altered when Nicole slept late after working long into the night.

Still, they were on their way to town by eight. While Nicole drove off in search of recipes for fish hash, clam fritters, and salmon quiche, Charlotte settled in at the Chowder House with Dorey Jewett, who, well beyond the assortment of chowders she always brought to Bailey's Brunch, would be as important a figure in the book as any.

They sat in the kitchen, though Dorey did little actual sitting. Looking her chef-self in T-shirt, shorts, and apron, if she wasn't dicing veggies, she was clarifying butter or supervising a young boy who was shucking clams dug from the flats hours before. Even this early, the kitchen smelled of chowder bubbling in huge steel pots.

Much as Anna Cabot had done for the island in general, Dorey gave a history of restaurants on Quinnipeague, from the first fish stand at the pier, to a primitive burger hut on the bluff, to a short-lived diner on Main Street, to the current Grill and Café. Naturally, she spoke at greatest length about the evolution of the Chowder House, whose success she credited to her father, though the man had been dead for nearly twenty years. Everyone knew Dorey was the one who had brought the place into the twenty-first century, but her family loyalty was endearing. It was particularly evident when Charlotte asked about Cecily's role in her cooking.

Pausing with her chop knife midair, Dorey was suddenly puffed up. "Jewetts have been cooking here since before Cecily was born. We did fine with our own herbs, thank you." The knife came down with a *thwunk*.

Charlotte modified the question. "Then, island cooking in general. You can't deny that her herbs play a role."

"No, I can't deny it," Dorey conceded, though the speed with which she proceeded to chop onions spoke of annoyance. "Some of your so-called cooks aren't what I'd call cooks. Their heirloom recipes would be downright awful if it weren't for those herbs."

"You do use Cecily's herbs, though?"

"Hey, I'm not stupid. If you need fresh basil or thyme on this island, there's only one source, and I'm not talking about her garden. I have Cole herbs in my own greenhouse. You won't find better anywhere else. I wasn't saying you could." She scraped the onions into a bowl with the broad of her knife, then ran a wide forearm across her watering eyes. "I'm just saying the Jewett recipes are more than herbs."

Charlotte was thinking that competitiveness was a side of Dorey she hadn't seen, when she saw another. Out of the blue, the woman asked, "What's Leo Cole to you?"

"Excuse me?"

"You were with him Tuesday night on Hayden Perry's boat."

Charlotte should have known Dorey would keep tabs on the harbor even at night. But there was a perfectly good explanation for what Dorey had seen. "I asked him to take me to Rockland. Nicole is my friend. We were picking her up."

Dorey studied her. Her tone softened, though her eyes remained serious. "Leo hasn't had it easy in life. Cecily wasn't the best mother. He's finally at a good place. I'm worried you'll mess it up."

Charlotte laughed. "Me?"

"He was different coming in here that night. He likes you."

"I like him, too."

"Why?"

Charlotte opened her mouth, then closed it and considered what she understood about her feelings. Finally, puzzled, she said, "I have no idea."

"You need to," Dorey warned. "He isn't one to play with."

"Because he's dangerous? That's what everyone says, but I don't feel it in him. Who *is* he?"

"What do you mean?"

"Is he a handyman? A carpenter? A *gardener*?"

"You don't know?"

"No. We don't talk much about personal things. It's the silence that kind of works—for both of us, I guess."

With a sigh, Dorey lightened up. "Well, I wouldn't know about silence. My life is filled with noise. If I didn't like it, I'd be doin' somethin' else besides running this zoo." She reached for another onion. "Gotta get back to work. Any more questions?"

"Actually, yes. Was there ever a father in the picture?"

"I meant, questions about the restaurant. Anything about Leo, you have to ask Leo. I know you've been asking other people, but I'll tell you one thing, Missy," she added, prodding the air with the tip of her knife. "For whatever else he is, Leo's a born and bred Quinnie, and we protect our own."

Hands up, Charlotte backed off. "Got it."

"That's good. No one here wants him hurt."

Charlotte did get it. She was summer; Leo was forever. He could be the worst of the worst, but Quinnipeague was his home. Islanders related to that. Black sheep or not, they would side with him.

Thinking how nice that was, she emerged from the Chowder House into the sun. It was ten thirty. Pickups filled the spaces outside the Café, suggesting that locals were taking advantage of the last hours of quiet before weekenders began to arrive. She looked through the lineup, but didn't see Nicole's SUV. Wondering if it was parked elsewhere, she looked down the street, then up. That was when she saw Leo. He was leaning against a dark blue pickup, parked nose-in at the head of a narrow driveway beside the library.

Her pulse skipped. With his hands in the pockets of his jeans and his booted feet crossed, he looked for all the world like he was just passing the time—except for his dark eyes, always his dark eyes. There was nothing nonchalant about those, and they were focused on her.

She started toward him, walking casually to avoid attention, though there was no one about. He had parked in a discreet spot. Their relationship—whatever it was—was secret.

She smiled, said a soft, "Hey," when she was close. He didn't answer, simply drew her in against the truck, and, with his hands flat on the window by her head, caught her mouth with his. It was the first time since Monday night, but as quickly as that she was back on the beach, naked in the moonlight, and turned on as that lean mouth moved hungrily over hers. Her arms were around his neck before it was done, holding on lest she fall, though his body would have prevented that. It held her against the truck, shielding her from the world. She was breathless when, after a final long kiss, he raised his head.

His eyes were wide and midnight blue. She couldn't look away. "What was that for?" she whispered.

"Wanted to see if I was imagining," he said in a low, rutted voice.

Imagining the fire. He didn't have to finish for her to know. Nor did she have to ask if the fire was real. She could hear it in the roughness of his breathing, could feel it in the lower body that wasn't lifting from hers so fast.

Those midnight blues roamed her face. "You haven't been out to the house."

"I've been with Nicole. She needs me around."

"For her cookbook?"

"There's also personal stuff. Plus, it's been rainy. You couldn't lay shingles in the rain, and now you have to wait at least a day for the plywood to dry."

"So you're not coming over tonight?"

"That depends on Nicole. If she's having dinner with other friends, I can get out."

"I'm Plan B."

"You're Plan Z, if you ask Nicole. She's afraid you'll sabotage her project."

He didn't respond to that. "What'd you tell her about us?"

"That I didn't know what in the hell it was, which I don't. Do you?"

"No. All I know is I want more."

So did Charlotte. Taking his face in her hands, she initiated the kiss this time. He let her lead it for a breath before taking over, and she didn't protest. Something happened to her when she was with him, like *this* was where she was supposed to be. When he raised his head this time, she should have been aching for more. But she felt peaceful, like she was home. With a contented sigh, she closed her eyes and rested her forehead on his chin.

"What was that for?" he asked in hoarse echo of her earlier words, but it was a minute before she was willing to draw back.

Then, with an inhalation to steady herself, she said, "Just wanted to make sure."

His eyes were inscrutable. Finally, he asked, "What's your cell number?"

She gave it to him and, sliding out from under him, backed away with a glance at the truck. "Is that yours?"

He nodded.

"Nice." It was dusty, but late model, which raised more questions, but she was tiring of them. So he had a source of income. What did it matter? If the island was in his corner, it couldn't be *too* disreputable.

Smiling, she faced forward and started walking. Her smile faltered, though, when she saw Nicole at the Chowder House. Apparently having come from the opposite end of the street, she had pulled up to the front door, set her blinkers, and looked to have been ready to go inside if she hadn't seen Charlotte. Having stopped beside the hood, she was staring at the dark blue pickup.

Frowning, she waited only until Charlotte was close. "Were you kissing him?"

Charlotte shrugged. "I guess so."

"Kissing him," Nicole repeated, like she wasn't sure she understood. When Charlotte nodded, she asked, "Is something going on? Like, more than helping with his roof?"

Good question. She remembered Leo saying, *Here you are, just perfect for me.* And Dorey saying, *He was different coming in here that night, he likes you.* Charlotte might have blamed making love on the beach to the moment, but there was the kiss just now. It had taken her out of herself.

Her escape. Not a mess of the summer as she had first feared. Her own personal escape from stem cell anxiety and deadlines.

Not that she could tell Nicole that. Needing a minute, she opened the door and climbed into the passenger's seat. Nicole stared, before rounding the car and sliding in, but she didn't let it go. As soon as she switched from reverse to drive, she asked, "Is there?"

"Yes."

"What?"

"There's a physical attraction."

"Is it real? Or for the sake of the cookbook?"

"It's real," Charlotte said. "For what it's worth, he hasn't mentioned the book. I think he's okay with it."

"Because he likes you?"

"Maybe. Or because he's knows I won't steal Cecily's herbs. I still want to take pictures. Those gardens are something." She was thinking of the white flowers with the incredibly arousing smell. She wondered what they were.

"Have you slept with him?"

Admitting it made her feel cheap. So she said, "No." It wasn't exactly a lie. There had been no sleeping that night.

"Do you think you will?"

"Why does it matter?"

"Because I worry about you. He's an ex-con."

"Oh, so was my dad," Charlotte tossed out in a second's exasperation.

"He was not."

"He was. He was convicted of domestic abuse and spent ten days in jail."

"Domestic abuse?"

"Of wife number two, who, not being a lush, didn't have alcohol to keep her from talking back. He didn't like back talk."

Nicole seemed horrified. "You never told me this."

"I'm not proud of it."

"Did he ever hit you?"

"He threatened to."

"Did he hit your mother?"

"No. She knew enough to steer clear when he was in a snit."

"I had no idea," Nicole said meekly and was quiet as they passed the road to Okers Beach. They were passing the clam flats when she returned to the other. "Still, ten days is different from four years."

Charlotte didn't want to discuss this. "Maybe Dad had a better lawyer than Leo. My point, Nicki, is that there are lots of reasons why people get sent away. We shouldn't pass judgment on Leo until we know what his are."

Nicole shot her a look. "You want to find out."

"Yeah, I do. He's interesting. So many things about him don't fit. I want to know who the real Leo is."

"And then what?"

Charlotte took a biding breath. "Then I get gorgeous pictures of his gardens for your book, after which I go back to New York, and then Paris, and then wherever work takes me. That's the lesson of *Salt*, is it not?"

Nicole's eyes lit. "You finished it?"

"I didn't. I got to the point of caring so much and feeling like things would end up wrong, so I read ahead."

"Charlotte!"

"I couldn't help it," Charlotte declared, unrepentant. "I refuse to finish. This is my protest."

"But you just said you'd do the same thing!"

"Right. That's reality. But fiction is fiction. Chris Mauldin took my heart and twisted it. That's pure manipulation."

"It's pure brilliance, if you ask me," Nicole mused and pulled up at the house.

Charlotte didn't argue. Not only didn't she want to further the discussion of *Salt*, which might lead back to her relationship with Leo, but now that they were home, she had other things to do. Having loved her interviews with Anna and Melissa, Nicole wanted her write-up of Dorey ASAP, so that she could impress her editor with their progress.

At the same time, Nicole began reading through the newest recipes in her pile and found a problem.

Chapter Thirteen

Charlotte was at the kitchen table when she heard a soft, "Strange." She stopped typing and looked up.

Nicole stood at the counter, frowning as she thumbed back and forth through a handful of recipe cards. "No thyme in Rebecca's fish hash? There's always thyme. It's one of the reasons I like her hash. And salmon quiche without parsley? Without *dill*? Marie's quiche has both. Goat cheese would be bland without dill, and even aside from taste, parsley adds color." Studying another card, she seemed baffled. "Mint extract in peppermint blondies? *Extract*? There's nothing organic in that. What happened to fresh mint?" She turned anxious eyes on Charlotte. "Quinnipeague is known for its herbs. They're supposed to be a major part of the cookbook. Remove them, and you lose what's so unique here. These cards have to be wrong."

Feeling a chill, Charlotte left the table. "All of them?" There were several dozen in the pile.

"Not all. Some are good. But these others? And *these*?" She singled out several lower cards that were marked with Post-its. "I got these earlier in the week. It's the same thing, either use of a commercial product or a clear-out omission. Two or three could be innocent mistakes. But eight? Nine? What is going on?"

Charlotte took the cards and glanced through. Original recipe cards would be dog-eared and stained; these were clean. "They're fresh copies. It could still be innocent."

But Nicole was shaking her head. "I know these people. They're not careless. This was deliberate."

"Sabotaging their own recipes?"

"Protecting them. Someone told them not to give away island secrets." Her implication was clear, her green eyes direct.

"You think it was Leo," Charlotte said.

"Who else could it be?"

"Dorey. Or Anna or Melissa." She had asked each about Leo. "They protect him."

"From what?" Nicole asked, clearly skeptical.

Charlotte searched for an answer, but her mind was stirring an uncomfortable brew. She had a personal stake in this. How to be objective?

"Aren't they protective of me, too?" Nicole asked, hurt now. "I've summered here all my life. They love my family—you heard how they gushed last week. Besides, these people aren't timid. If they didn't want me doing the cookbook, they'd have said so." Her eyes darkened. "It has to be Leo scaring them off. He didn't want us doing this in the first place. Ask him to stop, Charlotte, please? There are times when I feel like I'm hanging on by a thread. The last thing I need is a complication, when we finally have momentum going."

They did have that, in spite of the ongoing heartache of Julian. Nicole missed him—no doubting it—and he shared that, to judge from his frequent texts. *Tired, but okay,* he would say in response to her query. Or, *Just finished a great session with a bunch of top-notch MDs.* Or, *Taped a clip for the local news. Link to follow.* Charlotte assumed that their phone calls were more personal, since Nicole's anger had faded.

Not so the fear, which shadowed her eyes at odd moments. But she didn't talk about this as much now, either. *Tiresome* was the word she used when Charlotte asked. And true to that, she was upbeat and smiling when they were in town. Working on the cookbook gave her focus. She was right; the last thing they needed was a glitch.

Charlotte saw an easy fix. "Can you correct the herbs yourself?"

"If I alter the recipes, they won't sign a release. Please, Charlotte, ask him to stop?"

"I don't think it was Leo," she said, though she was unsettled. Hadn't Leo threatened to prevent their getting recipes? *I'll put out the word that I don't want you to,* he had said.

But that was before they were . . . whatever they were. Now it seemed impossible that he would do this. He had been too caring on the beach Monday night, too understanding on his front porch the next night. And his kiss this morning? Too honest.

"Then how do you explain this?" Nicole cried, holding up the cards. "I didn't sense guilt when I was collecting these. If leaving things out was deliberate, they were clearly comfortable with it. Did they not think I'd *notice*?" She grew beseechful. "Call Leo?"

"I don't have his number."

"Someone must. Maybe Dorey."

"Uh-huh, like she'd give it to me? She made it clear that I shouldn't mess with Leo Cole."

"She was right," Nicole said, deflating, "and *she* didn't see the two of you this morning. Are you going to his house this weekend?"

"I don't know."

"You don't have to babysit me, y'know."

"It isn't babysitting. I *choose* to be with you." That said, Charlotte's thoughts jumped ahead. If she wanted to get to know Leo, they needed more time together than an hour here and there. But she didn't want Nicole to be alone. "Has Julian committed to the Fourth?"

Quietly, Nicole said, "He can't come. He feels that since the doctors he's working with won't be leaving town, he shouldn't, either, and besides that, it's too far to travel. I think he means for him. And he's right.

Raleigh-Durham to Quinnipeague is a haul." She regarded the recipe
cards with renewed desperation. "What're we going to do about these?"

The answer, of course, was to go door-to-door getting corrections, but
that meant putting people on the spot when nothing about the under-
lying problem had changed. If island women were being pressured, the
pressure would remain until its source was found.

Leo was the logical first stop. Charlotte could have walked to his
house Friday night, but something held her back. It might have been
the fish hash that Nicole made with fresh halibut, the rest of Rebecca
Wilde's ingredients, and what she intuitively knew to be the right
amount of thyme. They didn't eat until late, and after finishing off a
white Burgundy from Bob's stash, they were too sluggish to do more
than watch a restored version of *Gone With the Wind*.

Then again, it might have been fear keeping her from Leo's that
night. If he had carried through on his threats, they had no future.

Or, it might have been simple procrastination. Better she learn that
tomorrow than tonight.

Saturday dawned foggy. Nicole played in the kitchen most of the morning, testing first a French toast casserole, then Anna Cabot's famed
layered eggs. Mercifully, these recipes were correct. They were actually perfect, she declared in an ebullient text to Julian following a tasting session with Charlotte.

No answer on the other? he wrote back.

Not yet. Maybe later. Charlotte has assured her Leo would be in
touch, and Nicole figured that collecting more recipes would be ridiculous until he was stopped.

On one level, she was stymied.

On another, she was freed. When the fog burned off, she took that
as an invitation to sit on the back patio and read.

*   *   *

Midway through the afternoon, Leo texted Charlotte. *I'm doing shingles tonight. Want to help?*

Since it was a clear, warm night, Charlotte walked. A navy dusk was just settling in when she rounded the Cole curve and saw him setting up the ladders. He wore his usual black, but his tool belt was still on the ground. Bundles of shingles were stacked on a pallet nearby.

Halfway down the drive, she stopped to wait. She smelled herbs, plus those white flowers, which were near the woods on her left. Refusing to be charmed by any of it, she thought of the recipe cards and stayed where she was.

Leo finished with the ladders and was about to open the first bundle when he saw her. He waited. When she didn't move, he gestured her forward. When she didn't come, he set down the box cutter and started toward her.

"Something wrong?" he asked as he neared.

She nodded. "We started collecting recipes cards. The herbs were misrepresented on a bunch of them."

"Misrepresented?"

"Given as dried, rather than fresh. Or left out completely. Like people were afraid to mention them. Like someone told them not to."

He seemed amused. "That so?"

"Was it you?"

His amusement faded. "No."

"You threatened."

"Yeah, and Bear was dangerous."

All talk, then? She wanted to believe it. "Well, it wasn't Cecily."

He snorted. "You sure about that?"

"Come on, Leo. Dead people don't go talking around town."

"Not in the traditional way."

"Which means?"

"The legend lives on."

Charlotte was intrigued. "Which *means?*"

"People believed things about Cecily. Most were wrong, but tell that to the faithful. If they think she can reach out from the grave, they might try to avoid upsetting her."

"By passing on recipes that used her herbs? Why would that upset her?"

He shrugged. "Go ask. She wasn't always the nicest person."

"Most Quinnies worship her."

"They weren't her son," he said with a head-on stare of those midnight eyes.

Charlotte caught her breath. "What did she do?"

He stared at her for another minute before looking away. "Not my place to criticize. I wasn't easy to raise."

"What did she do?" Charlotte repeated, but this time to his back. He was wandering off into the herbs. Halfway down the row, he bent to snap sprigs of tiny red buds from a broad-leafed plant. Stuffing them in his pocket, he reached for more. "What's that?" she asked, coming abreast of him.

"Sorrel." He shot her a quick look. "You know sorrel?"

"No."

"Most people don't. It isn't glam'rous," he said, sounding more Maine, "but it has a really nice lem'ny taste. The leaves cook up into a cream soup. Sorrel's also good for poachin' fish."

"What do you do with those buds?" Charlotte asked as he stuffed several more in his pocket.

"Throw 'em out. Sorrel grows easy, as long as you keep it trimmed. It's the young leaves that have the best taste. Buds like these"—he picked off another—"retard the new growth." He straightened, eyes resigned, enunciation less Maine and more Leo. "I know all this because I worked these gardens for her. It wasn't by choice. If I didn't do it, I didn't get fed."

Wondering why that sounded ominous, Charlotte was tentative. "That's a good work ethic."

"For a kid who's four? Five? Six? She home-schooled me to keep me around. I used to sneak off—jump on the back of a pickup headin' in town—and when I got there, I'd steal a little of this, little of that. Town was a whole new world. Candy? Potato chips? Comic books? They'd catch me and bring me back home, and she'd make me sleep outside with the plants. Great in summer, not in winter."

Charlotte tried to imagine it. "She imprisoned you here?"

"Not entirely. I used to stow away on fishing boats that left the harbor at dawn. She must've thought the male company would help because she didn't raise a stink. When I got a little older, she sent me around the island on my bike delivering her packets. They did help people. Gotta give her that."

"But you're describing child abuse. Didn't anyone know it?"

"How would they? They didn't come out here, and she wasn't telling. Me, neither. She was my mother."

He wandered to the end of the row, absently touching the white flowers as he passed. Following him, Charlotte asked, "How'd you finally end up going to the island school?" He didn't answer. She guessed there had been outside force. "Weren't they afraid of crossing her?"

"Islanders were. Not authorities on the mainland."

"Child welfare?"

He hesitated, then said, "Close enough. She did love me. She was afraid of losing me." Chewing on a corner of his mouth, he stood with his hands at his back, fingertips tucked in the waist of his shorts, and his eyes on the woods. With the sun gone and the moon not yet up, the trees blurred into a moss-green mass, making it a good place to get lost.

Not that Leo was lost. Entirely focused, he took several steps into the murk and scooped the fallen end of a branch from the forest floor. Studying it, he turned it slowly and with purpose, before tossing it gently toward the garden.

"What's that for?" Charlotte asked.

"Whittling. Pine's soft, but the knots can be tough." Retrieving the branch, he showed her. "There aren't many knots here. This one's good."

"What do you whittle?"

"Nothing much. I'm bad at it. It's about the process."

Like her knitting, but the thought was a distraction. "Go on," she urged gently. "About growing up. I want to hear." He looked at her then. Even with a minimum of light, she saw vulnerability—or felt it. "Friends tell friends things like this," she coaxed.

"Is that what we are?" he asked, sounding discouraged.

"Yes."

"Then that's a first for me. I don't have friends. I never learned how."

She had trouble believing that. He was a nice enough guy.

He must have seen her doubt, because his hand tightened on the branch. "I was ten when I started school in town. I'd never been with other kids. I didn't know how in the hell to act. Obviously, I did it wrong. Cecily saw that as a validation of what she'd been saying—that the plants were the only friends I needed, and that if you loved them, they'd love you and would thrive. They did. They still do. But they shouldn't." He glanced over the rows. "The climate here is all wrong for most of these plants. So maybe she was right. About the love part, at least." Hunkering down, he dropped the branch and brushed a hand over the grass. "How can something that grows in the shade be this green?"

It did look green, Charlotte realized. Even at night. But something else struck her. It had to do with the way he'd touched those white flowers and, now, brushed the grass. "You love the plants."

He shifted to sit. "I do. I like taking care of them." His knees were bent, boots planted in that surprising green grass.

"For her?"

"For me. I tried to kill them once," he confessed, sounding more guilty than proud. "It was right after she died. I was angry she'd croaked in that hospital, like she'd done it to show me how bad my judgment was, so I came back here and hacked all this down. It was fall. Most of it was gone for the season anyway, but I dug everything up, roots and all. Next spring, it all came back. Bigger, stronger."

"Did her ashes do that?" Charlotte asked.

He recoiled, staring up at her in distaste. "Hell no. I didn't cremate her. She's buried in town behind the church. I figured folks'd visit her there." His mouth quirked. "Part of the legend, y'know? She helped those people. Me, I was just the drug runner."

"A bad lesson."

"Hey, she gave it away for free. I was the one who sold it. She didn't know I was doing it 'til I got caught."

"Didn't she see her marijuana disappearing?" Charlotte asked, frowning back at the garden. "I don't smell it, by the way."

His expression turned wry. "It's the only thing that didn't grow back. Mother didn't want me tempted."

"So, you do believe that the dead reach out?"

"No. Hell, I don't know. But there's something poetic about the pot just dying off."

"Would you have been tempted?"

"Nope. Not to use, not to sell."

Charlotte wasn't surprised. Nothing about him spoke of either. All she could think about in the silence that followed, though, was the way Cecily had used him. *Wasn't the best mother,* Dorey had said. Charlotte hadn't followed then, but did now. Her own parents had never been that bad, their major crime being neglect. But she felt a new affinity for Leo. To have to struggle against a parent at home and then face the rest of the world . . . she didn't imagine it had been any easier for him than it had been for her.

Lowering herself so that she sat cross-legged between his boots, she leaned on her thighs. "Do you have a father?"

He snickered. "Cecily was good but not that good. Immaculate conception was beyond her."

"Do you know who he is?"

"Oh yeah."

"Do you see him much?"

"No. He doesn't come here, and I don't go there."

"Where's there?"

"Rockland."

The mainland, and so close. "But you two talk."

"Not if I can help it. He didn't treat my mother well. Just left her alone to raise me herself. I'm guessing she was bi-polar. The swings were dramatic. So it was hard. Money. Me. That."

Hard on Leo, Charlotte heard, though he tried to frame it otherwise. Needing to comfort—to let him know that he wasn't alone just then—she wrapped a hand around his calf. "You're good to take her side," she said, but he was staring at her hand.

"Is that pity?"

"No."

"What then?"

"Just me wanting to touch you."

"If it's pity, take it back."

She left her hand where it was—actually moved it in lightly. There was no padding here, just warm skin covered by a spatter of dark hair.

Slowly he calmed. "About what you said before. I have my own side. I just try to see hers is all. She helped a lot of people. That was her calling."

"So you keep up her house and her herbs."

"What else do I have?"

It was a throwaway line, but Charlotte took it to heart. He might have filled in a few blanks about the boy, but there were still major holes in the story of the man. He was an ex-con; that was fact. But other things didn't fit—like his talking as if he had an advanced degree in psychology. Giving his leg a squeeze, she said, "You tell me. What do you have?"

His eyes swept the night land. "This. My home."

"Did you never want to go elsewhere?"

"I've been elsewhere. It was worse."

"Where?"

Eyes glazing, he was suddenly years away and angry. "When I got out of jail, they set me up doing construction on the mainland. My boss was a woman who didn't like that I wouldn't fuck her. When she accused me of selling drugs on the site, they locked me back up faster'n you could say *frame-up*."

Charlotte gasped. "Did you?"

"Sell? Hell no. The prosecutor figured that out. That's when I came back here." He calmed. "I lived in an old shack down by the pier and did odd jobs. When Cecily got sick and wouldn't get help, I called the prison doctor. He'd been a kind of mentor, bringing me books and stuff. He said if I took her to the mainland, he'd meet us at the hospital. He never showed."

"Betrayal," Charlotte whispered.

"You could say."

She sensed he had other words for it, any of which he would articulate if she pushed him. He was intelligent and intuitive—unexpectedly so, she thought not for the first time.

But the silence was comfortable.

Finally, he came forward, took her hand, and linked their fingers. "Anyway, it wasn't me warning people against helping you out. I don't like the idea of your cookbook, but I wouldn't ruin it for you."

She could see it in his eyes, which in that moment were unguarded and direct. "Do you know who would?"

"No."

"Then how do we fight it?"

"We?"

She had meant Nicole and her. But he had a point. "Would you spread the word that Cecily's okay with the cookbook?"

"I'm not sure it'd help. I don't connect with her, Charlotte. I don't even go to the cemetery. Islanders know that. Cecily and me, it's definitely a love-hate thing."

"There," Charlotte said and, sitting straight, took back her hand. "That's what I don't understand. How do you know to call it a love-hate thing?"

He frowned. "Because it is."

"But how do you know that term? Have you been in therapy?"

"No."

"Which is weird. You describe a childhood that should have left you scarred, but you seem totally balanced to me. You live alone out here, but you don't sound like a hermit. You don't even speak Maine much. You do sometimes, but then it's like you forget to do it. Words, intonation, rhythm—you don't sound like a high school dropout. You say you have no friends, but you talk like you've been talking with friends all your life. Your dialogue is just right."

"I read," he said quietly.

"We all do—"

"I read," he repeated, eyes unblinking.

"I thought that started in prison."

He seemed to relax at that, giving her a curious smile. "Why?"

"Because I heard you were lousy in school."

"To put it nicely, but that had nothing to do with brains. I didn't like discipline. And I didn't like their books."

She considered that. It fit into the picture that was starting to emerge. "So you were reading back then?"

"Gotta thank Cecily for that. Next to plants, she loved reading most. I fought her—didn't like her books much, either. She called them her magic carpet, only her carpet didn't take *me* away. My own didn't take off until I was five and stole that first comic book. From there, I got into paperback books. Then I hit the big-time."

"Big-time?"

"The library. I used to love stealing from there. They knew I was doing it. Looked the other way, maybe out of compassion, maybe fear."

"But you returned the books when you were done."

"I did not. What fun would that be?"

"*Leo.*"

"I'm not saying I'd steal now. But those books were my lifeline. I'd be up all hours reading. I never needed much sleep."

Hence, his doing the roof at night. The question of what he did during the day remained. But she didn't want to ask just then and risk the good feeling between them. "What do you read?"

"Whatever. Reading's always been my out."

She studied his face. It was shadowed, but jaw and cheekbone were strong, and there was a depth to his eyes that the night couldn't hide. Or maybe it was that she knew it was there. Or that she was touched by his words. Or that her hand still shaped his skin. Or that his letting her into a place few had gone made him all the more attractive to her. Or, simply, that her heart was squeezed.

Whatever, coming up on her knees, she took his face in her hands and gave him a long, slow, nibbling kiss. Sweet scents hovered, adding to a sense of rightness.

When she finally allowed an inch between their mouths, he whispered a hoarse, "What was that for?"

"Because I like you," she whispered back, hard-pressed for a better answer, though it seemed to do the trick.

Pulling her so that she straddled his lap, he returned the kiss with growing hunger. She was starting to feel it in her belly, when he took off her T-shirt and unhooked her bra. The bra had been on the whole time at the beach, but his mouth on her breasts was not something she would have wanted to miss this time. She held his head, fingers in his hair. Needing more, she cried out.

As he had done at the beach, he paused at the sound. "Too much?"

"Not enough," she moaned.

He helped with her shorts, but she pushed his aside only enough so that she could take him in. They both went still then, forehead to forehead, taking deep, quivering breaths as they savored the possession, and when that wasn't enough, he rolled her beneath him and thrust.

He took her away—just took her out of herself to a place she could only go with him—but, when it was done, there was nothing scary about the return. He felt solid. Rooted. *Real*.

They sat for the longest time, his back against a tree with his arm around her and her cheek to his chest. That chest was finely textured, leanly muscled, and smelled of Leo. Feeling a sense of peace, she could have stayed there forever.

But Leo wanted to work on the roof. "Long's you're here," he reasoned a short time later as they climbed the ladders. The idea was to work sections from left to right, bottom to top, each section overlapping the next. "Two hammers or one?" he asked.

"One," she said. "I'll hold, you hammer." She had done it this way before and thought it the fastest and most efficient. After Leo positioned each shingle, she held it while he nailed. As he pounded in the last nail, she brought a new shingle up for positioning. Once they got into the rhythm, they moved right along. They stood close, arms or legs brushing at times. It wasn't sexual, but pleasant.

"Definitely anticlimactic," Charlotte remarked at one point, to which Leo chuckled. She had never heard him do that before, and eyed him in surprise. He seemed surprised, himself, to which she said, "It's a good sound."

"Y'think?"

A warmth spread inside. "I do." She might have kissed him again if they hadn't been standing on scaffolding clamped to the roof. And then came a *whoosh* in the garden. Looking back, she caught her breath. "The fawn." A sliver of blurred spots reflecting the moon, it darted here, darted there. "What's it doing?"

"Chasing a chipmunk. Or a mouse."

"I thought it was supposed to be sleeping."

"Did you always sleep when your parents put you to bed?"

Knowingly, she smiled at the fawn, then, feeling Leo's leg behind her, smiled curiously at him. "You think I'll fall?"

"Better safe than sorry."

Bob Lilly used to say that. Same with the hero of *Salt*. "I'm really fine," she assured him, but did brace herself with a hand when, at a renewed rustling in the garden, she turned quickly. The fawn was jumping and pouncing through the lowest of the herbs.

She watched in enjoyment for a minute, then had a thought. "Where's Bear?"

"In the shrubs. It's past his bedtime."

"Is he okay?"

"Oh yeah. Just old."

"Do you worry about him?"

"All the time. He's my best friend in the world."

Best *animal* friend, Charlotte might have corrected if she had wanted to get into that discussion, but she didn't. Each time she looked at Leo—each time their eyes met—she felt that spreading warmth. It might be pure chemistry. But she had known chemistry before, and it wasn't like this.

Their system worked. With Leo adept at repositioning ladders and planks, they lost no time moving from section to section. Still, it was close to midnight when they finished. Charlotte was yawning as he walked her down the drive, though she wasn't so tired as to be numb. The herbs were sleeping, but not those white flowers. They were night creatures like Leo, stronger than ever in the dark. Their pull kept her awareness of him high.

"Are you sure I can't drive you?" he asked when they reached the Cole curve.

"I'm sure." She needed to keep these parts of her life separate. He was here, Nicole was there—fantasy here, reality there.

Say good night, she thought. *Kiss his cheek. Give him a hug.* But the scent of those flowers was in her head, pushing for more. So she did nothing, simply stood in silence, watching him watch her.

"This is starting to make me nervous," he said quietly. "You're leaving at the end of the summer, right?"

"That's a ways off."

"But you are leaving."

She tried to keep it light. "Mid-August is the plan."

"So we should keep this low-key."

She laughed. "Like that would work? Like we should just tell our bodies there's nothing to feel?"

He studied the road underfoot, then raised questioning eyes. Even in the dark, their message was clear. What he was asking, she knew, was whether there was a chance she would stay.

But she had a life. She had friends in far places. She had assignments lined up. "I can't," she whispered, though the words tugged at her insides.

He took a breath and nodded. "Okay. Just so I know."

That, she thought, was reality. But these night hours, the moon, the fawn, that incredible smell—this was fantasy, wasn't it? Or not? Shouldn't he argue, fight, plead?

Annoyed that he was so accepting and apparently didn't feel the same tug she did, she glared back down the drive at the only thing that might have been its source. "What *is* that smell?"

"Me?"

"No, those white flowers. Back there in the garden."

His voice held a reluctant smile. "Jasmine."

"Jasmine."

"It's an aphrodisiac."

An aphrodisiac. She hung her head, then righted it and sighed. "Silly me. I should've guessed."

Chapter Fourteen

Nicole lay in bed Saturday night listening for Charlotte to return. Ten o'clock came and went, then eleven, and she grew uneasy. She wanted to know what Leo had to say about the recipes. More, though, she was starting to wonder what was really going on between Charlotte and Leo. If it would further hurt the cookbook, she didn't want it. She had a deadline to meet.

Somewhere around midnight, she fell asleep. When she awoke, it was two. Checking the hall, she saw that the front light was off and Charlotte's bedroom door closed. At least she was home; Nicole had half feared she would spend the night at Leo's. That kiss had been a wake-up call. Charlotte at thirty-four might be very different from Charlotte at twenty-four. For all Nicole knew, this Charlotte had lovers wherever she went.

Having married young, Nicole had never experimented much. Other friends had, and she didn't judge them for it. Nor was she judging Charlotte. She just wanted her here at a time when no one else was.

Feeling alone and lonely as she lay in a bed built for two, she decided to call Julian when morning came. He had sounded more tired than usual tonight. She was worried something else was going on.

As it happened, she didn't call Sunday, though she thought of it a hundred times. He had told her his plans, which started with rounds at the hospital and would be followed by brunch with the team he was training, then an afternoon with his laptop in a quiet alcove of the university library, drafting lectures for his fall series in California. He would be busy. She didn't want to disturb him.

But she couldn't not wonder how he felt. So she texted the question at seven, to which he texted back, *Starting rounds in five minutes,* which told her nothing. She wanted to know if the new drug was helping, whether he was feeling side effects, whether he was actively pursuing the stem cell route. She wanted to know how his hotel accommodations were and whether the laundry service was decent. Mostly, she wanted to know if he missed her, but was afraid to ask that, too.

After a subdued call from him Sunday night, her imagination was going wild. She shot off a handful of Monday morning texts, but his answers were unsatisfying enough to force her hand. Choosing her time with care, she waited until late morning, when he would be in his office-on-loan and hopefully alone before heading to lunch.

"Hey," she said lightly and, pulse racing, held her breath.

"Hey, baby. How are you?"

At the upbeat sound of his voice—that oh-so-intimate *baby*—she dared breathe again. "I'm good," she replied in relief. "You sound better."

"I slept well. Everything okay there?"

"It is. The weather's gorgeous." It was small talk. But after last night's worry and now his sounding like the old Julian, she could happily pretend there was no angst in their lives and enjoy what was right about them as a couple. "The stone on the patio is like a heater once it absorbs the sun. And the ocean is starting to warm up. I wish you'd come," she added, not nagging, but excited.

Good-spiritedly, Julian said, "I wish I could." Then, "Did you get the recipes fixed?"

"We did," she said, allowing for the evasion. She liked that he was concerned about her work. "We spent the morning in town. Leo wouldn't commit to calling around, but the people we talked with agreed to make changes. I'm guessing he told one person, who then spread the word."

"Did they say why they changed their ingredients?"

"They said they thought we'd want recipes that people anywhere in the country could follow, but it was kind of a canned line, you know? Like it was either the one he fed them or one they agreed on among themselves."

"It doesn't matter, as long as it's fixed."

"Assuming Leo lets it go at that. Charlotte still claims he had nothing to do with it, but she's biased. I don't trust him. If their relationship ends, he could attack out of sheer spite."

"Nicki. You're more positive than that."

She sighed. "I know. You're right. I just get frightened sometimes."

"Did you decide what to do with your father's clothes?"

It was another evasion, this one picking up on something she had said last week. She liked that he had remembered. "Well, I did, but Mom has other ideas. She called last night after you and I talked. She had a long list of questions, some of which I could answer and some I could not. It's be so much easier if she was here."

"It's an emotional thing for her."

"It is for me, too, but it has to be done, and she has opinions on all of it. You know what'll happen, Jules. She'll refuse to come here and will— quote, unquote—leave the decisions to me, then she won't like the ones I make. Dad's clothes are a good example. I thought I'd take them to the consignment shop in Rockland—and it's not about the money, which I was planning to donate to the animal shelter there, because it's a cause

Dad loved. When I mentioned this last night, Mom first said she didn't want me *touching* his clothes yet. In the next breath, she said the minister would know what to do with them. But honestly, I can't see someone here on Quinnipeague walking around in Dad's clothes. Whoever it is would look ridiculous—like an imposter. Books or furniture or pots and pans are one thing. But something as intimate as clothes?"

"Isn't it really about what your mother wants?" Julian asked gently enough.

"I suppose."

"It'll sort itself out, Nicki. So, with the recipes good, you're feeling better about the cookbook?"

"I am. Charlotte's profiles are great. Want me to e-mail you a few?"

"Sure," he said, but he was only indulging her. He had never been overly interested in Charlotte's contribution, preferring to think of the cookbook as Nicole's alone, and she did love him for that.

"Anything new?" she asked gently.

"I talked with Grendjin about the Beijing trip," Julian offered. Antoine Grendjin was president of the hospital. He and Julian used to play golf together, though they hadn't done it since Julian had developed chronic tennis elbow, or so he had told Antoine. It was a good enough excuse—tennis elbow being more of a problem for golfers than golfer's elbow, and an injury that fit in well with Julian shifting to a teaching role in the OR. "He's fine with my being gone the week."

"Did you sign the contract?" Nicole asked. The speech was for the following February; typically, there would be paperwork sent straight to him in Durham now.

"Not yet. I have it here."

She felt a glimmer of unease. "But you haven't signed it, because you're not sure how you'll be in February? Are you feeling any better now?"

"I haven't signed the contract because I haven't gotten to it," he replied sharply and, seeming to hear his edge, asked more quietly, "How about you? Now that there's progress, when do you think the cookbook will be done?"

"They want it by mid-August. I'll need all that time. Even after we have the recipes and Charlotte is done with her profiles, I'll have to pull the whole thing together—you know, write the foreword and the afterword, make menu plans, edit it so that my voice in the book is consistent with my blogging one. I still get the heebie-jeebies about it sometimes. Me, write a *book*? Charlotte was always the confident one. She's such a professional."

"So are you."

"Not in the same way. She knows what it's like to work under a deadline. She knows what it's like to see something of hers in print."

"So do you. Your blog is in print. I'd warrant a guess that your following is much larger than hers."

"Well, anyway, she keeps me in line. But we're not working over the Fourth," she ventured. "Everyone'll be here, Jules—all the people you like. You'd be able to sleep and swim and take a quick break from Duke. Are you sure you won't come? I miss you." She was careful to keep her voice light, not wheedling. She wasn't a nag, just a wife loving her husband.

"Maybe in another weekend or two."

"But this is a long one with the Fourth on a Thursday," she coaxed. "You could—"

"Not now. Gotta run, baby. Enjoy that sun."

He was gone before she could point out that he hadn't said how he was feeling.

But he had sounded good. And she hadn't wanted to rock the boat. With the connection cut now, though, she could only worry about what wasn't said.

She worried in silence—not venting more to Charlotte, simply so that she didn't have to hear it all again herself. There was nothing fun about trying new medicines and waiting for improvement, watching for side effects, praying that a tingling foot was an aberration and not a symptom. Charlotte found it upsetting; Nicole could see that. So she was protecting Charlotte by not going on and on—but she was also protecting herself. She couldn't be entirely sure of this Charlotte, who had done her own thing for ten years and now had something or other going with Leo Cole. There were parts of Charlotte that she didn't understand. But she needed her. She couldn't risk driving her away.

Besides, she had been silent for four years through no choice of her own. Being silent now because she did choose to be was okay. It was a comfort knowing that she could talk if she wanted to, and she no longer felt guilty doing it. This wasn't a betrayal of Julian. At a time when Julian was doing what he needed to do to survive, so was she.

So she kept up a bright front. They spent Monday afternoon throwing mugs on Oliver Weeks's pottery wheel, Tuesday morning focused on CHOWDER, and Tuesday afternoon at the beach. Nicole thought it was a good blend of work and play, though under it all the worry was there. Evening calls were increasingly brief, and Julian only texted in reply to notes she sent. Granted, she kept asking how he was feeling, which possibly irritated him, but she couldn't help herself.

You won't tell me how you are, so I imagine the worst, she finally wrote, to which he replied, *Status quo,* which did little to ease her mind.

Charlotte sensed it. "You're not sitting still," she said at breakfast Wednesday morning. "Last time you were like this, you exploded by ten. Tell me what's wrong."

The invitation was all it took for Nicole to let loose about the worry, the frustration, the anger. If she repeated herself at times, she didn't care. Charlotte hadn't seen Leo since Saturday, so Nicole felt like she had her back. "I have this sense of impending doom," she concluded.

"That's melodramatic."

"I'm serious. Impending doom."

"More now than before?"

Nicole considered that. "No. But doom can only be impending for so long. At some point, it has to hit, right?"

"No," Charlotte said. "Multiple sclerosis is a chronic disease. It can go on for years with little change."

Julian wouldn't put up with that, she knew, but she didn't want to repeat it. Better to try to believe what Charlotte said. "You're right. Definitely right."

"You're working yourself up for nothing."

"I am. You're right. And I shouldn't criticize Julian. He's doing the best he can." She took a deep breath. "That's better. Thank you."

"Want to go to Rockland?"

"Today?" she asked, liking the thought. "To play?"

"Absolutely. I didn't bring enough clothes. Besides, tomorrow's the holiday, so there'll be extra ferries shuttling guests in today. We've done a lot on the book. We deserve a day off."

They took the early boat to Rockland and spent the day shopping, viewing the Wyeth collection, even catching an afternoon movie at the Strand before heading back to the dock. In a different place, Nicole had an easier time focusing, though she regularly glanced at her phone. By the time they returned to Quinnipeague, every bit of her worry was back.

Charlotte was on edge simply because Nicole was. She didn't believe in the business of impending doom, but Nicole was so serious about it that she wondered if there were things she didn't know. There had been moments in Rockland when she was the same old chatty Nicole, other times when she was silent. Charlotte couldn't force her to talk. All she could do was to stay close.

That said, her mind did wander occasionally when she saw a man who was of the right age and build to be Leo's father. She didn't mention it to Nicole. Leo remained a sore spot with her.

*   *   *

It was late afternoon when they got back. They were dropping their things in the kitchen when Nicole's phone rang. Her heart was thudding even before she saw Julian's name. He didn't usually call this early. "Hey, Jules," she said in breathless surprise, praying that he had either changed his mind and was coming after all, or simply missed her enough to want to hear her voice. When he didn't speak, she asked a frightened, "Everything okay?"

His voice was quiet. "No. It's out."

She gasped. "What do you mean, out?"

"I was at a grant meeting with half a dozen surgeons when my right hand started to shake. I tried to put it in my lap, but it was pretty obvious."

"Maybe they didn't see."

"They were staring at it, Nicole. Surgeons don't like hand tremors."

"But these doctors don't know you. Maybe they think that's just how you are." The argument was absurd, of course. Shaking was shaking. "At least it wasn't in front of your team in Philly."

"Dan Ewing was there," Julian said quietly. "He flew down last night and was at the meeting. He stayed behind when the others left and asked point-blank. When I didn't immediately answer, he said he knew something was wrong—that he'd known it for a while—but didn't know what it was. So I told him. I didn't have a choice, Nicki. Giving evasive answers is one thing, lying outright is another."

"I understand," she tried, "but Dan's a friend. He'll respect your need for privacy. He won't go blabbing all over the hospital."

"Not all over the hospital, but he has an obligation to make sure certain people know. He's head of the department. That puts him in a precarious position vis-à-vis responsibility and liability."

"But you haven't operated in four years."

"It's about transparency. He said I needed to tell Antoine. I just called him."

Nicole gasped again. "Omigod. What did he say?"

"He went through the mumbo-jumbo about legalities and ethics, only it isn't mumbo-jumbo. It's what any hospital would do."

"He can't ask you to leave."

"He can, but he didn't. He was sympathetic."

"Like, upset?"

"Stunned. He asked all the right questions. But friendship only goes so far. As president of the hospital, he has to put certain wheels in motion."

"What wheels?"

"Whatever's needed to protect the hospital. I won't have to leave. I just have to pull back from everything related to treating patients. There's paperwork involved. I have to notify my insurers. I have to document the history of my illness, so that if there's a patient problem from two or three years ago, I can show that I'd already stopped holding the scalpel."

"It's all there in the records, isn't it?"

"Yes, but it'll take some digging to put it together. I took every precaution, Nicole. I was careful even before the diagnosis, because I wasn't sure of my hands." His voice shook. "The point is, it's over. I need to talk with the department head here. I can assure him that I haven't gone near patients, but he'll have lawyers at his back, too. He may or may not want me to stay." He exhaled. "Oh God. The consequences keep mounting. They may not want me here. I won't be asked to talk at conferences. Same with being on TV. My career is done."

"No, Julian," she argued, though her eyes had filled with tears, "it isn't done. It's just shifting."

"Same difference."

"But how are you feeling? You won't tell me that."

"Because you don't want to know."

"I do," she insisted.

"Okay, then. I'm feeling like this drug is having no effect at all. There's no improvement. It's just getting worse. The tremor today lasted for a good long time. The hand was shaking in my lap." Nicole swallowed, about to speak when he added, "If this drug was going to help, it should have done so by now. I've read the literature, baby. The old 'give it time' routine won't cut it, so save your breath. Once the holiday's done, I'm calling Hammon."

Remembering his remark about Mexico, she felt a tiny spark of hope. "You haven't gone looking elsewhere, then?"

He was silent, then very quiet. "No. I said I would. But I've had to think about it. This isn't an easy choice for me, Nicole. You think it is, but I do know the risks."

"I know."

"You don't. You don't know what I'm feeling inside."

"You won't tell me!"

"No man likes to tell his wife that he's scared."

Nicole's heart broke for him. "You have a right to be scared. I'm scared, too! It's nothing to be ashamed of."

"It is if it paralyzes you. I don't want to be paralyzed. I'd rather be a guinea pig."

Her stomach was churning. "Julian—"

"Don't worry. It won't happen tomorrow. He'll want to try an autologous transplant first."

Using his own cells was less risky, but her stomach continued to churn. "What would that entail?"

"Maybe nothing. If my blood counts are too low, it's a no-go."

"Then what?"

"We use donor stem cells."

And if he resorted to donor cells, she knew exactly which ones he'd go for. "You want to try umbilical cord cells, but that's *so* experimental," she cried.

"I have nothing to lose."

"You *do*," she argued, frantic. "You react badly to these things. Okay, so this drug isn't showing improvement yet, but if you've been tolerating it well—"

"I haven't. I'm jaundiced. Even Dan saw that. Jaundice means liver problems, which is what the blood work is starting to show. It'll only get worse if I stay on this drug."

She hadn't known about the blood work. He had kept that from her, knowing she would panic. Struggling for control, she tried to think. "What does Keppler say?"

"I haven't told him yet. This is beyond him now, Nicki. Mark will search cord blood banks to find as close a match as he can."

"There has to be another drug—"

"I've tried the best."

"Then something off-label."

He made a frustrated sound. "This isn't nicotine addiction. I've made up my mind, Nicole. I want treatment with umbilical cord stem cells."

"You could die."

"I could live. Either way, I'll have done something for medical research. Look at it from my point of view. I can't treat my own patients anymore. This is one way I can still give."

My point of view. My patients. I, I, I. "What about me?" she shot back. "What about our marriage?"

"Our marriage means the world to me, baby, but look at me. I can't be the kind of husband I want to be," he said with such defeat that her anger dissolved.

"I'm flying down," she said. "If I can't get a flight tonight—"

"Don't," he ordered, then entreated, "Please. I need to talk with Kaylin and John. And I need to call my parents. Explaining it is going to be hard for me. I need to be alone with it for a bit."

Nicole would have argued, if she hadn't been so devastated. She was losing him, and there didn't seem to be anything she could do to stop it.

Chapter Fifteen

CHARLOTTE HAD BEEN ROOTED TO the spot, barely breathing lest she miss a word. If it was wrong of her to be listening in on a discussion between husband and wife, her personal stake justified it. Besides, Nicole hadn't turned away, though she wondered if Nicole even knew she was there. Her eyes were glazed, her hand trembling as she very quietly lowered the phone.

Charlotte waited. When she couldn't stand it any longer, she whispered, "What?"

Nicole looked up. Her face was ashen, her eyes the palest ghost of green. She moistened her lips, then swallowed.

Rounding the table, Charlotte reached for her cold hand. "What happened?" She had been able to piece together parts of it, but not all.

Nicole's eyes welled. "It's over."

"What is?"

"Everything."

Horrified, Charlotte said, "He wants to *kill* himself?"

"Not directly. But that's what it amounts to." Tears trickled down her cheeks. "He's just giving up."

"Because someone found out."

Nicole nodded. She seemed numb, which was nearly as frightening to Charlotte as anything else. Pulling her friend down into a chair, Charlotte took the one beside it and, holding both of Nicole's hands tightly, said, "Talk to me, Nicki. Tell me what he said."

Nicole let out a long, tremulous sob and, in a broken burst, told her what had happened. By the end, Charlotte was holding her, trying to comfort her as she had done that first morning in town, though this time without success. Nicole was shaking all over when the story was done, eyes bleak, cheeks streaked with tears.

"I can't help him," she whispered, looking helpless and confused. "He won't let me in. Is that fair, Charlotte? Shouldn't this be a decision we make together?"

"It should be," Charlotte said, though her mind was rushing in a frightened direction. If Julian was determined to use umbilical cord stem cells, she had a decision of her own to make.

"He's become totally selfish and self-absorbed," Nicole cried. "I don't know this man."

"You love him."

"Not *this* man." Her eyes held shock at the words, then instant grief. "You're right. I love him. I'd do anything to help him. But I'm out of the picture."

"You're not—"

"He doesn't want to hear what I have to say. There's nothing I can do."

"Maybe there is," Charlotte begged, desperate to give her hope. "Maybe he's right about trying something totally different."

"He'll die!"

"He doesn't have to."

"Like you can prevent it."

"Not me, but maybe—" She stopped. She wasn't ready for this, knew that it would cause damage and that once out, it couldn't be taken back. She didn't know if it was the right thing to do at all. But remembering the sense of purpose she had felt in returning to Quinnipeague, she had to believe it was tied to this.

"Maybe what?" Nicole cried, then begged, "Tell me, Charlotte. Anything."

In mere seconds, with Nicole looking at her like she was the only one who could possibly help, Charlotte wavered a dozen times, weighing the knowledge that Nicole would be hurt against the possibility that Julian might be saved. In the end, it was a moral issue. Hurt could be handled; death could not.

"Umbilical cord cells," she said with barely a breath.

"No no! That's what I *don't* want! I don't care how close the match is, Julian's body will reject it. It's rejected everything else. If I'd had a baby, we'd have frozen the cord blood and had a better chance with that, but I don't *have* a baby."

"I do," Charlotte mouthed, afraid to say the words aloud.

Nicole's eyes widened. "What?"

"I had a baby," Charlotte said softly. "I gave her up for adoption, but there's cord blood. I own it until she turns eighteen."

Nicole let out a frustrated breath. "That won't help. You can't just take any cord blood and think it'll work, not with Julian's body."

Charlotte stared at her, frozen in a last minute of indecision. There was still time to take it back, just say that she'd gotten pregnant after she left here.

But she couldn't say that. It would have been an outright lie—and through all of this, ten summers before and now, she had never lied outright to Nicole. Sweet, innocent, generous, and kind Nicole. Impending doom? Absolutely. It was ready to hit. But as painful as the truth was, life was life and still the most precious thing in the world.

So she didn't take anything back, simply stared at Nicole until she figured it out.

It took a minute, not because the idea didn't come, but because it was so off the charts impossible that Nicole couldn't believe it. But

Charlotte had to know she was thinking it and didn't correct her. Not impossible, then. But wrong, so wrong that she had trouble taking it in. *"Julian's* baby?"

Charlotte's nod was so small that Nicole might have missed it if she hadn't been watching closely.

Sitting straight, she put a hand on her chest. "You had Julian's baby? You and Julian . . . together?"

"Just once. Before you were married."

In a sickening instant, Nicole saw a tangle of arms and legs, the lock of undulating bodies. With the scrape of chair legs on the tile floor, she rose and stepped back. "You and *Julian?"*

"It was an accident. We were drunk."

Nicole wanted to misunderstand, but the guilt on Charlotte's face wouldn't let her. She backed up farther, needing to distance herself from the words, but they didn't fade. Barely able to breathe, she continued to stare at Charlotte, seeing something totally different from what should have been there, someone she didn't know at all. And Julian? Her *husband*?

For a minute, she felt faint enough to pass out. All it took to recover was Charlotte coming toward her and she shot out a hand, *stop.*

"Don't *touch* me," she whispered and fled into the Great Room, which was as far as her legs would take her. Sinking against the edge of the sofa, she tried to take in what Charlotte had said, but her thoughts were fragmented, torn by questions that had nowhere to go but out.

Jumping up, she ran back to the kitchen. Charlotte hadn't moved.

"When did this happen?" she asked. She needed to know. Didn't know why. Just needed to know.

Charlotte looked terrified. "A month before the wedding. It was like a circus here. We were painting guest rooms, moving furniture, trying to decide where the tent would go."

It was a blur to Nicole. "What night?"

"Saturday, I guess, because he left the next day. You have no idea how sorry—"

"What time?"

Charlotte flinched. "I don't know. We were all exhausted. Julian had been making margaritas."

"Where was *I*?"

"You were with us for a while." She swallowed. "Then you went to bed. We could feel the margaritas, so we switched to wine. We were drunk, Nicki. It didn't mean anything."

And that was supposed to make it *all right*? Nicole stared at her in disbelief. Unable to even *begin* to respond, she walked out. Seconds later, though, she was back. There were more questions. Asking them seemed her only link to sanity. "When did you know you were pregnant?"

"Not until after I left here."

"And you're sure it was Julian's?"

"I hadn't been with anyone else in ten months."

"Ten months," Nicole echoed. "Exactly ten months." Were there that many men? "You keep count?"

Charlotte held her gaze. "Not the way you mean. I agonized afterward. Getting drunk isn't my style. I wanted to know why I did it that night. So I dug back. I remember feeling lonely. There was so much happiness here, but I remember feeling alone."

"We included you in *everything*."

"Yes, you did, but you were planning a wedding. I had been planning one the year before—not planning, just dreaming. I'd done a piece in Sweden and met a guy and thought that was it."

Nicole was skeptical. It sounded like just another excuse. "You never mentioned it."

"It ended badly. I couldn't talk about it. I didn't want to *think* about it. But after a few drinks, I must have been. I must have been wondering if I was right to break up with him and if there was something wrong with me that I couldn't find love and if I'd ever have *my* day walking down the aisle."

"So you screwed my husband instead."

"No, I got *drunk* instead. I'm guessing that I was desperate to feel wanted. It could as easily have been the gardener as Julian."

"Blind sex? *Indiscriminate* sex? You were my *maid of honor,* Charlotte. How could you be that after what you'd done?"

"How could I *tell* you?" Charlotte cried.

"How could you *not*? You were pregnant by my husband."

"Your fiancé, and I didn't know I was pregnant until after the wedding."

Unable to look at her a second longer, Nicole started out, but she hadn't even made it past the door when another, horrible thought made her pivot. "Did *he* know you were pregnant?"

"No. I haven't talked with him since I left here ten years ago."

"You didn't think he had a right to know you were *carrying his child?*"

"By the time I found out, you were married. I couldn't do that to you."

"You did it!" The words *carrying his child* were bleeping front and center. She started to cry, but stopped herself and screamed, "How *could* you, Charlotte? You knew I wanted a baby."

"I didn't plan it," Charlotte cried. "I didn't plan that night, didn't plan a *baby*. It was the most difficult thing I've ever lived through."

As was this for Nicole. Anger was the only thing keeping her erect. "Am I supposed to feel sorry for you?" she asked, tasting bitterness and hating that, too. But how not to resent Charlotte for having the baby she should have had? More quietly, unable to shake the image, she asked, "What was it?"

"Oh, Nicki, don't—"

"Don't ask? Don't *wonder*? If not now, when?" A detached part of her said she had to know these things, that as long as she kept asking questions, the awful, *awful* whole of it wouldn't hit. "What was it?" she repeated.

"A girl."

"Where is she now?"

"Washington."

"D.C.?"

"State. It was a private adoption. The parents were at the hospital for the birth."

"And you didn't think Julian should have been there?"

"He was married to you. It would have killed you."

"Didn't you think he should have had a say about what happened to his child?"

Charlotte's mouth tightened. "No. I didn't. We avoided each other that last month, then he was married to you, and I was gone. He never asked if there was a chance I'd get pregnant. Neither one of us wanted to remember that night." Her voice softened, pleading. "I agonized, Nicole. I was pregnant. I was terrified. I thought of every possibility. I knew you'd be the best mother in the world, but how could you raise a child conceived this way? And if I told Julian, he'd either have to keep it from you or risk ruining his marriage. Adoption seemed like the only choice."

"Did you hold her?" Nicole asked quietly. How many times had she imagined holding her own child immediately after its birth?

"This won't—"

"Did you?"

"For a minute."

"Did you name her?"

"No."

"Are you in touch with her now?"

"No."

"But you kept the umbilical cord cells." Charlotte nodded. "Why?"

"In case I had other children who might need them. Or me."

"What about Julian's other children?" Nicole added, thinking of children she might have had herself, children who would have been half siblings with this one. The question hung in the air without answer. "Did your friends know?"

"What friends? I was doing community outreach in Appalachia when I found out. I didn't know anyone there."

"They must have seen that you were pregnant."

"By that time, I was gone. I got my first writing assignment. It was for a story in Oregon. I spent most of the pregnancy there."

She looked ashamed, but that didn't help Nicole. Somewhere in the back of her mind was Julian . . . guilty Julian . . . *cheating* Julian.

But Charlotte was here, and Nicole wanted to hit back. "It makes sense in a sick way. Your parents were always fooling around. You said you hated that."

"I did."

"But then you did the same." The numbness was starting to wear off. Trembling inside, she wrapped her arms around her middle. "Do you have any idea how I feel? Did you think about that at all?

Charlotte nodded. "It's haunted me for ten years."

Resentment flared. "I loved you like a sister."

"And I you," Charlotte said, forearms on the table now, earnest and intense. "What I did was wrong, Nicole. I never wanted you to know. Then I got here and you told me about Julian, and I've been praying ever since that it wouldn't come to this. But if he needs those stem cells, how could I not speak up?"

"You could have told *him*," Nicole fired back. "Why me first?"

"Because you're the one I care about."

"By wrecking my marriage?"

"That's the last thing I want. I went away after the wedding and I stayed away. I tried to remove myself from your life. But you invited me back, and I've missed you. Everything seemed so right when we talked that I hoped the past was done and we could regain what we had. I did something awful, Nicole. If these cells give you hope, I'll have been able to give something back for all I've taken away."

"Really," Nicole said in a swirl of fury, because fury was the most obvious thing to feel. There was also disbelief and disappointment. There was emptiness. She had always thought she and Julian were the couple. Now to learn that it was *Charlotte* and Julian? She had no idea where that left her.

Charlotte didn't speak.

Nicole's fury did. "You had my husband's baby."

Still nothing.

"I can never forgive you for that."

"I understand," Charlotte said, turning beseechful, "but listen to me. This isn't *about* the baby. It's about stem cells. I have them. They could be the answer."

"Answer to *what?*" Nicole shouted, letting anger give her strength. "Saving my husband's life? Right now, I couldn't care less. He betrayed me as much as you did."

"Neither of us knew what we were doing."

Nicole didn't buy that. She could understand a lapse of morals in Charlotte, in whom they were poorly rooted to begin with. But Julian? Her *husband?* Even with his being married before—even with his dating other women between—she had assumed faithfulness, and if not on the eve of their wedding, when?

Charlotte drew her arms from the table and, in a faint voice, said, "Do you want me to leave?"

"Yes," Nicole said, then, "No." She thought about the cookbook, which was why Charlotte was here. On one hand, the cookbook seemed irrelevant right now. Food . . . place settings . . . tens of thousands of followers? Her whole *career* seemed irrelevant.

On the other hand, it was all she had. And Charlotte had committed to help. And kicking her out would only let her off the hook.

What to do? Nicole's thoughts were muddled by thick globs of emotion. Dismayed, she simply said, "I can't look at you," and, turning on a heel, ran through the Great Room and up the front stairs.

Charlotte waited for her to return. There was no sound from above—no crying, no yelling at Julian, not even the slam of a door. *I can't look at you.* Charlotte deserved that. She deserved worse. Still, it hurt.

Needing the comfort of the ocean, she went out the kitchen door. In the distance, the boom of fireworks at the pier marked the start of festivities for the Fourth, but festive was the last thing Charlotte felt. Crossing the patio, she settled on the beach steps and hunched over her knees. The tide was out, leaving a deep stretch of seaweed-blotched sand. Beyond it, the surf frothed in, broke, rolled out, echoing down the Quinnipeague coast. She tried to see the poetry in it; life ebbed and flowed. Bob Lilly had talked about that when she first came here, an eight-year-old child, troubled by what was happening at home. His voice, his words, and the echo of the poetry had given her strength during the loneliest times in her life.

None of it helped now. She had betrayed Bob, too. Wondering if Nicole was right—if she was as defective as her parents had been—she felt worse than ever. She rocked lightly. She put her head to her knees, listening, waiting, but though the ocean thundered rhythmically, it didn't soothe.

In time, she raised her head. Midnight had come and gone, but she doubted Nicole was asleep. She couldn't go to her. But she could wait in the Great Room, all night if need be, glad to be a whipping post if that would help Nicole.

She had just started back when the house lights went out. Uneasy, she made her way through the dark to the kitchen door and turned the handle, but the door didn't budge. She tried the patio sliders, then the front door, without luck.

She was wondering what to do next, when she heard footsteps inside. In a moment of fantasy, Charlotte imagined Nicole throwing open the door, saying that she understood, that people made mistakes, that those stem cells were the answer to a prayer.

The only thing reality brought, though, was the realization that the footsteps had been going *up* the stairs. Nicole had locked her out.

Chapter Sixteen

CHARLOTTE STOOD IN THE DARK, wondering what to do. She couldn't ring the bell. This wasn't a case of Nicole being distracted. She knew Charlotte was outside and didn't want her coming in.

Feeling like scum, she sat on the steps in the moonless night, arms around her knees, eyes on nothing at all. She had made a gross mistake ten years ago. It seemed she had compounded the error tonight. In weighing hurt against help, she had misjudged. Everything she had wanted *not* to happen *had*. And now the damage was done.

She thought to drive to the pier and wait there until morning to catch the ferry, but she didn't have money or even her car keys. Besides, running away wasn't the answer. She had spent her life running from one unpleasant relationship or another. But Nicole wasn't an unpleasant relationship. Charlotte loved her like a sister.

Anxious, she jumped up and started to walk. The night was cool. Still in the blouse and shorts she had worn to Rockland, she felt chilled, though she suspected part of it was grief. When easy walking didn't do it, she walked faster.

Five minutes later, though, she sat down on the side of the road. She had no business going to Leo's. She didn't deserve comfort. But she had never felt this alone. Even during the years when she hadn't seen Nicole, Charlotte had known the Lillys were there—an emotional, if fanciful touchstone. But no more. The loss was crippling.

She didn't know if Leo would understand. But she had nowhere else to go.

She walked with increasing speed, trying to escape an unspeakable sadness. Distracted, she didn't see the decaying road until her foot twisted in a rut. She caught herself and limped on, barely slowing, welcoming the pain. Shortly before the Cole curve, she started to run, pushing herself mercilessly down the dirt drive. She didn't notice the shadows of plants, the scents, the rustle of leaves. Not even the ocean registered.

Running straight to the house and up the steps, she sagged against the door. Her breath came in short gasps; her forehead, palms, and torso braced the wood. Shifting, she glanced at her watch. It was 2:10. All was silent inside.

She shouldn't have come. But she couldn't leave. She was cold and shaky, and that was totally apart from her mental state.

With only the faintest move of her hand, she knocked, then paused to listen for sounds from within. Hearing none, she repeated the knock. This time, Bear barked from the back of the house. She knocked again, still softly. The bark came closer.

When the door opened, she nearly fell forward. She caught herself just in time and looked up. Leo's hair was messed, but he didn't seem groggy. Though barefoot, he wore a T-shirt and jeans.

She must have looked like a madwoman, with her hair every which way and her face desolate, because he stared at her in stunned silence before whispering a frightened, *"Jesus,"* and pulling her inside.

As soon as the door shut, she slumped against it. In the next instant, her legs gave way and she slid down the wood to the floor. Covering her face, she burst into tears. Uncontrollable, they came in gut-wrenching sobs that went on and on. Mortified, she pressed her face to her knees and covered her head with her arms.

She felt a hand on her nape. "What *happened*?" he asked.

The connection was enough. Something inside her snapped, and the whole of it poured out. The words were broken, but, like the tears, they kept coming. She told him every last little private thing—about herself, Julian, the baby, Nicole.

He didn't say anything, just listened. When she ran out of words, he helped her up, led her through the dark house, and put her to bed.

She woke up feeling a wonderful warmth, a heartbeat under her ear, an arm around her back. Not daring to move, she opened an eye. The room was dark. It was a minute before she noticed a sliver of light where the drapes met, another before her eyes adjusted and she realized where she was. She sat up quickly, clutching the sheet to her chest, though she was fully dressed—and looked beside her. Leo half sat against the headboard with pillows at his back. His chest was bare, but he still wore his jeans. The arm that had held her lay empty on the sheet, the other was folded behind his head. His eyes, reflecting that sliver of light between the drapes, were on her.

Everything flooded back—her confrontation with Nicole, her flight here, her blubbering confession—and she was stricken. "My God," she breathed, thinking of Nicole, who was broken, then of Julian, who would damn her, then, in horror, of Leo. "I can't believe I told you all that!"

"Why not?" he asked quietly.

"It was private. I've betrayed her again."

"You think I'd tell anyone?"

"I don't know. Would you?"

He stared at her a minute longer, less relaxed now if the rigidity of his jaw was a clue. She was thinking she had offended him, when he rose from the bed and opened the drapes—and even then, she might have continued to watch him if he hadn't glanced around the room in daylight, inviting her to do the same.

The bedroom was a surprise. From the looks of the outside of the house, she would have expected something shabby, but nothing here was. The king-sized bed was sleek and black, the walls sleek and white, the carpet a nubby blend of both. French doors surrounded by windows faced the ocean, but there were also built-in dressers, paintings hung floor-to-ceiling, and Bear sprawled beneath a wall that held a huge flat-screen TV.

If this had been Cecily's bedroom, it was no more. Everything here was masculine, definitely Leo's. Everything in it was new and of fine quality, from the sheets and quilt to the carpet and art—all of which raised more questions than they answered. Confused, she looked back at him.

"We all have secrets," he said sadly and, opening a door to the outside, hitched his chin. When she joined him, he led her over a planked deck, across a well-kept beachfront, and down a long dock that extended out into the waves. At its end, sails furled, was an elegant sloop of fiberglass and teak.

A bell rang in Charlotte's head. This was the ghost ship she had seen the first morning she was here.

"Yours?" she whispered, stunned.

He nodded. Far from gloating, though, he seemed troubled. When her eyes asked why, he turned her so that she looked back at the house.

She sucked in a breath, thinking that this couldn't be the same house she had helped to reroof. That one was old, this one new. That one had peeling brown paint, this one was artfully set stone in myriad shades of sand. That one was two-storied and boxy, this one a single level with high ceilings, a handful of skylights, and an extension on the right that was nestled into the trees as sweetly as if it were part of the woods.

Oh, it was the same house. She could see the cupola up high behind the bedroom roof. But it had been totally rehabbed on this ocean side.

"When . . . ?" she asked, not sure where to begin.

"This year."

"You did it yourself?"

"I had help."

"Who?"

"Islanders."

"They *know* about this?" Being on the remote end of the island, it wasn't a part of Quinnipeague that they would normally pass.

"Some."

She hadn't been able to take her eyes from the house, but at his cryptic tone now, she did. He was chewing on the inside of his mouth, looking nervous, which, of course, made her wonder yet again where he got his money. Her first thought was grand theft, which would have been something a guy might do after he'd quit selling pot. But like the house, this guy wasn't what he seemed. Insider trading?

She finally had to ask, albeit in a confused hush. "Materials, labor— how did you pay?"

He stared at her with what actually looked like fear, and she might have questioned *that* if it hadn't slowly faded. Seeming resigned, he walked back down that long wooden dock and set off across the sand toward the room on the right. He didn't have to wave her along. Desperate for answers, she went.

As with the bedroom, the ocean-facing wall of this room was glass, reflecting the seascape so effectively that Charlotte couldn't see anything inside until he opened one of the doors, and then, her eyes were on him. He was chewing on the inside of his mouth again, clearly torn. But he did cock his head, gesturing her to pass him and go in.

Even with trees draping the skylights, there was enough sun pouring in over the ocean from the east to show endless shelves packed with a motley assortment of books. The only break in the shelves was for a machine of the copy-fax-scan variety. A large desk stood in the center of the room. Like the shelves, it looked to be cherry. It held a large computer screen that was surrounded by papers, some in neat piles, others not. This was a working desk, she realized and shot him a puzzled look.

He had his hands in his pockets. His jeans clung to lean hips, with his chest an inverted wedge above, but his shoulders seemed slumped. Clearly uneasy, he tipped his head toward one of the bookshelves.

She followed his gaze. The abundance of books was no surprise; he had already said he was a reader. As she approached the shelves, though, she was drawn to a familiar spine. She pulled it out. *Salt.* And it wasn't alone. There were three other copies—actually, *six,* if you counted three that, glancing around in bewilderment, she saw in the shadows of the copy machine. Eyes whipping back to the shelves, she spotted the title *Salt* on the spines of three others, though these were different. They were paperbacks.

But *Salt* wasn't out in paperback, at least not yet, or it would have been on sale in the airport.

Curious, she pulled out one, then another. Their covers had different designs, like someone was trying to decide which one to use.

Someone?

In the space of a stunned breath, little things came together—things Leo had said that reminded her of *Salt,* his familiarity with island life, the fact that the boat at his dock was like the one the hero built, even his disdain for the book, which might ward off suspicion.

Her gaze flew to his. *"You?"* she whispered, incredulous. *"You* wrote *Salt?"*

He didn't speak, didn't smile, didn't show a trace of emotion.

Trying to grasp it, she put a hand on the top of her head. "Self-published. Self-promoted."

"It isn't rocket science."

Disbelieving, she looked at the book again, then back. *"You* wrote this?"

A touch of color hit his cheeks. "Is that so improbable?"

"Yes! To hear Quinnies tell it, you're just a troublemaker who shoots gulls." Her own suspicion dawned. "None of it's true, is it. They were protecting you." That brought another thought. "They all know?"

"Mostly. The guy driving the mail boat sees me getting books and bags of forwarded mail. He's a gossip."

"Why 'forwarded' mail?"

"I have a P.O. box in Portland."

"So no one can track you here."

"I don't want publicity."

"Like the kind our cookbook could bring?"

He sputtered wryly. "Looks like I've ceded *that* fight."

Charlotte felt a dull pain. "Maybe me, too. Nicole won't want me touching it now." But she couldn't think about that, with the reality of Leo Cole sinking in. Feeling Bear's warmth by her leg, she touched his head for balance. "You wrote the hottest book of the year, and the world hasn't a clue. This is mind-boggling."

He said nothing. Clearly, he didn't think it was so mind-boggling. Clearly, he was feeling vaguely threatened that she knew his secret. "Does your publisher know your real name?"

He shook his head. "Everything goes through a lawyer in Boston."

"Even phone calls?"

"Those, too."

She scrunched up her face. "You don't want even a *little* of the glory?"

"No."

Well, he certainly knew what he wanted on that score at least. Fanning the three paperbacks, she held them out. "Which did you choose?"

"I haven't yet. The hardcover's doing well enough so that this won't come out for a while. Which do you like?"

Charlotte didn't have to study them. "The blue one," she said. It was a stylized ocean scene with a boat, though whether at sunrise or sunset, she didn't know, which added to the poignancy of it. She fitted the books back on the shelf and, puzzled, returned to Leo. "How did you learn how to do this?"

"I didn't design the cover. My publisher did."

"No, I mean, writing a book. I agonize over a piece that's twelve pages. *Salt* is four-hundred and eighty-three."

His mouth slanted, though not exactly in a smile. "You remember that."

"Oh, I do," Charlotte replied, clear-minded on this. "I was loving the reading so much that when I started to worry where it was headed, I skipped to the end. I hated that ending. I haven't finished the book."

"Are you angry?"

"Absolutely. You tugged at my heartstrings, then tore them all out and threw them away. I like my fiction happy. Real life is bad enough." Again, she thought of Nicole. Pushing the thought away again, she approached the desk. Some of the notes there were handwritten, others typed. One of the neater piles held what looked to be letters. "From fans?" she asked.

He nodded.

She was in awe. In the next instant, though, her eyes flew to the screen. "A sequel?" she asked excitedly, desperate for a happy ending.

"No. *Salt's* done."

"Then this is a whole new one?" She looked at the header. *Next Book,* it said.

He pushed his hands deeper into his pockets. "It's not going very well."

"Why not?"

He shrugged. "*Salt* wrote itself. This one's a struggle. Maybe it's the interruptions, you know, doing stuff on the Web to promote *Salt*. It's time-consuming."

"But you don't need much sleep," she remembered him saying.

"The issue isn't sleep. It's fear."

"Fear?"

"That a second one will bomb."

"What does your publisher say?" She pointed her chin, about *Next Book*.

"Nothing. I haven't sold it to them yet."

"Can I read it?" Omigod. *That* would thaw Nicole.

"No."

"Why not?"

"Because it isn't worth shit. I'm thinking *Salt* should be the first and last."

"But you have a special talent."

"Lots of people do. They just don't know what to do with it. I figured out that part." But he was reaching inward, troubled again. "It isn't just fear. It's the next part."

"What part?"

"Success. Fans, bloggers, the media—they all want a piece of you, and the more successful you get, the more demanding they are. I won't leave the island to do what writers usually do."

Knowing him even in a small way, Charlotte could understand that. He liked his privacy.

Actually, she liked his privacy, too, though that thought took her by surprise. She was trying to understand it, when he said, "What're you thinking?"

Perplexed, she was trying to decide. Touching Bear again, she said, "You wrote *Salt*. I'm not sure I like that."

"Why not?"

"I don't know." She was unsettled, but couldn't put her finger on it.

"It should make you like me more. It means I'm loaded."

She grunted at the absurdity of that. "Money means diddly to me. Actually, knowing you're loaded scares me to death."

"Because you're jealous."

"Of what?"

"My success."

"No *way*. I can't compare my job to yours. Every assignment is different. I get to go different places and talk with different people. I don't want to write a book." Thinking of the cookbook, she added, "At least, not a novel."

"So what scares you?"

She tried to think it through. What she liked about Leo was that he was self-contained, that his ties to the island were exclusive. Her future was strewn all over the world, but he wasn't going anywhere. He was rooted here. She found comfort in roots. When she was with him on his private little tail of Quinnipeague, she felt safe.

How to reconcile that with the concept of international bestsellerdom? And how to reconcile any of it with the future? She had no idea.

So she simply said, "I liked your life when it was simpler. The real world is complicated. Yours is basic and down to earth. At least, I thought it was." Needing a break from the hot seat, she asked, "Why are you telling me all this now?"

He didn't blink. "I know about you and Julian. You were worried I'd tell. Now you have something on me. That's insurance, isn't it?"

Insurance. Charlotte wasn't quite sure there was such a thing. Life did what it wanted whether you had insurance or not. Take the situation with Nicole. Julian could have had any number of other diseases, and this wouldn't have happened. That he should have MS, that no treatment was working, that his body had a rejection problem—Charlotte wouldn't have dreamed it in a million years.

And yet, it was all she thought about as she walked back to Nicole's. Leo had offered to drive her, but there was too much going on in her head. She needed exercise. She needed fresh air. She needed a buffer between his life and hers.

It didn't completely work. She got caught up remembering what he had said when she asked if she could tell Nicole about *Salt*.

He had shrugged his consent. "You have something on her. She won't tell."

"Is that what it's all about," Charlotte asked sadly. "Having something on someone?"

"It isn't the way I want life to be. But life never is."

She wondered if he was preparing himself for her leaving, which made her wonder exactly what their relationship was. She didn't know—didn't even know what she wanted it to be.

Inevitably, though, as she neared the house, Nicole replaced Leo. There were immediate issues here, starting with getting inside. For all she knew, the doors would still be locked and Nicole would refuse to answer the bell. For all she knew, her luggage would be on the front steps.

But oh yes, she did have a bit of insurance against that. She couldn't dream that Nicole was angry enough to turn her back on those stem cells.

There was no luggage on the front steps, and the door was unlocked. Cautious, Charlotte let herself in. She smelled coffee and was desperate for a cup, but didn't feel she had a right to help herself. For all she knew, Nicole had left the door open only so that she could get her things. Her welcome here remained in serious doubt.

Nicole was in the Great Room. She didn't rise or even turn, though she must have heard the door. Only the top of her head, blond hair uncombed, showed above the sofa cushions. She sat facing the sliders, which were open to salt air and a frothing surf.

Charlotte went only far enough to enter Nicole's periphery, and the sight tugged at her heart. She was a knot on the sofa—legs tucked under her, elbows at her sides, profile tense.

"I'm sorry," Charlotte said with her heart in her mouth. "If I could erase that night, I would. It meant nothing."

"I wish it had," Nicole murmured. "At least then someone would have gotten something out of it."

But someone yet might, Charlotte thought. "The stem cells are yours. Say the word, and I'll have them sent."

Nicole didn't acknowledge the offer. She lifted her mug, sipped her coffee, tucked the mug back in her lap. Finally, sounding curious but detached, she asked, "Why did you agree to work on the cookbook? Did you *want* me to find out about this?"

"God, no. I only agreed, because I figured you wouldn't. Ten years had passed. I was dying to see you. Maybe I felt that helping with it would go a little way toward compensating for what I did."

"Nothing can do that."

"Maybe not. Tell me what you want me to do. I'll leave, if you want."

Nicole turned her head only enough to suggest she was looking at Charlotte, without actually doing it. "And let you off the hook? No. I have to think of myself right now. The cookbook is my future. You agreed to help. You owe me."

"I do," Charlotte said, knowing it would be easier for her to leave, but feeling that for once she just couldn't run. "I'll help any way you want." She paused. When Nicole simply took another sip of coffee, she asked softly, "Did you tell Julian?"

"No."

That puzzled her. The stem cells alone would have been reason for her to call, and as for the affair? The old Nicole had been so angry last night that she would have yelled at him for an hour.

But the Nicole on the sofa seemed different. This Nicole was subdued. She was more controlled. In a cool voice, she said, "I told my mother. Not about you, just about Julian's MS. So that's one good thing. She's coming up."

Charlotte loved Angie and wanted her there for Nicole's sake. Facing her now? That would be hard.

Nicole did turn then, finally emotional. "You bet, it'll be awkward for you. But I don't really care. You should feel guilty every time you look at her. I hope you suffer."

It wasn't the suffering that bothered Charlotte, as much as the hatred. Nicole wasn't a hater. Knowing that she had caused this was as bad as everything else.

"But you'll have to look at me, too," Charlotte said deferentially enough. "Are you sure you want that?"

Nicole's nod was slow and long. "I want my cookbook done. Besides, if you think you can run off with those stem cells, think again. Julian will go after you." She paused, bewildered. "Did you always want him?"

"I *never* wanted him."

"Was it jealousy—you had no one and didn't want me to, so you did what you could to spoil my marriage?"

"If I'd wanted that," Charlotte argued, "I'd have told you about this long ago. I know you're trying to figure out why it happened, Nicole, but I've already told you all I can. I was lonely, so I drank too much. Julian wasn't any more aware of me than I was of him."

Nicole's eyes were cold. "But he wasn't calling my name when he made love to you."

"We weren't making love. There were no words at all. It was an animal act."

Nicole stared at the ocean again. Then, recomposed, she said, "You were at Leo's, weren't you?"

"I didn't know where else to go. For what it's worth," she added, because she couldn't let the inference go unchallenged, "there were no animal acts there. I was distraught, and he is a friend."

"Did you tell him?"

Charlotte wanted to lie. But that would only add to her guilt. "Yes." When Nicole shot her an alarmed look, she said, "He won't tell."

"How can you know that?"

"Because he told me something personal that he doesn't want getting out. If he talks about you, I tell the world."

"Like the world would care about Leo Cole?" Nicole asked in disdain.

Charlotte would have leapt on that disdain if the situation had been different. But leaping anywhere wasn't wise, when she was already on thin ice. She waited until Nicole sank deeper into the sofa before saying, "It would."

"Honestly. The *world*?"

"He wrote *Salt*."

Nicole snorted. "And I'm Lady Gaga."

"I saw his office. I saw the books there—including paperback copies that won't come out for a while. I was just as skeptical as you, Nicole. But think about it," she said, unable to keep the excitement from her voice. "He's the perfect one to write about island life."

"And about caring for women?"

"The bad things we heard were rumors. He isn't that way."

"So he says. But men lie." Another cutting look. "We both know that."

Here, too, Charlotte couldn't let the inference go. "Did Julian ever lie to you?" she asked, mildly annoyed. She was starting to hear self-pity, which never sat well with her. "Did you ever ask him if he'd slept with me? Did you ever ask if he even *liked* me?"

"Yes. When you two first met. You were my best friend. I was desperate that he like you." She seemed to know that Charlotte had made a point, though, because she hit back. "He didn't want you involved in the cookbook. He didn't want you here with me this summer. I don't think he ever really liked you at all."

"That's what I'm *saying*," Charlotte insisted, turning the argument around. "What happened between us was impersonal. It was once, and it was mindless."

"That doesn't mean it was right."

And what could Charlotte say, other than to return to the purpose of the firestorm? "You need to tell Julian about the stem cells."

"I don't need to do anything."

"Okay. You're right. But you said he might die. Using those cells would lower the risk."

"If they're a match."

"The match will be at least half, since he's the parent."

"Are we sure he is?"

Charlotte was suddenly weary. "Oh, for goodness' sake. If you doubt it, do a DNA test. Honestly, Nicole, would I lie about something like this, knowing it could be disproved"—she snapped her fingers—"like that? The bank I used did a DNA test before it froze the cord blood. Compare those results to Julian's DNA, and you'll have your proof."

Nicole was silent. Though her coffee had to be cold, she sipped it anyway. She was going through the motions, Charlotte realized, holding it together as she wouldn't have thought her friend could do. Not that she'd thought Nicole could build a hugely successful blog, either. But this was different. This was emotional. Maybe those four years of secrecy had given her a hidden strength.

Charlotte waited, allowing her time to ask more. Into the silence, she finally said, "So what do we do now?"

Nicole looked at her. "Now?"

"You don't really want to play Scrabble with me. So where do we go from here? I'd be glad to take a room in town if that'll make you more comfortable. Tell me what you want me to do."

Nicole was quiet for another minute. Then, "Stay here. The house is big enough for two of us. Today's the Fourth. Do what you want during the day, but we should go to the barbecue together tonight."

"Together?" Charlotte asked in surprise.

Nicole was impassive. "I don't want it any more than you do, but we have to pretend nothing's wrong. I don't want anyone doubting that this cookbook will come to be. We have to look like a team."

"Can you do that?"

"Easily. I'm good at putting on a show. I've been doing it for four years."

Since Julian had been diagnosed. "Nicole, about the stem cells—"

"Do you ever think about her?" Nicole cut in, albeit with a chink in her indifference. "Do you wonder what she's like?"

The child. "I try not to."

"You're her mother."

"Only biologically."

"But you have to wonder."

"I gave up that right when I signed the agreement."

"What if Julian wants to know about her?"

Charlotte should have seen where this was headed. Of course, Nicole would be worried about that. Suddenly, Charlotte was, too. "I hope not."

"Why?"

"She has a life."

"What if *she* wants it?"

"She's only nine. She's too young now. Besides, would he really want it? He didn't want you getting pregnant because he was afraid he wouldn't be able to do the things a father does."

"This is different. The child is born. Is his name on the birth certificate?"

"No. I told them I didn't know who the father was."

"Did you keep anything of hers—a hat or blanket?"

Charlotte shook her head. "Only the stem cells. You have to tell Julian about them, Nicole. That's the whole point of this hell."

But Nicole had risen. "I need to shower. I feel dirty. Try to interview Rose Mayes. Her cole slaw can fit in a couple of different places. Get the recipe while you're there. And check out the ingredients. Let's see what your precious Leo Cole does this time."

"Leo didn't—"

"Meet me here at six. We'll get to the barbecue when it's in full swing."

Chapter Seventeen

CHARLOTTE DROVE TO THE MAYES house, but there were so many children and grandchildren underfoot that Rose, who was a strikingly energetic seventy-five and totally apologetic, couldn't talk. She was, however, in the process of making her slaw, so Charlotte was able to copy the recipe while it lay on the kitchen table. She watched closely as Rose mixed the dressing—all the while wondering whether she was one of those who might have feared Cecily enough to be secretive. If so, someone had assured her that sharing was fine, because she specifically said that the mustard seed she used was a descendent of Cecily's plants, and the rest of her ingredients were organic and fresh.

Wanting to validate Leo, Charlotte returned to the house, only to find it empty. Nicole's laptop was gone as well, likely taken to a place where she could work without seeing Charlotte. And though Charlotte felt the sting of that, a small part of her was relieved. They would go together to the barbecue. That would be bad enough.

Making herself a ham sandwich, she unearthed her copy of *Salt* from under the sofa cushion and took it out to deck. This time around, reading the book was a different experience. For one thing, since she knew the ending, the worry was gone. For another, knowing the author, she read it thinking about the prose, the vocabulary, and the plot in terms of Leo's life. Several times, she stopped to reconcile a remark or event with what she knew of him. More often than not, though, it raised more questions.

Even forewarned, she cried at the end. The characters were so well drawn that she felt what they felt, and their parting hurt. No doubt, given the turn her own life had taken in the last twenty-four hours, she was hypersensitive. But *Salt* had become personal.

She cried herself to sleep right there on the lounge chair, awoke late in the afternoon to find that the wind was blowing in, that she had no Leo to warm her, and that either the glass slider had blown shut—an unlikely prospect—or Nicole had returned. Fearing she was locked out again, she quickly tried the door, but it opened easily.

Nicole had her laptop open on the kitchen table. Charlotte might have asked how she was, if she hadn't been typing steadily, clearly ignoring her. Nor did she want to talk during the drive to town. When Charlotte complimented her on her blouse, which was red and sleeveless with touches of lace, she simply nodded. Same when Charlotte asked if she'd written another blog.

The silence was so uncharacteristic—so telling and sad—that Charlotte might have cried again. And once they parked and walked together to join the crowds on the field beside the church, Nicole spotted friends and, with a superficial smile for Charlotte, smoothly moved off.

Wisely, Charlotte had her camera. On the chance that Nicole would want to include pictures of island events in the book, she photographed everything in sight. Huge grills lined the sides of the field, serving up hot dogs, hamburgers, and grilled chicken. Long tables, covered with the requisite red-and-white oilskins, held platters of buns, baskets of chips, and condiments of every kind. More interesting, Charlotte thought, was the lineup of sides for which recipes would be printed. There were pasta salads and vegetable salads. Mayes slaw was only one of several slaws. And there were bean casseroles, with meat and without.

Charlotte photographed them all. She photographed groups sitting on quilts that were strewn across the field, and others getting refills of soda and beer. She photographed squealing children playing tag.

In time, the light got too low for pictures. She was debating getting something to eat herself, looking back over the crowd to see which group she might join, when she spotted Leo. Wearing a muted plaid shirt and jeans, he sat alone on a split-rail fence at the far end of the field. Overhanging trees might have hidden him in the lengthening shadows if he hadn't already been in the back of her mind. His feet were on the bottom rail, his legs splayed, elbows on knees.

Taking her first deep breath since leaving his house that morning, she decided that he hadn't eaten, either. Loading a plate with enough goodies for two, she crossed the field. After setting the plate on the flat of a post, she went between his legs and looped her arms over his shoulders.

His smile was small, but so sweet that it took her breath. He kissed her softly. When he drew back, she mirrored the smile. "You came," she said.

"I don't usually."

She had figured that. Even here, he was solitary. "Why now?"

"I wanted to see you."

A warmth spread inside, clogging her throat so that she couldn't reply.

His smile faded. "How'd it go?"

Her confrontation with Nicole. For those few seconds, she'd actually forgotten. Finding her voice now, she said, "It went."

"Uncomfortable?"

"Very."

"If she doesn't want you under her roof, you can stay with me."

Charlotte might have loved that, but she had vowed not to run away. "Her mother is coming. I want to be there to help."

"Is her mother trouble?"

"Could be. She doesn't know about Julian and me, but she will. There's no way Nicole will be able to hold it in." Retrieving the plate, she settled beside him on the fence and shot him a wry look. "Keep that invitation open, though. I may need it."

He took the hamburger she offered. After several big bites, he asked, "Have you thought about the other?"

"What other?" Charlotte asked back.

He was self-conscious. "My writing the book."

She chewed and swallowed, then said, "I finished it this afternoon. It's brilliant."

"Not the book. Have you thought about me as the writer."

"I'm trying not to."

"Because it's too complicated?"

She nodded. "I need simplicity right now. And friendship."

And sex, his dark eyes said. *A given,* hers replied. She could feel it even then, as they sat thigh to thigh on the fence. His hair looked like it had been combed before the wind had fingered through, and the lines of his nose, cheeks, and jaw were marked. He wasn't attractive in the classical sense, though something about him screamed *man.* At least, it did to her.

He glanced at the crowds on the field as he finished off his burger. "People are looking, y'know."

"I'm surprised they aren't mobbing you."

"They know I'd leave if they did." He took a handful of chips. "Being with me could ruin your reputation."

She laughed. "Sorry, but my reputation is long gone."

They didn't talk again until every chip, every bean, every bit of salad on the plate was devoured. He handed her his beer to wash it down, then said, "She's headin' our way."

Charlotte choked on a gulp and wiped her mouth with the back of her hand. "Nicole?" she whispered. He nodded. "Does she look angry?" When he shook his head, she looked around.

To the unknowing eye, Nicole looked on top of the world. Her blond hair swung comfortably at her jaw, the red blouse was chic, her white slacks snug. Even in the hovering dusk, she glowed. No one but Charlotte would see the faint smudges under her eyes as anything other than the style. Nor would anyone but Charlotte see past the stunning green of those eyes to their bite.

They were on Leo. "Charlotte tells me you're Chris Mauldin," she said civilly enough.

Leo gave a faint shrug.

"*Salt*, huh?" she went on. "Where'd you get the name?"

"Sea salt. Sailor. Tears." Nothing was new here. He had given similar answers in numerous online forums.

"No," Nicole said. "Where'd you get the name Chris Mauldin?"

"The phone book."

"You said it was real in one of the posts."

"It is. Just not mine."

"Was it the Quinnipeague phone book?"

She would check it out, Charlotte knew.

But Leo muddied the waters of that plan. "The library has phone books from all over Maine. It was a random choice. I don't remember what town."

Nicole gave the kind of soft *hmph* that could have shown either admiration or frustration, if her follow-up hadn't been telling. "I hear it's being made into a movie."

Charlotte hadn't heard that.

Nor, apparently, had Leo. "Not that I know of," he said.

"It should be," she stated. "I mean, how can you resist a love story like that? Arizona and Maine—they come from such different places."

"Actually," Leo corrected politely, "she's from Texas."

Charlotte knew that Nicole knew exactly where the heroine was from. She was testing Leo, and none too subtly.

"And her mother?" she asked, pushing further. "That's a tough one. There's no way she could disregard the feelings of *that* woman."

"Nicole," Charlotte chided softly.

Leo was more blunt. "You and I both know her mother was dead." His voice held an edge. "You don't have to believe me. I'm fine with that."

"You have to admit, it's a pretty preposterous story."

"So's yours," he said.

Here was the unpolished Leo, Charlotte realized, charging when charged, and it didn't bother her. She rather liked that he said what he felt, and that she could choke on her beer and not be ridiculed.

But Nicole was startled and that quickly brought her back to being the woman whose life had suffered a series of shocks. "I couldn't dream mine up."

"Nor me mine." When she had no comeback, he said, "Let's call it a draw."

She didn't answer. Seeming wounded, she turned to Charlotte. "Can he drop you home? The Matthews invited me over for coffee after the fireworks."

"I can do that," Leo said before Charlotte could ask.

"Great," Nicole said to no one in particular and, turning, walked away.

Charlotte slid off the fence and ran after her. "Are you okay?" she asked, catching her arm.

Nicole stopped and stared at her. "He's despicable. My story preposterous? Like I could have made it up? Like I was responsible for *any* of it?"

"You attacked him. He lashed back. His skin isn't very hard."

"And that's the kind of guy you like?" Pulling her arm free, she set off again.

Charlotte watched her for a minute, hurting for her but unable to help. She could help Leo, though. Returning, she settled in between his knees. "I'm sorry," she said softly.

"Don't be. It could have been worse."

"She's feeling humiliated."

"Because her husband was with you before they were married?"

"Because she didn't know, and because now *you* know."

"Did I mention it?" he asked with a last bit of defensiveness.

She slid her arms around his waist. "No. She just feels exposed."

He snorted. "I know *that* feeling."

Charlotte studied his face. The light had faded enough to make its lines more stark, reminding her of those first nights at his house. Recalling how little she had known of him then, she realized how much there still was to learn.

"Who was she?" she asked gently. When Leo seemed reluctant to answer, she said, "*Salt* had to be partly autobiographical."

His eyes fell to the place where their bodies met, middle to middle, though there was nothing sexual in it.

"Was she from Texas?" Charlotte asked to get him started.

"Arizona," he said. "Ironic?" That was how Nicole had tried to trip him up. "She was here for the summer."

"A regular?"

His head moved no. "She came with her family. First and last time."

"When was this?" Charlotte asked, and, moments later, felt his surrender.

He met her eyes. "I was back here two years. I was living in town, doing construction or renovation or handiwork—whatever. Her father was a real estate developer. He was successful—y'know, headed an empire. He bought the house that April and wanted to do it over. I was doing a lot of the work."

In *Salt*, the father was an investment banker and his daughter a partner in the firm, but the house in that version needed work, too.

"We met. We clicked. We had an affair."

"What was she like?"

"Physically? Like Nicole. Fragile-looking. She was sweet. She wasn't the kind of person you'd picture in finance. She wasn't tough." He paused. "Her daddy was tough enough for two."

"What about her mom? She wasn't dead, was she?" He would have changed that kind of detail.

"She might as well have been. She was a ditz. That's probably the only way she could avoid her husband's iron hand—y'know, zone out. She didn't know what to do with herself up here other than sit in the sun and burn to a crisp. Two brothers came and went, but when push came to shove, it was just the dad and his little girl."

"How old was she?"

"Twenty-seven."

"She wasn't a little girl."

Leo seemed puzzled. "Her father accepted that on some level. He didn't freak out when she met me at night. He didn't even freak out when she told him she loved me. Marrying me, having my kids, that was different."

"Did she say she would?"

"To me? Many times. She hated her life. She hated the pressure and the expectations. She hated the fact that her father favored her over her brothers. She said she could set up a little office in town and still work for the firm. She thought it'd be easier if she wasn't under his thumb. I was her escape."

"So she said?"

"Oh, she meant it." His eyes held hers. "But Quinnipeague isn't the real world. Leave here, and the best of intentions fall apart." Slipping a hand under her hair, he cupped her nape. He might as well have flashed his message in neon lights.

"I can't promise you anything," she whispered.

"I know." Lowering his head, he opened his mouth and, done with talk, kissed her until her knees were weak. "Can I drive you home?" he asked in a voice whose huskiness went further.

Fireworks lit the rearview mirror, but Nicole's house was dark when they reached it. Charlotte felt only a brief hesitation. Nicole wouldn't be back for a while, and she wanted Leo too much to wait. So she led him up the stairs, closed the door to her room, and quickly undressed.

He watched, not so much waiting as entranced, though there was nothing seductive in what she did. When she was naked, she helped him undress, leaning in to kiss his neck, his chest, his belly as each was bared, and when they joined, they held still for the longest, most trying moment, before breaking into a movement that could only be called fierce. They made love against the door, the floor, the bed, none of it gentle, but this was about truth. It was about needing to be together and needing release. It was as raw as anything Charlotte had ever felt, and it was real.

Afterward, mindful of Nicole's imminent return, they lay together for only a few minutes before silently dressing and, hand in hand, walking down the stairs and out to Leo's truck. He was behind the wheel, Charlotte standing on the running board, kissing him again, when he made a noise against her mouth. She drew back.

"I almost forgot," he said and lifted her to the ground. Climbing down, he went back to the bed of the truck and pulled out a trio of pots, each containing tall, staked stems. Above fernlike leaves on each were clusters of white flowers. "For Nicole's garden," he said.

Catching a sweet scent—not arousing like jasmine, quite the opposite—Charlotte leaned in. "Mmmm. What is this?"

"Valerian," he said. "The root was used during World War I to treat shock. You know, PTSD. You don't need to touch the roots with these plants. The smell usually does it. I meant it as a peace offering to Nicole, but from the looks of her, it'll have to be pretty potent to work. I'm not sure even my mother has that much power," he remarked only half joking, then added, "Plant these in the sun, but don't worry after that. Cecily will take care of them. She likes you."

Charlotte might have asked how he knew that, but he was off, carrying the pots around the side of the house, setting them carefully at the edge of the garden before straightening and dusting off his hands.

She followed him back to the truck, kissed him lightly before he climbed inside, then watched his taillights until a cluster of trees blocked their view, and even then she didn't move. *I can't promise you anything,* she had said, but feeling a new ache as she watched him leave, she wished it wasn't so.

Chapter Eighteen

By the time Nicole pulled into the driveway, she was exhausted. Putting on a show was hard work when she was being pulled every which way at once. She missed Julian, but dreaded seeing him. She missed Charlotte, but didn't want to talk. She wanted to tell all to her mother, but didn't want to tell the half.

She had never thought of herself as a prideful person, but she was too proud to tell her mother that her marriage was failing. She had never thought of herself as unreasonable, but she couldn't listen to Charlotte's apologies. And Julian? She didn't know where to begin. She had never thought of herself as cynical, but wondered why he had married her; had never thought of herself as mistrustful, but wondered if he had a woman at work; had never thought of herself as *spiteful,* but couldn't tell him about the cells. She was furious at him, but thought about him all the time. He had called while she was at the Matthews', which excused her distant tone, but she didn't offer to call him back.

Letting herself in the front door, she went through to the kitchen. Charlotte's purse was on the kitchen counter, meaning that she was back but apparently asleep. Nicole would have given anything to sleep.

Her eyes were heavy and her thoughts spent, but her body was keyed up. Caffeine with dessert? Not a good idea.

Blog, she told herself. But she wasn't in the mood. Check for messages from Sparrow, she suggested. But it could wait. Shop online for organic tea, she proposed, but why do that when she already had the best in the cupboard?

After steeping a mug of Cecily's passionflower tea, she carried it through the Great Room door and, pulling out one of the patio chairs, sat in the dark at the table outside. The ocean soughed gently over midnight sand. She took one deep breath to calm herself, then another, and, puzzled, turned toward the garden. Something smelled good, but it wasn't lavender. Rising, she followed her nose to the three pots that hadn't been there earlier. She touched the green fronds and, bending to the white clusters on top, inhaled.

She wasn't sure what they were, but she was pretty sure where they'd come from, and while a part of her wanted to hurl them into the sea, her better instinct held back. Sitting down on the garden path, white pants and all, she inhaled, exhaled, inhaled, exhaled. In time, she felt calmer—possibly from the simple act of breathing deeply, more likely from the plants. She couldn't be prideful when it came to these. They were definitely medicinal. They were also pretty. And she was tired of being angry.

Reasoning that since she had already benefitted from the tea, she wouldn't be damned for accepting a second Cole gift, she looked at them and breathed of them until she was calm enough for bed.

Friday had the dubious distinction of starting a weekend that had effectively begun two days before—meaning that the ferry schedule was off, which Nicole didn't discover until she reached the pier and waited twenty minutes for a boat that didn't come.

"Not due 'til eleven," advised the harbormaster, Roy Pepin, as he sauntered toward the dock from the Chowder House kitchen with a take-out mug in one bony hand and a half-eaten cruller in the other. "Ten minutes mow-a. G'won up and see Dorey."

Nicole smiled, nodded, and was grateful when Roy went on his way. Since there wasn't much for a harbormaster to do in a harbor as small as this, he tended to talk even more than other Quinnies. Holidays always brought him out, and if he was rarely seen on the pier itself, it was because he was chatting it up at one slip or another.

But Nicole wasn't in the mood to socialize with Dorey, either. She was trying to gear up for her mother's arrival, feeling the old pull and push, wondering how much to say when. Before leaving the house, after filling a ceramic ewer with fresh-cut peonies from the garden, she had snipped off a few valerian sprigs. Yes, valerian, Charlotte had said. Taking them from her pocket now, she held them to her nose. That they remained fragrant was a tribute to Cecily. That the scent alone, rather than tea brewed from the roots, brought relief, was also a tribute to Cecily. Nicole refused to credit Leo with this, much less Charlotte—though that anger was less raw this morning. The hurt remained, along with a certain disgust. But breakfast hadn't been as awkward today. Granted, Nicole had finished her own before Charlotte came down, so it wasn't a question of having to cook for or eat with her.

Nicole no longer felt she owed Charlotte for coming to Quinnipeague. A few profiles for the cookbook were a drop in the bucket, given what Charlotte owed her. Nicole feel guilty? No more! Still, she was able to ask about the flowers in what she thought was a reasonable tone, and, when Charlotte said they were from Leo, she actually told her to thank him.

She also didn't ask the impossible—which, in hindsight, was what she had done, expecting Charlotte to approach Rose Mayes on the holiday. She did suggest talking with the minister and his wife, who, being parentless and childless, had no weekend guests and would be eager to talk. Given the number of island events held at the church, they were major players in Quinnipeague's social scene—not to mention the mean banana-raspberry smoothie the wife kept in reserve as an alternative to popcorn on movie nights.

The wind blew her hair about, and still Nicole held those petals to her nose. When the ferry finally appeared on the horizon, she felt a yearning. She needed her mother here—needed to talk about MS and babies and the future, all of which Julian had forbidden her to discuss. And yes, she needed to talk about Charlotte and Julian. Angie was the mother, and, right now, Nicole the child.

But it wasn't Angie who stepped off the ferry when it turned and backed up to the pier. It was her stepdaughter, Kaylin. Long dark hair caught up in a ponytail that had lost stray wisps to the wind, she wore jeans, layered tops, and tall UGGs. A large duffel hung from one shoulder, a backpack from the other.

Confused, Nicole ran to her and gave her a hug, but in the next instant she was searching the boat. Other weekenders had debarked. There was no one left.

"Mom was supposed to be here," she said worriedly, knowing that Kaylin, who had spent so many summers with Angie, loved her, too.

"She's coming Sunday," the girl said.

"No. She said tomorrow, which is today."

"She was planning to," Kaylin explained, words coming in her typical rush, "but when she saw me at the dock in Rockland, she said you and I needed time alone."

Nicole didn't understand. Angie was the one she needed. "So where is *she* supposed to go?"

"She's driving up the coast."

"*Alone?*"

"She was grateful to see me. She said she needed more time to gather the courage to come. There's no cause for worry, Nicki—"

But Nicole was already on the phone and, moments later, heard the same thing from Angie. The call was brief. Angie sounded fine.

Nicole was disappointed but relieved—though she couldn't dwell on either, because Kaylin said in a frightened rush, "Dad told me he has MS, Nicki. I. Am. Staggered. I mean, thank God I wasn't at work when he called, because I was a total mess. I don't know anyone with MS but I've heard plenty, and now my own father has it. I can't believe it, I just can't *believe* it."

Nicole took her backpack. "How was he when he called?"

"Tired. I mean, like, I've seen his hand shake, but I thought it was too much caffeine. And his balance is sometimes off. I've seen him kick at the carpet like it's the carpet's fault, which I always thought was just how he was getting older. But he sounded really, really down. He's been sick for four years, and I didn't know? What was he *thinking*?"

"He was trying to protect you."

"Like I'm ten or something?" Kaylin asked, sounding indignant. She had her father's dark looks and regal carriage, but her mother's attitude. "I'm twenty-one. I'll be graduating from college next year."

Attitude had served Monica well, propelling her up the corporate ladder, but Kaylin wasn't quite there yet. "Speaking of which, why aren't you in New York?" Nicole asked. "You said summer interns don't get time off." The girl had landed a plum spot at a major television network, hence no time planned on Quinnipeague.

"I left after Dad called. And I'm not going back. You're right. We don't get time off. It's sweltering in the city, and they have us running all over the place for stupid little things like mauve-and-white polka-dot place mats for this set or a red linen scarf for that personality— which is what my supervisor calls his anchors, though the only personality those people have is on air. They treat us like furniture."

That fast, Nicole was on overload. She had spent the night preparing to be a daughter and wasn't up for being a mother. Struggling with the transition, she heard her father's voice, and, in the void, repeated his words. "It's called paying your dues."

"Dad said that, but I've been there a month, Nicki. That's long enough to know what I don't want. Besides, his being sick puts it all in a new light."

"He'll be okay," Nicole said.

"Not to hear him tell," Kaylin remarked and, during the drive back to the house, gave a rapid-fire blow-by-blow of the discussion. "He says he's taking part in a trial," she ended. "He says it's his best hope, but it's dangerous."

"He told you the risks?"

"He had to. I made him." Kaylin could be dogged when she wanted something, very Monica at times. More than once over the years, Nicole had been a buffer between father and daughter.

But she felt little sympathy for Julian now. He had made his own bed, which was another of Bob's pithy points.

Suddenly Kaylin was more frightened than confrontational. "Maybe he was exaggerating the danger. Do you think he was?"

"He was probably talking worst-case scenario."

"I told him I'd be a donor, but he says umbilical cord cells offer more hope. Is it true?"

In lieu of taking a stand, Nicole shared what she knew. Without quite dissing stem cell treatments, she tried to put the emphasis on more conventional ones. Kaylin, bless her, kept coming back to the other.

When they reached the house, Nicole made fresh lemonade and led the girl to the garden. "Talk with me here," she said. "I want to plant these flowers." She needed a little soothing herself, but if the valerian helped Kaylin at the same time, so much the better.

Besides, garden work was therapeutic. Having no garden back home, Nicole only did it here, and then only when George Mayes wasn't around to put in his tipsy two bits. In passing, she pulled spent blooms from her mother's red snapdragons and drying leaves from the purple lisianthus, but her goal was those white valerian plants. They were doing just fine in their pots, but Nicole knew they would do better in the ground and, though she doubted the soil was right, Charlotte had insisted that Cecily's spirit would make them grow.

Okay. So maybe Cecily was trying to butter her up into thinking more highly of Leo and Charlotte. But Nicole could play the game, too. She could pretend she felt better about them as a couple. She was good at hiding things. And she did like these plants.

"Here or there?" she asked Kaylin, indicating the site options.

Never without an opinion, Kaylin pointed. "There. Dad shouldn't be alone, y'know."

"He isn't alone," Nicole said as she took a gardening fork to the soil to loosen it up. "He's in Durham surrounded by doctors."

"That's his job, and it isn't the same. Shouldn't you be with him?"

Nicole kept working. "It's been four years, Kay. He and I know what to expect." She looked up. "Did he call your brother?"

"Johnny?" She make a sputtering sound. "He's no help. He's been working on my mom's cousin's farm, which is two hours from Des Moines, and they were in the middle of some soybean emergency."

Nicole twisted the fork in the soil. "How did he take it?"

"Oh, he's Mister Cool. He says Dad's a doctor and knows what he's doing, and I always thought so, too, only he was wrong for not telling us. I mean, like, we have a personal stake here, too, don't we?"

Nicole pointed at the trowel and, when Kaylin passed it to her, lengthened the hole to allow for three sets of roots. "They don't know that it's hereditary."

"They don't know that it isn't," the girl argued. "Okay, so if MS has to do with the autoimmune system, maybe that's the hereditary part, which means that I may have the same disorder but it'll develop into some whole *other* disease."

She sounded frightened again, clearly needed a mother's reassurance. But Nicole wasn't her mother, damn it, and right now, she was emotionally handicapped. Julian really needed to be here answering her questions. Hell, Julian really needed to be here answering *Nicole's*.

But he wasn't. And Kaylin was.

Grasping at straws, she eyed the valerian. Handing the girl a bag of fertilizer, she nudged her nearer the blooms. "Mix a little into the soil while I get water."

"Will I?" Kaylin called as Nicole put a watering can under the nearby spigot.

"I don't know," she said when she returned. "None of us knows when it comes to health. Look at my dad. He dropped dead out of the blue."

"That's my *point*," Kaylin said with feeling. "I could kill myself working as hard as Dad always did, then get sick, and, zappo, it's gone."

"Excuse me," Nicole said, darting her intermittent glances as she poured water into the hole, "your father isn't done working by a long shot, and even if he were, he's already contributed more to his field than many doctors do in a lifetime." Nicole might fault Julian's judgment on personal matters, but she couldn't fault his work. "He's made breakthroughs that totally justify the effort it took to get there. Even if he doesn't discover another single thing, he'll always have that."

"Well, he was lucky. He didn't get sick until he was forty-two, but most people get MS in their twenties or thirties, and I'm twenty-two, which puts me right in the line of fire. If I have limited time—"

"You don't have limited time!" Nicole cried, unable to bear that thought. Taking one of the pots, she held the flowers to her nose and breathed deeply.

"But if I do," Kaylin said in a more measured way, "shouldn't I be doing something I like? I won't ever be a news anchor or host a talk show, and I know more about set design than my bosses do, because I've taken courses that they haven't. This internship sucks."

After another inhalation, Nicole gently pulled the plant from its pot, positioned the roots in the hole, and scooped dirt around them. When the stalks stood on their own, she reached for a second pot. "There must be something you can get out of it."

"Oh, yeah. A line on my CV and maybe a reference, but if it leads to another job like this, what's the point? I'm not having fun."

Nicole thrust the pot at her to hold and reached for the third. "There's more to life than having fun."

"But look at you. You're here having fun, while he's back there alone."

Having *fun*? Nicole might have laughed at the irony of that if she hadn't known the laugh would speak of hysteria, which would open up a can of worms she couldn't possibly, *possibly* discuss with Kaylin.

So she simply emptied the second pot, secured the roots in the ground, and sat back on her heels. Only then, when she was feeling a little calmer, did she answer the criticism. "I offered to be there, Kaylin. He thought it would be better if he made those phone calls himself."

"I don't mean right now. I mean all summer. You knew he was sick. How could you come to Quinnipeague?"

The question was so like one Charlotte had asked, that it seemed only right for Charlotte herself to return from town just then. When Nicole looked up, Kaylin swiveled. "Omigod," the girl cried. "Charlotte?"

They had spent only that wedding summer together—Kaylin and John here for the first time, getting to know the island, Angie and Bob, and even Nicole—but ten weeks of living in the same house with a person involved more shared time than could be forgotten.

Charlotte smiled. Rather than launch into social niceties, though, she was typically blunt. "Your dad had a full schedule in Durham and wanted Nicki here. It wasn't her choice." She glanced at Nicole. "Sorry. I overheard. Do you guys want to be alone?"

"No," Nicole said. Charlotte, Cecily's valerian—she would take whatever help she could get.

Kaylin picked up where she'd left off, challenging Charlotte now. "He may say that, but I don't believe him."

"He wanted Nicole to work on her book."

"He was totally lonely. Why else would he have suddenly decided to tell John and me?"

Nicole broke in, puzzled. "Didn't he tell you why?"

"Tell me what?"

She wasn't protecting Julian in this when there was a perfectly good explanation. Taking the last of the three pots from Kaylin, she said, "He was outed down there, and word spreads. He wanted to tell you himself before you heard it from someone else." That someone else would have been Monica, who had been married to Julian long enough to know his colleagues in Philadelphia, any one of whom might be learning momentarily that Julian had MS.

"And anyway," Charlotte said, playing bad cop to Nicole's good, "if you're so worried about his being alone, why aren't *you* down there?"

"I offered, but he said no. So I'm doing the next best thing, coming here to get Nicole to go."

Setting down the pot, Nicole caught the girl's hand. "He doesn't want that."

Kaylin's face crumbled. "You guys *are* breaking up?"

She gave the hand a little shake. "*No.* I talk with your father all the time."

"Did you agree with him not telling Johnny and me until now?"

As angry as Nicole was at Julian, she didn't want to bad-mouth him to his daughter. But if she was dealing with character issues in him, this related to one in her.

Releasing Kaylin's hand, she removed the last plant from its pot and said a quiet, "No."

Charlotte was less restrained. "Different people handle problems different ways. Nicki wanted to be in Durham; he wanted her here. She wanted you to know way back; your dad didn't."

"But he's right about the internship," Nicole put in, because he had shared Kaylin's earlier complaints. "He told you to stick with it, didn't he?"

Kaylin nodded and, finally calmer, said, "He said I was being impulsive, but he doesn't understand what I'm feeling. I tried to tell him, but he didn't get it. Bob would have understood."

"Excuse me?" Nicole burst out. "Mr. Law and Order? He was a push-over with you and Johnny, because you never tested him on big things, but this is a biggie, which is what he'd tell you if he was here. He believed that if you made a commitment, you had to stand by it."

"It's called paying your dues," Charlotte added.

Smiling, Nicole fitted the plant in the hole. "I already used that one on her."

"It bears repeating," Charlotte stated, focused on Kaylin. "I worked for no-name publications, writing pieces *no one* read, before I finally sold to a magazine big enough so that the byline got me better assignments. All that early time, I kept remembering what Bob said."

Kaylin knew how successful Charlotte was. Nicole had told her back in the spring, had even looked over Kaylin's shoulder while the girl read several of Charlotte's articles. Nicole might criticize Charlotte, like Julian, on moral grounds now, but that didn't take away from the quality of her work.

Kaylin was properly subdued.

"So you'll go back?" Nicole ventured, tamping soil around the plant.

"I can't," the girl said meekly.

"Why not?"

"I called my boss this morning." When Nicole eyed her in alarm, she hurriedly said, "There was only a month left anyway. They let you go after the first week in August so you have time before school."

She had quit. Stunned, Nicole sat back on her heels. "What did your father say?"

"He doesn't know."

"So you just did it. Can you call your boss back?"

Kaylin looked sheepish. "It wasn't a good ending. I told him there was a family emergency. He actually asked me what. I couldn't tell him about Dad, and I think I stammered a little and then finally said it wasn't really his business—and he and I hadn't been on good terms anyway, so the discussion went downhill." Her voice went now.

It was done then, Nicole realized in dismay as she pounded the last of the loose soil with her palms. She wondered if Kaylin had picked her timing, thinking that Nicole would be more understanding than either of her parents. As flattering as it was, it put her in the position of having to call one of the others.

But no. Kaylin was of age. The decision had been hers.

"You can't stay here," she warned, gathering up the garden tools. Kaylin couldn't ever know about Charlotte and Julian.

"Why not?"

There were plenty of innocent reasons. "We're getting ready to put the place on the market, which means weeding out and cleaning up. Besides, the summer's just starting. You can't do nothing for the next six weeks," she said as Julian would have, though she did agree with him on this. Having Kaylin hanging around, watching, listening, already worried that her father was heading toward his second divorce—it would be beyond dismal for Nicole.

"I could hostess at the Island Grill like I used to," Kaylin offered.

Nicole stood. "The season's underway. They've already hired their staff."

"I could help with your book."

"I have Charlotte for that." She grabbed the watering can with her free hand.

"I could help pack up the house," the girl tried, adding a timid, "or babysit Angie."

"Angie won't stay long," Nicole said, though it suddenly occurred to her that she had no idea how long her mother would stay. It suddenly occurred to her that she might have *two* more houseguests for however long, watching her every move through what had to be the darkest period of her life.

For the first time since Kaylin stepped off the ferry, she felt a moment of panic.

"I can work with Kaylin," Charlotte offered quietly, beside her now. "We'll make it a journalism internship. There are personal stories here that have nothing to do with the cookbook—like Oliver Weeks and Isabel Skane. Kaylin can hang around with them on my behalf. She can even do online research for my fall assignments."

Nicole was uneasy, but she was in a bind. As wounded as she was herself, she did love Kaylin. None of this was her fault. She had deserved better from Julian, too.

Besides, much as she didn't want it to be so, Charlotte's plan made sense.

Nicole was no pushover. But as soon as it was decided that Kaylin would stay, she knew she had to call Julian. Sure, Kaylin could do it. But Nicole owed him a call, and here was something relatively neutral to discuss.

Not wanting to be overheard, she took her phone to the beach and, facing the house to make sure no one came, punched in his cell number. With each digit, she grew more tense, but that was a good thing. Anger kept her spine straight, her hand steady, and her resolve intact.

He picked up after a single ring. "Hey. I was starting to worry. You okay?"

She had been abrupt the evening before and hadn't called him back. Hearing his voice now, it all rushed back. She wanted to tell him what a bastard he was, wanted to scream and carry on about betrayal—and maybe she would have done that once. But the ocean was at her back, grounding her to a world she had been safe in long before Julian had entered it, and as for the anger, rather than pushing her into hysteria, it gave her control.

She refused to apologize for not calling sooner. Nor could she get herself to ask how he was. "Kaylin's here," was all she said.

He was silent for a beat, then resigned. "I figured she'd try that. She wants to quit the internship. She wasn't happy with me when I said she couldn't."

"She's twenty-one."

"And thinks she knows everything. I assume you told her she had to go back."

"Actually, she's staying here."

"For the rest of the summer? Who made that decision?" he asked, marginally indignant, the father whose child hadn't behaved.

Nicole refused to cower. *She* wasn't his child. "Kaylin did. She's twenty-one." It bore repeating. "She called her boss and quit before she ever got here. Charlotte offered her an internship. She'll help with interviews."

"*There?*"

"Yes." With Charlotte. If that made him nervous, so be it.

He was silent again. Then, "Are you all right? You don't sound like you."

No more childish voice? Funny, how disillusionment made you

grow up fast. In many ways, his betrayal was worse than MS. At least, MS hadn't been his fault.

"I'm fine," she said, and the steadiness anger gave her was only the half. The other had to do with stem cells. She knew something that Julian did not. That was empowering.

"Are you sure?"

"Absolutely."

"Does this have to do with Charlotte?" he asked in a way that might have been casual if she hadn't known what she did.

She couldn't resist. "What could Charlotte have to do with anything?"

Problems with the book, he might have said. Or getting under each other's skin at the house. He might have even come clean. But he let it pass and simply said, "Nothing. You just sound strange. I worry."

Of course, he did. And she said nothing to ease his mind. He didn't need to know it all now—and if there was some reason he did, he certainly wasn't telling her. Was she being spiteful? Yes. Did she hate herself for it? Yes. Could she reverse it? No. After feeling powerless for so long, she needed to cling to this just a bit.

Besides, if he was worried about her for once, maybe that was good. For four years, he had been totally self-absorbed. Four, she caught herself? Try *ten*. He hadn't thought about her—hadn't considered how small she might feel learning he'd had sex with her best friend on the eve of their wedding. Small. Yes. That was it. Small. Insignificant. Worthless.

But she wasn't. If her parents' faith had meant anything, she was substantial and significant and worthy of being respected and loved. *He* was the small one here—at least, when it came to marriage. He had accused Monica of leaving him out of her life. Wasn't he doing the same to Nicole, and if so, was he the problem? Had he never considered that?

If not, it was time he did.

Actually, it was long *past* time he did.

That thought strengthened her, but her resolve lasted only through the call. The instant it was done, everything rushed back like the incoming tide, dumping at her feet the debris of ill health, a rotting marriage, and a muddy future. When the waters receded again, she was left with the realization that Julian might be the biggest asshole in the world, but he was still her husband, and that though she might hold a winning card in those stem cells, that didn't make up for the loss of love. Love was all she had ever wanted.

Turning toward the sea, she burst into tears.

By the time Nicole was composed enough to head for the house, Charlotte was approaching. They met at the patio's edge. Done being the perfect hostess who had to greet everyone with a smile and kind word, Nicole pulled her sweater tight and waited.

"Kaylin saw you crying," Charlotte said quietly. With her hands deep in the pockets of her jeans and her hair pulled starkly back, she looked subdued. "She's convinced you're lying about you and Julian."

Nicole glanced at the house. Kaylin stood at the glass sliders. "She thinks we're separating? Maybe we are."

"You confronted him then?"

"About you two? No. If my marriage falls apart, it won't be because of that. It'll be because my husband is an uptight jerk who refuses to include his wife in his life."

"He's sick, Nicki. You said it way back—he isn't himself."

Nicole remembered those words. They had totally new meaning now. "Maybe not completely," she said, "but I'm suddenly wondering about all the things I didn't see. I wasn't looking for anything wrong. He dictated and I obeyed. I was too soft."

"But we all *love* you for that."

Nicole wanted to say that it hadn't gotten her far and to ask whether Charlotte thought she should obey now or hold her ground, to rush to Durham or stay here, to give on the issue of stem cells or object. She wanted to pour out her fears, confiding in Charlotte as she'd always done, and not only during summers. During those growing-up years, they talked on the phone during winters, too. Charlotte had known about her first bra, her first kiss, her first serious crush. She had helped Nicole write her college essays and had been the first person Nicole called when she got into Middlebury. During their sophomore year, they had driven hours, meeting halfway between schools to sing their hearts out at a Shania Twain concert.

Nicole wanted the closeness back. She wanted Charlotte's help with Julian. Charlotte was smart. She would know what to do.

But she was still the enemy. Nicole wanted to forgive her, but couldn't.

Feeling a pervasive sadness, she said, "I never could understand why we grew apart. I told myself you were giving me space, like you knew you couldn't be part of my marriage and were stepping back. When it got worse, I blamed it on your work. Then on our having such different lifestyles. But all along it was the other, wasn't it?"

Charlotte's eyes were dull. *Yes.*

That quickly, Nicole was stung all over again. "You were my BFF."

"I *am*."

"A BFF is supposed to be loyal. She's supposed to be honest and considerate and generous. She's supposed to sacrifice something she wants if she knows that getting it will hurt the other."

"I did all those things," Charlotte claimed helplessly.

"You did *not*."

"Once. I screwed up *once*—and I was so drunk I didn't know I was doing it. Haven't you ever made a mistake?"

Oh yes, Nicole thought. She had trusted blindly. But no more. "Don't tell Julian about the stem cells, Charlotte. He doesn't need to know yet."

"But shouldn't he at least know they're an option?"

"He needs to consider other options first."

"You said he was going straight to stem cells."

"He will if I tell him what you have. Don't you see? Even with cells from his own child, he could die."

"Do you care?"

"Yes!" Nicole exclaimed, then quieted. "I shouldn't. But I do."

They stood for a moment, facing each other in silence while the ocean pounded and the gulls screeched. Finally, Charlotte said, "Are you afraid he'll want to know the child?"

Nicole considered the question. She wanted to deny it, but her anger wasn't that strong. "Maybe."

"The adoption papers forbid our contacting her."

"You. But not him."

"Both of us. The parents know how to reach me, but they've never tried."

"Why did they let you keep the stem cells?"

"She can use them if she needs them. That was part of the agreement."

"But why did you want them? Was it to keep some little last thing of hers?"

Charlotte looked vulnerable now. "I thought that if I had other children—"

Nicole cut her off, feeling a trace of impatience. "Yes, you said that, but wasn't there even a little bit of wanting something of hers?"

There was silence, then a reluctant, "Maybe subconsciously. But they're yours, Nicki. I'm serious about that. I can't think of a better use."

Nicole had wanted the admission. She wanted Charlotte to know she did understand the emotions involved. Now, though, she turned away. "I don't want them."

"He might. Please tell him."

"I can't."

"No one would have to know," Charlotte argued, her voice low and quickly taken by the wind. "You could just say he used donor cells. No one but the three of us would know their source."

Nicole knew it wasn't that simple. Kaylin was here, still watching from the sliders. And Angie was coming. And then there were Johnny, Julian's parents, and Monica, plus dozens of friends and colleagues, all of whom would ask questions if a stem cell transplant went bad.

But she couldn't think that far. One step at a time was all she could manage. "I'd better go talk with Kaylin." She set off, then stopped and, wary, turned back to Charlotte. "What about Leo? Will your working with Kaylin interfere with that?"

"No. He has his own work."

Nicole still wasn't sure what Charlotte saw in Leo Cole. She found him abrasive. But she hadn't been able to trip him up. "He really did write *Salt*?"

"Yes."

"Has he sold the rights to a second book?" Charlotte shook her head. "Why not?"

"He's keeping his options open."

"About writing the next one, or about who to sell it to?"

"Both."

"So if the world already knows Chris Mauldin is male, why's he's hiding out on Quinnipeague?"

"This is his home."

"But he never leaves. Is he agoraphobic?"

"No. He just prefers life here."

"Is he not interested in broadening his horizons? In growing as a writer?"

"He's not interested in what it would cost him. He figures he can grow just doing more of what he's done."

Nicole thought it a waste. Not in her wildest dreams did she have publishers fighting each other for the rights to her second book. Leo Cole was either very brilliant or very stupid—though she couldn't say that to Charlotte, who was clearly biased. So she settled for, "Well, anyway, thanks for giving Kaylin a job."

"Don't thank me," Charlotte insisted. "*Use* me. Please?"

Nicole knew Charlotte was feeling guilty—but so was she. Yes, she should tell Julian about the stem cells, but she wasn't ready, just wasn't ready. So she converted guilt into productivity. On a wave of antisentimentality, she attacked her bedroom closet, bagging up clothes she hadn't worn in years. That took her into Saturday, when, with Kaylin's help, she opened the Great Room cabinets and boxed up childhood games, jigsaw puzzles, old cassettes and CDs. After dinner at the Chowder House with her stepdaughter—Charlotte had gone down the road in the opposite direction, the details of which Nicole didn't want to know—she blogged about lobster rolls, adding a photo from her stock source, and when the posting was done, she spent several hours reading farm journals.

The thought did cross her mind that with Kaylin here, Charlotte could leave when the interviews were done. Kaylin could help organize the book, and if not Kaylin, her own editors. Wasn't that what editors were for?

She was getting ahead of herself with this, but it was nice to have a choice.

Feeling marginally in control, she slept soundly and awoke Sunday morning on the same positive note. She lost a little of it during the drive to the pier as she faced the thought of her mother again and wondered just what to say. But it wasn't until the ferry ramp lowered and her mother came down that her confidence imploded.

Driving up the coast these last few days, Angie hadn't been alone.

Chapter Nineteen

NICOLE KNEW THE MAN. TALL and robust, Tom Herschel had been one of Bob's law partners and was an old family friend, a widower who had lost his wife to breast cancer three years before—all of which, *including* two nights in motels along the coast, might have been totally innocent, if it hadn't been for the look on Angie's face. Her eyes were larger than normal, and it wasn't from makeup, though Angie was an expert at that. She was also an expert dresser, and though she weighed five pounds more this summer than last, she was still stunning in her sweater and slacks. What Nicole saw most, though, in these first instants, was nervousness.

Perhaps she was uneasy coming here for the first time without Bob? Or she was anxious about Nicole's mental state?

"You remember Tom," Angie said after they'd hugged—and it was such a ridiculous comment, what with Tom having been at the house all the time during the dark days after Bob's sudden death, that Nicole just *knew.*

How to behave? Speechless, she kept her right arm around her mother and extended her left for a genial clasp of Tom's hand, but she faced Angie again in the next breath.

"Up the coast?" she managed to say.

Angie's smile was stilted. "We went to Bar Harbor. Acadia is a fabulous place to hike."

Nicole had never known her mother to be a hiker but couldn't say that with Tom right there at her elbow. Rather, an inbred politeness kicked in, and she nodded and smiled, at which point Angie drew her into a motherly hug and deftly changed the subject. "I've been worried about you since I learned about Julian. I talked with him again this morning. He's worried about you, too." Holding Nicole back, she scowled. "For what it's worth, I'm furious at him for making you keep this all to yourself. There was no *reason* why you couldn't tell me. You poor thing."

Not wanting to dwell on what "poor thing" could mean, Nicole reached for her mother's bag before Tom could and led them to the car. Once the engine turned over, though, Angie picked up where she'd left off. "He sounded okay. But, of course, I couldn't see him. This has to have been such a strain on you. He was right to want you here, though this has to be bittersweet for you, too. Well, maybe it's different for me. My memories go so far back. Even standing on that ferry and watching Rockland recede, how many times your father and I did that." She sucked in a breath. "Has the island given you any kind of a break?"

Nicole checked the rearview mirror, then turned left and started down the neck road. She didn't have time to answer before Angie said, "Of course, you have the cookbook to do. That must be a diversion. How's it coming? Have islanders been cooperative? I don't suppose they wouldn't be, but asking for something as intimate as a personal recipe has to be challenging. Recipes *are* intimate, don't you think? Many of them have been in families for generations. I was telling Tom about the project, and he raised the issue of getting signed releases for everyone whose recipes you print. Have you thought about that?"

"My publisher did. They gave me a form."

"Oh, good. Do you think that's okay," she called to Tom, who was in the backseat, "or should we have someone in the firm check it out?"

"I'm sure it's fine," he reassured her, much as he had done dozens of times during the funeral planning—and suddenly Nicole had a thought that would have made her apoplectic, if she hadn't already been numb. Angie and Tom, even before Bob died? She couldn't bear to *think* it!

But here was her mother, giving a running commentary on whose drive they passed and how *were* the Warrens or the McKenzies or the Matthews? Yes, she jabbered. Normally Nicole would have given her competition, but since she wasn't saying much now, Angie had the airwaves all to herself. Still, she sounded . . . what? Apprehensive? Uncomfortable? *Guilty?*

By the time they were home, Nicole's head was throbbing. While she filled a glass with water and downed two Tylenol tabs, her mother opened the refrigerator and, after studying its contents, extracted boxes of blueberries, raspberries, and strawberries. Setting a colander in the sink, she put the berries under the spray.

She paused only to ask, "You haven't washed these, have you?"

"No. Uh, Mom . . ." What to say? "I was going to grill steaks for dinner, but I don't have enough for five."

"No problem. I thought we'd go to the Grill."

Nicole swallowed. "Okay. And, uh, how do you want to handle bedrooms? The master is the only one free—"

Hands stilling, Angie gasped. "Oh no, I couldn't sleep there. The memories would keep me up all night! When your father and I walked out of that bedroom last September, we had no idea he would never be back." She resumed washing the fruit.

"So you came here with *Tom?*" Nicole asked, because berries were nothing next to the memory of her father, which felt like it was being shoved into a dark, dusty corner.

Angie shushed her and glanced at the door. "Don't rush to judgment, honey. Tom didn't have to come. But he knew I'd have trouble here."

"Well, you can't both sleep in my room," Nicole said, bewildered.

"Why would either of us want to, when there are six other perfectly good rooms in the wings?"

In two bedrooms or one? That was what haunted Nicole. But it wasn't until after lunch, when they had exhausted the issues of Julian's diagnosis, treatment history, and current symptoms, that she was alone again with Angie and able to ask. Charlotte had offered to show Tom around the island, and had drafted Kaylin to narrate the tour.

They were on the patio, Angie rearranging the furniture there as though nothing was wrong, while, in Nicole's world, nothing was right. With growing astonishment, she watched her mother bend to check under the table for traces of where the legs had stood on the stone the summer before. Straightening, she moved one chair after another aside, all the while ignoring Nicole, who simmered.

"What is going *on*, Mom?" she finally cried. "Are you *with* Tom?"

Having pulled out all six chairs, Angie was struggling to move the table. "Take that end, like a good girl, would you?"

Nicole helped her inch the table to the very spot where it had likely been last year, then dropped her hands and asked, "Are you?"

Angie began returning chairs. "Would that be so awful?"

"Yes! Dad hasn't been dead seven months!"

"It's been seven months and three weeks."

"You said you loved him."

Angie stared at her. "I did love him. With all my heart and soul."

"Did you always have a thing for Tom?"

"Nicole," she warned. "That is very wrong. I've always loved Tom as a friend. So did your father. What you're suggesting is an insult to all of us."

Nicole knew her mother enough to recognize honest outrage, but she was only marginally appeased. She couldn't get her head around the idea of Angie dating. "He wasn't around the last few times we visited. All this time, I've pictured you alone."

"I've been telling you about dinners with friends."

"I assumed you were talking about couples, like the Farringtons or the Spragues." But that raised another awful thought. "Does the firm know about this? Dad's friends?"

"They don't think twice about Tom's support. In some regards, they're happy to have me off their hands, and they trust Tom." She grew crestfallen. "I knew you'd be upset."

"How could I not be?" Nicole cried.

"Tom is a *friend*, honey. When someone dies, everyone gathers around for the first week, then little by little they wander off. Tom didn't."

"But he's nothing like Dad." Bob was affable, outgoing, a rainmaker. Tom was none of those things.

"That's the point. I'm not looking for someone to replace your father."

Nicole barely heard. "I thought you loved him."

Angie's voice shot up. "I *did*. *Listen* to me, Nicole. This has nothing to *do* with Dad. Dad is *dead*." There were tears in her eyes. She held the chair so tightly that her knuckles were white. "Maybe I shouldn't have brought Tom. But I wanted to be here with you and didn't think I'd be able to handle it all on my own. Look at this table. I remember when your father and I bought it. And that planter . . . and those mushroom lights. Back home, I took care of these kinds of things while your father worked, but up here, we did everything together. This house may not much resemble the one your grandparents built, but I look at this one and see that one. It's where your father and I were married."

Nicole tried to understand, but she kept picturing Bob looking down from heaven at the sight of his best friend in this house with his wife. Wasn't it a betrayal, not totally unlike Julian and Charlotte?

She must have looked like she would cry, because Angie had a quick arm around her. "I'm sorry, sweetheart. I didn't think you'd take it this badly."

Nicole couldn't speak.

"So much happening in your life," Angie cooed, squeezing her sweetly. "I can understand why you're numb."

Nicole had a hysterical thought. *Numb? After four years? No way. It's seeing my mother with another man after seven months!*

There was more to it, of course. She had taken a breath—tempted, oh so tempted by that loving arm to let loose about Charlotte and Julian, trust and betrayal, and how little Angie knew of it all, when she spotted movement in the Great Room. The island tour was apparently done.

Angie gave her a last squeeze before letting go. "There's a fellow at our church whose wife has had MS for thirty years. You'd never know she was suffering from anything worse than aging. Julian will be fine, honey. I know he will."

"How can you be sure?" Nicole asked, knowing that no two cases of MS were alike, but willing to grasp anything that would make her feel better.

"Because God wouldn't take your father and your husband in the same breath."

"Mom—"

"Remember what Dad used to say when things didn't go the way we wanted? What doesn't kill us makes us stronger."

Nicole was stunned. Mention of death did not make her feel better.

Angie must have taken her inability to speak for thoughtfulness, because, after pressing a cheek to hers, she went inside.

Nicole watched in despair. There was no PDA, but Angie was smiling for Tom. Or maybe the smile was for Charlotte or Kaylin. She didn't know what to think.

Retreating into numbness, she wandered up the path and into the garden to sit with the plants. The valerian was thriving. Same with the lavender. She didn't know which would help her more and didn't care, as long as one of them worked.

Charlotte joined her a short time later. "I'm sorry. I tried to draw it out, but there just isn't much to see." She settled down on the path, not quite invading Nicole's space in the garden, but not going away, either.

And Nicole didn't want her to. There was something to be said for not feeling entirely alone. "Are you scandalized?" she asked Charlotte with a sideways glance.

"About Tom? Surprised when I first saw him."

"Do you think she's wrong?"

"I'm not one to judge," Charlotte had the good grace to say.

"But what do you think?"

Another person would have given Nicole the answer she wanted, but Charlotte would be truthful. This was why Nicole had asked.

Her dark hair was a wild riot caught in a hair tie, but her brown eyes were more restrained. "I think they're both alone," she finally said. "They're not breaking any rules."

"What about Dad's memory?"

"That'll always be here."

"But buried under a mountain of new ones?"

Charlotte smiled sadly. "There would be new ones anyway. Angie is young—"

"Sixty-two."

"That's young," Charlotte remarked. "Women in Appalachia—or Ethiopia or Zimbabwe? Sixty-two is old in those places, but not here. Not the way Angie has lived. She's still full of life. She'll never forget Bob—never in a million years—but you can't expect her to close up like a clam and wait to die. You wouldn't want that for her."

Nicole supposed not. "But so *soon*?"

"He's helped her through a hard time. He seems like a nice enough guy."

"He's bland."

"Anyone would be bland next to Bob."

True, Nicole thought. Still, having Angie show up with another man was not what she needed just then. "She should have warned me. All these months, and she said nothing. Did she have to hide it?"

"Did you ask?" Charlotte argued gently. "She was protecting you, Nicki. Think about it. Would this have been easier two or three months ago?"

No, Nicole admitted and watched a bee hovering over the sweet William, which were in full bloom and lovely, their frilled edges framing petals layered with deep shades of pink. The buzzing was loud enough to survive the rumble of the nearby surf. She listened, breathing in wisps of the spicy clove scent of valerian, a soother in the salty sea air.

One thing about Charlotte; she knew when not to talk. She waited a full five minutes, until Nicole was feeling calmer, before quietly asking, "Did you tell her?"

About the affair, the child. "No."

"Will you?"

Nicole had come close. But something had stopped her, and it wasn't only the return of the others.

"If I'm going to talk about stem cells, I have to," she said, though Charlotte had already made the opposite point. No one had to know the identity of the donor. Anonymity was expected with donor banks. Julian would have to know, of course, but he wouldn't want the source of the cells advertised. Nor would Nicole. What had happened was humiliating enough without.

But she had no intention of sharing those thoughts with Charlotte, who deserved to worry a little.

Chapter Twenty

CHARLOTTE WAS APPREHENSIVE ENTERING THE kitchen Monday morning, wondering whether Nicole would have spilled all to Angie overnight and, if so, what manner of condemnation would greet her. But Angie smiled brightly at her from the counter, where she was slicing kiwi, and someone must have already driven into town, because not only was Tom reading the *Wall Street Journal* in print, but Nicole was slicing bagels, fresh from a Quinnie Café bag.

Kaylin was a no-show; she wouldn't be up until ten. Charlotte might have stayed in bed late, too, if she hadn't been edgy thinking of Nicole and Angie alone. If it was going to happen, it would happen, but she wanted to be able to defend herself when it did.

That said, there was safety in numbers. Nicole wouldn't spill the beans in front of Tom, and since Tom sat there through breakfast, seconds of coffee on the patio, and cleanup back in the kitchen, Nicole and Angie weren't alone. By the time Angie took Tom back into town to browse in the shops, Kaylin was awake, so Charlotte was safe for another little while.

Under the guise of scouting out potential interviews, she left the
two on the patio in the sun and went to visit Isabel Skane. There were
others in the shop, two browsing the floor-to-ceiling bins of yarn,
three at the table knitting. Charlotte had brought her sweater, which
elicited more *ooohs* and *ahhhs* than it deserved given the number of
mistakes, and Isabel quickly saw the problem with the cables.

"Once you slip stitches to the holder for a cable, whether you place
the holder in back or in front determines the look of the finished cable.
See these early ones?" Isabel spread out the lower sleeve. "You've con-
sistently given the cable a left twist here, meaning the holder was in
front, but you lost track of that as you moved up the arm."

Charlotte didn't like the implication. "So I need to tear all of this
out?"

"Not if you think the Native American way," Isabel offered gently.
"They deliberately knit a mistake into each piece to let the recipient
know it was hand-knit with love."

"Well, that would work," Charlotte remarked, "except for two things.
A, I'm the recipient and, B, there was nothing deliberate about these mistakes."

Soft laughter, a grin, and a knowing nod came from the three at
the table.

"Want me to rip?" Isabel whispered. She was definitely a perfection-
ist, though that had never been in doubt in Charlotte's mind, given the
samples on display in the shop. Each was flawless. Charlotte wasn't
sure she would ever reach that stage.

"You're doing a great job," Isabel encouraged her, taking the sleeve.
"This pattern would challenge even me."

Charlotte doubted that, but the remark opened the door for her to
dig deeper into Isabel's knitting background and, unaware of her own
professional purpose, the two shoppers joined in. Day-trippers, they
were avid yarnies, asking questions Charlotte wouldn't have known to
ask but the answers to which were fascinating.

Isabel paused from ripping only to ring up their sales. By the time she had the sleeve back to the first wrong cable, Charlotte was on her third chocolate almond candy and feeling no pain.

The pain returned, of course. Driving back past the beaches and flats, she could think of nothing but that Nicole had either told Angie or *hadn't* told Julian. Either way, there would be increased tension in the house.

But lunch was underway with no added tension, just hearty turkey sandwiches on thick slices of Melissa Parker's anadama bread. And so went the day. Nicole read through recipes with Angie for a while, then they all went to the beach. Charlotte stayed behind to edit photos, and when they returned she held her breath, searching faces to see if anything had changed.

Something actually had. Nicole confided to her in a private moment that Angie was urging her to fly to Durham despite what Julian wanted, because, after all, a wife should be with her husband, and what did Charlotte think about that?

Charlotte thought it was a good idea. She hoped—but didn't say— that if Nicole were there, she might be more apt to tell Julian what she knew about the affair, the baby, the stem cells. Charlotte was starting to think of telling him herself, and not only for his sake. Nicole was suffering holding it in.

But Nicole was adamant about picking the time. And since Charlotte didn't want to betray her again, she waited.

By the time the patio grill had cooled and the dishes were done, Charlotte needed to get out. Staying nearby to help Nicole was all well and good, but the tension was getting to her. When Trivial Pursuit, which was best played with exuberance, was retrieved from the giveaway box, she pleaded a need to see the ocean and excused herself from the room.

Can I come over? she typed into her phone as she climbed the stairs for a sweater.

Since when do you have to ask? Leo texted back, then, seconds later, *Want to go sailing?*

Now?

Why not?

Don't sailors return to shore at night?

Not me. I know these waters. Do you trust me?

Charlotte thought about racing with him from Quinnipeague to Rockland for Nicole, pouring her heart out to him in a flood of tears, and believing all the unbelievable things he said. Did she trust him? She figured she did.

Be there in five, she typed and, pocketing the phone, went for her keys.

For the first time, she drove right past the Cole curve and down the dirt drive between all those well-tended rows of flowers and herbs. Leo was a dark shadow on the front steps. Dropping his knife and wood as she approached, he rose and gestured her to the side of the house. Once she had parked beside his truck, he opened the door, helped her out, then pressed her against the car for a slow, tongue-dance of a kiss. She was beginning to think he had changed his mind about sailing, when he took her hand, led her out back, and picked up a duffel.

"Jackets and a blanket," he explained. "In case you're cold."

She wouldn't be for a while after that kiss, and, anyway, she had her fisherman's sweater along. But his consideration was endearing, as was his care when he lifted Bear onto the boat after the dog followed them down the dock.

In no time, he had stowed the bag, pulled in bumpers that hung between the boat and the dock, and released the lines. When he turned a key, navigating lights came on. With the press of a button came a healthy thrum.

"Motor?" she asked, surprised, since there was a good wind.

"Just 'til we clear the rocks," he said as they moved away from the dock. "They come on with no warning."

One did just then, seeming barely a foot from Charlotte's side, though she wouldn't have seen it if Leo hadn't pointed. A chiseled mound of wet granite, it rose only enough to break the waves. But he steered comfortably around it and between several others before he finally cut the engine and hoisted the sails. There were two, one fore and one aft; both winched up in no time.

Though the air was mild, the wind held steady as they tacked away from Quinnipeague. When they were far enough out so that the crash of the waves against the shore was barely a beat, he steered into the wind until the sails flapped, then lowered them and secured the lines. Pulling a thermos of cocoa from the duffel, he produced mugs and filled each.

"Warm enough?" he asked, settling beside her on the padded bench.

"With Bear on my feet, cocoa in my hands, and a hot guy beside me?" She gave a satisfied sigh, then, looking up at the star-filled sky, said, "Tell me what I see."

He began to point. "Saturn's too low this late, but there's Jupiter. See it? And way over there's the horse, Pegasus." His finger shifted, drawing. "Big Dipper. Little Dipper."

Charlotte had to focus hard to see each. Then she saw something else. "A shooting star." She squeezed her eyes shut.

When she opened them, Leo was watching her. "Wha'dya wish for?"

"I'm not telling. That'll jinx it."

"Tell me."

But she wouldn't. Instead, she nestled closer—which, if he had known her a little better, would have told him what her wish was—and said, "It's nice being out here, just floating." She listened. There was the lap of the water against the hull, the soft clink of the rigging as the boat swayed, Bear's low snoring, and Leo's steady heart. "It's quiet."

"Are things loud at the house?"

"Tense. Nicki still won't tell Julian about the stem cells."

"Can you?"

"I'm trying to respect her wishes. But she can't hold out forever. Those cells are a valuable tool."

"She's using them as one."

Charlotte was about to say that she wasn't using them at all—when she realized what he meant. "A tool against Julian."

"Punishment for the affair."

She tipped her head back on his shoulder so that she could see his eyes. "How did you know that?"

He shrugged. "Just a guess."

"It's the kind of thing the hero of *Salt* knew. Natural intuition. Have you worked more on *Next Book*?"

"Some. I got distracted by hate mail."

"What kind of hate mail?"

"One guy says I stole his story and wants a cut of my royalties or he's taking me to court. Another says my research sucked, because if anyone built a boat the way I described, it'd sink."

"People like finding fault. It's the culture."

"You don't get hate mail."

"Only because I'm small-time. Ninety-nine point nine percent of your mail must be positive."

"It's the point one percent that haunts me. Like the lady who says I'm irresponsible not addressing birth control with so much sex going on." He stopped talking, watching her intently.

"I told you."

"Tell me again."

"I'm not an impressionable young girl." Pregnancy was not a worry. She made sure of that.

"Once burned?"

"You could say. For the record, there haven't been many men."

"I wasn't asking that."

"But I want you to know. I'm particular about who I'm with."

The night sky was bright, accentuating his eyes. "If you wanted to have my baby, I wouldn't walk away."

Charlotte's heart stopped for a split second before resuming its beat. The remark might have been innocent but for the intensity in those eyes.

"Be careful what you say," she warned softly.

"I'm serious," he said. "But you won't stay here, will you." It wasn't a question.

"Would you come with me to Paris in September?" she asked. It wasn't a question, either, though, so she simply slipped back into fantasy by nestling closer.

They drained the thermos and drifted for a time until Leo raised the sails again and returned to the dock. "Come in for a few," he whispered when they reached the beach.

And how could she not? She wasn't able to put into words what she felt for Leo Cole, but making love came in a close second.

Chapter Twenty-one

ANGIE STAYED THROUGH THE WEEK. Nicole certainly couldn't ask her to leave, since it was her house, but increasingly they were at odds—and not about the small things they bickered about when Nicole was growing up, like music, makeup, and clothes. Their disagreements now had to do with the role of a wife, and it was two-sided. Nicole felt Angie was disloyal; Angie felt Nicole was negligent. Bob had always been the great diffuser, which gave Nicole double reason to miss him now. Add to that her turmoil about all the things her mother still didn't know—things about which Nicole was so torn—and she was touchy whenever her mother appeared.

On Tuesday, when Angie again raised the issue of her joining Julian in Durham, Nicole snapped, "He can come here, too, y'know," which led to a remark about *Tom being there,* which led to another argument about that.

On Wednesday, when Angie asked how Julian was feeling, Nicole said, "I haven't talked with him today," and when she asked why not, Nicole said, "Mother, it's barely eight. He needs sleep. I am not waking him up." When Angie argued that Julian was *always* up early, Nicole said, "Well, he isn't now," and left the room in a huff.

On Thursday, Angie waited awhile longer to launch in, but that only made the words more pointed when they came. "Do you *ever* call Julian?" she asked, and when Nicole said that they talked *every night,* Angie said she seemed angry and that if the anger was toward Julian, it was disappointing. "He didn't ask to be sick, Nicole, and if your anger isn't at him, it's at me. Where did this selfishness come from?"

Stung, Nicole held up her hands in surrender and turned away.

"She's worried about you," Charlotte tried to reason later, but when Charlotte, too, asked how Julian was feeling, Nicole was more defensive than ever.

"I could call him ten times a day, and there wouldn't be anything new. He's tired. He's *always* tired. End of conversation."

And then there was Kaylin, who announced she was returning to New York.

Nicole was bewildered. "But you have no job."

"I can get a job waitressing."

"What about working with Charlotte?"

"She doesn't need me, Nicki. I mean, like, it was sweet of her to offer, but she always does her own stuff herself, and you guys are totally on top of the cookbook." Her ponytail swished as she turned away, then quickly back. "And don't ask what Dad will say, because waitressing is a totally responsible job. And besides, Mom says it's okay."

Feeling shut out and separate, Nicole didn't share the text she received from Julian a short time later. He was returning to Philly. Having had done most of what he wanted to do in Durham, he was tired.

He was tired. He was always tired.

But something felt different this time. *Tired how?* she texted back.

Just tired.

Is it the drugs?
I think I just want to be home.
End of conversation.

Nicole worried.

She worried that his MS was getting worse.

She worried that everyone knowing about it now had demoralized him.

She worried that there *was* another woman in Philly, and that he missed her.

And yet, she couldn't get herself to call him. *It'll upset him,* she rationalized. *It'll make him angry. It'll cause a greater rift.* She knew she should offer to meet him at home, but there was no way she could see him and not confront him about Charlotte, and she just wasn't ready for that.

Burying herself in work, she spent the afternoon reviewing her to-do list for the book and seeing far more there than on the all-done list. Actually, she realized in a frightened moment, there was precious *little* on the all-done list. Yes, they had addressed BRUNCH, CHOWDER, FISH, and SWEETS, but not all of the recipes had come in—and those were only four of ten chapters. They hadn't even started the other six, and her deadline was barely a month off.

"Can we do all this?" she asked, offering the lists when Charlotte found her on the patio in a particularly discouraged moment.

Charlotte studied them briefly and looked up. "Absolutely."

But Nicole's stomach was churning, as it used to when she was eight or nine or ten, facing something new and different. She hadn't felt panic like this in a while.

Charlotte must have known that. Taking her friend's arms, she looked her in the eye and said a quiet, "It's been a rough week for you with everyone here. I love your mom, but she brought new issues with her, and she raises all your old insecurities. For what it's worth, I'm disappointed in Kaylin, too, but you can't control her. They're leaving Saturday. Once things settle, we'll work through these lists. I've had deadlines before, and I promise you, this one's doable."

Doable. Doable. Doable. Nicole chanted the words, and it helped.

What helped most, though, was Nickitotable.com. This was her escape. Community farms, pure food, spreading the locavore word— this was her mission. Whether describing the fresh-from-the-sea haddock they grilled for dinner and served with corn salsa, pushing handwoven place mats that Bev carried at the island store, or promoting the return of roadside food stands, she was in a world she could manage. She took to using her laptop in a far corner of the patio, where she immersed herself and, with the sea providing white noise, refused to look up.

Charlotte had taken to using her laptop at Leo's, though she wasn't as productive as she might have been on the patio with Nicole. After moving his computer over to make room on the desk for hers, he produced a second chair, which was totally sweet. But seated so close, she was distracted—first, by the glasses that he put on when he was at his computer for a stretch and which startled her each time he put them on; then by his surprisingly speedy forefinger pecking; then by the way he would sit back after a sentence or two, mouth the words, come forward and type more, lost in the world he created for however brief a time.

And brief it was. Though he never discussed specifics, and continued to refuse to let her read what he had written, he always grew frustrated. Inevitably, Charlotte would hear him swear, tap the keyboard to bring up new screens, and settle in to do marketing. This he shared with her—posting responses to Facebook fans, responding to questions posted on his Web site, tracking down blogsite reviews of *Salt* to thank a reviewer, or weighing in elsewhere on a discussion of his characters or plot. When she asked why he made the effort, he said he did it for *Salt,* and when she asked why it mattered, given the book's jaw-dropping success, he said it was a fair substitute for the touring his publisher would rather he do.

At one point toward the end of the week, he set down a thick folder. She hesitated before opening it. "More hate mail?" she asked warily.

He shook his head and hitched his chin at the folder, urging her on.

She opened it to find letter after letter from publishing houses and production companies, all addressed to his post office box in Portland. In some instances, there were multiple letters from the same source, sent when he hadn't responded to a first or second one. With each, the money increased. The amounts were staggering.

"This is every writer's dream," Charlotte breathed in awe.

He looked terrified. "Y'think?"

"I do." She singled out a glitzy header. "This one's for a feature film. So's this," she said, pushing at another. "And these?" She fanned out several more. "These are the best publishing houses in New York." She looked at him. "Have you called any of them back?"

"No. That's my lawyer's job. But he knows I'm not ready to sign another contract, not with my current publisher or any other. I like being in the driver's seat and working at my own speed. I don't want to have to finish the next book if I don't want to. And if they get fed up and lose interest, I can do another e-book myself."

"What about a movie? You can't do that yourself."

"Do I need a movie?"

"No." Neatening the letters, she closed the folder.

"You think I'm crazy," he said. With his hair slanting in short, dark spikes, his jaw hard and his lips thin, he looked tough, but the toughness didn't reach his eyes. Those eyes always betrayed his vulnerability, which was what Charlotte saw now. But there was more. She sensed he wasn't only thinking of his future as a writer. He was thinking of his future with her.

"You're not crazy," she said, addressing the first, easier to do than addressing the second. "Anyone who offers this kind of money isn't going to let you stay anonymous. If you were to take any of these, your life would change."

He seemed to relax a little.

"And I know what you mean about being in the driver's seat," she reasoned. "That's how my work is, and I love it. I couldn't have come here this summer without that freedom. I just wish . . . just wish . . ."

"What?"

She wished he would give a little, wished he would agree to go to Paris with her or at least visit her in New York. As for the rest, she didn't care about it any more than he did. Sure, the money was good, but if it wasn't what he wanted, it wasn't worth a dime. She loved him the way he was—honest and pure, naïve in his way, certainly vulnerable, all of which might be lost if the world found out who he was, and then where would her haven be?

Leaving the desk, she wrapped her arms around his waist and put her head on his chest. "This is nice," was all she said, and he seemed content to leave it at that.

Driving home a short time later, she thought of just how nice it was. She liked working with Leo. Distractions and all, she had done some good work. Whether it was the man, his beautiful office, or poor old Bear—who had taken to finding her leg wherever it was and sleeping against it—she was inspired.

Nicole knew it, too, because the interviews Charlotte gave her were top-notch. They captured the spirit of the island in ways Nicole couldn't have done herself, which—totally aside from Charlotte being her sole cheerleader—justified Nicole having insisted she stay. The rawness of her anger had passed, leaving a nagging hurt, but even that paled in the face of Angie's needling.

She did her best to regroup after each argument, determined to be more mature and restrained. But with Angie's departure near, and few mentions made about how sad the house was without Bob, how strong his presence remained, or what to do with his clothes, Nicole was growing suspicious.

Saturday morning, when they were in the kitchen alone and Angie remarked that being here wasn't so bad, that they should put a hold on packing, that maybe selling the house was a rash idea, Nicole lost it.

"Rash?" she cried. "Mom, you've been talking about selling since Dad died. You haven't had a single doubt, not once. The only thing that's changed here is Tom."

Angie drew back. "Was he unpleasant to be around? Did he get in your way? I know you avoided the west wing, but if you'd gone there even once, you'd have seen that Tom and I did not share a room—and if we had, would that be so bad? Would it be so bad if I kept the house and spent time here with someone other than your father? Bob loved having people come."

"Tom is not people," Nicole argued.

"Right you are. Tom is special. He's the one person your father would have trusted with me. Tom knows me. He respects what I had with Bob and lets me talk about him. He would never ask me to give up those memories, any more than I'd ask him to give up his memories of Susan, rest her soul. But this week has been really good. So no, I'm not selling."

Nicole swallowed hard. If this was Angie's call, it was done. "It's your house. You can do what you want." But there was another side. "I don't have to be here."

That caught Angie, who looked suddenly stricken. "You wouldn't want your children to experience Quinnipeague?"

"I don't *have* any children!" Nicole shouted, wondering how her own mother could be so insensitive.

"But you will."

"*When?* My husband is sick. He might die."

Angie straightened. "So you'll sit around and wait for that?"

"Mother!"

"I'm serious. Are you counting on his death?"

Nicole took a short breath. "Please don't say that word."

"So what's planned for the fall?" Angie asked with a calm that took nothing from her momentum. "Julian says he has a week of work in California and then something in China in the spring. Are you going, too? There's great sightseeing in China. Or are you afraid to make plans?" Her face was suddenly harder, the lines over her lip more pronounced. "Life doesn't follow our orders, Nicole. Things haven't worked out the way you want, but you have to accept them—"

"I can't."

"Accept and move on," Angie finished.

"Is that what you're doing, just giving up on everything you had that was good?"

Charlotte appeared at the door and stopped. At the sight of her, Nicole took a deep breath, held up her hands, and started to back off.

But Angie cried, "Oh, no no no, don't run away. We need to discuss this right now. You are stuck in the past, Nicole. Your father is dead. Nothing can bring him back."

"I refuse to forget him."

"Then remember this," Angie said in a rising voice. "He wasn't perfect. He never made the bed or did the laundry, not even when I was sick. We would eat in five-star restaurants, with him using their fine linen napkin to blow his nose, though I can't tell you how many times I asked him not to." Her voice kept rising. "He never wanted to hear complaints about my day, because my problems were petty compared to the ones he saw. He could be judgmental, and he was impatient. It was fine for *us* to wait for him, but he didn't like waiting for us. And he *died* on me, Nicole," she charged as her voice hit a high note. "He left me alone just as we were reaching what should have been the easy years of our lives. There are times when I'm *furious* at him for that." Winded, she sagged. "Does that mean I didn't love him? No. I loved him faults and all."

Nicole wasn't so angry that she didn't hear what Angie was saying.

She just wasn't sure where it was headed. "What does this have to do with me?"

"Do you love Julian?"

"Of course I love Julian."

"Then make it work." The words hung in the air along with all that Nicole hadn't said about the state of her marriage. Nicole was trying to decide whether to deny problems or admit to them, when Angie said, "And while we're talking about your father, here's one more thing. I lived through dozens of court trials with him, and the one thing he always said was that you had to look at the hand you're dealt and be creative. That's how he won cases. Look at the hand you're dealt, Nicole, and be creative. Make your own reality!"

Nicole couldn't be creative with so much else going on in her mind. One step at a time. That was all she could handle, which was why she did laundry, made lunch, made marginal peace with Kaylin as the girl packed, and, at the appointed time Saturday afternoon, drove the trio to the ferry. She was pleasant enough saying good-bye to Tom, and felt true emotion saying good-bye to Kaylin.

How to deal with her mother? She had wanted to tell Angie about Julian's illness for so long, yet now that she had, she was as bottled up as before.

Seeming to sense it, Angie let the others board first, then took Nicole's hands. Her voice was gentle, her neatly made-up eyes sad. "I can't know everything that's going on with you," she said. "I shouldn't. You're a grown woman. But you always used to be tolerant. I don't see that now. Honey, life isn't black or white. There isn't only one picture that's perfect. It's about piecing together shades of gray to make something quite stunning. And the picture shifts. That's another Dad-ism. Remember his sea shadows? Each time the shadow moves, there's a new image. Only sometimes those clouds are stuck up there, so we're the ones who have to move to see it."

*   *   *

At some point during the night, Nicole moved. Come dawn, she saw a different picture. Angie was right; she was a grown woman. She would never act on the say-so of her mother, though the phrase that stuck in her mind came from her. *Make your own reality.*

And with that came the conviction that she had to go home.

Charlotte drove her to the ferry. "Are you sure I can't come?" she asked as she lifted the Rollaboard from the back.

That scenario was actually one of many Nicole had considered during the night. But what had happened before her marriage was something that she and her husband had to work out. Same with their future. "I need to do this myself."

"If you want me to talk with him, I'll be here."

"What I really want," Nicole said, "is for you to keep at the book. I'm freaking out about that. The timing of all this couldn't be worse. I've done the menu planning, and if I'm not back right away, you have my notes on the rest." She had added more during breakfast. "Will you keep things going?"

"Absolutely," Charlotte said, looking her most earnest. "I'll do anything, Nicki. Name it, and it's yours. I'll even blog for you."

Feeling sad, Nicole smiled. "And take away the one thing I do well?" She gave Charlotte a spontaneous hug, only afterward realizing that she probably shouldn't have. But it was done, certainly the tolerant thing to do. Her mother would have been pleased. Forgiveness? She wasn't quite there yet. She had to hear Julian's side of the story. For now, though, that hug had filled a void.

"Don't underestimate yourself!" Charlotte called when Nicole was at the top of the platform. Moments later, with the rumble of its engine, the ferry cast off, and she was on her way.

Chapter Twenty-two

Having made the decision to return to Philadelphia, Nicole was impatient. Unable to find a taxi in Rockland, though, she had to wait for the shuttle bus, then wait again at the Portland Jetport for her flight. She didn't land in Philly until early evening, but even in all that time, she didn't change her mind. The only qualm she had as her cab neared the condo was whether Julian would be alone. She hadn't called to say she was coming. There was nothing she wanted to say on the phone.

She felt a headache coming on, but willed it away and produced a smile for the doorman, who took her bag from the trunk and wheeled it inside.

"Good to see you, Mrs. Carlysle. Would you like help taking this up?"

"No, thanks, John," she said, reaching for the handle as she entered the elevator. "It's light enough." The only things she had brought were ones she didn't have doubles of, like makeup and a favorite outfit or two, though generally she wore different clothes here. She didn't know how long she'd be staying. That depended on what she found.

John pressed the button for the eighteenth floor and, seeming unaware of Julian's illness, gave her his usual smile as the door closed. By the time it reopened, she had her keys in her hand.

Quietly, she let herself into their place. Julian's wallet and keys were on the nearby credenza, but there were no signs that anyone was with him—no handbag, no shoes or discarded clothing. Part of the reason she had come without warning was to check, and though she hated herself for the suspicion, it was one of the things they had to deal with.

He wasn't in the living room. Nor was there sound from else-where—no television, no music, no shuffle of feet in the kitchen. Guessing that he was working, she set her shoulder bag on the carpet by the suitcase and went down the hall, but the study was empty.

When she turned from there, though, she saw him. He stood at the bedroom door, wearing khakis and loafers, but that was where normalcy ended. His shirt was unbuttoned, his hair messy and his skin sallow. Most uncharacteristic, though, was the fear in his eyes.

Because he wasn't alone in the bedroom?

No. She knew in the instant that he was *profoundly* alone, his eyes tearing up now—her husband, whom she loved with the kind of irrationality that kept love alive even when anger should kill it.

"I'm sorry," she whispered, that quickly becoming the deferential Nicole who had been told not to come. "I can't leave you alone. I have to be here."

She approached, but he was reaching for her even before she arrived, pulling her close and holding her to him with a strength she wouldn't have imagined he had from the looks of the rest of him.

"You came," he murmured, his voice shaky in her hair. "I wasn't sure you would."

"You didn't ask me to come," she said in surprise, pulling back. The fear remained in his eyes.

"You sounded so distant. I thought you wanted out."

"I thought you did."

"I'm not good at talking about some things," he said, but before she could tell him that had to change, he ducked his head and caught her lips in a kiss that, yes, held fear and relief, but also the warmth of the good times. When it was done, he held her close for a while, right there in the doorway, and she didn't complain. When he kissed her again and she felt his arousal for the first time in months, her own excitement grew.

Nothing mattered then—not Charlotte, not the stem cells, not even a tremor in the hand that searched and uncovered. She gave him what he wanted, but the hunger was mutual—and if there was a subconscious anger in her greed, it became desire. She was forward in ways she had never been, reacquainting herself with his skin and his scent, taking the lead when his arms tired, refusing to let him rest until they were both sated.

Mine. The word echoed in her mind when finally she lay against him on the bed, listening as his heartbeat grew steady, as her own did the same. Tired or not, he kept an arm around her, holding her close, and when he dozed off, she followed.

She woke up to see city lights glowing under a purpling sky. Pushing up in alarm, she found him awake, head on the pillow, eyes watching her. "How long did we sleep?"

"A couple of hours," he said, then quietly added, "This is the best I've felt in days."

"Really?"

"Really."

She took a deep breath, let it out, and, when he gave a tug, returned to his side. No way was she raising the issue of Charlotte and spoiling the moment. Yes, she wanted what she'd had in the past. She wanted nothing more than to turn back the clock to the days before Julian got sick. And yes, she knew she couldn't. But if, for whatever reason, this intimacy had survived, she needed it.

Apparently, so did he, because he didn't speak, simply continued to hold her, letting her go only to get food, which she did in the form of grilled cheese and arugula sandwiches, but once those were gone, he wanted her with him again.

She was tired enough, relieved enough to sleep in his arms through the night. When morning came, though, she couldn't put it off. They were lying together in bed, his fingers moving lightly on her shoulder.

She spoke against his chest. "Tell me what happened with Charlotte."

His fingers stilled. When she didn't try to modify the question and let him off the hook, he let out a defeated breath. "I was afraid it was that. There had to be a reason you were different."

"I want to hear your side," she said, sitting up now, with the sheet under her arms and determination in her eyes. In fact, she didn't want to hear *anything*. But knowing Charlotte's side, she had to know his.

He began with the obvious—exhaustion from juggling work and wedding plans, too much to drink, little remembered the next day except that what had happened was wrong. But he had looked deeper, too. "At some level," he confessed awkwardly, "I was worried about getting married again. It was easy to blame Monica for what happened the first time, but a marriage takes two. You were younger and more vulnerable. I felt a greater responsibility for you." His voice fell. "I wasn't sure I was up to the task. But there we were with the wedding coming closer and closer, and the arrangements growing more and more elaborate. I panicked and drank too much. I was trying to forget the fear."

"Were you hoping to call off the wedding by having sex with someone else?" Nicole asked. It was a logical follow-up to what he was saying. She had to ask or would forever wonder.

"*Lord no,*" he said with force and, reaching for her hand, hung on. "It was an insane thing—an *animal* thing that had nothing to do with what I wanted."

"Was the wedding too over-the-top?" she asked, still trying to understand.

"No. No, baby. The wedding was perfect. The problem was me. I got overwhelmed and did something I have regretted ever since. I am so, so sorry." He had always been modest. But humble? Ashamed? Never before. "It's the worst thing I've ever done. I told myself that I hadn't betrayed a vow, since we hadn't exchanged them yet. But that was a technical distinction. The whole thing was wrong." His eyes skittered off, only to return seconds later. "I was hoping it would go away. I thought it had."

It might have had it not been for the baby, she knew, but she wasn't mentioning that yet.

He had pushed himself up against the pillows, though there was nothing relaxed about the pose. "When did you learn—" He stopped himself. "Ahh. Right before the Fourth. That's when you pulled back."

She didn't apologize, didn't say anything at all. In the morning light, his jaundice was unsettling, but she wasn't ready to deal with that. He still had more explaining to do, and though he was visibly uncomfortable with it, she held her ground.

He sighed and looked away. "I barely knew her. I had only met her that summer, and I was only on Quinnipeague weekends. It wasn't something I planned." He looked back at Nicole, more troubled than ever. "Did she?"

"No." Nicole believed that. "She regrets it, too."

"Why did she tell you?"

Because she had to, Nicole might have said. *Because I was falling apart thinking that you were desperate enough to sacrifice your life for the sake of experimental medicine, and she wanted to give me hope.*

Still she held back. The argument now wasn't about stem cells. It was about her marriage.

So she simply said, "She probably thought I already knew."

"Did you ask her to leave?"

"No. I need her help with the cookbook."

"How can you stand looking at her?"

"How can I stand looking at you?" Nicole replied. "I'm trying to understand, Julian. I tell myself it was a long time ago, but I'm suddenly seeing things differently."

"Like what?"

"The late nights you work. Business trips."

He gave a spasmodic shake of his head. "Never."

"Not even while I'm on the island for weeks at a time?"

"Never," he repeated.

She started to rock, couldn't help herself. "But it happened with Charlotte. My best friend." Her breath shook, with deep, dark fears breaking through. "I know women whose husbands cheat. I never saw myself as one of them. But I am. It happened."

He came forward fast. "Not an affair, not willful—"

"Was it *me*?" she had to ask. "Was I not strong enough or smart enough or independent enough?"

He cupped her face with tremorous hands. "It wasn't you. You're all I wanted. It was me, feeling inadequate and being stupid enough to try to drown my own insecurities in drink."

"You? Inadequate?"

"You put me on a pedestal, Nicki. But I'd already fucked up one marriage when I met you. Have I fucked up a second?"

"I don't know," she said. The MS issue had to be discussed. But they weren't done with the other. "I hear the excuses you both give, and she's doing everything she can to help, but I still feel betrayed and angry."

"I'm sorry," he said, but mention of anger had stirred it up in her again, so she reached for a robe and went into the kitchen.

Minutes later, knife in hand, she had emptied the refrigerator of apples, pears, kiwi, and pineapple, and was chopping them to bits. After scooping the tiny cubes into a bowl, she added lime juice and sweetener and put the bowl in the fridge. Ten minutes later, she had turned frozen baguettes into cinnamon French toast enough for two, added a mound of fruit salsa to each plate, and put them on the breakfast bar—not because Julian deserved it, but for the sheer therapy of it.

Wearing a sweatshirt and jeans, he watched from the door. His hands were tucked under his arms, his feet were bare. "Feel better?" he asked when she was done.

Had he been smug, she might have lashed out. She still felt threads of anger. But the only thing in his tone was a knowledge borne of familiarity, a reminder that they had been married for ten years and that she wasn't ready to end it.

Yes, she felt better. Not great. But better. Nodding, she pocketed her hands, and met his gaze.

"So help me God, Nicole, there have been no other women. What happened that night was sobering."

"You were with women before me—"

"But never while I was married to Monica," he broke in, "and never while I was married to you. For what it's worth, I haven't had any contact with Charlotte since the wedding."

Nicole knew that. The whole issue of the baby made it so, because there was no way in hell Julian could have known about that and not let it slip now.

Coffee. She wanted coffee. Turning away, she was in the process of making it when he came from behind, wrapped his arms around her middle, and buried his face in her hair.

His voice was muffled. "I don't want to lose you, Nicole. You are the best thing in my life."

The words haunted her. She finished setting up the coffee, then turned. "Would you have said that even if I didn't know about you and Charlotte?"

"Yes. I would have told you last night if we'd stayed awake."

"Why did it have to take my going silent for you to realize it? Because I'm normally so sweet and trusting? Because I was an airhead ten years ago and too naïve to make you worry about it before now?"

"No," he insisted, framing her face with his hands, but he was frowning again. "And you aren't an airhead. You're an amazingly smart woman who never gave herself credit for that. You never demanded much. I took you for granted. And now with MS? You were the only one I could take my anger out on."

"Is the anger gone?"

"No. But I have to make a decision, and I can't do it alone."

"Other people know now," she argued. "You could talk with them."

"They're not you. I need you on my side. I've been miserable these last ten days."

She wanted to believe, wanted to think that the tears in his eyes last night had been sheer relief that she was here. It was an encouraging thought.

Gesturing for him to sit, she poured two juices and was in the process of carrying over their coffees when he took a mouthful of salsa and set down his fork. The tremor in his hand had been pronounced.

"No better?" she asked softly, taking the stool beside his.

He shook his head.

"How did your parents take it?"

"Stoically." He cradled his coffee with both hands. "Dad was quiet. My mother refuses to consider the ramifications for my career." He hesitated. "They haven't called you?"

She shook her head. She had never been close to Julian's parents, had always guessed that they viewed her as the second wife, maybe the trophy one. Maybe it was her childlike voice, or the fact that she hadn't given them a grandchild. She bought them Christmas gifts, sent birthday cards, and pulled out all stops when they visited Philadelphia, though that wasn't often. And she had her own parents, little more than an hour away.

"It's okay," she said to Julian now. "They're dealing, just like you. Has word spread at the hospital?"

"Some. I didn't get in until midday Friday. A few friends came by then. It's awkward until they realize I'm still me and"—he tapped his head—"all here. Dan was great in Durham. And Antoine wants to play golf. He says it would be good for me, though I think it's guilt on his part. But I have to hand it to him. He isn't running away." He stopped short.

"Others have?" Nicole asked.

Julian held up a hand and left the room, walking with the slightly uneven gait that he usually tried to hide. He returned a minute later, wearing wool socks.

"Who ran away?" she asked.

"The support staff. Hey, I was only in for half a day, and the whole idea is still strange to them. They don't know what to say. You'd think they would, given what they do for a living. But this isn't a patient. It's me."

"How's the limp?"

"You saw. It comes and goes. There's some relief not having to worry that someone will see." He rose again and, heading for the living room this time, fiddled with the thermostat.

When he returned, Nicole touched his hand. It was cold.

"I get chills," he admitted quietly and busied himself with the French toast.

Chills were a side effect of the meds he was on. Between that, the yellow tinge to his skin, and the pronounced tremor in his hand, it was obvious they weren't helping.

She ate silently beside him for a short time, liking the good will between them, liking that he was eating, liking that he seemed more relaxed with her, his old self in some regards. From having sex? Maybe. Men took pride in that.

But there was an elephant in the room, looming hairy and large. Sitting back with barely half of her breakfast eaten, she said, "Have you done anything about the other?"

"Stem cells?" He eyed her French toast, and asked, "Do you want that?"

She moved her plate closer and waited until he had finished most everything there. Naturally lean, he was now leaner than ever. For missing her? Disinterest in food? Nausea, which would be another side effect of the meds?

"Stem cells?" she prompted softly, gearing up for what she feared hearing. Impending doom? It seemed so long ago that she'd used the phrase with Charlotte. She had managed to push it aside for a while, but here it was again, front and center.

Setting down his fork, he rested his bad hand in his lap, and looked at her. "No. I haven't done anything yet."

"Why not?" she asked in surprise. He had been so determined when they'd discussed it last.

He reached for his coffee, but she took the cup before it reached his mouth, and topped it off with hot, fresh brew. As before, he held it with both hands.

"Why not, Julian?"

He was studying her strangely. "This is not a discussion you want to have."

"I know that. But I don't want to be ignored anymore."

"I never ignored you." He considered, modified. "I just turned away when you said things I didn't like."

"If you want me involved in your life, you have to let me in."

"I want you involved in my life," he said. "That's one of the reasons I haven't moved forward on this. I knew you were against it."

Wow. "Does that matter?"

His eyes were intense. "Yes. It matters a lot."

"Because you want me to support what you do?"

"No, because I want your opinion. You have common sense. I depend on it."

"You do? But you're the doctor. You know more."

"Maybe about medicine. Not about life."

Nicole didn't know what to think. Julian depending on her was a heady thought.

As she watched him, he grew self-conscious. "I also have questions. It isn't an easy decision." He looked out the window, then back. "Can we go for a walk or something?"

"Don't you have to get to the hospital?"

"Why?"

Here was bitterness. She was waiting to see if it would become anger and snowball into an accusation against her, when he let it go.

"I have a two o'clock meeting," he conceded, slipping into the old Julian, professional and composed. "It's a first pregnancy. There are early signs of left ventricular hypoplasia in the fetus and, understandably, the mom is off the wall. I can't do the surgery myself, but since it's my technique, I may be able to reassure her. My name is still worth something." He rose. "Out?"

*   *   *

They walked leisurely. Though the heat and humidity were high, the familiarity of the city was reassuring at a time when their lives were in flux. Julian held her hand and, later, looped her elbow through his. He seemed to want the connection. Hungry for it herself, Nicole refused to think beyond the moment.

Eventually reaching the park at Rittenhouse Square, they found an empty bench by the fountain, where the movement of water could soothe. Pedestrian traffic was light, but the normalcy of other people was calming as well. Julian stretched out his legs, ankles crossed, and though his arms were folded, their elbows remained linked.

When he asked about Kaylin, Nicole described her visit in a level-headed way. She even remained composed when he asked about Angie. From the perspective of Philadelphia and Julian, the issue of Tom just didn't seem as important, though Julian asked all the right questions regarding loyalty to Bob. Same with not selling the house. Nicole was still trying to process the meaning of that.

The questions ended. Tearing her eyes from the fountain, she found him studying her. She smiled, puzzled.

"Your voice is different," he remarked. "The way you speak. It's more blunt."

"Like Charlotte?" she asked, feeling a fondness she wouldn't have thought herself capable of not so long ago. Either old habits died hard, or new ones were, yes, more forgiving.

Whatever, he gave a short shrug with his brows. "I couldn't say. I barely knew her."

Accepting that at least, Nicole explained, "She's had to deal with a lot in her life, so she doesn't waste words. When she speaks, you listen. People tune me out sometimes. I feel like I need to fill the silence, whether I have something to say or not. It's the insecure me."

"It's the sociable you, and I like your voice," he said gently. "It's unique."

"Childlike?"

"Sweet."

She sighed. "Then along came reality." She waited. He looked torn, but they had to discuss the next medical step. Sitting in the midmorning quiet of a public garden was as good a place as any. "Your turn," she cued.

Releasing her arm, he leaned forward, put his elbows on his knees, and knotted his hands. He was slow to speak, seeming to struggle, unsure where to start. Finally, with the quickest glance back at her, he said, "I've been reading MS blogs."

That surprised her. He had always resisted. "You said they didn't relate to you."

"They don't in the sense of work. It's what I do for a living that makes this so bad for me. But that doesn't mean others don't have problems. And some of them don't have access to the kinds of doctors we do."

She might have said he was right, that it was about time he moved past self-pity and looked outside himself. But that would have been filling the silence again, and she was through doing that. Julian needed to talk. She waited for him to go on.

Finally, frowning at the ground, he said, "I feel like I'm on a precipice. I know that sounds melodramatic, but I've never been in a situation like this. My patients have. They put the lives of their babies in my hands all the time, or they used to. I was the one in control. But I'm not now. I can't control the doctor, can't control the process, can't control the results. I read those blogs and tell myself that if I return to a more conventional treatment plan, I could go on for a long time with maybe minimal decline. Then I think of the things that I love that I wouldn't be able to do." His frown deepened, dark brows more pronounced in profile. "I ask my patients to take risks. Can I not do it myself?" He considered that, hands clenched tighter. "So I'm here on the edge, knowing that if I decide to jump, I could either fly or fall." When he looked at her, he was fighting tears. "I don't know what in the hell to do."

Heartbroken, she came forward so that they were arm to arm, thigh to thigh, and leaned into him for several minutes. Then, feeling trepidation, she turned her head on his shoulder. "You still want that cure."

His eyes were frightened when they met hers, his voice low. "Yes."

His fear somehow modulated her own. "Umbilical cord stem cells," she breathed, just to be sure.

He nodded. "If I'm going for it, I'd rather go for it all."

"In spite of the risks?" she asked, and held her breath.

He hesitated, then said softly, "I want a cure. I tell myself that it doesn't matter as long as I'm alive. Only it does. I want it for me, but I also want it for you, for *us*, so that I can be the kind of husband you deserve. And I want it for others who are facing what we are." Voice still low, he said, "Here's another way I'm different from those bloggers. I've seen the success that can come when you take a chance on a new technique. I know how breakthroughs happen. It has to start with someone being willing to try."

"It could go bad," she whispered, feeling like she was on a precipice herself. He wanted her support. She could be the one pushing him over the edge.

"I know. That scares the shit out of me. But these meds aren't working. I don't need blood work to tell me what's happening. If I'm not off them soon, my liver is gone." His breathing was unsteady. "I want to try, Nicole."

And there it was, a choice as simple as loving him and wanting him happy. This was the hand they'd been dealt. The cards said that if he ever had a shot at winning, he needed this.

His eyes mirrored that need. She was lost in them for a final, pleading moment, before ceding the fight. "Then you should."

He gave a little jerk, clearly surprised. "You didn't think so before."

"I didn't understand how torn you were. I wasn't sure you'd thought it through."

"Oh, I have. I've thought it through six ways from Sunday. I could die. I could live and be cured and still not be allowed in the operating room. I could live but be severely debilitated just because of the treatment. I could live and be a vegetable. I know the risks."

The final, pleading moment was hers now. Once the words were said, they couldn't be taken back. But he wanted this. She could only imagine how much.

Taking a last breath, she swallowed, then said softly, "There's something that could lessen them." She loved him and, fly or fall, she owed him this. "Charlotte had a baby."

His expression was blank. *Which has to do with what?* it said. After a minute of utter silence, though, the blankness dissolved.

"She had *my* baby?" he whispered in horror. Sitting up straight, he exhaled in a sharp gust. "*My* child?"

"It isn't yours or hers now." Briefly, she explained.

His expression went from shock to confusion. "She said nothing."

"What could she say? Think about it. What were her choices?"

He sank back against the bench. To his credit, he remained stunned. "And you're sure it's mine?"

"She says she wasn't with anyone else. If she had been—if there was the slightest chance the baby wasn't yours—she wouldn't have confessed to having the cells."

"Cells from a child guarantee at least a partial match." But he was still struggling with the other. "She carried my child for nine months without a word? Who helped her?"

"No one. She was alone."

He considered that in silence.

"Would you have fought her?" Nicole finally asked, because that did impact her. Oh, abortion wasn't an option. None of them would have wanted that. But had Julian taken the baby, Nicole's life would have radically changed, and not only in the sense of having a baby to raise. Surrogate motherhood was one thing, but a baby conceived in a moment's betrayal? Charlotte would have forever been part of their marriage. The marriage might not have survived.

He was a while thinking about that, before finally shaking his head.

"Do you want to know about the baby?" she asked cautiously.

He thought again, then shook his head once more. "I can't. Not now. Tell me about the cells."

"They're frozen. Charlotte owns them until the child is eighteen."

He considered that, then let out another breath. "I'm not sure if this makes my decision easier or harder."

"Why harder?" she asked.

"It's suddenly real." Un-Julian-like, he pushed a hand through his hair, then clung to the back of his neck. "If there's a match, I'd have an edge. That may be too good to pass up. But it could still backfire." His eyes shot to hers. "I could still die."

"Not a good word, Jules," she warned quietly. "Do you trust Hammon?"

"Yes."

She took his hand—so cold again—and held it to the pulse at her throat. "Like your patients trust you?" When he nodded, she said, "Then if anyone can minimize the risk, it's him."

They were quiet returning to the house. Julian didn't rush to pick up the phone, but sat in the living room, brooding. Nicole guessed that a small part of him was still trying to process the fact of that night ten years ago having produced a child. More, though, to judge from the indecision on his face, he was revisiting those six ways from Sunday with this new information.

When she came to sit on the arm of his chair, he slipped his own arm around her waist. When she brought him lunch, he ate everything she served. And when he went off to his two o'clock meeting, she gave him a hug and let him go. She didn't ask what he was thinking, and though she was dying to know, she wouldn't hover. They were in this together. She believed that now in ways she hadn't before. She knew her husband. He was a self-contained man. He would speak when he had something to say.

When he returned from the hospital, he did. While there, he had called New York. Peter Keppler agreed with him about the liver problem and, understanding the next step, returned him to a more conventional drug. Julian also called Mark Hammon, who apparently began the conversation holding to the idea of an autologous transplant, until he electronically accessed the latest blood work.

"My counts are too low," Julian told Nicole now. "We won't be able to get a good collection of cells from me, so it'll have to be donor cells. If Charlotte is telling the truth, those UCB cells would be a gift. Mark is excited. That's the first time I've heard it from him. But he's cautious. He wants me to think through everything again. He also wants me to recuperate." Cautious himself now, he said, "I want to go to Quinni-peague, Nicki. It's the best place to rest. And Charlotte's there. She and I have to talk."

Nicole's first high little voice cried *no no no*. She had just found her husband again and couldn't bear to risk losing him to a woman with whom he'd had an affair, or whatever you wanted to call it. Seeing them separately was one thing, but together—and on *Quinnipeague? Her* island? Her *haven*—which wasn't the haven it used to be, thanks to these very same two people?

When the deeper, grown-up voice emerged, though, it said that, of course, Julian had to talk with Charlotte. Nicole had opened the door to that herself by telling him about the cord blood. He and Charlotte had a connection that wasn't ending anytime soon.

She wasn't sure which frightened her more—his having a stem cell transplant or his seeing Charlotte. But both were part of the new real-ity. If Angie was right, Nicole had to accept it and move on.

That said, moving on involved Charlotte in more ways than one. That cord blood could either save or kill. Having encouraged Julian to use it, Nicole felt the weight of responsibility. She wanted to share it with the woman who had made it possible.

Chapter Twenty-three

CHARLOTTE FELT THE WEIGHT. IT had been on her shoulders for more than a month, heavier after she told Nicole about the baby and even heavier now. Hour after hour with no word? She was dying to know what was going on but was reluctant to inject herself into what had to be a difficult time between Nicole and Julian.

When finally, *finally* on Wednesday morning Nicole texted, she was relieved only until she read the note. Sitting at Leo's desk, she reread it in dismay, then held the phone away and cried, "I've been waiting to hear for two days, and this is the best she can do? *Returning tomorrow, can u pick up at pier?*"

"Text her back," Leo suggested and, of course, it was the sensible thing to do, only Charlotte hadn't been good at being sensible since Nicole had left. Too much was at stake—Julian's health and Nicole's marriage, not to mention the future of her friendship with Nicole.

Now she texted, *What happened?*

I'll tell you tomorrow, Nicole replied, to which Charlotte made an exasperated sound.

Leo was reading over her shoulder. "Write her back."

Does he know? Charlotte texted.

Yes.

And . . . ?

Tomorrow. Can't talk now.

Tossing the phone across the desk, Charlotte turned on Leo again. "Here is a woman who can find a dozen different ways of saying the same thing in one conversation, and she refuses to talk now? Does she not know that I've been waiting?"

"Waiting *anxiously*," Leo remarked, dropping into his chair and tipping back.

Supersensitive, she studied him. "Are you mocking me?"

"No no. But your mind hasn't been here." He glanced at her laptop. "Get any good work done today? Yesterday?"

"You know I didn't," she remarked, "but look who's talking. You say it's because *Next Book* sucks, but you won't let me read it, so I can't even give you encouragement. I want encouragement, Leo." If they had any future as a couple, he had to learn. "That's what I need right now."

Lowering his brows, he considered, then said, "I think you've done all the right things."

She sighed.

"What?" he asked defensively.

"Tell me that Julian and Nicole will be okay."

"You want me to lie? I don't know what's going to happen." His brows went even lower. "And anyway, why does it matter so much? You hadn't seen her in ten years. You drifted apart."

"Which was totally my fault," Charlotte stated, "and which I seriously regret and had hoped to move past by coming here this summer. Nicole's the only friend I have who knew me when we were kids. There's something to be said for that."

Leo righted his chair. "I wouldn't know," he said quietly, his dark eyes penetrating. "But you weren't close to your parents, either."

Livid, she said, "Excuse me, is the pot calling the kettle black? My parents are as dead as your mom, but your dad is not. What does he do, by the way? When Nicki and I were in Rockland, I kept thinking I'd see someone who looked like you."

"Not likely. He'd have been the one strutting around in khakis with a bill cap, dark glasses, a patch on his arm, and a gun at his hip."

"He's a *cop?*"

"Chief of."

"*Seriously?*" But he wouldn't kid about something like that. His father, the chief of police? Whoa. "When was the last time you talked with him?" Leo was silent. "Don't you think you should? Don't you think he should know what you're doing with your life? He isn't a nobody, Leo. Don't you think he would be *proud?*"

He stared at her. "No. He would not be proud."

"Why not?"

"Because he said I'd never make anything of my life if I stayed here, so he'd have to eat crow, and that's not his favorite meal."

Leo rarely spoke of his father. The fact that she rarely spoke of her parents was a thread they had shared. But his father was alive, and clearly a sore point. Speaking of him now brought the vulnerability to his stare that got to her every time. Parts of his past were as dark as his eyes.

Remorseful, she reached for his hand. "I'm sorry. I didn't mean to push."

"You did," he said flatly. "It's been in the back of your mind."

"Maybe, but it isn't my business."

He didn't answer, simply continued to stare at her in a way that said it was her business, because whatever they had was growing deeper by the day, so they had to know each other better if they had a prayer in hell of understanding why he wouldn't leave Quinnipeague and she couldn't stay.

So much unspoken. Charlotte knew it, too. A cop? Amazing. "What do you hate most about him?"

He finally blinked, took a breath, lowered his eyes to their linked hands, seeming to take comfort in them. "That he never came here.

Like it wasn't worth his time." He studied their fingers, woven so well it was hard to tell whose was whose.

"He must have been here when you were conceived."

"It happened there."

"How do you know?"

He met her gaze. "When I realized I didn't just sprout like her plants, I asked Cecily."

"At which point, she explained the facts of life?"

"Oh no. I got those from other kids. Took a lot of crap for not knowing. Not that they knew much. They knew nothing about the beauty." Lifting their hands, he separated out fingers enough to kiss hers.

And again, her heart clenched. He could do this as no other man ever had—could turn distance into something utterly sweet. Or maybe it was his way of expressing love, because she sensed that he felt that, too.

"I'm sorry," she said again. "I can be a bitch."

"Not all the time." He smiled his tough-guy, poignant smile.

She lingered on it a minute before sliding a discouraged glance at the phone. "I tell myself that I'm just the messenger. They tell me they want the cells, I make a call, that's it. Only it isn't. Each step of the way, I care what happens." She thought about the moment. "And then there's the cookbook. I expected Nicole to be gone a week. You're right. I haven't written much."

"But you knitted." The yarn bag lay on the floor. Having gotten the knack of the cables, she was nearly done with the second sleeve. "Who's it for?"

She sighed. "Me. I guess. At least, the process is. I feel better when I knit. Like you do when you whittle." Totally the process for him. Though he never seemed to finish anything, he wasn't bad at it. She could always tell what he was trying to make.

His expression turned wry. "My alternative isn't wandering around aimlessly."

"Do I do that?"

"Sometimes." He gave her hand a little shake. "Why don't you call her? Be honest. Tell her the wait's killing you."

She considered doing that. "But if Julian is there, she wouldn't be able to talk and, besides, my impatience is petty compared to what she's living through."

Leo tipped back again, though nowhere near as nonchalantly this time. He looked like he wanted to help but didn't know how. "You're a good friend," he finally said, which did help, as did a reprise of that poignant smile, not to mention the rest of him. His hair was tousled, his eyes intimate and direct. He wore his black gym shorts and a tank top that showed a little chest hair and a lot of shoulder. He was barefooted, which seemed to be his preference, though she was barefooted now herself. The day was warm. The French doors were open; the ocean rolled in on the shore less than fifty feet away, directing the sweetest of salt scents their way.

Taken as always by both it and him, she wheeled her chair around so that she faced him, slipped her hands up his thighs, and sighed.

"What?" he asked in amusement—because he could read her thoughts, which were lewd. What with the splayed way he sat, the shadow on his jaw and the engaged look in his eyes, he was good enough to eat.

But she had already done that earlier.

Sex with Leo continued to amaze. And the amazement wasn't hers alone. A lot of what they did was new to him, too. They were well suited to each other in this regard.

But sex couldn't sustain a relationship. And it didn't work long distance. Having been on Quinnipeague for four weeks, she had another four to go. Then Paris. Which she loved. Then Tuscany. Which she loved.

She sighed again. "Can we do something?"

He smirked. "That?"

"No. Like sail."

He thought for a minute. "How about Jet Ski?"

She eyed him askance. "I do not see a Jet Ski at your dock."

Hauling her up by the armpits, he kissed her firmly on the mouth and said, "Being a best-selling novelist has its advantages. People are eager to please. I know one we can borrow. Interested?"

In a distraction? "You bet."

Zooming around the island on a Jet Ski was a fine distraction.

Same with having dinner at the Chowder House, which meant confirming what most Quinnies already knew about their being involved. Even Dorey Jewett's arched brow, less warning than intrigued, gave Charlotte a warm feeling.

And making love on the sand that night? Lying naked under the stars afterward? Washing the salt off in his Jacuzzi, then making love all over again in his bed?

Distractions all, but finite. Wednesday came soon enough, and Charlotte woke up worried. That was when Leo led her through the garden and into the forest. He spent a few minutes searching before Bear sniffed it out, at which point Leo knelt and pulled back a mass of fern fronds to reveal low clusters of what appeared to be red four-leaf clovers. They looked oddly mystical.

"What *are* they?" she asked, squatting beside him.

"I don't know. But they make wishes come true."

"Seriously?"

"That's what Cecily said. She hid them around the forest."

More than happy to set reality aside a bit longer, Charlotte was charmed. "Make wishes come true, huh?"

"That's what she said."

"Like regular green four-leaf clovers?"

He shrugged.

"Then you don't know for sure?"

"If they work? Cecily claimed they did. She only gave them to very special, very loyal friends, and they don't talk." Picking one, he held the bud by its tiny stem. "Close your eyes and make a wish."

Charlotte closed her eyes and wished for Leo. Then she looked at the bed of petals. Regular four-leaf clovers were one in ten thousand, but when it came to red, there had to be hundreds in the clump. "Can I make more than one wish?"

Tucking the first clover into her tank top, under the lace of her bra, right by her heart, he picked another. "Close your eyes."

She closed her eyes and wished for a cure for MS. "One more?" This time, she wished for Nicole and Julian to live happily every after.

She now had three petals tucked in her bra, but when she went to remove them, Leo covered her hand.

"They have to stay with you for three days."

"On me?"

"Or in a pocket."

"What happens after three days?"

"They dry up and die. By that time the wish is either rooted or not."

Charlotte eyed him skeptically. "Are you kidding me?"

"Would I risk Cecily's wrath by lying?" he asked, fully serious.

No. She guessed he wouldn't. Still, red clover that made wishes come true? "Could I take a little clump and plant it in Nicole's garden?"

Leo looked like he was about to refuse. Then he paused, frowned. "I guess you could. The valerian is still alive." He held up a hand, *stay*, and loped off for a trowel and pail.

Charlotte planted the clover with care, encircling the small patch with wire mesh so that one of the Mayes men didn't mistake the clover for weeds and pull it out. She tamped the soil a final time, watered it, then went inside to clean up. Taking the petals from her bra, she showered, dressed in a clean tank and shorts, and slipped them into her pocket. They were wilting, much as ordinary clover would do. She wasn't sure they were magic at all, but could she risk it and throw them away?

* * *

The ferry was due at two and, sure enough, several minutes before that it appeared on the horizon, etching a V of foam in the waves. Reaching the pier, it turned and slowly backed in.

Of the half dozen passengers waiting at the top of the ramp, Nicole was the most stunning. She wore white capris, a turquoise silk blouse from her Philly stash, and a multicolored scarf, just taken from her hair, which, with just a touch of the wind, looked as chic as ever. Eyes on Charlotte, she waited until four others debarked before starting down.

That was when Charlotte saw Julian. Startled, she caught her breath.

But of course he would come. He would want to talk with her, which she didn't particularly want, which was likely why she had blotted out the possibility and why Nicole hadn't mentioned it. Not that Nicole had mentioned much.

Ten years, four of them ill, had aged him. He still stood straight, and was trim and well dressed. But leaving the ramp, he walked with a deliberateness that wasn't quite natural, and he looked exhausted. That didn't keep him from staring at her with a handful of questions and a glint of accusation.

The accusation hit her the wrong way. This was the first time she'd seen him since learning she was pregnant—and he was accusing *her* of something? What about *him*? While he had been enjoying newly married bliss, she had been dealing with loneliness, fear, and pain. *Why hadn't he worn a condom?* A responsible man would have done that, drunk or not—or so she had reasoned quite unreasonably when life had seemed dark.

Once the baby was gone, she had put the anger behind her and moved on. Now it roared back.

What to do? She touched a cheek to Nicole's in token greeting. But Julian? What could she bear? A nod? A handshake?

Following his lead, she did nothing. Ignoring him as best she could, she took Nicole's bag and carried it to the car.

*   *   *

Her anger eased during the drive to the house, but not without great effort and ongoing internal monologue. *It's over, Charlotte. Let it go. You were the one who chose to freeze cord blood. Focus on that.*

Julian rode shotgun for the sake of legroom, but Nicole proceeded to fill what would have otherwise been an uncomfortable silence by leaning up between the seats to talk to him about seasonal changes. Charlotte might have asked her to put on her seat belt, if she hadn't been so grateful to have a head between Julian's and hers. Each time she felt his stare, she wanted to shout, *Yes, I had your baby and gave her away, but you were married and I was alone.* Each time, she returned to her mantra. *It's over, Charlotte. Let it go.*

Anger and guilt mixed in waves, building on an awkwardness that neither the ocean air that blew through the open windows nor the bursts of coral and red flowers that lined the route could touch. As soon as they had settled in at the house, with Julian on the patio and Nicole searching the fridge for dinner-makings, Charlotte approached her.

"Would you rather I not be here? I could stay at Leo's. That way you'd have the house to yourselves."

"What would you rather?" came a distracted reply.

"I asked first."

Nicole rifled through the vegetable bin, then the freezer. "He needs red meat," she murmured, straightening with one hand on the refrigerator door and another pushing up the back of her hair. "I want fresh everything. I'll go back to town."

"I'll go," Charlotte offered, perhaps a bit too readily, but if she couldn't get answers, she needed an out.

Letting the fridge close on its own, Nicole went through the kitchen door to the garden. Following her for a shopping list, Charlotte found her bent over the valerian.

"These are doing well," she said, putting her nose to the petals and inhaling. Still doubled over, she peered up at Charlotte. Her distraction was totally gone. "What did it feel like seeing him? Be honest with me. I need to know."

Oh, she did. It struck Charlotte this was why Nicole hadn't given her fair warning that Julian was coming. She also suspected that he hadn't known she would be at the pier. Nicole had wanted candid reactions.

Like Charlotte could hide hers? "It did not feel good," she stated.

Nicole studied her with sharp green eyes. "Worse than during the wedding?"

"Way worse. I mean, hell, he was looking at me like I was an ogre, but it wasn't like I did this on my own. He was careless—"

"I thought he was drunk."

"Drunk *is* careless," Charlotte cried, not caring if Julian heard. "He's a fine one to be accusing me of *anything*. I was the one who took the hit for that night—and since it nearly killed our friendship, you did, too. *He* got off scot-free. I didn't have to mention those stem cells, Nicole. If he wants to use them, he should be damn grateful I did."

Nicole was taken aback. "I hadn't realized you were angry."

"Yeah, well, seeing him brought it all back. So there's your answer." Taking the lavender for herself, she leaned in, closed her eyes, inhaled, calmed. When she straightened, she felt better, not that she regretted the outburst. Catharsis had value on many levels. "Besides," she went on, in answer to Nicole's question, "during the wedding, we could ignore the whole thing. Now we can't." *It's over, Charlotte. Let it go.* "Does he want the cord blood or not?"

With a last inhalation, Nicole stood. "Yes. He wants it. We're here because he needs to rest first. He fights the fatigue, but it's constant, and you saw how jaundiced he is. The neurologist put him back on safer drugs. He needs to stabilize and regain strength before the other."

The other. Charlotte tried to interpret her tone, but this Nicole wasn't as transparent as the old one. So she asked, "Are you still against it?"

"*Terrified*," Nicole cried. "I mean, have the two of us signed his death warrant?" Seeming desperate for comfort, she eyed the flowers. "But how can I tell him no, when it means the world to him?" Her gaze wandered, stumbling into the fenced-in patch. "What is that?"

"Red clover," Charlotte said, explaining the how and why of it as she approached. Picking a single leaf, she offered it to Nicole. "Make a wish."

"You believe in this kind of thing?"

"Don't you?" Charlotte asked in surprise, because where gullible went, Nicole usually led the pack. "This is a Cecily thing."

Nicole let out a breath. "I've grown up. I don't believe like I used to." But she was eying the clover with something that looked suspiciously like longing. Finally, grabbing the tiny leaf, she said, "Screw that. I am in dire need of a wish," and closed her eyes tightly. When she opened them, she seemed calmer.

Taking advantage of that, Charlotte repeated her original question. "Should I stay with Leo while Julian is here?"

"Were you with him while I was gone?"

"Back and forth."

"What do you see in him?"

"There are times when I haven't a clue. He has serious baggage."

"But you're spending nights with him."

"I *love* him."

Nicole's green eyes widened. "Seriously?"

Startled by her own admission, Charlotte considered the words. Thinking them was one thing, saying them aloud another. Forcing herself to breathe, she said, "I guess so."

"But you're leaving in four weeks."

"I know."

"And he won't leave."

"No."

Shifting to the adjacent topic, Nicole asked, "How's work going?"

"It's going."

"What's left?"

Charlotte reeled off the list. She tried to make light of its length, but with most entrées and their related interviews still not done, not to mention intros, connectors, and closings, there was lots to do.

Nicole let out a frightened breath.

"We can do it," Charlotte assured her.

"But I may have to leave again," she warned. "If the doctor wants Julian in Chicago, I can't let him go alone. Should I ask for an extension of my deadline?"

"No." An extension wouldn't help Charlotte. She had to be on a plane in four weeks. "I'll make it happen if I have to pull all-nighters the whole last week," she promised. This wasn't only about work ethic. It was about atonement and redemption.

That said, three was a crowd. Tension between Julian and her could make for uncomfortable days. "I'm happy to work at Leo's."

"No," Nicole said, suddenly decisive. "Work here. Julian needs to talk with you, anyway. You're one of the reasons he came."

Julian didn't seek her out until the next morning. Charlotte had already been into town for an interview and was at the patio table, typing it up on her laptop, when he emerged from the house. Wearing surprisingly stylish cargo shorts and a wool crewneck sweater—Nicole's doing, she bet—he looked marginally rested.

Deliberately, she finished typing her thought. Then she sat back in the chair and waited. He owed her something after all she'd done for him.

"I'm sorry," he said wisely, conscious at some level of her anger. Nicole's doing, too?

"Do not judge me," she warned softly. "My sympathy for you only goes so far."

He glanced at the nearest lounge. "Do you mind if I sit?"

She moved her head. *Whatever.*

He stretched out, crossed his ankles, and pushed his hands into his pockets.

And since he had opened the dialogue, Charlotte was only too happy to take part. "The last thing you should be is angry at me," she said. "I did what I had to do. I wanted Nicole to be happy."

He sat, seeming deep in thought. As she watched him, she wondered for the gazillionth time how she could have ever been in his arms. She felt no physical draw at all.

Finally, he said, "I had no idea." About the child.

"That was the point. I never wanted this to spoil your marriage."

He made a sardonic sound. "Funny how health issues can trump most else."

He didn't have to elaborate. Annoyed as she was—unsympathetic as she wanted to be—Charlotte hadn't missed the tremor in his hand when he ate or the way he favored his right leg and too casually touched the backs of chairs to steady himself when he walked past.

"Did she look like one of us?" he asked quietly.

Feeling a twist of the old pain, Charlotte was somber. "I don't know. She was covered with gunk. And I was crying, so everything was blurred. They took her away right after that."

"Did you ever regret it?"

"Of *course* I regretted it. She was my child, my baby. But keeping her would have been wrong. I thought it then, and I think it now." She was clutching the wrought-iron arms of the chair. With a conscious effort, she relaxed her grip. "It's done, Julian. You can hate me forever, but she has a happy life."

He still seemed troubled. "Did you ever think about looking for her?"

"I'm not allowed to do that. Nor are you." She glanced up at the pergola with its lavish canopy of small, peach-colored roses, but their fragrance failed to take her to a happier place.

"Even just going to her school and watching her on the playground without her knowing?"

She struggled to stay composed. "What I'm *saying*, Julian, is that letting them take her from my arms was the hardest thing I've ever done, but she isn't mine anymore. Do I wonder sometimes? I wouldn't be human if I didn't. But to spy on her, then walk away a second time?" She gave a slow headshake.

"What if she comes looking for you someday?"

"Please. I can't go there. This isn't about the baby. It's about the cord blood."

"That's fine for you to say," he argued with an anger of his own. "You've had ten years to come to terms with it. I haven't."

He stared at her. She stared back.

"Does she know about the stem cells?" he finally asked.

"I doubt it."

"If she needed them and her parents came to you, what would you do?"

"If I had them, I'd give them. If they've already been used, I can't."

"Is she well?"

"I do not know. There is no contact at all. Nothing."

Seeming to finally get the point, he stared at the ocean again, before meeting her gaze. "How do you retrieve the cord blood?"

This was better. This she could handle.

Then again, perhaps what she felt was relief. Venting her anger at Julian gave a kind of closure to that night on the beach. What came next was part of moving on.

"I call. The bank will overnight whatever you need. They froze separate one-milliliter samples for the sake of matching. They also did DNA testing when the cord blood first came in."

"Is that standard?"

"I don't know about other banks, but it is for this one. They use the results for identification purposes as much as anything, kind of like a serial number. So if you doubt she's your child—"

He waved off the possibility.

Grateful for that at least, Charlotte mellowed. "You should know, Julian, that I hadn't planned on telling Nicole any of this."

He swallowed. "It worked out. We're stronger, she and I."

"I'm glad. She's my best friend. I would do most anything for her sake."

He took a deep breath and raised his eyes to hers. "Then it's time. I want the cord blood. Will you make the call?"

Chapter Twenty-four

SINGLING OUT THE SMALL RECTANGULAR tag from others on her key ring, Charlotte called the number there and gave the necessary information. After a follow-up fax to confirm her identity, the cord blood was on its way to Chicago.

And what was there to say then?

Julian had already been in touch with the doctor, but called back now with shipment details.

Nicole sat beside him on the patio, looking like her heart was in her mouth as the arrangements were defined. She left him only for the minute it took to go to the garden, pick another clover, and return.

And Charlotte? With her part done, she headed for the beach and walked until she found a sheltered rock. Nestling in, she hugged her knees and stared out. Under a steady wind, the ocean was a mass of whitecaps that hit the shore in a reverberating rush, all wet and mired with spume. But she didn't feel the wildness inside. She wasn't upset. Nor was she gratified, though. And she certainly wasn't smug. Sitting alone with granite at her back, cold sand under her butt, and the wind whipping her hair over her face, then away, over and back, hiding then exposing, she wasn't sure what she felt at all.

"You okay?" Nicole asked, seeming surprisingly strong against the elements in her jeans, sweater, and thick-wrapped scarf.

Charlotte felt a prick of annoyance. She had left the patio to give Nicole and Julian private time. But this was hers. "Everything good back there?" she asked in what was, in essence, a polite dismissal—as in, *unless you need me, please leave.*

"I guess. Once Hammon gets the cells, he'll start work in the lab."

With a brief nod, Charlotte returned to the sea, but the hint must have been too subtle, because rather than leaving, Nicole began to talk.

"Once the cells are thawed, Hammon has to select out the regulatory T cells. They're the ones that hold the secret to a cure, and you only find them in umbilical cord blood. Know why? A baby may not be compatible with its mother—like, different blood type or whatever. Regulatory T cells make it possible for the baby to thrive in the womb regardless of that. This is the same reason you don't need a perfect match when you do a transplant using regulatory T cells. They're like magic bullets. We're just beginning to understand the kinds of illnesses they may help."

Holding her hair back on the side farthest from Nicole, Charlotte glanced up as a seagull flew past, but it was another subtle gesture missed.

"He cultures the T cells and expands them," Nicole went on. "I mean, the numbers are ridiculous. He may get a few million from the original sample and then expand them in nineteen days to, like, a thousand *times* that, so he'll have enough for an adult transplant. This guy is good, Charlotte. This is all research for him, so he'll keep track of every little detail. He's going away in September, so he wants to do the transplant by the middle of August to make sure he's around for two or three weeks afterward to be sure Julian's okay."

She was trying to sound confident, like this was all just another medical procedure, and she wanted reassurance. But Charlotte wasn't in the mood to coddle her. Pushing up from the rock, she said, "I think I need to walk," and set off.

"Want company?" Nicole called, sounding frightened.

But Charlotte tuned that out. "No." She didn't understand what she was feeling, she only knew she didn't want Nicole around.

Walking toward the tail of the island, she crossed patches of sand, skirting boulders and low rocks. She stopped when she reached the spot where she had been with Julian. There was no pain from that memory now. Nicole knew what had happened and was benefitting from it.

But Charlotte felt pain from something. Trying to figure it out, she stood for a time, oblivious to the punishing wind, before continuing on.

As she neared Cole land, the route roughened. Boulders were larger at spots, spilling at length into the sea. She debated swimming around them. Hell, she was wading in and out of the shallows already, and with the gush of the incoming surf, her sneakers and lower jeans were wet. If the rest of her got wet, too? She would dry.

That said, she wasn't suicidal. The water was wild, the depth of the rocks unknown, and undertow a possibility. So she turned inland, climbing up over granite, plodding through heath and thick grass, then scrambling back down when sand reappeared. Two, three, four times she did this, the last being the hardest. Here was the forested patch bordering the spot where she first swam with Leo. The boulders were more jagged here, the woods dense. She stumbled over roots and tangled underbrush, and scrabbled on all fours over the trickiest rocks before reaching sea level again.

The beach where they had made love was a puddle. Splashing through, she continued on over a floor of stones, over a last granite patch, through the overhang of trees and around the curve to the tip of the island and Leo's house.

The office door was open. He would be working.

But she didn't go in. This wasn't about him. It was about feelings that disturbed her but that she couldn't name, and about needing to be at the most soothing spot on Quinnipeague.

So she walked all the way to the end of the dock and sat cross-legged with her elbows on her knees. The ocean was as wild as before, but the last outcropping of rocks over which she had climbed was a natural breakwater, calming the surf at the dock. In keeping, his boat rocked gently against its lines.

No, this wasn't about Leo. But she didn't feel the full effect of the soothing until his footsteps vibrated on the dock.

Bare feet was all she saw. He scratched the top of her head, then leaned over her. "You okay?" he asked just as Nicole had, but with an entirely different effect. Lowering her face to her knees, she began to cry.

"Hey," he whispered, lowering to his haunches. His hand slipped to her nape, stroking gently, but he let her cry.

In time, she took a ragged breath and, wiping her face, raised her head. "Oh God," she whispered, embarrassed. "Where did that come from?"

He didn't answer, simply sank down, folded his legs, and faced her.

"He wants the stem cells, so I made the call," she said, looking any-where but at him. "I should feel pleased that I was able to help. Or re-lieved that it's done." Her eyes filled again, her voice high and broken. "So why do I feel so . . . nothing?"

"Empty."

She pushed her fingers against her eyes. "Yes."

"They were yours all this time, Charlotte. Now they're gone."

"But it was just blood, frozen away in some anonymous repository."

"It was a link."

"I gave her up. I've been just fine without her."

"It was a link," he repeated quietly.

Chin in her hands, fingers spread over her face, she admitted a soft, "Yes." And now the link was gone. "But that isn't why I kept them—" She caught herself. "Or maybe it was and I didn't know it? Why else would I be upset now?"

Unfolding his legs, he turned her and pulled her close. With her back to his front, he cinched her in with his arms, but the quiet of that only lasted until she looped her fingers around his wrists.

"*Jeez*," he breathed in horror, "what in the hell happened to your hands!"

She straightened them, only then seeing the scrapes. Some were a superficial white, some more pink, others outright crusted with blood. "I had to hike to get here. It was either that or swim."

"You couldn't *drive*?"

"And spoil my dramatic departure from the house?" she asked, self-mocking. "Absolutely not."

"Let's get those cleaned," he said, but when he started to stand, she clamped her arms on his to prevent it.

"Let's sit here. Just a couple more minutes, okay?"

After a healthy disinfecting with sage soap and a cup of passionflower tea sipped for calm, Leo dropped her back at the house. Nicole was at the kitchen table with her laptop, eyes on the door in anticipation when she came through, but she didn't speak, for which Charlotte was grateful. The cells were gone. Nothing Nicole said could bring them back.

Determined to move on, Charlotte asked, "Are you blogging?"

"Just finished. There was an interesting piece in today's *Wall Street Journal* comparing farm-raised and wild salmon. Readers always wonder. So I talked a little about PCBs. I mean, we don't know exactly how harmful they are, but they're definitely there in farm-raised fish. Right now, I'm writing the introduction to the chapter on FISH."

Charlotte heard nervousness in the chatter. But if the talk was of fish, she could bear it.

"No PCBs here, it's pure sea-to-table," Nicole went on, "but I want to change the name to SEAFOOD. A lot of people think of FISH as white fish or fish with a soft skin as opposed to SHELLFISH, like lobster and scallops. But I don't want two separate chapters. SEAFOOD covers it all, don't you think?"

"Yes."

She frowned, thoughtful. "That's actually a good idea for a blog—fish versus shellfish, what each includes and why. Cookbooks sometimes confuse the two, but they really are different."

She babbled on, definitely nervous energy, Charlotte realized. She would be second-guessing the stem cell route, wondering if these weeks would be the best she'd ever have with Julian again and whether he would be functional after this treatment was done.

Had Charlotte been the frenzied type, she might have babbled, too, though not about fear for Julian's health, and not about losing the cells. She understood herself more now, and while she hadn't expected to feel buyer's remorse, it was what it was. Leo had said it; those cells were a link. Gone now, she had to let go.

Her own nervous energy was quieter, and it had less to do with UCB cells than with time. She was leaving in four weeks. The comfort Leo had given her just now was sweet, so sweet, and perfect for her. She would never find it in another man. She had been around long enough to know that. But it was the same old same old. He wouldn't leave and she couldn't stay. What to do?

"Hel-lo?" Nicole called softly.

Charlotte blinked. "Sorry. What did you say?"

"I said we need to brainstorm. I am freaking out about what we have left to do in a very short period of time, and the only way I can see us getting through is to make lists and assign dates and put everything on a schedule. They want a completed draft by August fifteenth, but I don't even think I'll be here then. Can we redo the schedule to speed things up?"

We just spent two hours with a calendar, Charlotte e-mailed Leo later that afternoon, while she was organizing the interviews on her laptop. *Made an accelerated outline for the rest of the cookbook. She printed out four copies of the schedule—one for each of us to keep in clear sight, one for the note board in the kitchen, one for her purse. Nicole likes organization.*

Too much? he wrote back.

Maybe, but who am I to judge? I slipped through Yale on the seat of my pants, while she graduated magna from Middlebury, so clearly this works for her.

I didn't graduate from college. I didn't even go.

And look at you now, Charlotte replied, knowing he was testing her to see if she cared. *You're more successful than any of us.*

That was beginner's luck. I'm writing squat today.

Because you were busy playing shrink. Thank you, Leo. You helped.

Anytime, Charlotte. Another session tonight?

Charlotte wanted to be good. That meant trying her best to be attentive to Nicole, perhaps out of guilt for still feeling annoyed, more likely because the cookbook was her project, too.

That said, the time issue loomed. *Be there at nine,* she e-mailed.

Late dinner?

I'd like that.

Leo knew how to cook. His offerings were simple, like the strip steak he grilled that night, but he had a wicked way with herbs. Not that she was surprised, given his background. Still, the sight of his lean, long fingers expertly wielding a chopping knife in his new, relatively sleek, definitely state-of-the-art kitchen was such a contrast from dirt-crusted ones wielding a hammer, callused ones hauling up sails, and literary ones typing a book, that she found herself watching him in awe. Barefoot, he wore jeans and an open-neck shirt. When she found herself imagining how well he would fit into her Brooklyn neighborhood, she determinedly dragged herself back to the reality of the moment—which was tarragon butter, freshly drawn and dribbled over the steak, served with a salad that contained chives, basil, and a slew of other herbs she couldn't name.

"You know parsley," he said and pointed in turn at dill, marjoram, and arugula.

"Arugula? Huh. With these others, it looks like an herb."

"It is an herb."

"I thought it was a lettuce?"

Midnight-blue eyes were indulgent as he shook his head.

"Do you grow it in your garden?"

Amused, he nodded.

She took another taste of the salad. The dressing was a simple blend of olive oil and lemon juice that she had watched him squeeze. He had added fresh-ground pepper, but no salt. The salad didn't miss it. "Can I have this recipe for our book?"

He shook his head no.

"Even if I keep it anonymous?"

Another headshake. "You'll get other recipes like it. Herbs are a Quinnie thing."

You were right about that, too, Charlotte texted from town the next morning. *I just interviewed Carrie Samuels, and she gave me three different herb salad recipes.*

Three? he typed back.

Parsley, mixed herbs, and fennel.

Fennel. Good one. Why were you interviewing Carrie?

Age. And family. She's younger than me but with six siblings and four times that in aunts, uncles, and cousins, she has very deep roots. I envy that.

You envy roots?

Yeah. I don't have any.

Roots can be shackles.

Her thumbs hovered. Shackles were a negative, right? Was he complaining? If he wanted to cut roots and wander afield, she could help.

But he typed before she could reply, *I have plenty to share. Want some?*

She sighed. *You're the root guy, I'm the wanderlust girl. Is there a way to graft the two?* She sent the question, then, fearing a discussion that texting couldn't handle or, worse, an argument, quickly typed, *What's with fennel? Carrie gave me a quart of fennel soup for Julian. She says it's medicinal.*

It is, he replied, *but not for MS. Ask about her mother's pregnancies.*

Carrie's mother's pregnancies. That had not come up during the interview, but she figured if he had mentioned it, it was something to add. Climbing from the Wrangler, she ran back to the small cottage where Carrie lived with her husband and three kids, knocked on the door, and smiled apologetically. "One last question?"

Back in the Jeep a short time later, she typed, *Constant morning sickness, for which only fennel helped, and with seven babies in twelve years, she lived and breathed the stuff. Carrie wanted to know how I knew to ask, and while I was trying to think up an answer, she said she knew it was you. Is there something I don't know, Leo Cole?*

I used to deliver fennel to her mom. Carrie followed me around.

Puppy love?

(Snort.)

Well, Charlotte wrote, *I didn't confirm or deny that you were my source, so your virtue is safe.*

Thank you, Charlotte.

Thank you for the tip, Leo.

That afternoon Charlotte was pro-active. *I'm off to interview Mary Ellen Holloway,* she e-mailed before closing her laptop. *Anything special I should ask?*

The zucchini lady? I thought you were doing salads today.

Nicole says we have too much to do to limit ourselves.

What about the schedule?

She revised it again. So while she does a blanket sweep for recipes, I'm interviewing whoever commits to a time. She set up matching files on our computers for sorting. Zucchini is both a side and a snack. I've never had zucchini chips like Quinnie ones. (Sigh.) Why aren't you working????

Because I'm e-mailing you.

That won't pay the bills.

Neither will Next Book. I told you. It sucks.

When can I read it?

When it starts getting better. (Sigh.) Ask Mary Ellen about blossoms.

Blossoms?

Zucchini blossoms. She fries them.

OMG, Charlotte texted when, after two hours with Mary Ellen, she returned to the Wrangler. *ZBs are AMAZING. She just fried up a batch. Why didn't I know about them?*

Because she doesn't make them for island events. Didn't Nicole know?

She must not have, since she didn't have them on our list. Mary Ellen sent me home with what we didn't eat just now, plus zucchini bread for Julian. She knew all about him, BTW.

Quinnies talk. Are you coming over tonight?

Nicole wants to work. But I told her I'd be gone for the night tomorrow. Are you free?

They spent Saturday night grilling fat hot dogs on sticks over a fire on the beach, and, undressing only enough, made love on the sand in the embers' warmth. Taking refuge in his bed from the cool of the night, she fell asleep in his arms while he read Grisham's latest. His body heat held her close until the arrival of Sunday's sun, and when she awoke to his hands on her body, she was ready again.

"How do you do that?" she breathed after an orgasm that was stronger, deeper, more mind-blowing than any other.

His heart was thudding under her cheek. "Do what?" he asked hoarsely.

"Make me feel so much."

He didn't answer at first, simply stretched a hair-spattered leg between hers. Gradually, his pulse steadied. "Do I?"

She tipped her head back. Her fingers had left his damp hair a mess of dark spikes. The lines of his face were softer, but the midnight blue of his eyes was dark, and not with passion, she realized. She saw worry.

"What?" she asked softly. She wanted him to say it—say that he loved her and that she should stay. They weren't texting. They were together and naked. They could discuss this now.

But he simply drew her closer, kissed the top of her head, and held her until it was time to bring her breakfast in bed.

Charlotte spent Monday with Eleanor Bailey, owner of a must-have recipe for mini crab cakes as well as the biggest Quinnie heart. If there had been a formal hospitality committee on Quinnipeague, Eleanor would have chaired it. Since this was the crux of Charlotte's profile, they drove the island roads together, stopping to visit shut-ins, deliver groceries to others unable to get to the store, even prepare lunch for the four young children of a woman whose preemie baby was taking huge chunks of her time.

Eleanor was storing the leftovers from lunch in the fridge, when Charlotte's phone pinged.

S'up? he wrote.

I'm at the Blodgetts' with Eleanor. Too noisy to think. I'll get back to you. An hour later, she typed, *What a zoo.*

Lotsa little creatures?

Oh, yeah. S'up with you?

Down. Weekend sales. Just got word.

Why? When he named a new release, she wrote, *Ahh. That author's a biggie. Give him a week or two, and Salt'll be up again. Are you writing?*

No. Counting my direct deposits. Is it OK to text that? Which is safer— e-mail or text?

Text. It's through phone lines and doesn't go anywhere but your phone. E-mail sits on a server.

Why don't we talk on the phone?

Because Eleanor is two feet away.

I hope you're not driving and texting.

She's driving.

She's hell on wheels.

Now you tell me.

Can you come over later?

We're testing recipes.

Later later, then.

Absolutely.

Ten tonight? I'll be waiting between thyme and turmeric.

Turmeric. Sounds phallic.

TURMERIC, not tumescent. You have a dirty mind.

Takes one to know one. I've never seen turmeric.

It's related to ginger. The rhizome treats arthritis.

Rhizome?

Root.

That won't help me find you, she typed. "Work," she told Eleanor. "I'll be done in a sec." *Describe the above-ground part.*

It's phallic.

She snickered. *Ha ha.*

I'm serious.

So it'll look like you?

Am I phallic?

Part of you is.

Is this sexting?

No. We're not sending pics.

Want to?

Funny boy.

Is that a no?

Absolutely. You may be Mr. Anonymous, but I am not. She sent the note with a touch of resentment but quickly sent another. *Back at Eleanor's. Gotta finish up here. See you at ten.*

Nicole and Julian were upstairs when Charlotte left the house that night. She hadn't said she was going out. She didn't owe this to Nicole, especially after the ton of work she'd done for her that day, and when she crept back in early Tuesday, the kitchen was empty.

Feeling guilty for negative thoughts, she put on a pot of coffee. It had just finished brewing when Nicole appeared in her fluffy robe and slippers. Her face was bare and pale, her eyes tired. She reached for a mug. "You went out last night."

"Uh-huh."

"I heard the door."

She seemed about to say something more, but simply closed her mouth and reached for the cream—which was wise, in Charlotte's humble opinion. She had no intention of discussing Leo. She didn't want to be explaining herself, much less invite criticism.

But Nicole's worry lay elsewhere. Holding back a swath of blond hair, she said, "I know you're pissed at me, Charlotte, and I'm not sure why, but here's the thing. I jump every time the phone rings, because, if it's Hammon, we may have to leave. He needs time to culture the cells, but if he wants to run tests on Julian before the nineteen days are up, and if I'm in Chicago and not here, the cookbook is in trouble. The cookbook may be totally silly compared to MS, but it's like"—her green eyes went foggy as she tried to explain—"it's like something of *me* is in it, and I need that to make it through all this." Scowling, she pulled a handful of red petals from her pocket. Some were faded, others more fresh. "Do these actually *work?*" she asked in despair.

"Do we know that they don't?" Charlotte countered, closing Nicole's fist with the clover inside. "We're making good headway on the cookbook—"

"But mostly on collecting raw material. There's still so much left to write." She scooped her hair back again, baring frantic eyes. "Five chapters are done now, but another five are not, and that's not including the long, detailed, *witty* foreword and afterword that my editor wants."

"Write them now," Charlotte suggested calmly.

"I am so not in the mood for witty."

"You'll add wit later."

"What if I can't?" Her eyes foreshadowed the horror of paralysis, coma, death.

"Nicki. You have to think positive. Give me the chapter intros you've already finished," she suggested, coming up with Plan B there and then. "If you have to leave, I'll use those as a model and write the rest myself."

Nicole studied her, then sighed. "What a mess. I should never have signed that contract. I knew Julian was sick."

"Which is why you signed it, and it's good," Charlotte argued, taking her arms. "Don't do this to yourself. You made a commitment. It's done."

"But you're with Leo all the time."

Silence.

Astonished, Charlotte dropped her arms. "Much of the time I'm with Leo, I'm writing for you, and the rest, you're with Julian. Why do I need to hang around here? You have the cells. I paid my dues. Don't bring Leo into it."

"But I'm losing you *anyway*."

The silence this time was sadder. Charlotte felt it and let out a tiny breath. "No, Nicki. You're not. I'm just having a hard time accepting that the stem cells are gone, but I'm telling *me* the same thing I'm telling you. It's over and done. Get. A. Grip."

"This is a nightmare."

"Given everything, that is probably an understatement," Charlotte acknowledged, folding her future with Leo into the mix, "but we'll get through. Trust me on this. I've done it before."

When Wednesday dawned cloudy and cool, they headed for the island store, where the potbelly stove filled the sitting corner with the scent of glowing pine logs and warmth. Though they knew that this was the place to see and be seen, their real target was Bev Simone, who, as owner of the store and the Café, was second only to the postmaster in the daily number of Quinnies she met. Indeed, through the hours Nicole and Charlotte were there, Bev rarely sat, but talked about the evolution of the store while standing at the ready, elbows on the back of a fat armchair. When the door jangled, she was off, but she always returned with something that helped—either a recipe card, a release form, or a foil-covered package for Julian.

Quinnies were curious, but tactful. They could easily pass an hour chatting up the weather, the radish harvest, or a bad stretch of planks on the pier, but to make small talk with Nicole at this time would have been considered gauche. Likewise making a big deal about bringing a plate of brownies, a bowl of fresh-picked strawberries, or a pan of lasagna. As for their curiosity, Bev was able to satisfy that with the bits of information Nicole purposely gave.

Did you ask Bev about her arthritis? Leo e-mailed midday, to which Charlotte replied, *I didn't have to ask. She knows I'm with you and mentioned it right off. Devil's Claw. She says it's indigenous to South Africa, but, if so, how did Cecily grow it?*

Under lights inside. When I tore the greenhouse down, I stuck the roots in the ground and it keeps coming up. It's ugly as hell, but it just won't die. ARE you with me?

She wasn't thrown by the change of subject, since it was never far from her mind. *I am if you'll come to Paris.*

I don't speak French.

I do.

I don't own a suitcase.

I do.

I don't have a passport.

Apply now, and you'll have one in time.

He didn't respond to that, and Charlotte didn't see him that evening. She and Nicole worked late, and by the time they were done, she was too tired to do more than fall into bed. She woke up Thursday morning thinking about him and wanting to tell him as much. But he had to write back first. It was his turn.

*　*　*

You're very quiet, he finally texted after Charlotte had suffered through a long morning.

Waiting for word on your passport, she wrote. She had been able to distract herself with work, but seeing his text brought a rush of emotion. She was feeling relieved, impatient, and needy, all of it unsettling.

Why Paris?

Because it's where I'm going after here.

Why do I need to see Paris?

You don't. Her need to type kept her from throwing her hands up in frustration. *It could be Tuscany. Or Montreal, or Boston, or Brooklyn. The point is that it isn't Quinnipeague.* If he didn't see that, then she had over-rated his brain.

What's wrong with Quinnipeague?

NOTHING! I just can't live here full time. Some of the time, yes. But if you can't spend some of your life elsewhere, we have no future.

There was a brief pause then. She wondered if she had gone too far. It wasn't an ultimatum, exactly.

Yes, it was.

Why are you raising this now?

Because it's been weighing on me. I love you.

The instant she clicked SEND, she would have pulled it back. Texting wasn't the right place to say this. But it was done. Too late. Gone.

Chapter Twenty-five

CHARLOTTE HAD TYPED THE WORDS in exasperation, and no, texting wasn't the right place for a first declaration, but wasn't she stating the obvious? The man had written *Salt*. He was sensitive and insightful. He had to have felt what was going on here.

But the flow of notes abruptly stopped, leaving her suspended, wondering if she had misjudged him, fallen for an irreparably damaged soul or, worse, an empty shell. At the very least, it looked like she had scared him off.

But she refused to take back the words. *Aim high, hit high,* Bob Lilly had always said, and, emotionally speaking, Charlotte was finally doing it. She had never fallen in love—as in, aching at the sight of someone, wanting to live with him and have kids with him and to grow old with him, and being willing to modify her life to make it happen. But she felt all that now, and it *couldn't* be all one-sided. The recluse, who had once accused her of trespassing and told her to leave, had opened up. Totally aside from physical attraction, he seemed drawn to her thoughts, willing to listen, wanting to share with her what he did for fun. He had taken her into his own private space—had *let* her fall in love. He wouldn't have done that if he hadn't felt even just a teeny little bit of the same, yet with each minute that crept by, she grew more distressed.

After a full hour of silence he wrote, *I've heard that before,* at which point she gave up all pretense of working, went outside, and phoned.

He had barely picked up when she said, "I know you've heard it before, but she was not honest. I am trying to be, and it isn't only for your sake. It's for mine, too. I stand to be hurt really, really badly if this falls apart, because I feel things for you that I've never felt before. I don't want to be hurt, Leo. I can't afford to lose everything again."

"And you think I can?" he argued flatly. "This isn't easy for me, either."

"Why not?" *Say it,* she thought and held her breath. *Say it.*

But he was quiet. Finally, "Can I come over?"

Releasing a breath, she lowered her head. "No. Not now. I need to work and you need to think."

How's it going? he texted later that afternoon.

It's going, she wrote back.

Can I see you tonight?

No. I need to think, too.

She knitted for much of the night—knitted frenetically—first propped up in bed, then curled in a chair, later standing by the floor lamp when she got up for a drink of water and couldn't quite get herself to return to bed. Her fingers weren't kind to the sweater; working on the front now, she made constant mistakes. Leo was a thread worked right into the popcorns, cables, and twists, but no matter how long or hard she pondered their relationship, no new insight popped up. She loved him. How many ways could you parse that? It wasn't rocket science.

By Friday morning, she was in a snit. It must have been written all over her face when, after a whopping two hours of sleep at dawn, she awoke to the smell of coffee.

Julian was reading the paper, while Nicole made bacon and many more pancakes than the two of them would eat. "Blueberry," she told Charlotte, gesturing toward the pile. "Help yourself." Then, "You don't look great."

Charlotte poured coffee into the largest mug she could find. "I didn't sleep well."

"Did you go out?"

"No."

"Problems with Leo?"

The woman didn't have a mega-following for nothing, Charlotte thought dryly, wondering at what sounded like satisfaction in her voice. But of course, Nicole would like the relationship to implode. She had been against it from the start.

Not wanting to discuss it now, Charlotte asked, "What's on for today?"—which was a ridiculous diversion, what with printed schedules everywhere. But if Leo was off-limits, what else did she have?

Work would save her. It always had. After all, what was wanderlust if not having nowhere better to stay?

Hey, he texted at ten.

That was it. *Hey.*

At eleven, he wrote, *Are you there?*

Yes.

Ignoring me?

Trying to. I have work to do.

I'm wounded.

He had been kidding. She was not. *That makes two of us.*

Can I take you to lunch?

In town? She couldn't bear it. Or at his house? With dreams scattered everywhere and Bear—she hated dogs but loved Bear—plopped against her leg? Worse.

I have to work, Leo. Really.

You're pushing me away.

Yes, so I can work. Please respect that for a change.

For a change?

Sighing, she typed, *Delete that. It begs a whole other discussion. I'm working now. Please.*

She put the phone in her pocket, determined to ignore it, reasoning that the beauty of being uncommitted was that you didn't owe anyone anything. The downside, of course, was that you felt unloved, which was why she kept checking for notes from Leo. By the time he finally texted, her hackles were back up.

Do I have a prayer in hell of dinner? he wrote.

She might have considered it if he had texted sooner, but while he'd been taking his own sweet time, she had made other plans. *I can't. We're going to the Warrens.*

So after. I'll pick you up at their house.

But Nicole had wanted her for the evening, and Charlotte had every intention of drinking enough wine to put her to sleep as soon as she got home, thereby keeping her from agonizing over why Leo couldn't commit. *Tonight isn't good, Leo. Sorry.*

She dressed up, which by Quinnipeague standards, meant a blouse and skirt. That the skirt was short and paired with high wedged sandals made her feel like she might have been able to pick up a guy if there had been anyone there of interest. There wasn't. Moreover, the wine plan didn't work, largely because Julian's presence reminded her that bad things could happen when too much wine was consumed. So she simply smiled a lot, nodded a lot, and spoke when addressed, but her heart wasn't in any of it. Slumped in the backseat on the way home, she felt empty, which annoyed her, which was why, when they approached the house and she saw a dark blue pickup parked on the edge of the road just past the driveway, she rediscovered her spine. The instant the SUV parked, she was out and, ignoring the echo of slamming doors behind her, strode toward the house. She wasn't halfway there when a hand closed on her arm.

"We need to talk," he said.

She stared at his hand. "Not tonight."

"Don't shut me out."

Her eyes met his, but the night was dark, making them as opaque as his jaw was tight, all in a shadowed face. "Should we discuss who's shutting who out?"

"We can discuss whatever you want."

Charlotte felt she'd been doing that internally for the better part of the day, and hadn't she told him tonight wasn't good? "I'm tired."

But his hand was insistent, its grip just shy of hurtful as he drew her toward the truck.

"Hey," Nicole shouted. "You can't just drag her off. What part of *no* don't you get? She doesn't want to go."

He stopped and murmured, "Tell her to mind her own business."

"She loves me," Charlotte said.

His hand fell, his mouth went flat. "Fine. She's your future? Fine. She's all you need? Fine." He took a step back.

Charlotte's heart was curling up on itself, aching with want and need. "She's not my future, and she's not what I need, but she's my friend and she loves me, so she cares."

"I care."

"Is that the best you can do?" she shot back.

"No."

She glared at him, thinking that one word didn't do it—*two* words didn't do it—that she *knew* there was more inside him, and that she couldn't turn away from him yet.

Glancing at Nicole, she held up a hand, said a terse, "I'm good," and stalked off across the grass, across the road to the truck, around the truck to the far side, where she stopped, leaned against the door, and angrily folded her arms.

Leo was there in a heartbeat. Pinning her to the metal with his hips, he pried her arms free, anchored them over her head with one hand, and held her face with the other. His mouth tore at hers, lips angry, tongue insistent in ways it had never been before. In those seconds, he was the dangerous recluse who threatened trespassers and shot gulls for sport.

But she wanted the man she knew. So she returned his aggression with aggression, asking for more, tearing her arms free so that she could search with her hands. She was clutching his hair when his mouth found her neck, and when his hands found her breasts, she slipped hers in the back of his jeans to pull him closer. Mouth to mouth, he gave her breath, and when he began rocking hard against her, she forced her hands between them to touch him there.

"Jeeeez," he groaned and, covering her hand, held it still. Struggling for control, he leaned into her, pressing his mouth to the top of her head.

Charlotte gasped for breath, but with each breath came more of Leo. He always smelled clean, though not in the herbal way she had once imagined. He might bathe her with peppermint and sage, but he was Irish Spring all the way. Now, between that and man and arousal, she was desperate with need.

"Do it," she gritted between her teeth, pulling at his snap.

He swore when her hand closed around him.

"Here?"

"They're inside. *Do* it," she ordered, aching for him. If this was the only way they could communicate, she would take it for the sake of sheer affirmation.

Frenzied, he pushed her already-hiked skirt to her waist, tugged her panties until they tore and, lifting her legs, slammed inside.

She cried out at the sudden fullness, then again when her back lashed the truck, but if he had tried to slow down, she would have screamed. He was rough, but she wanted rough. In this, too, she gave as good as she got, kissing him, clutching his shirt, riding him fiercely until a guttural sound came from his throat, at which point she broke apart herself.

After a climactic eternity, he sagged against her, holding her up when her body went limp. And he stayed in her for a while, panting with decreasing force, before slowly withdrawing. Even then, he held her close.

The truck, the muted crash of a distant surf, their state of undress, her anger—item by item, her awareness returned. With it came the idea that he had just punished her for the hurt he had suffered years before, but if that hurt was exorcised now, she couldn't object. They needed to move on.

She let her legs slide down his until they took her weight, pressed her face to his chest, and listened to his heart. It calmed, but only to a point.

"I can't say the words you want," he finally murmured.

She didn't move. "Because you don't feel it?"

"Because I can't say the words. I don't know where to go with this."

"What do you *feel*?"

"I feel . . . like I'm doing what I swore I would never do. I told myself I would never commit that way again."

Though it wasn't quite the declaration she wanted, it was something.

"Things change."

"Do they? Look at me. I am what I am." He pushed a hand through his short, dark hair not so much in frustration as bewilderment. "I didn't expect any of this—the book, you. I'm clueless here, Charlotte. Don't know what in the hell to do about any of it."

Hearing the echo of Angie's thought, Charlotte said, "Life is like a game of cards. It deals you different hands at different times. You don't have that old hand anymore, Leo. Look at what you have now."

"I'm looking at her," he whispered. And she was lost in the midnight blue complexity of a deep, darling man.

Framing his face with her hands, she kissed him until that lean mouth softened. She didn't say anything else. He was uncomfortable with words, and she couldn't bear to spoil the moment. Back at his house, though, when she bundled up in one of his sweatshirts and they went out to the dock, she thought about the few weeks she had left.

Words weren't necessary; she could show him how she felt. She would get under his skin so that by the time she left, he would feel the loss. And yes, he'd been there before, the difference being that she was willing to meet him halfway.

It was his choice.

Nicole had remained in the dark at the front window long after the truck pulled away. Lost in thought, she gave a start when Julian slipped his arms around her waist. She leaned into him, appreciating that he'd sought her out.

Quinnipeague had been good to him. After nine days here, he was rested and stronger. He had even put on a few of the pounds he had lost while on that last dismal drug. His symptoms remained, neither better nor worse. Even now she felt a tremor in his hand, but steadied it with her own. He wasn't debilitated by a long shot. And yes, she was committed to the stem cell transplant. Hadn't she been the one to suggest it? Still, a tiny part of her wished that they were taking it more slowly, adapting to his illness, waiting before taking this next iffy step.

His thoughts were elsewhere as he rested his chin on her head. "Why does he make you so angry?"

Leo. She sighed. "Because he's all wrong for Charlotte."

"How do you know?"

"Because he's nothing like you."

"Nicki," he said with a curious laugh, "why should he be like me? Charlotte's nothing like you. You're sweet and giving. She's independent and edgy."

"Do you ever wish I was more of those things?" Nicole asked, because always, *always*, in the back of her mind, there would be an image of them together—always, *always*, in the back of her mind, there would be the worry that she was somehow lacking as a woman.

"No, I do not. I love you for who you are," he said, giving her the reassurance she feared she would need again and again.

Closing her eyes, she turned her face to his neck. These nine days had been good for them as a couple, too. They had talked, made love, slept close. Fear of the future was never far, though she knew that the stronger he was, the better he would withstand the transplant. Still, she wondered if he was living on borrowed time. She guessed he was wondering it, too. He was softer, gentler, mellower.

And forgiving. When she said that one aloud, he asked, "Where does forgiveness come in?"

"Charlotte's baby."

"It was my baby, too," he said, mellow indeed. "I can accept that she's gone, but having a shot at these stem cells is something. Charlotte didn't have to come forward with them. She didn't have to come here at all this summer."

"You didn't want her to."

"No," he said with a modicum of shame for his evasiveness then. "But it worked out. And now she deserves happiness, don't you think?"

Nicole truly wanted that for her, but something about Leo rubbed her the wrong way. "Can she get it with him?"

"I don't know. But neither do you. Only Charlotte can answer that."

She angled her head to try to see his face in the dark. "She says she loves him. After five weeks? That's all it's been, Jules. Five weeks. Did you see how rough he was tonight?"

"He wasn't all that rough. And she handled him."

"But what is he? Okay, so he lucked out with *Salt*, but can he repeat that? People may buy his next book, but if it isn't as good, they won't buy him again. And how can it be as good? The guy is *Quinnipeague*, Jules. I mean, I love it here, but living nowhere else—oh, he was in prison for a while, sorry, I forgot about that. Like he'd get material for a follow-up to *Salt* there? I mean, really. *Salt* was a place just like this. He can't repeat it. My dad would call him a flash in the pan."

"Wrong," Julian said quietly. "Your dad would have been intrigued. He'd have invited the guy over for dinner to talk about how he made his book such a success."

Nicole was appalled. "You want me to invite Leo to *dinner*? Omigod, Julian. That would be like giving Charlotte a green light to do whatever she's doing with him."

He sighed. "Baby, you are not her mother."

"But I love her, and she is being totally stupid. He's taking what he can get while he can get it."

"You may be wrong," Julian said more firmly, at which point Nicole grew defensive. She was going along with what he wanted when it came to treatment, even though it wasn't what she wanted. And still he found fault.

"Wrong, like I hover? Like I smother you?"

He pressed her lips closed. "I was taking my frustration out on you when I said those things. But you're doing the same thing now. You're worried about the cookbook and angry at your mother, and we're both on edge waiting for Hammon. But none of this is Leo's fault. You're making him the receptacle of every other bad thing. That's not fair, Nicki. It's not right."

Nicole wasn't sure if she agreed, but she didn't want to argue more with Julian. Things had been too good between them for that, and if time was short, she couldn't waste it. So she turned in his arms and kissed him. "I love you," she whispered against his lips.

She felt his smirk. "Is that meant to shut me up?"

"Yes," she mused, then reflected. "It's like right now, at this moment in time, I'm arguing with Charlotte about Leo, Leo about Charlotte, Mom about Dad and Tom and the house—or I would be, if I was talking to Mom—even Kaylin, who is doing absolutely nothing but playing in Manhattan until school starts again, and when I ask her about it, she starts in on MS, and I can't go there with her right now. I don't want to argue with you."

He didn't pursue it, simply guided her up to bed, though when he teetered on the stairs, she was the one to steady him.

She hadn't shut him up, she knew. If she were to resume the argument the next morning, he would pick up his side of it again. And maybe he was right. Maybe she was demonizing Leo for no reason. Only it did feel like a reason. And she was worried about Charlotte.

Whatever, she'd be damned before she would encourage Leo Cole.

Charlotte didn't have to encourage him. In lieu of not saying The Words, he was attentive and gentle all on his own. Whether it was prepping her for interviews while driving her into town, making the effort to talk with other Quinnies at the end-of-July potluck dinner Sunday, or making sweet love to her in the shower, the bath, the bed, or the boat—he was an interesting companion, a devoted helpmate, an exquisite lover. And the irony of that? Despite her determination to sink her teeth deeper into *him,* she was the one falling harder herself.

Nicole was the thorn. She clearly hated Leo and kept her distance the few times their paths crossed. Charlotte told herself she didn't care. But she did. She wanted Nicole's blessing. Wasn't Nicole one step removed from Angie and Bob? Wasn't she as good as a sister in Charlotte's lonely-only family of one? She was going out on a limb with Leo and wanted someone to say she was doing the right thing.

Knowing Nicole wouldn't say it, though, she didn't ask. When they were together, she focused on work, but the silence regarding Leo would have been comical if it hadn't been so sad. After all, Charlotte was with him whenever she wasn't either with Nicole or working on her behalf. She was with him most evenings and some overnights. She was brushing her hair more, using mascara more, buying a sweater, scarf, or necklace at the island store—all because she cared more about how she looked. Nicole had to notice, but she said nothing.

"She's preoccupied," Charlotte told Leo when he came to pick her up for dinner Wednesday night and Nicole turned away. "She's worried about what's coming for Julian. She isn't herself."

"Hey," he said, opening the door for her to climb into the truck, "if you're afraid my feelings are hurt, don't be. I'm fine."

If he was fine, she decided, she was done making excuses. "Well, I'm not. This hurts me. What is her problem with you?"

"Maybe her problem's still with you."

She waited until he rounded the truck and slid in behind the wheel before saying in an indignant tone, "*Why?* I could have blamed *her* for what happened with Julian. I mean, why wasn't she with us on the beach that night? Was she afraid of getting sand in her pretty little open-toed shoes?"

"She's angry about that night, about the baby she wanted but you had, about the fact that you've come through with stem cells that could save his life." He cupped her face, fingers skimming her ears. "Don't agonize over this, Charlotte. She's afraid. She can't take it out on Julian so she's taking it out on you."

"On you," Charlotte insisted. He was right about everything else.

"Okay, on me, but I have a hard skin." He started the truck. "I'm hungry."

The Island Grill was packed. As luck had it, a window table opened minutes after they arrived, adding an ocean backdrop to blue linen, a vase of balsam, and the scent of sizzling steak. Having had steak the day before, Leo ordered swordfish, Charlotte ordered scallops, and they shared—and during the time they ate, no less than three people approached to quietly ask if Julian had gotten his call. All three were longtime family friends, which explained why Nicole kept them in the loop.

None of the three were year-round Quinnies, and still *they* weren't bothered by Leo, Charlotte observed. He was well dressed, well groomed, and ten times better looking than any other man in the place, which made her wonder if Nicole was plain old envious. There was nothing rakish about Julian. Distinguished, yes. But not exciting.

Leo was exciting. At least, Charlotte thought so, but then, she knew how he could be in private. Here at The Grill he was comfortably reserved. Though he was polite when people approached, he didn't seem to care if they did. He didn't look around for familiar faces, didn't need to see people he knew. He didn't order the most expensive wine on the list, though he could easily afford it. And while he looked the part of someone comfortably disposed, no outsider would have taken him for a number-one *New York Times* bestselling author, which served him well this night.

Their strawberry-rhubarb crostini was brought to them with two spoons by no less than the owner of the restaurant. Michaela Bray never failed to startle Charlotte. While the food here was unfailingly straightforward, the fifty-something woman had pink streaks in her short, silver hair, exquisitely made-up blue eyes, and a tattoo that crept up the side of her neck. She had only last week returned to Quinnipeague after tending to a sick mother in Sacramento, so Charlotte hadn't interviewed her yet. They had set a time; she assumed Michaela was delivering their dessert herself to confirm it.

But she pulled up a chair, leaned in close, and murmured, "Don't both of you look at the same time, but there's a woman in a red blouse at the back corner table. She's media."

Charlotte looked only at Leo, who barely glanced around. Though he showed no outward change, she felt a new tension in the leg that touched hers.

"Why's she here?" he asked, eyes on Michaela.

"Her parents are renting for a couple of weeks."

"So she's not working," Charlotte said, wanting to define the threat.

"Not officially," Michaela warned, "but she let everyone know she just finished a piece on Clooney for *People*. When you get ones like that who are full of themselves, you know that if they get whiff of a scoop, vacation or not they'll grab the nearest camera. No Quinnie will let on who you are," she told Leo, "and you're not loud, so she won't hear it by accident." She stood, leaning back in for a last, "Just wanted you to know," before straightening again and saying to Charlotte in a fuller voice, "Friday at ten?"

Charlotte nodded. "I'll be here."

The crostini was the restaurant's signature dessert, but neither of them could appreciate it fully—Leo, because he was working too hard to be nonchalant, and Charlotte, because she was wondering how to help him.

When they were back in the truck, she asked, "Does that happen much—you know, outsiders?"

He backed out of the space, shrugged, and, shifting gear, set off for home.

"Would it be so awful if the outside world knew?" she asked.

"I don't know." He drove down the neck before leveling off and asking, "Do you?"

"No."

They continued on past the clam flats. "But if I go public, and readers come here in droves, I'm not the only one who suffers. Tourism is great, but not when it decimates the feel of the place. That's why Quinnies keep my secret. They're scared, too."

Charlotte had a thought. "So you're deliberately letting it die?" When he shot her a quick look but said nothing, she added, "Not really wanting *Next Book* to happen?" Still he was quiet. "What about the offers you've had? You got a privacy clause once. You could do it again."

"Don't put money on that," he warned. "My lawyer says they're hounding him. He says they want the publicity of a public appearance when the paperback comes out."

"If they want a second book enough, they'll agree to whatever you want, and if they don't, another publisher will."

"Like I have a second book to sell?" he murmured. "I do want it to happen, Charlotte. I'm just not inspired."

"What inspired you with *Salt*? That book was so rich. All from Our Lady of Phoenix?"

The epithet made him snicker. "No."

"Then what?"

"My dreams." He kept his eyes on the road.

"You didn't have it with her?" she asked in surprise.

"I thought I did. Looking back now—" He shook his head no. "It was all a dream. With her, with *Salt*. I wouldn't have chosen that ending, but the rest of it was what I'd always wanted to happen."

The fact that he didn't look at her, that he seemed self-conscious, touched her deeply. She thought of the opening line of *Salt*: *Every man wants love, if he can get past the fear of exposure*. Here was exposure. *Salt* might be fiction, but the man behind it was sensitive and complex. And then there was that *looking back now*. If he was saying that Charlotte was the one who had shown him what true love really was, this was huge.

He parked behind the house and helped her out of the truck, but then, seeming lost in thought, wandered off. She followed him into the garden, where the scent of lavender rose above the rest.

Sitting beside him on the dirt, she tucked his hand in the crook of her arm. "You don't have to hide, Leo. You have so much to be proud of."

"One thing."

"More than one. You have depth."

He studied their fingers, rubbing a long thumb against hers. "I've let you in more than anyone else."

"More than her?" Charlotte asked, needing confirmation of that at least.

"Our Lady of Phoenix?" A wry smile in the dark. "No comparison. I was young. If I'd been a little smarter, I'd have known she wouldn't stay. The signs were there. She didn't like Quinnies. She hated Bear. She was allergic to fish." He smiled sadly. "I never talked to her like this."

"The conversations in *Salt* were imagined."

"They were what I wanted a relationship to be."

We have it, Charlotte thought, but she knew that he knew.

"I've gotten better, haven't I?" he asked.

"From the uniword guy on the roof?"

His smile was as beautiful a thing in the dark as the crescent moon. "Uniword?"

"Grumpy. *Guarded*. But yeah, you're better." She paused, thinking back to those first days, and swept her chin toward the herbs. "So when are you going to let me photograph all this?"

"How about tomorrow?"

She gasped. She had been fully expecting a refusal. "Seriously?"

"The herbs need to be thinned. I'll have to get supplies at the hardware store so I can pot and deliver."

"Deliver?"

"To Quinnies who'll grow them. Now's the time to divide the plants."

"You'll let me use pictures in the cookbook?" She had to be sure she understood.

He nodded.

"For Nicole?"

"For you. Come at dawn. The light's best then."

Charlotte was dying to tell Nicole. Forget bragging rights, though she certainly could claim those. This would make Nicole feel better about the cookbook. More important, it would make her feel better about Leo.

Nicole was in fact waiting for her at the kitchen table, her fingers opening and closing around a handful of tiny red leaves. When she spoke, though, her voice was low and filled with fear.

Mark Hammon had called earlier that evening and wanted Julian in Chicago the next day.

In the frenzy of packing, last-minute instructions, and getting Nicole and Julian to the pier, Charlotte pushed everything else aside. Pictures of herbs were petty. This was life and death.

To Nicole's credit, where Julian was oddly scattered, she held it together. Only after the mail boat sputtered to the dock and he boarded, did Charlotte pull her into a tight hug.

"You are incredible," she said quietly. When Nicole's resistance gave way to trembling, she said, "You're strong. He'll do fine; you'll get him through." Holding her back, she gave her a stare. "Do not argue with me about this. You are *so* doing the right thing. I will always love you for that."

Nicole's eyes were awash with uncertainty. She was the one to do the pulling this time, clinging to Charlotte until the mail boat beeped. "You're the best," she finally whispered and, drawing back, took a breath. Putting on a confident face, she turned and climbed aboard to join Julian.

Chapter Twenty-six

As she watched the boat disappear that Thursday morning, Charlotte wondered what condition Julian would be in when she saw him again. Given the experimental nature of UCB treatment, he could end up anywhere between cure and death. Add to that the testing, waiting, and worrying that she knew would come in Chicago, and she figured her own days would crawl.

That didn't happen. Leo had put off thinning the herbs for a day, knowing she wouldn't have had the heart to leave the house that morning, so she began at the top of her to-do list, interviewing a few last Quinnies, collecting late recipes, cross-checking for releases and going after ones that hadn't yet come in. She still had most of her profiles to write, but she knew she could do that under pressure at the end.

More important first, since Nicole was stressed about it, was reading the rest. Not that it took much effort. Nicole was a good writer. Her style was warm and personal, much as in her blog, and it set a perfect tone for the book. Charlotte found herself smiling as she read, hearing Nicole's voice with its enthusiasm and pop, all the more remarkable considering the darkness in her life during the writing. She caught a few typos and removed the occasional "like" or "I mean" that interfered with the flow, though she was careful not to change the flavor.

After e-mailing those files to Chicago, she pored over the notes Nicole had left and, emulating her style, which actually turned out to be a hoot, wrote the last few chapter intros from scratch.

And then, yes, came the photos. Leo had been absolutely right about the time. The light of dawn gave a magical glow to the garden. But then, midmorning light was flattering to the taller plants, while noon light more evenly lit the leafier ones. All told, she took hundreds of pictures, both of the garden and of Leo working there. None of the latter would appear in the book; he had made that clear at the start.

"Trust me," she said at the time. "These are for me." And they were. After transferring Leo shots to a separate SD card, she spent hours editing the rest.

Once she had sent Nicole enough material to keep her spirits high, she turned to her own work and the southwest of France. She hadn't thought about the assignment in weeks, but it was suddenly rushing at her. After two nights in Paris, she would be taking the high-speed train to Bordeaux to profile the owners of a small winery. Her editor called to confirm travel arrangements and to share thoughts on the piece, after which Charlotte spent hours at her computer getting background information. She e-mailed a heads-up to her *amie Parisienne,* Michelle, with whom she would be staying at the start and the end of the trip, and since she was heading to Tuscany after that, she touched base with the editor who was paying her for that piece.

All told, she would be gone for three weeks. For the first time in her life, the thought of being so far for so long was unsettling, and she had Leo to blame. More than once as she studied him, with his dark head bowed to computer or phone, his lean legs splayed, his clever hands holding or poised, she heard the clock ticking so loudly that she considered rescheduling her flights and staying on Quinnipeague until after Labor Day.

But that would only defer the inevitable. Her work was part of who she was.

That said, with Nicole gone, she made no pretense of sleeping alone. She stopped at the big white house each day, the caretaker of this, too, and though Leo often went with her, he wasn't comfortable there. His own home was truly his castle; it was where he felt safe. And he had plenty to do. If he wasn't studying e-book sales analytics, relaying lawyer-to-publisher new thoughts on the paperback release, or surfing the Web for marketing ops, he was removing summer storm debris from his roof or cleaning the boat. He seemed to have temporarily given up on *Next Book,* though she guessed it was in his mind as he walked around in the night, dressed in those long gym shorts or nothing at all. He got regular deliveries of other authors' books and read while she slept, leaving whatever novel, memoir, or biography it was open and facedown on the bed. Always, he had breakfast ready when she woke.

Three weeks without Leo, three weeks back in the life she had known before him, three weeks with no guarantee he would want her when she returned—the fear never quite left her. And she *knew* he was feeling it, too. She could see it in his occasional lost look, and that, too, needled its way to her heart.

And then there was Bear, in some regards the more vocal of the two, who growled his way into a blissful purr when she rubbed the lean leg that he favored or stroked the silky spot on his brow. She had no idea how she could have ever thought him vicious. He was a softie, but an old one. She did worry about him—and about Leo come the day Bear died—and about herself if she learned of it after the fact.

Yes, Bear was definitely a player in her desire to stay, but so was the island. Quinnipeague in August was a lush green place where inchworms dangled from trees whose leaves were so full that the eaten parts were barely missed. Mornings meant *thick o' fog* that caught on rooftops and dripped, blurring weathered gray shingles while barely muting the deep pink of *rosa rugosa* or the hydrangea's blue. Wood smoke filled the air on rainy days, pine sap on sunny ones, and wafting through it all was the briny smell of the sea.

At Leo's, still and always, the smell of herbs rose above. She would miss this, too.

No. Time didn't crawl. It was slipping away with alarming speed.

Slipping away. Nicole had thought the same words often of late. Memories of her father, communication with her mother, interest in food and clothes and even the cookbook—she was losing a grip on the familiar.

Part of it was leaving Quinnipeague with its link to her past.

Part of it was the silence on her mother's end.

Part of it was spending hour upon hour at the hospital, where individuality gave way to utilitarian scrubs and sterile gowns.

Mostly, though, it was Julian, whose preoccupation had grown deeper since they landed in Chicago. Time and again, she found him staring blindly at the carpet, the window, or whatever TV was in view. When he opened his iPad, he was more apt to zone out on the home page than read any of the journals he had loaded there. He responded when she spoke, looking at her then, even smiling, but he didn't initiate conversation on his own.

They offered Nicole a counselor. *Often harder on the family than the patient,* they said. But Nicole doubted that. Julian was suffering emotionally. She didn't need a counselor to tell her he was terrified, but when she reminded him that he didn't have to go ahead with this, he insisted he did. In her darkest private moments, she wondered if his slipping away from her was a prelude to what might be.

Friday morning, members of Hammon's team did scans of Julian's brain and spinal cord. Both tests were brief and noninvasive. The spinal tap that afternoon was more involved. He tolerated it well right up to the recovery, which required that he remain lying down for ninety minutes in the care of a nurse who was constantly asking—hovering, *nagging*—if he felt a headache or tingling or numbness. *I'm a doctor,* he finally snapped. *I know what to look for, thank you.* Nicole might have reminded him that the woman was only doing her job, that he demanded the same attentiveness from his own team, and that doctor-patients could be pains in the butt, if indulging him hadn't been more important. Mercifully, there were no headaches, and the only tingling or numbness he felt were the same-old-same-old from his illness.

Saturday, after a morning of blood work, he began to drag—literally, his left foot worse than ever, though whether from MS or simply the enervating effect of giving so many vials of blood, Nicole didn't know. But she couldn't complain. Clearly, Mark wasn't leaving anything to chance. He wanted to be sure that every one of Julian's vital organs was functioning well before attempting something as risky as this transplant would be.

While the tests were being done, Nicole either sat in a nearby waiting room or stood alone in a corridor just beyond the room where Julian lay. And this waiting wasn't so bad. Though she knew that each test inched the process forward, she was in a personal holding pattern, wherein Julian was alive as long as the testing went on. Moreover, the fact of others tending to him gave her a break, because if Hammon was the director of the event, she was its facilitator. She had a written schedule, a watch, and a mandate to keep track of where they had to be when and get them there on time. This was no small feat with Julian spacing out.

"Are you okay?" she asked him at first, but after a few days, it was more a statement of affection than a question demanding a response. No, he was not okay. He was on a train that was picking up speed, headed to a place none of them knew. He was physically shaky and increasingly tired. He missed seeing patients, worried about his kids, and couldn't talk about any of it. She might have asked if *he* wanted to see a counselor, if she hadn't known the answer. Her Julian prided himself on being self-contained. With Hammon's team scrutinizing his every bodily function and the dignity he lost in the process, she couldn't force him on this.

*   *   *

Sunday was a rest day. Hammon ordered it, and Julian was tired enough not to argue, but it did mean that he had idle time in a strange hotel with little to ward off unwelcome thoughts. While on Quinnipeague, he had kept in touch with people at work, albeit with declining frequency. They knew where he was now and why, and sent notes of encouragement. But his passion in life was working with patients. Since the satisfaction of that had been taken from him, contact with colleagues was only a reminder of what he missed.

Had he been stronger, Nicole would have taken him to the Art Institute. She had never seen the Modern Wing, though she had studied much of the art housed there and might have been able to distract them both by playing the docent.

But Hammon had suggested he catch up on sleep, and he seemed exhausted.

So, leaving him with the bedroom drapes drawn, she settled in the living room of the suite to catch up on work, which was a touchy subject itself, now that he was without his. But she did have a deadline, and her work was her joy.

Focusing on immediate experience, she blogged about defying convention by having eggs, sunny-side up, with bacon and wheat toast for dinner at the hotel restaurant the night before. She talked about what made organic eggs organic, how organic bacon differed from regular bacon, and where pork could be found that was antibiotic- and hormone-free.

When Julian continued to sleep, she turned to the cookbook. Charlotte had been sending files, both edited and new, but she hadn't had the wherewithal to look at them until now. With that deadline only eleven days off, though, she read each file, made counteredits, and sent them back. *These are awesome,* she wrote in the accompanying note. Had she really not written those new chapter introductions herself? Hard to tell. *Did Michaela come through with the recipes we wanted?*

She did, Charlotte replied with barely a moment's lag. *I sent them on to New York.*

Why are you working today?

Same reason you are.

I doubt that. Unless Leo's sleeping.

She sent off the last, wondering if Charlotte would answer. Leo's name had been conspicuously absent from their notes, and it wasn't that Nicole was fishing for information. But Charlotte had been unfailingly solicitous in the last few days, texting to ask about her, Julian, the tests. A small mention of Leo seemed only right.

Not sleeping. Reading Sue Grafton, Charlotte wrote back as though discussing him was the most natural thing in the world. *He knows I want to get this done. Is Julian sleeping?*

Out cold. Two days of tests did him in. At least they're done. We get the results tomorrow. Hold your breath that Hammon doesn't see a problem that will nix the trial. Nix the trial, kill the hope, destroy stem cells that then could not be refrozen. *I lose sleep thinking about this.*

Why? Charlotte wrote back. *His liver was the only question, and those symptoms are gone. Hammon wouldn't have come this far if he didn't think Julian could go all the way. He's still culturing the cells, right?*

Right. They could be ready by Thursday. He'll have to medicate Julian first, but if that goes okay, he'll do the infusion Friday. Her stomach turned at the thought. Five days until the reckoning.

Medicate how?

He'll give him a chemo drug to suppress his immune system and lower the risk of rejection. The cells aren't a perfect match, only four out of six, which is totally consistent with his being the father, she added, lest Charlotte think anyone questioned that. *Hammon actually prefers a partial match like this. I'm not sure why. I know that if a baby inherits a genetic condition, his own cells won't help him because they would carry that condition, so maybe with Julian, it's the mismatched cells that hold the most hope. Hammon actually thinks T Reg cells may work with no matching at all, but at this stage, the FDA won't let him use a total mismatch. They want the extra precaution.*

She sent the note, thinking how much she knew about this and how little it mattered if the experiment went wrong. She had to be strong for Julian. But those dark private moments kept coming.

Her e-mail dinged again. *Is the Wi-Fi there good enough to handle a super big file?*

Absolutely, she wrote back, suddenly in desperate need of a lift. *E-mail marble macadamias, and I'll eat every one.* Warm, soft, fragrant brownies would go a long way toward covering up the smell of hospital that had taken over her life.

Of course, Charlotte couldn't e-mail brownies. Wondering what would be in a super big file that hadn't already been sent, she waited for the computer to ding again. When it did, she found a photo album waiting. She caught her breath at the title. *Cecily Cole's Garden.* Inside, one after another, were portraits of plants, some individual, some grouped into thick clusters of herbs and flowers, captioned left to right like guests at a party. Some were tall, some short, some broad of leaf, others narrow, some spiked, some feathered. They covered the spectrum of green, from olive to pea to lime. The flowers were in different states of bloom, but all looked rich, healthy, and so . . . so *Quinnipeague* that Nicole felt a wave of homesickness that brought tears to her eyes. What a comfort it was to be back there for these few virtual moments!

And oh yes. The pictures would be *amazing* in the cookbook.

Grabbing her phone, she pressed in Charlotte's number and said a breathless, "He let you do it."

"I wore him down."

"And we can use them in the book?"

"Of course. He wouldn't have let me shoot them if he wasn't okay with that."

"Do I have to pay him for the pictures?"

"Absolutely not."

"Are there any conditions?"

"Only that we not use his name. We can label them as Cecily's plants, but the implication should be that the pictures were taken all over the island. Obviously, he doesn't want readers coming to his house—not his readers or ours."

"I understand," Nicole said, willing to grant him as simple a request as that. At the start of the summer, she had feared he would sabotage the cookbook, which he could have easily done, since his herbs were at the heart of island cooking. To this day, she believed he might have been the one inhibiting those early contributors. The fact that he was helping them out now spoke either of remorse for that, his feelings for Charlotte, or generosity. If the latter, he was also forgiving. Nicole hadn't been particularly nice to him.

Admitting that to herself, she was humbled. But the sound of Charlotte's voice more than compensated. It warmed her, soothed her. She did want Charlotte to be happy. What had happened ten years ago was at this moment very far away, and totally aside from the stem cells, Charlotte had been beyond-belief-helpful this summer. These photographs would make the cookbook special.

"He's not a bad person," Charlotte said softly.

Nicole wasn't ready to fully concede that, but she offered a conciliatory, "Please thank him for me. And Charlotte?"

"Yes?"

She lowered her voice. "Pick another clover for me?"

"I do. Every day."

Nicole insisted that they have lunch in the lobby restaurant, where she had a grilled salad to Julian's short rib sliders. She took notes and snapped pictures of both, telling him that this was food for a blog, which was a good excuse for having gotten him up and out for a little while at least, but she didn't push for more. If Hammon wanted a quiet day, there was nothing more quiet than golf. Julian loved the game, and the PGA Championship was on. So they went back upstairs after lunch to watch in their suite.

Since he was with her now, she wasn't comfortable working, and since she didn't want to leave him, she couldn't shop, walk, or go to a movie. Not being a lover of golf, she sat beside him, trying to get caught up in the game, but her mind wandered.

She didn't like where it went.

Opening her iPad, she downloaded what sounded like a good book, but when she started reading, the characters didn't grab her. So she pulled a magazine from her growing collection and flipped through. Magazine articles were usually short enough to hold her attention. But she had already read the good ones.

She pulled up the pictures Charlotte had sent and showed them to Julian. Needless to say, pictures of herbs intrigued him about as much as golf intrigued her, which meant he was quickly back to watching the game.

Staying with the photographs, she found comfort in the profusion of green. That led her to think about Quinnipeague, which led her to think of the house that apparently wouldn't be sold. Her feelings about that had changed since returning to the island with Julian. In the past, her parents had always been around, but if she could have time alone there with Julian, it wouldn't be bad at all. That had been nice—or would have been, if there hadn't been a sword hanging over their heads.

The weight of that sword grew heavier as Sunday slowly ticked away.

Monday morning, with a report that the test results were good, the ticking sped up. Once Julian nodded his agreement, Hammon produced a ream of release forms.

I didn't expect that, Nicole e-mailed Charlotte a short time later. *Julian did, since his patients have to sign releases, too. He says it's as much about educating the consumer as it is about avoiding a lawsuit, but, geez, is it intimidating. You sign your life away in multiple copies. I mean, we knew about most of the potential side effects, but seeing them in print? It was bad.*

Anything would probably seem bad to you right now, Charlotte replied, making total sense as Nicole knew she would, which was one of the reasons Nicole had been quick to e-mail her. *He plans to do it Friday?*

Unless something goes wrong between now and then, but he doesn't see that happening, Nicole wrote. *I guess I'm glad, since this is what we came for. And I'm being calm. You'd be proud.*

Do you FEEL calm?

Are you kidding? I'm terrified!

Is Julian?

Nicole considered that. *Not right now. It's strange. He's been so out of it since we got the call to come here, like the reality of it hit him over the head and he was stunned. He's been in a daze. Then, as soon as he signed the papers, he woke up. Just like that, he's lucid. And eager. I thought it was just being there in the office with Hammon, but when Hammon left the room and Jules looked at me, his eyes were clear and he smiled, like he was back.*

Does he worry about the risk?

He does, but it's a measured worry. He says it's like with his own work. He's scared when he tries something new on a patient, but if he's done the testing and practiced the technique, and if he knows the risks and has plans for handling them, he's excited. That's what he says. But how crazy is it to be excited about something that could kill you?

He believes in the trial.

Oh yeah. He and Mark get what this could mean for people everywhere with MS, and it's true, only Julian isn't just "people" to me, he's my husband. The old Nicole returned. She needed reassurance. *What if it goes bad, Charlotte?*

It won't. It can't. When does he start the drug?

They just did! It's called fludarabine. The infusion takes a little while, and they'll keep him here for a couple of hours to make sure he doesn't have an allergic reaction. Me, I'm the one who reacted. I got light-headed and turned green. They told me to wait out here in the hall. I should probably go back in now.

He'll do fine, Nicki. So will you.

Keep telling me that.

I will. Xoxox

Charlotte clicked SEND and, whispering a what-a-nightmare groan, raised her hands high in the air and stretched to ease the tension from her shoulders. Suddenly Leo was behind her, leaning between her arms to read the last of the exchange on the screen. Looping her hands around his neck, she watched him read. Talk about light-headed? From this angle, she couldn't see more than a square chin and jaw and his neck, but the neck was strong. She loved that, loved how clean he smelled and how solid he felt.

When he finished reading, he held her arms and looked down. "Bet you want to be with her."

"I do. She's been hit with a lot, and she's been so strong. I know she's with Julian. But the frightened part of her is all alone."

"Why don't you go?"

"Because you won't." When his eyes grew ocean-turbulent, she said, "Would it be so bad? You could wear a ball cap and your Ray-Bans. No one would know who you are—not that anyone knows you're Chris Mauldin or even what Chris Mauldin looks like. And you'd be with me. I know my way around."

"I don't like off-island," he said in his old, flat, stubborn voice. It was an old, flat, stubborn *wall,* she decided, and, twisting, went up on her knees on the chair.

"You don't *know* off-island. You know prison. You know a construction crew headed by a bitch. You know the father who ignored you. But there's a whole other world out there, Leo, and it isn't bad. I could show you that."

His eyes were clouded. "Don't you like Quinnipeague?"

"I *love* Quinnipeague. But I also love New York and Paris. And Juneau and Rio and Oslo. I love the variety."

He thought about that, clearly troubled. "Do I bore you?"

Feeling helpless, she breathed. "*Never.* But a person can love clams cooked a dozen different ways, and still love steak." She framed his face with her hands. "Know what the best part is about going different places?"

He knew the answer. He had read enough, dreamed enough. He was certainly smart enough. But he was in the moment, a silently turbulent package of pigheaded fear. Eyes holding hers, he shook his head.

"Coming home," she chided softly. "My place in Brooklyn is tiny.

It's shabby, and it smells of whatever my downstairs neighbor is cooking, and clouds in New York aren't like clouds here. My furniture is secondhand, my refrigerator may be dead when I get back, and there are *roaches*." Mention of those made her shudder, in response to which his mouth quirked, but she went on. "Brooklyn is nothing like Paris or Tuscany, or Ireland or Bali, but right now it's where my roots are."

He didn't blink. "Roots can be moved. Look at the herbs. We transplant them all the time."

"Right," she said with meaning and held his gaze.

Still he resisted. "I am who I am. If you loved me, you wouldn't want to change me."

Deep inside, she felt something deflate. If he didn't know she loved him after the last few days, he was thicker than that wall he had built to protect himself from the outside world. She had certainly said it enough, and not only when they had sex.

But it was test time. She let out a quick breath. "I could say the same to you."

"I never said the words," he said.

She sat back on her heels. "Right again." But he got an F. Shifting around in the chair, she rose and headed for the office door.

"Where are you going?" He sounded afraid.

"To the dock."

She barely made it halfway before he caught her arm and pulled her against him. "We don't fight. It's not who we are."

"Who *are* we?" she asked weakly.

The ocean rolled in, washing over the sand before being sucked back.

"I don't know," he finally said against her ear. "I'm trying to figure it out."

Charlotte didn't sleep well that night, but found herself obsessing over the larger picture. She felt fear for Nicole and guilt at not being there. She worried that she had inherited her parents' dysfunction in matters of the heart. And when she projected herself into the future and tried to anticipate adventure in Bordeaux, all she could think of was the weirdness she always felt the first day in a new place.

Between each thought came Leo. She imagined spending a lifetime here on Quinnipeague and realized she had a problem: She could do it in a heartbeat. While she lay here in bed, curled to his back and held there by his hands, which grasped hers in the dark, she could feel the pull of nascent roots. She had come to know the island more this summer than ever before, thanks to the cookbook, thanks to Leo, thanks even to her own maturity. She liked the people, liked the pace, liked the sweet salt air. She also liked the feel of those roots.

But there was still the rest of the world, which she loved. And the fact that she was tired of going places alone. And the realization that if downtown Quinnipeague counted for anything, she liked going places with Leo, which brought her right back to the rest of the world. She wanted to travel with Leo.

He knew how she felt, but wasn't budging. And when she was no longer here? That might get him going. He might be lovesick enough to act. Or he might just suck it up and do fine alone again, might even get another book out of it. If his writing was his catharsis. If he wanted revenge for her leaving. If he really didn't love her all that much.

The last possibility was like . . . like the pea under the mattress of the princess. And where had *that* thought come from? She had to dig back to remember. Her mother. Her mother had been into fairy tales. She would have liked Quinnipeague for that reason. With its wood smoke curling, its mystical herbs healing, and its symbiosis with the sea, it was the ultimate fairy tale.

How to fold that into real life? Lacking an answer that would work for Leo, she could do nothing but lie there and listen to the soft, steady sound of his breath.

Nicole did the same thing, though she didn't take the steadiness for granted. Hammon hadn't expected that Julian would react to the light dose of fludarabine he had prescribed, and the nurses who moni-tored him in the hours after the infusion had seen no cause for alarm. She was the one who had visions of sudden death, to which end she kept one body part or another—arm, leg, or hip—touching him at all times on the premise that as long as he was warm, he was fine.

She glanced at the clock: 2:27 A.M. Returning her head to the pillow, she went still and listened, but his breathing was steady.

She dozed and woke again to what sounded like wheezing, but turned out to be laughter in the hall.

She drifted off again, bolting up this time to what sounded like choking, but turned out to be the rumble of a truck on the street far below.

Charlotte's words became her mantra. *He'll do fine, Nicki. So will you.* She had Team Quinnipeague rooting from afar—lavender to calm, valerian to uplift, red four-leaf clover with the alleged ability to make wishes come true.

Nicole hadn't told Julian about those. He was a scientist. Scientists didn't do alleged.

Nicole wasn't as doctrinaire. Had she been on the island, she would still be picking that clover, still be holding it close for three days to let her wish take root. She liked knowing that Charlotte was doing it for her now that she was gone. With Friday only three days off, she needed all the help she could get.

Chapter Twenty-seven

*E*ARLY TUESDAY MORNING, JULIAN HAD a second chemo infusion, and when there was no sign of trouble this time, either, he said he was bored. He couldn't run, couldn't work. He wasn't interested in the art museum or the planetarium, and as for other options, there were limits. Hammon didn't want them going far on the chance of a delayed reaction. Nor did he want them in tight spaces where, with Julian's immune system low, he might pick up an infection.

For Nicole, finding the right distraction on a moment's notice was a challenge, which was in turn a welcome distraction. Taking to heart her mother's advice on creativity, she worked with those medical parameters and the hotel concierge, and came up with a plan.

By noon on Tuesday, in a rental car that came with a programmed GPS and box lunches, they drove to the Brookfield Zoo and, on Wednesday, the Botanical Garden. Julian's gait was more stilted both days, perhaps from the fatigue he was trying to ignore, but since they walked arm in arm, she could help. Both venues were quiet and open, with plenty to see. At night, they either watched movies in their room or slept, all of which took their minds from The Main Event, as

Nicole thought of the transplant in her sane Jekyll moments. The harried Hyde moments were when she texted Charlotte, who had a stake in this, too, and who could calm her.

Julian had no injection on Thursday. Hammon wanted to check him out a final time and review the details of the procedure with them, which precluded another day trip. So they simply walked through Navy Pier that afternoon, stopping when Julian tired but otherwise just . . . walking. They ate dinner at a restaurant that Nicole had heard about, taking care to sit at a secluded table, and watched another movie in their room, but they had more trouble this last night denying what was to come. There was a poignancy in the arm Julian kept around her. He was the one who seemed to need physical contact through a toss-and-turn night.

All too soon, it was Friday morning. As instructed, they were at the hospital by six, at which time Julian was admitted, settled in a room, and hooked up to monitors and an IV. With Hammon supervising, he took a single Tylenol by mouth and a ten-minute IV infusion of Benadryl, both prophylactic treatments of possible reaction to the T-regulatory cells. The Benadryl made him seriously drowsy, which was a good thing, Nicole decided, since she was a bundle of nerves. It was worse once the actual infusion began. She studied first Julian, then Mark, looking for a reaction from either of them to what was finally happening.

Julian was fuzzy. She saw no clues there.

But Mark? Intense. As he stood by the IV pole on the opposite side of the bed, she couldn't decide whether he was simply concentrating hard or downright frightened. He was more a thinker than a talker; she knew that. But she needed to know now if he was having second thoughts.

"Doubts?" she asked aloud.

Her voice startled him, he was that absorbed. His eyes flew to hers, but it was a minute before he raised his brows and pressed his glasses to the bridge of his nose. "I always have doubts. The process wouldn't be experimental if I didn't."

It wasn't the unequivocal thumbs-up she needed. But he had to have a feeling one way or another. "Are you worried?"

"I'm always worried." He glanced at the monitors that showed Julian's vital signs. "That's why we're watching so closely."

"I'm fine," Julian murmured sleepily.

Nicole rubbed his arm. "Mark was about to tell me that." Her eyes put the question to the doctor. She didn't care if he made it up. She needed the reassurance and wanted Julian to hear.

Hammon pushed at his glasses again and finally said, "If I didn't have faith in T-reg cells, I wouldn't be trying it. The lab tests were good. The first human trials were good."

"Those weren't with MS," she whispered.

"No," Mark confirmed. "Julian's my first."

At mention of his name, Julian opened his eyes. "How'm I doing?" he asked Mark, seeming to have drifted in and out of the conversation. Turning the arm with the blood pressure cuff, he reached for Nicole's hand.

"So far, so good," Hammon said.

With a satisfied murmur, he closed his eyes again. He looked pale but peaceful. The monitors held steady.

"Don't take my distraction for doubt," Mark said, finally opening up to Nicole. "Someone in my position is constantly reviewing a huge amount of information. The responsibility can feel overwhelming at times. Julian knows how that is. He's a risk-taker, too."

Eyes closed, Julian nodded, at which point Nicole decided that she was with two men who were either very brave or very reckless. Whatever, watching the slow drip of the cells, she was a nervous wreck. She had half a mind to ask for a little of that Benadryl herself.

They stood in silence for a time, she to Julian's right, the doctor to his left. Her eyes went from the IV, to Julian, to Mark, and back.

They reached the fifteen-minute mark; the infusion was half done.

"So, if something happens, when would it be?" she asked Mark. And it was strange. No one here was talking about the effect the cells might have on MS. At this point, it was solely about getting Julian through the treatment alive.

Mark shrugged a brow. "It could be any time—now, tonight, tomorrow. Different bodies react different ways. Some patients have no reaction at all."

But others did, Nicole knew. Stroke, heart attack, respiratory failure—these were three of the worst possibilities, but the list included dozens, running the gamut from mild to severe, all of which Julian had signed off on, as if complications were expected, as if they were perfectly acceptable. Of course, he'd had no choice. Without his signature, the procedure would have been off.

The infusion ended. Julian remained the same. Mark watched him for a while, then left to monitor vital signs from an office down the hall.

Alone, Nicole held her husband's hand. He opened his eyes from time to time, and gave her a smile, but it was small. "Feel okay?" she asked, to which he nodded each time. She poured him water and held the straw while he sipped. She poured herself a cup, but it didn't slow her own inner shakes.

After a bit, she began to feel dizzy. Not wanting to leave Julian's side, she ignored it, but it didn't ease. When the world went a milky white, she backed into a chair, hung her head to restore the flow of blood, and focused on breathing in and out, in and out. In time, she was well enough to look up again. Julian continued to sleep.

Pulling out her phone, she texted Charlotte. *He made it through the infusion. Now we wait for a reaction. Tell me we did the right thing.*

The speed of Charlotte's reply said she had been waiting for news. *We did the right thing. Julian wants this. Is he nervous?*

No. Dopey. They have him on a heavy dose of Benadryl.

When will you know if the transplant works?

Nicole took a tempering breath. She had asked the same question not only of Mark, but of various members of his team, not to mention the nursing staff, and the answer was unsatisfactory each time. *That depends on how he reacts. Seizures will mask the disease. Same with stroke.*

Why are you expecting the worst?
Because I'm terrified. So much is riding on this.
But it's done. You can't take it back. You have to look ahead. Be optimistic.

Charlotte set down the phone. She was sitting cross-legged on the single step outside Leo's office while, across the beach and in the surf to his thighs, the man himself was sanding the dock.

She had promised to help. Right now, though, she wished she were in Chicago, and it had nothing to do with messy jobs like sanding and restaining a dock. If Julian was groggy and the doctor was focused on looking for trouble, who was there for Nicole?

Catching her eye, Leo waved her over.

Raising a just-a-sec finger, she opened her contact list, selected a name, and put through the call.

Nicole felt washed out. She wasn't dizzy now, more sick to her stomach, but she hated to leave the room. Something could happen at any time. She had to be there if it did.

Julian awoke enough to ask for the TV. Encouraged, she turned on a news station, though he seemed to drift more out than in. Nurses came to check the flow of fluids from the IV, and they couldn't have been nicer. They brought him Jell-O. They brought him pudding. They even brought Nicole chowder and crackers, which she ate only because she knew she needed nourishment, though it was the worst chowder she'd ever had. Naturally, she was comparing it to chowder on Quinnipeague, where she was desperate to be.

She texted Charlotte. *Are you working?*

Yes. Just sent you SIDES and SNACKS, all done. Do NOT look at them now.

Nicole was torn, more Jekyll and Hyde stuff. While her heart was with Julian and about as distant from the cookbook as could be, Nicki-totable stamping her foot, pointing at the computer, telling her to work. *Maybe tonight,* she typed. *My editor wants everything by Thursday.* She had been so caught up in the countdown to the transplant, that she had slackened off. But Thursday was less than a week away.

Your editor won't even look at it until after Labor Day, Charlotte wrote back. *Trust me. The last two weeks in August are dead in New York. Let me call her and explain. You have more than enough reason to ask for extra time.*

I hate to do that. It says something about me.

Are you kidding? Every writer is late. Deadlines are a starting date. Editors give them out in hopes of seeing something a month later.

Nicole was tempted. Six days from deadline meant six days from Charlotte's departure, after which she was truly on her own. *How close are we?*

You need to review the last of the recipes. I need to write the POTPIE intro, collect three releases, finish two profiles for SWEETS, but that's it.

Nicole tried to grasp all that Charlotte had done—and, P.S., it wasn't like nothing was going on with *her* life. There would be Leo, surely an issue for Charlotte with only six days left on Quinnipeague. And though Nicole was starting to get used to the idea of their being together, she still couldn't ask. So she simply typed, *What would I have done without you?*

You'd have gotten an extension on your deadline, and you still should. You need to read everything I've written, and you'll want to make changes. It'll be easier because the structure is there, but this is your book. Can I call your editor?

Nicole let out a shaky breath and typed, *Not yet. Let's wait another few days and see what happens.*

She sent the last, but continued to stare at the words. *See what happens.* If Julian had a stroke, it would be more than a few days before she could focus on food. Likewise, if he was paralyzed or recovering from a heart attack, and if he died?

No. Better to get the cookbook done before Charlotte left.

*　　*　　*

She spent hours that evening at her laptop in Julian's room, poring over what Charlotte had sent. Each time Julian stirred, though, she was quickly up and leaning over the bed, asking how he felt, telling him how well he was doing.

Mark, who had been in and out all day, stopped by at ten to say that he was going home for a few hours of sleep. He looked more ruffled than his usual neat self. She doubted he was often at work this late.

"Are you worried?" she whispered again, not wanting Julian to hear.

The doctor's reply was similarly low, though likely more from exhaustion than secrecy. "No cause for worry yet."

"Is this a good sign for the success of the treatment?"

He shot her a glance over his glasses. "It's too early to tell. You should probably get some sleep yourself. Can I drop you back at the hotel?"

"No. I'll stay a while longer."

"They'll call if there's a problem. You're only five minutes away."

The night nurse said the same thing a short time later and again an hour after that. By the time she said it a third time, the room lights were low and Nicole had fallen asleep curled in the chair. She jolted awake at the touch of a hand on her arm.

"He's still sleeping," the woman said, "and that's a good thing, because if he sees you here at this hour, he'll worry."

Nicole went to the bed, saw for herself how peacefully Julian was sleeping, and gave in.

The call came at five on Saturday morning. Having fallen asleep only three hours before, she was dead to the world when the ringing jarred her awake. She was a minute getting her bearings and another searching for the phone in the folds of the sheets.

"Yes?" she breathed, sitting up. She was shaking as much from being startled awake as from fear.

It was Mark, his voice tight. "His temperature spiked. I'm at the

357

hospital now. I won't call it an emergency yet. But I told you we'd let you know if there was any change."

"Temperature spiked," Nicole echoed and swallowed, trying not to panic. "What does that mean?"

"He's having some kind of reaction. This may be the worst of it."

Or the start, she knew, pushing the sheets aside. "But you can get his temperature down, right?"

"I'm upping the acetaminophen, but I have to be careful."

He didn't have to elaborate. The fear was damage to a liver that hadn't fully recovered from the last MS drug.

They should have waited. She knew it, *knew* it. Another month, and he'd have been stronger. Another *two* months and he'd have been even stronger.

"Is he awake?" she asked, pulling a blouse from the closet.

"Yes. He says he's okay."

Of course, Mr. Cool-and-Calm would say that. Mr. Risk-taker would say this was part of the game.

Nicole was neither cool, calm, nor risk-taking. "I'm on my way," she said, and, ending the call, rushed to get dressed. Having in essence cut Mark off, she didn't know whether he would have told her to wait, that it wasn't crucial, that she should just come at eight. But it didn't matter. No *way* could she have gone back to sleep.

The sun hadn't yet risen when she was through the lobby and out the revolving door. Hopping into a cab, she hugged her bag to her chest, only marginally aware of a paler horizon between buildings to the east. In no time, she was at the hospital and taking the elevator to Julian's floor.

At first glance, there was no imminent trauma—no red lights flashing above his room, no emergency gear in sight. Mark stood just outside the door talking with two of the doctors from his team. Pushing at his glasses, he separated himself from them as she approached. She saw concern on his face, certainly fatigue, but no panic, not yet.

How is he? she mouthed. The floor was still in night mode—lights dimmer, sounds softer—but her own lack of sound wasn't so much consideration of others as pure anxiety.

"Still hot," he said quietly.

"Getting worse?"

"Up a notch."

She was still clutching her bag, needing to hold something solid with the bottom of her world shifting. "Not what we want."

"No."

And what more was there to say? Frightened, she entered the room. Julian's eyes were closed; he would still be on Benadryl, still half zonked. Flags of red touched his cheeks just above the shadow of his beard. His forehead was damp.

He opened his eyes, saw her there, and gave a vague smile. "Hey."

"Hey, yourself," she said brightly.

"What time is it?" The words were slurred.

"Early." She didn't want to alarm him with the actual time, which was five fifty. Slipping her bag to the floor, she leaned in to softly kiss his lips. They were as hot as his cheeks looked. "I couldn't sleep. How do you feel?"

"Okay."

"You look like you've just finished a run."

"Don't I wish," he murmured and held out a shaky hand for hers. He had a surgeon's long, slim fingers. She had always liked their warmth against her usually cold ones, but this intense heat was something else.

She told herself that it was the fever that was causing his hand to shake.

He closed his eyes. "This is a blip. It'll pass."

"Absolutely," she said and brought his hand to her throat. "Mark expected things like this." She glanced at the tray table with its small pitcher and half-filled plastic glass. "Is that drink still cold?" Ice had to be the way to go.

But he said, "It's fine."

And she didn't want to let go of his hand. "Are they letting you eat yet?"

"Only Jell-O."

She saw none on the tray. "Can I bring you more?"

Eyes still closed, he shook his head. If she couldn't bring him drink and she couldn't bring him food, she could at least cool his face. She ran her free hand along his jaw, up to his temple, across his brow and down. He hummed his pleasure.

She repeated the circle once, twice, three times, by which time her fingers had warmed. He was hotter than ever.

Hugging his hand to her neck, she put her elbows on the bed rail and watched him. He didn't actually sleep but seemed to hover in a twilight one step above, opening his eyes to smile at her every so often before drifting again. Nicole didn't move, not when the nurse checked him, not when Hammon checked him. She counted his breaths, reassured by their steadiness. She wasn't reassured by the color on his cheeks, though, which was flaming compared to the pallor elsewhere. When her legs tired, she pulled the chair close and, clasping his hand now between the rails, put her forehead to the cool metal and closed her eyes.

"Tired?" he mumbled.

"Mmm."

"Go for coffee."

She looked up. "For you?"

"You," he said, clearly wanting to sleep himself.

Still she stayed. She might have even dozed, vaguely knew that others came and went, but she was tired enough not to move and encouraged enough by the curl of Julian's hand around hers not to bother with anything else.

She was starting to stir, needing to stretch and use the bathroom, when Charlotte texted. *How's he doing?*

He has a fever.

As in a reaction? Call me when you can.

Rising then, she leaned over the bed. "Jules?" she whispered.

When, with visible effort, he opened his eyes, she asked, "How do you feel?"

"Okay," he mouthed and returned to wherever he'd been, but he didn't look as peaceful as he had earlier. His skin was moist, his brow furrowed; he seemed to be concentrating. Trying to control the fever through sheer force of will? She touched his cheek. He was burning up.

"I'm going for that coffee now," she said softly. "Can I bring you anything?" His headshake was small. She kissed his forehead. "Be right back," she whispered and slipped out of the room.

"I only have a sec," she said the instant Charlotte picked up. "The fever was 102 when I got here at six and it's 103.5 now. They can't control it. I want to bathe him with cool cloths, but they say no." She had just checked, frantic to do something.

"Is Hammon worried?"

"He doesn't say it in as many words, but he's not a word man to begin with, and when I talked with him a minute ago, he was down to two per response. *This isn't trending the right way*, I say. He says, *I know. Isn't there anything you can do?* I ask. *Not yet*, he says. So I'm thinking," she told Charlotte, "that a reaction means his body is aware of the treatment, but when I ask Mark if this is good or bad, he says, *We'll know soon*. Three words. Yay."

"You have a right to be upset—"

"*Scared*."

"Scared, but if this is the worst it gets, it isn't so bad. I'm sure Hammon's doing what he can," Charlotte reasoned and, coming from anyone else, Nicole would have shot back with a dozen arguments to the effect that Mark knew this might happen and should have had a plan, that it was a fever, for pity's sake, and if a teaching hospital couldn't deal with a fever, *it* had a serious problem, and that maybe Mark's best wasn't good enough.

But this was Charlotte, whose voice brought comfort.

"I wish you could come," she pleaded. "Any chance?"

After a pause came a soft, "I can't, Nicki."

"Because of Leo?" There. She'd had to ask.

Charlotte didn't deny it. "I only have five days left here," she said, sounding like she was agonizing. "I need this time. Besides," she hurried on, "given the circumstances, it isn't really appropriate. I still regret what happened that night. I'll always regret it."

"I don't," Nicole said, unable to hold anything against Charlotte just then. "He would have had MS with or without you. Same with this treatment. He was itching for it, and if it wasn't these cells, he'd have used donor ones. These ones feel better to me. I just want it to work, Charlotte. I keep wondering what I'll do if it ends badly. Julian has his heart set on a cure. If there's no hope, what's left?"

"If he's alive—"

"He'll be devastated. I want to criticize him for putting all his eggs in one basket, but there just isn't any other basket."

"There will be," Charlotte reasoned. "Research is ongoing. If this doesn't work, something else will. You have to keep telling yourself that."

"That's fine for me, but what do I tell Julian?"

Discouraged, she bought coffee and a muffin, and carried them back upstairs. Hammon was just leaving the room. The stark lines of his face said there was no improvement.

Setting her food on the tray table, she sat on the side of the bed where the rail was down and held Julian's hot hand in one of hers while she nibbled and sipped with the other. When she'd had enough, she pressed his fingers to her mouth, willing the scent of coffee and blueberries there. They smelled antiseptic, but his hands often did, given his work. Everything else was strange, though, from the heat of his skin to his utter stillness. She told herself that he was conserving energy, focusing on fighting rejection of strange cells in his body, but it was small solace.

His temperature continued to rise. It had hit 104 by noon and 104.5 by three.

"How high can it *go*?" she asked in a panic.

"Higher," the nurse said calmly, clearly used to fevers.

They gave him more acetaminophen. Hammon came and went, came and went, assuring her that Julian was strong enough to fight this, but she could see that he was concerned.

"Is there nothing more you can do?" she begged. "Nothing else to lower the fever?"

"Not yet," he replied but seemed disinclined to say more.

What are you waiting for? she thought frantically when he left her alone again with Julian, who continued to float, tethered to the bed by a tangle of sensors and wires and the hum of the mother machines.

Then she knew what they were waiting for—or, at least, what they feared. The humming went on, but there was something else. At first, she thought Julian was snoring and gently shook his arm. When he opened his eyes, though, she could hear each breath he took.

"Call Hammon," he managed.

Racing to the hall, she was looking around in bewilderment when a nurse, having seen the problem from her station, rushed past. Minutes later, Hammon and his team came at a clip from the computer room behind the desk.

Nicole followed them in, but stayed clear of the bedside while they listened and examined and discussed what to do. In addition to the wheezing, Julian's blood pressure had dropped, both of which raised mention of anaphylactic shock. From time to time, she heard Julian speak in a low, whistly voice, and even in spite of the sound, he was forceful. He clearly had an opinion. Nicole guessed what it was.

Separating himself from the others, Hammon joined her. "We could use steroids. They'd control the reaction. But they might kill the T-regulatory cells."

"Julian wants to wait."

"Yes. He knows the risk."

Of killing the cure. But the risk went beyond that, and in a moment of panic she could only see the other. "At what point do you opt to save his life?" she asked in a high voice.

"When we feel it's in danger. Let's see how long this lasts."

She held her tongue. Raw with emotion in a world of science, she was out of her depth.

Hammon returned to Julian's side. Feeling weak, she backed up to the wall by the door and listened as they went back and forth, weighing pros against cons with none of the emphasis she would apply. After a time, she didn't hear the words, only the awful sound of Julian's laboring breath.

It went on and on and on. She must have begun to look sick, because a nurse gently took her arm and guided her out to the hall for air. No, she didn't want water. No, she didn't want tea. She stood there feeling frightened and alone, arms wrapped around her middle in an attempt to self-soothe. And when the nurse asked if there was anyone she could call to be with her through the evening, she gave a jerky shake of her head.

Oh yes, she had friends. And family. And a following that clung to her every word.

But the friends were back in Philadelphia, thinking that Julian was on vacation in Maine. They didn't have a clue about this.

Same with Kaylin and John, both of whom should be there if their father was failing. They knew he was in Chicago consulting on a new treatment, but he had refused to tell them the rest.

And the following? They knew Nickitotable, not Nicki Carlysle.

Had her father been alive, she would have called him. He would have boosted her spirits.

Or . . . or maybe not. She didn't want to hear *Aim high, hit high* right now, and as for *What doesn't kill us, blah blah blah,* that was *so* not what she needed. She had adored Bob, but he was optimism to the point of denial. It struck her now that if he had been more proactive about his family history of heart problems, he might still be alive.

Realism was her mom's domain. Just then, she wanted Angie. They had parted badly, with ill will and ugly words. But she wanted Angie. She looked down the hall toward the elevator, willing her to emerge, aching for it.

And then suddenly there she was, a blurred image through Nicole's tears, surely a mirage. But the closer she got, the more real she was.

They hadn't talked in the four weeks since Angie had left Quinnipeague, but four weeks couldn't negate thirty-four years.

"Mom," Nicole breathed. Just Mom, and the estrangement was done.

Angie's face held only concern. When her arms opened, Nicole went there and began to weep, and those arms tightened around her, which was what she needed most. She had been strong for Julian, supporting his decision, steadying his limbs, filling in the blanks when they had time on their hands. And she had vented to Charlotte. But it wasn't the same.

Angie was her mother. Mothers were for those times when only a total meltdown would do. And tears were only the first part. After that came talk. As they sat side by side in the family lounge, Nicole poured out every bit of her fear—the rising fever, the falling blood pressure, the wheezing that could escalate to anaphylactic shock, the ominous hand tremor, the steroid dilemma.

Angie was sympathetic and concerned—but yes, realistic. She didn't pretend to have answers, simply listened and asked questions. Her presence alone was calming. It was also well-timed. Nicole was about to take her to Julian's room when Mark appeared in the lounge. "We're transferring him to the ICU," he said quietly.

She was on her feet in a flash. "He's worse?"

"No, but we can watch him more closely there."

"He's still refusing steroids, isn't he?" Julian wasn't flashy in manner or dress, but when it came to medicine, he was definitely out there. Granted, he was careful. He studied every angle. But once committed, he didn't turn back.

"He's still hoping to preserve the T-regs."

"Do you agree with him?"

"I see his point. I also see the other side. Right now, I'm torn. That's why we want to watch him more closely. If he gets much worse, we won't have a choice."

"Should I try talking with him myself?" Nicole asked and answered, "No, no point. If he wouldn't listen to you, he won't listen to me."

Mark gave her a brief smile. "You're probably right. I admire him, though. He'd rather die trying."

Die trying, Nicole thought and turned frantic eyes to her mother.

Angie stood then and put a restraining hand on her arm. After introducing herself to the doctor, she said, "Can we do anything while you move him?"

"You can take Nicole somewhere for dinner."

Since Nicole refused to leave the hospital, they went to the cafeteria, but she couldn't think of a thing she wanted to eat. She sat at a table, fingers knotting, while Angie filled a tray, paid the cashier, and set the tray neatly before her, but all she could hear-see-feel was ICU ICU ICU.

"It sounds worse than it is," Angie offered gently as she divvied up napkins, forks, knives, and food. "It's just a precaution."

"What if he does die?" she asked as she could only with Angie.

"Don't go there, honey. He's a long way from that."

But Nicole couldn't stop. If the doctors were worried enough to want intensive care, *they* were thinking he might die. She had known this was a possibility. But a future without Julian? Unthinkable. She should've told him that back in Philadelphia, should've said it on the island and again last Friday morning at the hotel, before all of this had begun. She could've made him fight harder. She would've done it, if she hadn't been determined to be strong for him herself. And now, intensive care?

"An ICU is just another room with more machines," Angie mused, taking a forkful of chicken salad. "Dr. Hammon simply wants to get as much information as he can. He's covering his bases, and I don't say that in criticism. He doesn't strike me as the type who'll let his patient die trying unless he's pulled out every stop. He'll overrule Julian when he feels the time is right." She eyed an unappetizing piece of fish before pushing the chicken salad toward Nicole. "Please eat."

Nicole picked up a roll. Setting it down again, she eyed Angie in despair. "I'm trying to be realistic. That's what this whole summer's been about. It's what this whole *year* has been about. Talk about wake-up calls. Talk about *growing up*."

"Oh sweetheart, you've been grown up for a while. Look at the last four years. Keeping all that to yourself, accepting Julian's limitations, dealing with flare-ups? And your blog? And the *book*? You don't give yourself enough credit."

Charlotte had said the same. But Nicole couldn't take credit for anything when Julian was en route to the ICU. "How does one prepare for something like this?"

"One doesn't. It's all about how you react when it happens."

"This isn't what I wanted."

"No." Her mother smiled. "But look at it this way. If you'd died at twenty-five, you wouldn't have had to deal with it."

"What an awful thing to say!"

But Angie didn't take it back. She simply straightened the straw in her diet Coke and sipped—and of course, in the silence, Nicole realized she was right. This was what always happened. Mother-daughter disagreements were, in hindsight, basically mother stating the truth and daughter taking her own sweet time coming around. That had been the case with boys and sports. It was certainly the case with Tom.

"I was not nice to you when you were on Quinnipeague," Nicole said softly.

"No, you weren't."

"I'm sorry."

"Apology accepted."

Nicole paused. "Just like that? No discussion."

"No. Not now, at least. I understand what you're feeling, sweetheart. Trust me, I've felt a lot of it myself. I also know how frightened you are right now. You're thinking that you can't lose Julian, that your life would be totally empty without him, that there has to be something you can do; only you don't know what it is. Your mind is filled with coulda shoulda wouldas."

Nicole was amazed. Hadn't she thought those same words five minutes before? "How did you know?"

"Because I loved your father like you love Julian. He was in the ICU,
too—the difference being that he was basically gone when he got there.
Julian is not. You will have your life with him, sweetheart. I have to
believe that. You will."

Nicole breathed more deeply. Angie couldn't know for sure that Julian would survive. Plus, there were different levels of survival, any
one of which might be worse than what they'd had before now and, in
so being, impact their lives forever more.

But she did trust her mother. And she did want to believe.

Reaching for Angie's hand, she linked their fingers as she used to do
when she was little and whispered, "How long can you stay?"

"As long as you want, honey. I'm here for you."

Moments later, when Angie went to dump the uneaten food and buy
cheese to nibble on upstairs, Nicole pulled out her phone.

Thank you, she typed very simply and pressed SEND.

Chapter Twenty-eight

CHARLOTTE WAS ROWING. THE BOAT was an old wooden thing that she had spotted in Leo's shed, but since, unlike the sailboat, it was something she could drive herself, she had made him take it out. Leo, being Leo and a handyman, had sanded, painted, and sealed it before he would launch it, and then, though he let her row, he insisted on going along.

The sun hadn't set, but it was heading that way, spattering gold across the waves under a brooding sky. As mild as the waves were, the boat bobbed more than it actually moved. Pulling on the oars with her back to the bow, Charlotte was fully absorbed for the first time that day.

When her phone vibrated against her hip, though, Chicago came back in a rush. Dropping the oars in their oarlocks, she pulled it out, saw Nicole's text, and smiled in relief.

"Her mother got there," Leo guessed. Facing her in the stern with his bare feet braced wide, he was uncorking a bottle of wine and, with remarkable steadiness given the rock of the boat, half-filled two plastic cups.

An OK exec decision? she typed.

Very OK, Nicole replied.

Satisfied, Charlotte took the cup he offered. After tapping it to his—they always did this—she sipped.

"How is he?" Leo asked.

Charlotte glanced at the phone again before sliding it into her pocket. "Must be the same, if she didn't say."

"She should have called her mother herself." As sympathetic as Leo was for the situation, he hadn't warmed much to Nicole.

"Uh-huh," she said, sipping the wine. "We know all about that." He still refused to call his father.

With a you-know-what-I-mean look, he reached into a plastic baggie, pairing cheese with pear slices for her and with crackers for himself.

She took a bite, then said, "If it were me, I'd call Kaylin and John, too. They ought to be there. She needs all the support she can get." She pushed the rest of the snack in her mouth.

Leo's eyes were level. "Go to her."

She shook her head no, leveled a gaze right back at him as she swallowed. "I choose you." It was one step removed from *I love you,* which she didn't say other than in moments of passion, when she had no control over what came out. Those words were too threatening for other times. And that was fine. He knew how she felt.

The oars clinked loudly against their locks. Leaning forward, he pulled them into the boat, then reached into the baggie and doled out seconds.

"Maybe you shouldn't," he finally said. "There are too many problems."

"Tell me something new." He didn't travel. That wasn't new.

"Kids," he said.

Whoa. That *was* new. He hadn't mentioned kids before. *Salt* hadn't gone that far, and she hadn't dared ask. "You want them?"

"Yes," he said, seeming wounded that she wouldn't have known.

"That's part of the dream, but we can't have kids if you're flying all over the world."

The fact that he was thinking of these things was something. But a step forward or just an extension of the wall? "So the problem is me."

"It's *me*. I'm Quinnipeague."

"You're sophisticated, educated, and worldly on paper. You could do it in real life," she argued.

But he was stuck on the other. "And even if you went back and forth from here, we'd still be apart for weeks at a time. That's a recipe for disaster."

"Oh, come on, Leo," she said gently, "that's what we see on TV and read in books, both of which need trauma to keep the plot moving. But I know lots of couples that have families and jobs and still travel. Everyone gives a little, and it works. If you're talking babies, though, you'd *really* have to meet me halfway."

"You don't want more kids?"

"I do. *Absolutely*. But I did it alone once, and I won't do that again. And excuse me," she frowned, "where would I give *birth* to these kids? There is no hospital here." Quinnie babies were customarily born on the mainland in the kind of hospital where Cecily had died after Leo had dragged her there, for which he still felt deep regret.

He seemed confused, clearly hadn't considered that. Brows knitting, he leaned forward, then sat back again, elbows on the transom, long legs splayed outside hers. The pose was more defiant than relaxed. "What if someone finds out who I am? That'd be a problem if you were my girlfriend, wife, mother of my kids, whatever."

"Wouldn't be a problem for me. You're the only one who has a problem with success."

"Okay, then the reverse. What if I can't write another book? What if the money I've made on *Salt* is a one-time thing? What if I can't support a wife and kids?"

Charlotte stared at him. "Listen to you, Leo. You're dreaming up problems, and every one of them is small. Money is not an issue. You have enough to last a lifetime, even *before* the paperback comes out, and that's not counting what you could make if you let them turn *Salt* into a movie. You invest. I've seen you do it. You're making money on top of money."

"I worry."

"So do I, but not about that. Right now, I worry that Julian Carlysle might die. All the money in the world didn't keep him from getting MS, and it can't assure his survival now." She felt a chill just thinking about it, though perhaps that was a murky cloud crossing the path of the setting sun. They were definitely in a sea shadow. She had to move, but to where?

Nicole would have said sea shadows were for fools because, try as she might to hang in there and be positive and maybe see things differently—as in, these reactions are just part of a larger picture that includes reduction of MS symptoms—come Sunday morning, Julian was no better. As Angie had warned, there were more machines in the ICU. And the staff checked on him so often that it was like having a private nurse. But his temperature remained high, and the wheezing was exhausting him in a way that went well beyond the drowsiness of Benadryl.

Still, he refused to take steroids.

By Monday morning, when there was no improvement, she was worried enough, frustrated enough, angry enough to take a page from Charlotte's book and to make an executive decision of her own. Julian's parents, being in San Diego, were too far away to come running, but his children were not. They were adults, or close to it. They had a right to be there.

Charlotte was constantly checking her phone for word from Nicole, but other than the occasional *Still the same* or *No change*—all sent from outside the ICU, since cell phones were banned inside—there was nothing of substance until Monday afternoon.

Then, *I called Kaylin and John. They'll be here tomorrow. He's going to be mad, but tough shit. It was the right thing to do.*

Absolutely. They SHOULD be there. You did GOOD, Nicki. Any improvement yet?

No. Hammon is still agonizing over steroids. If Julian asked him to do it, he would. I'm telling you, my husband's priorities are fucked up.

The language was totally uncharacteristic of Nicole, but she was clearly at her wits' end. Not that Charlotte was about to scold, since every other thought in her mind was that *Leo's* priorities were fucked up, too, in those very same words. She knew that Leo loved her at some level. But enough to admit it? Admitting it meant you acknowledged what it meant, which meant you did have to give a little, and he wasn't ready to do that.

Time was running out. She was up late Monday night working on the cookbook and at it again at dawn on Tuesday, working straight through midafternoon, when she was finally able to call Nicole.

"How is he?" she asked first, because that remained the priority.

"The same," Nicole replied, sounding tense. "Kay and Johnny just landed. They'll be here any minute. He won't be happy. I'm gearing up for that. So tell me something good."

"I think we're done."

There was a moment's silence, then a surprised, "You and Leo?"

"The cookbook," Charlotte corrected with barely bridled excitement. In spite of everything dark going on, there was still a sense of accomplishment when she finally closed her working file, sat back, and let her hands fall from the computer. As for Leo, he was in her good graces at that moment, having been genuinely excited for her. Knowing she would call Nicole, he had gone into town to pick up groceries for a celebratory dinner.

Nicole's voice lifted. "Seriously?"

"I just e-mailed you the last of the files."

"Omigod! You. Are. Amazing!"

"Don't say that until you read what I sent. I love the profiles, but you may want to reorder which goes where, and tweak menu plans to coordinate with that, and there's still all the me-writing-as-you business."

"I'm barely halfway through. I'm so far behind!"

"But that's the second part of my news." Charlotte was nearly as pleased about this. "You have more time."

Nicole's laugh was shrill. "Not from what *I* see."

"So I called my favorite editor," Charlotte went on. "She and I get along really well, like we have lunch together just for fun, and I asked if she knew yours. Turns out that they're good friends. Do you know about the baby?"

Nicole was clearly puzzled. "Yes. It's due at the end of September."

"It came last *week*. She must have e-mailed you."

There was a pause, then a gasp. "Omigod. *That* e-mail?" She switched to speaker phone, apparently checking her inbox while she talked. "I didn't open it, because I felt so guilty not being done." She gasped a second time. "A little girl. Five pounds, one ounce. Deadline extension until the end of September, when she'll start working from home." She let out a long, soft, clearly relieved sigh. "Omigod. I don't believe it. This is the best news!"

So, just like Charlotte when she'd called, Nicole had two pieces of good news to share with Julian. She knew he would be pleased about the cookbook, but she didn't get to that until much later, because just as she turned off her phone, Kaylin and John arrived. Kaylin looked the New Yorker in skinny jeans, blousy layers, and impossibly high heels, while John, with an untucked shirt, jeans, and an impossibly pale face, just looked scared.

Nicole had called them for Julian's sake. Seeing them coming toward her, though, she felt a little of the same relief she had felt seeing Angie. This was her family. With each new arrival, she felt less alone.

Though Angie was included in the hugs, Nicole was the one to explain what was happening. She had told them on the phone about the treatment and his reaction. Now, without quite saying he might die, she detailed his symptoms. "He sounds worse than he is," she said, which wasn't necessarily the truth, but they would be frightened enough.

Leading them into Julian's unit, she directed them to the hand sanitizer, and then, leaning over the bed, gently shook his arm. He opened his eyes, but it was a minute before they focused on his children. There was an initial instinctive flare of pleasure, then understanding and a glower at Nicole.

"I didn't want them to worry," he croaked between wheezy inhalations.

"They're here to cheer you on." She stood back to give each of the kids time. Kaylin took more, though she talked so steadily about how glad she was that Nicole had called because she wanted to be there, that nothing was demanded of Julian. John was more emotional, as, ironically, was Julian.

"I'll be fine," he managed to tell his son while struggling for air and composure, but he seemed to find new strength when the kids retreated and Nicole took their place. His brown eyes, still dull with fever, were full of censure, his words sharp around the whistling of his breath. "I told you not to."

"They love you."

He rasped, "What's love." It wasn't a question, more a holier-than-thou dismissal, and that hit Nicole the wrong way.

"It's *everything*," she said, eyes wide open. "It's why I've been here with you for the last week and a half, even when I would have rather waited longer to do this, and it's why you need to *fight*."

"But not . . . the kids."

"Yes, the kids," she shot back with a fire she wouldn't have dared a day or two ago, but if not now, when? *If not now, when?* Her father had been big on sayings; this one was hers. It was what reality was about. Growing up—being strong—this was her summer. And it absolutely felt right. "They love you. They want to be part of your life. Well, illness goes with that. They aren't babies, Jules. They're young adults with lots of good sense and positive vibes, and they *love* you." With Julian staring at her, seeming stunned by her voice, listening with greater awareness than he'd shown since Friday, she felt a surge of strength. "They're here because I called them, because this is what people do when they love each other, this is what families do—and aren't you lucky to have this? Some people don't." As an inner steam built, she pressed a hand to her chest. "Omigod, I feel so blessed to have them here right now. You should, too, and if you can't see that, then you don't deserve us." Clutching his hand, she leaned in and, more determined than ever, said, "If you can't fight for yourself, fight for us. Do not throw this away, Julian Carlysle. Do not be a total . . . total . . . *prick.*"

He stared at her. His forehead was still dewy and his cheeks flushed, but something gave in his eyes, and his lips curved. "Prick?"

She hedged. It was an ugly word. "I was going to say asshole, but that's what came out."

He made a strangled sound that might have been a chuckle. "Prick, huh?"

"You can be," she said softly.

"But you love me anyway."

"I do."

Smiling, he closed his eyes. The smile lingered, but he said nothing more. He was quiet. Too quiet.

Dead.

The thought stole her breath.

Terrified, she leaned close again and gave his hand a sharp shake. "Julian."

He opened his eyes. "Just resting. Want to ease up on the hand?"

* * *

He's better! Charlotte read a short time later. *Wheezing, blood pressure, fever—everything broke. It'll be a while before he's totally out of the woods, but Hammon is beside himself. Me, I just can't believe it. More later. Going back in now.*

Tears in her eyes, throat tight, she showed the text to Leo, who hugged her until the kitchen timer drew him away. Beyond joy for Nicole, she felt extraordinary relief, as though the hell of the summer—memories of the affair, Nicole's anger, the loss of this only link to her own child—had a purpose.

The book was done, and Julian had turned a corner. It was a double-celebratory dinner.

Leo had bought lobster fresh from the sea that afternoon, and cooked it live, which she refused to do herself after hearing the scrabbling of the claws against the pot years before. He also grilled ears of sweet corn and sliced zucchini, both fresh from Quinnipeague fields, while Charlotte heated a round of Melissa Parker's buttery rosemary bread.

Silence between them had never been a problem, and it wasn't now. Charlotte couldn't help but think of Julian and smile in relief from time to time, but increasingly her thoughts were of Leo. His features were soft now, his midnight eyes warm. He tucked a strand of hair behind her ear; she wiped butter from his lip with a thumb. Again and again, they raised their wineglasses in wordless toasts, and when the wine was gone and the food eaten, they lingered over coffee, sitting on the dock with Bear. When Charlotte leaned down at one point to rest her head on the dog's neck, her eyes filled with tears. By the time she straightened, though, the tears were gone. She refused to cry on this special night.

Later yet, when the moon was up and the surf down, they walked the beach, toes gripping the sand, hands separating only to scramble over large rocks. In time they reached the spot where they had first made love seven weeks before. It might have been their destination all along, but they didn't speak of it aloud. Leaving their clothes on the beach, they swam, though once they were in over their heads, it was more treading water, with Leo keeping them afloat while Charlotte wrapped her legs around his waist and her arms around his neck, and their mouths fused.

They made love once there in the water, then again, slower and more savoring, on the beach. When it was done, they stayed until the ocean air chilled them. Then, carrying their clothes in the hands that weren't linked, they returned to the house, where they lay in bed for the longest time, bodies curled into each other as they listened to the roll of the tide, which was as rhythmic as Leo's breathing when he finally fell asleep.

Charlotte didn't sleep, simply listened to the ocean, his breathing, and that life-sustaining beat of his heart. Minutes passed, then hours. If she dozed, it wasn't for long. More important, she knew, to feel the soft brush of his chest hair against her cheek and the strength of his thigh under hers. More important to commit his scent to memory.

Shortly before dawn, leaving Leo prone on the bed with his head turned away, she quietly rose. Bear looked up from the floor, but a simple touch to that silky spot between his eyes had him sleeping again. Her duffel was on a chair; never having formally moved in, she had never fully unpacked, which made the task easier now. Adding the last of her clothes and toiletries, she carried the bag to the kitchen. Wanting to say some last thing to Leo, she took paper and pen from a drawer, but words escaped her. Finally, with a simply XOXOX, she left the note on the pillow, let herself out the front door, walked down the drive with her duffel and on to Nicole's.

Leo didn't follow. He didn't come or even call, but she hadn't expected either. She wasn't even sure he had been totally asleep while she was packing. They both knew this had to be done.

That said, the hole inside her gaped. She tried to fill it by doing laundry and cleaning her room, but both were quickly done. So she knit. After a summer of it, she was totally familiar with the pattern and, miraculously, made no mistakes. By early afternoon, she had cast off and was driving to Isabel Skane's for instructions on putting the pieces together. She took detailed notes, thinking it might take her a while to get it done. But the finishing turned out to be the easy part, especially since she had nothing else to do but sew on the patio, seeking comfort from the last of the pergola roses, the salty breeze and the thunder of the surf.

More than once, she wandered to the garden where lavender, valerian, and red clover thrived. She smiled, pleased that they remained alive, though they had certainly done their job. Word from Chicago was good. Julian was better, steadily recovering from the transplant. Even his MS symptoms were improved, Nicole reported, though only time would tell if that would hold. Likewise, only time would tell whether the stem cells could actually mend damage to the myelin sheath that four years of the disease had caused. But Nicole didn't care about that. She had her man back. She couldn't be happier.

In a moment's whimsy, thinking that the plants remained alive and fresh just for her, Charlotte picked a single clover, made a wish, and tucked it by her heart. She didn't know if she believed in all this. Too often in her life, she had dug deep inside and come up with the same calming that the plants had offered, and as for making wishes on red clover, was this truly why Julian was better? Medicine was medicine, science was science, physiology was physiology—and had Leo said he loved her, for all the clover she'd picked and wishes she'd made? No!

Discouraged, she returned to the sweater, working into the evening, weaving in ends and wrapping it up just before exhaustion hit. Having not slept the night before, she slept soundly—a good sign, she decided Thursday morning as she made a last check of the house, packed up the Wrangler, and set off.

As planned, she reached the pier before the ferry arrived. Taking the tissue-wrapped package from the passenger's seat, she went into the Chowder House. The scent of chowder was strong, accompanied by that of fried clams. Dorey was in the kitchen, getting ready for lunch. One look at Charlotte, though, and, wiping her hands on a cloth, she left the stove.

"You look like you lost your best friend," the woman said, uncharacteristically subdued.

"Actually, there's good news." Smiling, Charlotte told her about Julian.

"Good news but not surprising," Dorey decided. "The heart of Quinnipeague was with them." She paused. "It'll be with you, too."

Charlotte struggled not to cry. "A favor?" she managed to ask and held out the package. She didn't have to say who it was for or what to do with it. Dorey nodded and took it. Then her crinkled eyes grew pleading.

"Are you sure you can't stay?"

"Yes. I have to work."

"Will you be back?"

"I don't know." Choking up, she turned to leave. When she felt a stocky arm around her shoulders, she paused, eyes on the old wood floor.

Dorey's voice was filled with compassion. "And I was worried about him," she remarked with a *tsk*. "Take care of yourself, Missy. I'll keep the chowdah hot for you."

Chowdah. So Maine, so *Quinnie*, the word echoed in her head until the ferry horn blasted it out. Once she'd driven the Wrangler aboard and the ramp was raised, she took a seat in the stern. How not to look for him then? How not to hope he had changed his mind? How not to envision a happily-ever-after in this place that was a fantasy in so many ways?

All she saw, though, was the island growing smaller as the ferry plowed through the waves toward the mainland.

She did fine all the way to Rockland, did fine all the way to New York. She even did fine when she got to Brooklyn and found her third-floor walkup sweltering, the AC on the blink, and no air to be had outside. She called her landlord, stopped at her coolest favorite sushi place for dinner and, after, at her coolest favorite café for a tall, iced raspberry tea to go. Back in her apartment, she was fine going through her closet for clothes to take to France.

It was when she was taking Quinnie things from her duffel, reaching in a final time, that she touched something hard. Puzzled, she pulled it out. It was a piece of pine, six inches of increasing detail from tail to nose, its head a near-perfect replica of Bear whittled by the man who knew him best.

Charlotte's heart began to pound. For all the nothings Leo had started that summer, all the while claiming that he wasn't good at it and that, like her knitting, it was all about the process, this was exquisite.

Holding the tiny dog, with its small, widespread ears, its muscular flanks and lean legs, and, in her mind's eye, seeing the real thing with its master close behind, she burst into tears.

Chapter Twenty-nine

*P*ARIS WAS AS MUCH FUN as Paris could be without a beating heart, or so Charlotte felt. In the two days she was there, she robotically followed her friends, smiling and nodding even when their French babble went over her head. She didn't tell them about Leo, didn't want to talk about him, and they were excited enough just seeing her and taking her from market to market, café to café, club to club.

Did she think about Leo? Of course, she did. She had deliberately packed different clothes from ones that would remind her of Quinnipeague, but she had tucked the little whittled Bear in their midst—couldn't leave it home alone, much less sleep without it—and she thought of Leo each time her hands warmed the wood. He had taken great pains, particularly with the detail of the head, and with pine being knotty and soft, she wondered how many times he'd had to restart with a fresh piece when one didn't work. While she slept? While she was at Nicole's or in town? Was it a 'til-September gift or a final good-bye? She just didn't know.

She also thought of him each time Nicole sent an update, which was often. Julian had been removed from intensive care on Thursday night, and when Charlotte landed in Paris early Saturday morning, a waiting e-mail said he was up and walking around. Charlotte was pleased for them both, though here, too, it was a knee-jerk response.

By the time he was discharged from the hospital, it was Monday, and she was en route to Bordeaux. Here, amid imposing châteaux and lush vineyards, she was more engaged. This was her baby; she had to be *on*. Her assignment was to profile an American family who had recently bought a small vineyard here. It was a remarkable clan—three generations' worth, including two grandparents, two sons and their wives, and seven children under the age of ten—facing a remarkable challenge. Having owned a smaller vineyard in California, they were following a dream, and though the former owners were there to guide them, it wasn't going quite the way they had planned. Between a weakened economy, a foreign infusion that was driving prices too high, and the sheer veneration of the competition, they had been forced to rethink their goals. Marketability was their new byword. Their wines had to be affordable, which meant cutting margins of profitability, which meant retooling the dream even more—all of which meant stress. And yet they were happy. During the ten days Charlotte spent in their aging château, she saw optimism at every turn.

For the first five of those days, Nicole and Julian stayed in Chicago to return to the hospital for daily checks. By the time Charlotte left Bordeaux, they were back in Philadelphia, and Charlotte was welcoming Nicole's texts as ties to her past. She knew the minute they settled back into their condo with new hope, the minute Nicole hit her favorite farmers' markets, the minute she realized—again—that nothing was as fresh as Quinnie-fresh.

Fresh described Tuscany, though in totally different ways from Bordeaux. Rather than verdant rows of manicured vines rolling up and down hillsides, in the small Italian village where she stayed, the olive groves were more drab, their trees rangy and staggered. Rather than the moist scent of Bordeaux, the smells here were drier and more piquant, often of *focacce* or fish or meat stew, all cooked with olive oil straight from the press.

The challenge here wasn't optimism, but evolution. The subjects of her story were an olive farm and the Italian family that had run it for generations, and their constant reinvention had more to do with the personal interest of the members than the economy. Money meant little to this family. To them, life was about trying different things, most notably—and the reason Charlotte was there—establishing a cooking school to showcase the glory of the olive.

She spent hours with growers, pruners, pickers, and pressers. She interviewed local chefs and sat in on a session with current students. Much like what she'd done those last days on Quinnipeague, she was in the process of choosing recipes for her piece, when Nicole and Julian returned to the island.

His tests are all good, Nicole wrote, *so Hammon says the risk of further rejection is remote. He's still weak, but it'll be a while before we know whether it's from the transplant or the disease.*

Is he discouraged?

Hard to say. I don't think he's thought about work yet. He's focused on getting out and walking. He's determined to be running in another week. That's his litmus test for recovery.

Picturing them on the road, the patio, the beach, Charlotte felt a wave of homesickness. *What's it like there?*

Gorgeous. The nights are cooler and start earlier, but the crowd's gone. I've been taking my laptop to the Café and working there. Am almost done. I mean, there are no changes—NO changes—to what you did. How do I thank you—for that work, for the stem cells?

He'd have made it through. It was meant to be.

But so much more meaningful this way.

More painful? Charlotte had to ask, because nothing could ever erase the betrayal behind those cells.

Maybe a little, Nicole typed. *But being back here, I miss you. Are you okay?*

I'm good, Charlotte replied. *Back in my old routine,* she added. Only she wasn't really. Try as she might to recapture the excitement of traveling freely without ties to home, she failed. She was with people all day long, but she was lonely. And then there was the whittled dog.

What's the word from Leo? Nicole asked.

Charlotte felt a deep, dark pang. *Zip. We aren't in touch.*

Why not?

Taking a break. That was the gentlest way to put it.

You BROKE UP?

No. Yes. Maybe. I don't know. Having typed the words on impulse, she positioned her thumb to delete. But this perfectly expressed what she felt, which was total confusion. She loved Leo but didn't know what to do with it. She had hoped he would text, or call, or get on a *friggin' jet* in a burst of courage, and surprise her with a declaration of undying love on the banks of the Seine, in a vineyard in Bordeaux, or under a Tuscan olive tree.

Such romantic notions. This wasn't who she was. It might be what she liked to read. But in real life?

Leaving the first words as is, she typed, *It's like Julian, I guess. Time will tell.*

Then you're not coming here after Italy?

To Quinnipeague? No. I take the train back to Paris Wednesday and fly to New York Friday. I'll work there for a while.

I'm sending you flowers. When do you land?

You are not sending me flowers. Flowers were unnecessary. *Thanks* were unnecessary. She would never quite feel she deserved either, where Nicole was concerned.

When do you land? Nicole repeated.

Knowing that she was determined enough to figure it out, which meant that arguing now was absurd, and that, anyway, flowers would be pretty and bright in her lonely walkup, she typed, *1:25 P.M. Friday.*

In fact, she arrived a day early. Once in Paris, she felt a yearning for American soil, and when a can't-hurt-to-try phone call offered a flight change, she booked it. The flight was smooth and, despite headwinds, landed early. Her duffel was one of the first to emerge; she sailed through customs, and was still early enough to be in a cab en route to Brooklyn before the Friday afternoon rush. The AC worked perfectly, quickly cooling her apartment. In no time, she had unpacked, putting clean in the closet and dirty in a basket. Her laptop, camera, and a folder of pamphlets and notes went on the breakfast bar in her galley kitchen.

What to do then?

Craving to reconnect with her roots, she began calling friends, some of whom she hadn't talked with since spring. She left three messages before, desperate for a human voice, she called her friend-the-editor, took the subway into Manhattan, and met her for drinks. Whether being jostled on the subway, crowded in pedestrian traffic, or ignoring pick-up looks in the bar, she was comfortable. This was her old stomping ground, loud and busy and familiar. She was glad to be back.

Since she was on Paris time, she was asleep by eight, and the next morning she met one friend for breakfast, another for coffee. Keeping busy seemed the way to go, so when she returned to her apartment she did laundry, dusted, vacuumed. After checking for e-mail, she went down the street for lunch. The café was a favorite of hers, another familiar spot. The yarn shop, though, was new. She went in, introduced herself, and browsed, but left empty-handed when nothing there was as beautiful as what Isabel Skane sold.

Home again, she kicked off her shoes, put on shorts, and, after tacking her unruly hair into a tortoise-shell claw, opened her Bordeaux folder and shifted papers around. And shifted papers around. And did it a little more.

Lacking incentive, she looked around for something else to do, but nothing appealed. Feeling hollow, she went to the window, folded her arms over her middle, and stared out through the thin blinds at nothing at all.

It was a minute before she saw the man. Leaning against the stoop of the town house across the street, he wore a ball cap, dark glasses, jeans and sneakers. A backpack lay by his feet. He was looking up at her window, his body alert. She might have thought he was casing the joint if it hadn't been for the bunch of yellow flowers he held. From Nicole? Not quite. Something about the way he stood—the way his jeans fit his hips, not quite loose, not quite tight—the way his legs were braced like he was on a boat—was very familiar. And then there was his sweater.

Her heart nearly stopped when the last registered. She had dreamed, but hadn't dared hope. Romantic wasn't reality. And this wasn't Quinnipeague on a cool, *thick o' fog,* wood-smoke summer morning, but Brooklyn on a warm and hazy September afternoon.

In a split second, heart pounding now, she realized what it had taken for him to come here, and still she stood for disbelieving seconds after that, feet rooted to the faded carpet.

She blinked, and he remained.

Real.

Suddenly not rooted there at all, she flew from the apartment and raced down two flights in her bare feet. Flinging open the front door, she darted out, but stopped on the top step. With the glasses and cap, with the jeans, sneaks, even the flowers, he might have been any man. But no other one would be wearing an Irish knit sweater in 78-degree heat, much less a sweater with a lopsided cable on the left front and bunchy shoulders.

Holding the wrought-iron rail, she went slowly down the stairs, never once taking her eyes from him lest he disappear. She didn't stop at the bottom, but crossed the sidewalk and stepped off the curb without a glance either way.

His face was bronzed after a Quinnie summer, but his cheeks were flushed beyond that, and though she could see little of his brow beneath the big Q on the visor of his ball cap, his jaw, throat, and what little neck showed above the sweater looked damp.

"Do I know you?" she asked with her heart in her throat.

"I hope so," he replied in a low and shaky voice. "I sure as hell don't."

"Feeling strange?"

"Very."

"Because of the city?"

"Partly."

The thought crossed her mind that he had come to say good-bye, which would surely account for unease. But all this way? "Did you fly?"

"I don't fly."

"You don't leave Quinnipeague, either," she reminded him gently, inching closer as hope gained strength. "So you drove."

He shot a nervous glance down the street, where his dark blue pickup was parked. In that split second, she remembered making love against its side and felt a stab of want deep in her belly.

Inching closer still, desperate to touch but afraid to assume, she said, "You'll get a ticket parking there."

"I can pay a ticket. Will they tow?"

"Depends how long you're here." But she didn't want to go there yet. "How's Bear?"

"Nosin' around looking for you."

Her throat closed up. Bear always did that to her. But why Bear and not Leo? Perhaps because Bear's love was unconditional. And because loving a dog was allowed.

But Bear wasn't here, and Leo was—and she ached to be allowed to love him, too. Eyes filling, she pressed her lips together to stop their trembling, but it wasn't enough. On tiptoe, she snaked her arms around his neck and buried her face in his throat. He smelled of sweat and soap—and balsam and pine, lavender, valerian, sage, thyme, and mint, and fried clams and *chowdah*, and the beach, and the ocean. He smelled of Quinnipeague, because he *was* Quinnipeague.

Unable to contain the sheer fullness of it all, she began to weep—Charlotte, who never wept except with Leo. With a guttural sound, he wrapped one arm around her, anchoring her tightly to him, while the other smoothed tendrils of hair from her face before pressing the back of her head to his throat. He kissed her hair and was inching closer to her temple when she drew back.

"What *took* you so long?" she charged in a nasal voice.

He might have argued that she had been away and only now returned, and that she was the one who had left in the first place—and she would have thrown back words like cell phone, e-mail, and text.

Instead, succinct and wry, he said, "I'm a slow learner."

Just like that, her anger was gone, and her heart was melting in puddles. She could live with this kind of honesty—speaking of which, as she tried to blot her tears, she said, "I look awful."

"You look beautiful." He held her gaze.

But his eyes were only shallow shapes on the far side of dark. Needing to see the whole of them, she lifted his Ray-Bans—and then barely breathed. Here was a stunning midnight blue with not a trace of defiance or disdain, nothing of the wall, just deep, deep need and want and fear.

Then his lips moved. Had her eyes not been wet, she might have read his lips. But tears blurred the words. So she asked, "What?"

He whispered it this time.

Her heart caught. "Again," she whispered back.

"I love you," he said, not quite full voice, but intimate and exposed and so *Leo* that she had to believe.

Her tears threatened again. But his eyes remained so dark, so worried, so fearful, that she could only blink and hold her breath.

"Is it still there?" he asked in that same not-quite-full voice.

Releasing the breath, she smiled. "It doesn't go away, Leo. It's always there. That's what I've been trying to tell you. When it's real, it stays."

"This is real?"

She nodded. Her eyes fell to the bunch of flowers that still hung from his hand. And suddenly, with a clumping of little threads of thought, she frowned. "When did you get here?"

"An hour ago. I was thinking you'd come in a cab. Your flight must've been early."

"Nicole told you."

"Oh yeah," he drawled, facetious in a way Charlotte totally got. "In no uncertain terms. She hates me."

"She does not. I'm sure there's pride involved, and stubbornness. But if she called to tell you when I was landing and that you had to be here with flowers—"

"The flowers were my idea," he said and, as if in proof, a van pulled up just then with the logo of a local flower shop on the side.

Minutes later, Charlotte was holding the bushiest arrangement of wildflowers she had ever seen. It was actually pretty ugly, but of course, Nicole was making a statement about how much prettier wildflowers were in a Quinnipeague fall, and that Charlotte needed to come see for herself.

"These'll be dead in no time," she decided as her eyes moved to the yellow roses, "but not those. They need water. Want to come up?"

"Christ," he breathed, "I thought you'd never ask. It's hot as hell out here."

"That's because you're wearing a heavy old handmade sweater. Why in this heat?"

"It was the only thing holding me together."

They were barely able to put the roses in water, before the sweater came off, then shirts and pants and the rest—all this with perfect air-conditioning, but the need to be together was overwhelming. They made love a dozen ways, from floor to bed to shower and back. Charlotte had never been as insatiable, but then, she had been without Leo for a month, and she was in love.

Not that Leo flagged. He was, in a word, awesome. Actually, he was also *wordy*, telling her that he loved her over and over again. She didn't think she would ever tire of that.

As afternoon morphed into evening, though, there were practical matters to consider, like stashing the truck and buying food for dinner, but both were easily handled. The truck went behind the Jeep in the alley of a friend several streets over, and they brought in Thai, which Leo had requested, and since he'd never had it before, Charlotte ordered a selection. He liked some dishes better than others, but long before the food was gone, he was starting to drag. Having made the crossing from Quinnipeague to Rockland with the truck the afternoon before, he had left there at three this morning to allow for traffic and terror and getting lost.

So Leo, her man of the night on Quinnipeague, dragged her back to bed in Brooklyn and made sweet, sweet love to her one more time before falling asleep. Not her. She wasn't tired in the least. She was too pumped up to sleep, too enthralled by the sight of Leo in her bed to want to close her eyes at all.

Besides, moments before dropping off, he had reached into his backpack and pulled out a manuscript.

"Next Book?" Charlotte asked excitedly.

He shook his head and nudged the wad of papers into her hand. Then, lying on his side facing her, he pushed the pillow to fit his neck, and closed his eyes.

Charlotte stared at him. When it became clear that he wouldn't explain—that he was actually that quickly asleep—she turned to the cover page. *Roots and All That Other Dirty Stuff,* it read. She turned to the next page. *For Charlotte.*

Swallowing, she started to read.

It would never be published, of course, though not because it wasn't beautifully written. He was a natural; that was clear from the start. He had put several hundred pages together in three weeks, and the prose was as lyrical as in *Salt,* though Charlotte knew he couldn't have had time for much editing. Here was catharsis in its most raw form—a spilling out of thirty-eight years of brief victories overshadowed by anger, resentment, and fear.

This was Leo's own, very personal story, written perhaps for Charlotte but surely finished for himself. He had told her the basics before, but now he elaborated on the feelings he'd had for his mother and the island. He wrote of his dreams of having a father. He wrote of defiance and sadness, of confusion and floundering. He wrote of island girls and sex and his lover from Phoenix, none of which Charlotte found offensive, what with the wrongness of those relationships so clear in light of the man she knew. He wrote about seeing Charlotte in the dark of his drive that first night, of what their summer together had meant to him and how, when she left, he was paralyzed at first, then disgusted enough with himself and his fear to know what he had to do.

And what he had to do, for starters, was to see his father. It wasn't an easy visit for either of them, what with no history of communication, no guidelines for father-son relationships, no filters to soften hair-trigger emotions. Leo had been brutally honest, largely angry and accusatory, surely arrogant when he told the man about *Salt*. He hadn't planned on doing that. He knew the risk of exposure, and he didn't trust this stranger.

But *Salt* had seemed a vital connection to make. With its ties to the sea, to longing and dreams, it was a big piece of who he was.

His father was older than he remembered, newly retired from the police department, outwardly defensive at times, but listening. Would there be a détente? Leo didn't know. But hours of blunt talk—this act of tearing up negative roots and leaving the ground tilled and waiting, as Leo put it—was what he had to do before leaving the State of Maine for the first time in his life.

And he did have to leave, or, at least, had to be able to do it. Having taken Charlotte's arguments to heart, he spared himself nothing on that score. Narrow-minded, he called himself. Selfish. Cowardly. As insecure as that little boy sleeping outside with the herbs, he didn't paint himself in the best of lights, not even with the success of *Salt*. And yet he came across shining in Charlotte's eyes.

By the time she finished reading, it was three in the morning, and his words had brought her to tears a dozen times. Leo slept through it all. She didn't know how. Hadn't he wanted to see her reactions? But no, she realized. He was using sleep so that he wouldn't see, wouldn't worry or fear. Through it all, though, he kept a physical link, be it the touch of a toe, a hand, a leg.

Seeming to sense when she finished, he stretched, opened one eye, then the other as he regained awareness, and quickly grew wary. He waited for her to speak, but what could she say? He had lived through the kind of angst that, for all her own loneliness, she couldn't imagine. And his father? The man claimed Cecily had threatened mayhem if he interfered with Leo's life, and he had felt just bewitched enough by her to believe it. Cecily hadn't known that he was the one directing the lawyer who got Leo off with five years in prison rather than ten, or that he was instrumental in having charges dropped the second time around, when Leo was falsely charged.

Reaching up, he touched the tears on her face, but she didn't want that. Nor did she want sex. Sliding down, she squirreled one arm under, stretched one arm over, and held him tightly enough so he'd know she wasn't ever letting go. In time, he switched it up, holding her while she slept with her ear to his heart.

When she finally awoke, a midday sun was heating the carpet, and he announced that he wanted to go into the city. Charlotte was startled. "Manhattan?" She would have thought he'd have wanted to take it slow, fanning out from her neighborhood in baby steps. Manhattan was a shock for people from other cities, let alone those from tiny islands.

But he nodded. "Fifth Avenue." He was sure.

That said, when they left open air to go underground for the subway, he held her hand as though his life depended on it. Stop to stop, he was guarded, and when they emerged in Midtown, his eyes held a mix of terror and awe. But he was cool—oh, he was cool. Betrayed only by the bob of his Adam's apple, he studied the street signs. He had clearly done his homework; he knew how the grid worked. After several blocks, he began checking numbers. When he found the one he wanted, he opened the large door and stood aside.

Charlotte, to whom the number meant nothing, but the store name etched over the stone portal did, shot him a questioning look. He simply hitched his head, indicating that she should precede him. Once inside, he went to the nearest salesperson and, in a quiet, confident voice, asked for Victoria Harper, who, it turned out, was the assistant manager with whom he had talked earlier that week. If Charlotte hadn't already been stunned by his *savoir-faire*, she would have been moments later when the woman guided them to a display case filled with diamond rings. The elegant Ms. Harper proceeded to pull out several that, apparently, she and Leo had agreed to on the phone.

Charlotte pressed shaky fingers to her mouth, though she couldn't have talked if she'd wanted to. All she could do was to stare at the rings, then at Leo, who smiled with equal parts shyness, excitement, and pride. "What did you expect?" he asked.

Blindly, she groped for his hand, which seemed the only real thing in the place. "I, uh . . . I didn't . . . I-I hadn't planned—"

"Is that a no?"

"It's a yes yes *yes*, but . . . *Tiffany's*?" she cried and added in an astonished whisper, "It's too *much*."

"Not for me," he said, "not if you love one of these."

She loved Leo. She didn't need a ring. But he had planned it all out, and he seemed to know exactly what he was doing. If he had learned sophistication from fictional characters, they had taught him well. As suave as he was in as fabled a store as this, his eyes were earnest. He wanted her happy.

She studied the rings. Each was stunning. Most women didn't have a choice; she could see the advantage of that. With a hand pressed to her chest, she went back and forth, but it was overwhelming.

"If you don't like these, there are others," he said, nervous now. "Or we can have one designed."

"Omigod, *no*, Leo," she said, clutching his hand to her throat. "These are *exquisite*."

"He knew what he wanted," said Victoria with a hint of something British in her voice. "He has very good taste."

Charlotte doubted that her own taste was as good, but her eye kept returning to one of the rings. It was a pear-shaped diamond flanked by tapering baguettes. She liked the simplicity of it, liked the spark the diamond emitted.

Within minutes, it was on her finger. She could hardly breathe.

It had to be sized, but smart Leo had made that part of the deal. The chosen ring went to the in-store silversmith for an hour, during which time they walked outside and, for the first time, he took in the grandeur of Manhattan in general, and Rockefeller Center and St. Patrick's Cathedral in particular. Charlotte was the one who clung now—to his arm, his hand, his side—more amazed at the courage of her husband-to-be than anything the city had to offer.

When they returned to Tiffany's, the ring was waiting, sparklingly alive in a velvet-lined box. Charlotte inhaled a stunned gasp, again thinking it was way too expensive, way too large, way too *flawless* for someone as flawed as she. But Leo was removing it from its bed, dropping to one knee, and offering himself to her. He didn't speak. Didn't have to. She heard the words loud and clear in the sweet, shy, vulnerable look on his face.

Grinning, she held out a shaky finger. He slid the ring on, then rose and, slipping his hands into her hair, tipped her face up for the simplest, most honest kiss. Only when it was done did she hear the applause of onlookers, at which point, embarrassed in a delighted way, she tucked her face into his neck.

It couldn't have been better scripted if he had written the scene himself.

Epilogue

JUNE WOULD ALWAYS BE CHARLOTTE'S favorite month on Quinnipeague. She loved the purples and pinks of new flowers and the smell of moist earth. She loved the frothy roil of the sea as it recovered from a day of rain, and in those early mornings, before the fog lifted and sun warmed the island, there was nothing, *nothing* better than a wood fire, wool socks, and hot chocolate made from scratch.

She had the hot chocolate this morning, but with Leo back in bed, she didn't need the fire or the socks. Propped against the headboard, he was typing away, but looked over when he felt her eyes on him.

"Happy anniversary," she whispered, cradling the warm mug as she lay on her side.

He raised a brow. "Not 'til October."

"It was one year ago tonight that I first walked here and saw you on your roof."

Amused, he considered that. "Only a year?"

"Weird, isn't it."

He opened an arm for her to scoot closer. Hadn't they been this way forever? But no. They had come from totally different places, which should have made compatibility a challenge. And yet, as easy as it was for Charlotte to see his side, what gratified her most was how safe he now felt in moving toward hers.

Not that they had ever disagreed about getting married quickly and on Quinnipeague. Leo wanted a small wedding, and Charlotte would have been happy exchanging vows at the end of the dock or in the herb garden. But Quinnies were vocal about wanting to attend, and she loved this community she was marrying into. "It's a tribute to you," she told Leo when he hedged at the thought of a crowd. "They're saying that they know your childhood was hell, they're sorry they didn't do more, and they really like you. They do, Leo."

In essence, Quinnies ran the wedding, which was fine with Charlotte, who didn't know the first thing about running anything beyond a dinner for four . . . and that, with take-in. Nicole had offered to help and did take her wedding-gown shopping. But Nicole was busy shuttling between Philadelphia and New York, working with her editor to get the cookbook into production, and giving Julian emotional support at a time when his future hadn't quite taken shape.

The ceremony was held in the church. Charlotte wore a stunning white gown, which was as close as she came to traditional, what with her hair loose and curling, her fingernails painted blue, and Bear walking her down the aisle. They went slow. Bear's excuse was arthritis, hers the four-inch heels Nicole had insisted she wear, though the heels came off for the progressive celebration that followed, starting with champagne on the front steps of the church, moving on to appetizers at the Island Grill, dinner at the Chowder House, and dancing under a heated tent on Nicole's patio.

Leo's dad, though a Mainer with a long history of public service, was awkward with Quinnies. He knew many of those there, but if they didn't resent him for abandoning Cecily, they did for abandoning Leo. They were polite, but there was clearly no love lost on his behalf. Julian, who didn't know all that many Quinnies, enjoyed discussing law enforcement, so kept an eye on him.

"What're you thinking?" Leo whispered now. He had a hand on her belly, which was seriously swollen. She was seven months pregnant. Four more weeks on the island, then they would shift to New York for the duration.

"Your dad. We should take him to dinner on our way to New York."

"Why?"

Charlotte gave him a chiding pinch. "Because he's your dad. And because he's LL's grandfather." LL was little Leo, though Leo was adamant about not naming the baby after him. He wanted Ethan, after the hero of *Salt*. Charlotte loved that name, too, though she felt that, in the absence of in-utero clothing, LL was more boyish than LE.

Leo didn't reply. She knew he would come around about his father. He usually did, not that they saw the man often. He certainly wasn't an active player in their lives. Still, he and Leo did share genes. Charlotte, being Charlotte and incorrigibly curious, had found common ground with him discussing granite quarrying, which was part of the midcoast Maine history and about which it appeared he knew a great deal.

It was about roots. Charlotte was finally growing them now and was greedy. Not the least bit ashamed of that, she snuggled in.

He drew his head back to see her face. "That's a smug smile. What now?"

She shrugged, grinned, eyed his computer. "I'm thinking how far you've come."

"Literally?"

"That, too."

He was on his second book—actually, the second one after *Salt*—and just starting Chapter 16, if the screen was to be believed. He claimed Charlotte was his muse, but she knew better. Having exorcised a raft of demons, his mind had opened. He would never love traveling as much as he loved Quinnipeague, but his world had begun to grow. After New York had come a honeymoon in New Zealand, then a week in Eastern Europe, where Charlotte was on assignment, then one in Iceland. Though he would only admit it when forced, new places inspired him. Once the baby was big enough to tuck in a carrier, they would be traveling not for her work, but his.

With the help of his lawyer, Leo had hired an agent who sold the second Chris Mauldin for bigger bucks than he had ever dreamed. He had written it in four brief winter months, and, having proven to himself that he *could*, had signed another contract. The deal specified that Chris Mauldin would neither tour nor do anything else to reveal his identity, and though his publisher fought him on the issue of confidentiality, Leo wasn't budging. Moreover, he would only meet with his agent or editor in the office of his attorney. Slightly paranoid? Perhaps. But they were hungry enough for his books to agree.

With the advance he received for *Salt's* successor, he had bought a brownstone in Brooklyn, where they spent much of their work time at catty-cornered desks. Bear was with them, sleeping through the long drive, too old to care about the change in location or even about having to wear a leash. Leo was probably more aware of the leash than Bear was. Tethered to the dog, he ventured farther afield on his own. And then there was the reality of a hospital. Having accepted that Charlotte absolutely would *not* give birth at home, he used tours and birthing classes to mitigate his unease. It helped that Nicole and Julian were doing the same in Philadelphia; Nicole was due three weeks after Charlotte.

And Julian? Eight months after the transplant, he was remarkably well. Though his symptoms had improved, the hospital wouldn't allow him to operate. He had known that would be so. Still, it was a door that had closed once and for all, and he took it hard. Then alternatives had sprung up. He was on television more than ever, as something of a poster child now for MS, a motivational speaker at events, an advocate for pushing the envelope of medical trials—all of which was great publicity for Nickitotable and her cookbook.

A vibration sounded on Charlotte's nightstand. Rolling herself over, she put the mug there in exchange for the phone.

"Just wanted to hear your voice," Nicole said. Pregnancy had left her breathless, which ratcheted up her voice to the pitch it used to be. But she didn't babble as much. She had grown up that last summer. It wasn't a bad thing.

Actually, it was a good thing for Charlotte, since they were in touch every day—often multiple times—sharing advice, complaints, fears. And since Charlotte was trying to get ahead on her own assignments, brief calls or texts worked best.

"Feeling okay?" she asked now.

"I do not like this extra weight. But there's good news," Nicole said, clearly struggling to contain her excitement. "We're into a third printing." The cookbook had come out in time for Mother's Day, with promotions planned for summer sales. Since those had yet to begin, something was working even without. "They are thrilled. And my editor says, by the way, that heartburn is not necessarily a sign that the baby will have hair, since she had heartburn the whole time and her baby turned out bald."

Charlotte laughed. "I don't have heartburn, just hiccups. What does that mean?" She felt the bed move as Leo slid down behind her.

"ADHD?" Nicole ventured.

"I seriously hope not," Charlotte said, covering Leo's hands when they covered her baby bump.

"Maybe he'll be a dancer."

"Uh-huh," Charlotte drawled. "Tap."

"Or a workout guru. Hit it big in that, and you can do really well. Mine, now mine will be an inventor, kind of like its dad."

Charlotte only heard part of the last. Leo was nibbling her ear. "Okay, Nicki, I have to run. Talk later." She hung up, pushed the phone under the pillow, and smiled at the far wall. "What are you up to?"

"Up," was all he said, though she could certainly feel that. He snaked a hand under her tee—his actually—and stroked her breast. "When's she coming?"

"Soon," Charlotte murmured, there so quickly, given his clever fingers and mobile hips.

His breath was warm against her ear, his smile audible, his up larger. "Not you. Nicole."

"Next week," she managed, breathing shallowly. Angie was already on Quinnipeague, beside herself in anticipation of *two* births as she opened the house for the season. Tom had come to help, but would be leaving before Nicole arrived. That said, Nicole was starting to come around, with Bob gone now for eighteen . . . uh, twenty . . . uh, however many months—Charlotte couldn't think straight with Leo's hand between her legs. When his leg raised hers and he entered her from behind, she gasped at the beauty of the fullness. There had always been physical chemistry between them, but add emotional chemistry to it and the pleasure exploded. This was one of the pieces that Charlotte had never had with anyone else.

Though he barely moved, the heat was searing. Ever so slowly, it built and burst, and for a time after that, all she knew was a residual panting at her ear, the rapid rise and fall of his warm, now-damp torso against her back, and fading spasms inside.

When it finally ended, she rolled herself over, cupped his chin, and met the deep blue eyes that she desperately wanted their son to have.

"I hate not looking at you," she whispered.

"I don't want anything between us."

"Not even your own child?"

"Nope, not even him," Leo said and grinned. He did that a lot now. It wasn't the mean grin of a guy with a chip on his shoulder and a fear of flying, but the smug one of a happy man.

Lost in it, she couldn't speak, but could only look at him and feel the love link they shared.

Raising a brow, he made a show of turning his ear her way. "Nothing to say?"

She smiled back, as smug and happy as he was, and simply shook her head.

Acknowledgments

Sweet Salt Air marks the start of a new phase in my career as I begin work with the talented and energetic team at St. Martin's Press. There are so many people to thank. Topping the list, though, have to be my editor, Hilary Rubin Teeman, whose in-depth notes reflect the in-depth thoughts that I need, and my publisher, Matthew Shear, who quickly asked me where I want to go and, as quickly, pointed me there. Still, yet again, I thank my agent, Amy Berkower, for her sound advice and unflagging support, both professionally and politically.

Thanks to my assistant, Lucy Davis, for one very special contact above and beyond the rest—to wit, Dr. John Wagner, whom I thank profusely for his dedication to umbilical cord stem cell research. I asked him to share his thoughts of the future with me, and he did. I dreamed that by the time this book was published, treatments such as the one described here would be the norm. They aren't yet, but we're getting there.

In that sense, I would be remiss if I didn't acknowledge the estimated 2.1 million people who, at this writing, have multiple sclerosis. You helped me understand the frustration, pain, and fear this disease brings. I wish you all the very, very best as medical breakthroughs approach.

More generally, I thank my readers for their loyalty and patience as they allow me time to write a better book.

Finally, always, I thank my family for its love. I am one very lucky soul. I wake up every morning knowing that.

SWEET SALT AIR

by Barbara Delinsky

Reading
Group
Gold

About the Author

• A Conversation with Barbara Delinsky

Behind the Novel

• "The Art of Friendship"
An Original Essay by the Author

Keep on Reading

• Recommended Reading
• Reading Group Questions

*A
Reading
Group Gold
Selection*

For more reading group suggestions,
visit www.readinggroupgold.com.

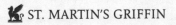 ST. MARTIN'S GRIFFIN

 *A Conversation with Barbara Delinsky*

The main characters in *Sweet Salt Air*, Nicole and Charlotte, are old friends now in their mid-thirties. Is there something about that age for women that particularly interested you?

Absolutely. I had my kids in my early twenties when we were young and stupid. But for a lot of women now, their early- to mid-thirties is a time for saying, "OK, is this the career I want? Or should I be heading in another direction?" In Nicole's case, she's built a whole career, but it's about to take off in a different way because of her contract to write a cookbook. Charlotte, on the other hand, is just not sure if she's satisfied with where she's been. I think the mid-thirties is a vulnerable time for a lot of women. They aren't so stuck in what they're doing that they can't change. I like change in my characters. I like to see them grow.

You've returned to coastal Maine, a setting you've used in many of your novels. What's the allure of that landscape?

I am my quintessential reader. I need to be in a setting that speaks to me. When things are really hectic, I love nothing more than to be able to go and stand by the water. The North Atlantic coast is a bit wild and there's a rocky shoreline, but it does soothe me. There is also something very romantic about it.

"I like change in my characters. I like to see them grow."

Nicole's husband has MS. How does this impact their lives?

Nicole's husband is a prenatal cardiac surgeon. His work requires intricate detail, and suddenly his hands shake. He is hoping that there is some kind of cure. He's done a lot of research, being a doctor, and he knows that there might be some things on the horizon, such as umbilical cord blood transplants, but he also knows that everything is experimental. He wants to preserve his future, and to do that he needs to be very secretive. He doesn't tell anyone that he has MS—and that means Nicole can't tell anyone either.

When I was diagnosed with breast cancer almost twenty years ago, I didn't tell anybody except for close family and very close friends. Honestly, I didn't want publishers in New York to think I'd be dead in five years and not bother pushing my books. That's the blunt bottom line. For that reason, I perfectly understand why he didn't want to say anything.

What are some of the other dynamics at play in their relationship?

Nicole doesn't have a parallel career to his. That's a biggie. My husband and I do have parallel careers—he's a lawyer and I'm a writer, and we each have similar clout in the marriage. My career has given me a kind of courage to speak up when I need to, even though we got married at a time when marriages were more conventional. When my kids were little, my husband never changed a diaper, but my sons all change diapers and they cook. In so many regards, Nicole and Julian adhere to more traditional gender roles. Nicole defers to him.

Your characters Charlotte and Nicole are collaborating on a cookbook in this novel. Are you much of a whiz in the kitchen?

No, I'm not. Isn't that hysterical? I was just talking with my publicist about why I chose to discuss the farm-to-table movement. The reason I did is because I like to deal with things that are current and in the news. Also, as a breast cancer survivor, I wonder about environmental factors. I am glad my granddaughters drink organic milk. My being a non-cook was only an issue when my publisher asked if I had any recipes I could share. I had to say no.

So the dark secret of Barbara Delinsky is that she hates to cook?

That's it! I love reading cookbooks, and I love eating out, but I don't like cooking. I buy a lot of stuff ready-made—dinner tonight is chicken cacciatore from Whole Foods.

You've written traditional romance novels as well as contemporary women's fiction. Are those genres closer than we think? What are the differences?

Length is the first. The romances I wrote were two hundred pages, as opposed to four hundred like my more recent novels. The other difference is scope. I wanted to deal with topics that were considered a little too serious for the romance genre. My romances were always 80 percent romance, 20 percent something else. When I moved into mainstream fiction, the equation reversed. Actually, at my publisher's request, *Sweet Salt Air*

"I love reading cookbooks, and I love eating out, but I don't like cooking."

has more romance in it than the books I've written in the last ten years. When I write contemporary fiction, I can divide the book as I want, as opposed to being restricted to the romance.

That said, you have a lot of experience writing sex scenes. What's the key to writing a believable one?

Emotion. If a sex scene is purely physical, it doesn't work for me. Conversely, when a sex scene incorporates the emotion ongoing in the story, it can be richer. I don't write gratuitous sex scenes, as in sex for the sake of sex. Every scene has to move the plot forward.

Do you ever read them aloud to your husband?

No. My husband doesn't read my books, but then I don't read his law briefs. He knows what every book of mine is about. I talk my plots through with him and he may help with legal matters in them. But my books have no place in our bed at night.

I read that your first book took you three months to plan and draft. Are you always this fast?

Try three weeks! That was one of the category romances and they were very short: 55,000 to 60,000 words. At the beginning I was that fast. I had three young boys at home. We didn't have any money. My husband was a lawyer in public service at the time. With a house full of boys, it was constantly noisy and dirty. Writing was my escape. I spent every spare minute doing it. There were a couple of years early on in which I wrote eight books!

Describe a typical day spent writing. Do you have any unusual writing habits?

Unusual? Not really. A typical day writing is probably 6 a.m. to noon, Monday through Friday, and my office is pretty standard. It's a room above the garage; a nice, bright room with skylights. There's a sitting area, lots of bookshelves, and Post-its everywhere. They are the best invention since bagged lettuce.

What authors, books, or ideas have influenced you?

I read a very eclectic selection of books. I'm in a book group that's been meeting for twenty-six years. My own reading choices are usually new releases which show me what other writers are doing right now. [You can learn more about Barbara's book club in the Recommended Reading section in this guide.]

Excerpted from an interview by Margaret Wappler for Goodreads. Reprinted with permission.

"Writing was my escape. I spent every spare minute doing it."

"The Art of Friendship"

Friendship has always intrigued me. Go to a restaurant on a Thursday night, for instance, and you see some tables with eight women, others with two. Watching the women at one of those large tables, all laughing and comfortable, clearly good friends, a tiny part of me is often envious. But only a tiny part. My own preference is sitting with a BFF and talking one-on-one for several hours.

Behind the Novel

BFF is an easy term. The closest I can find to a documented origin is 1997 in the TV show *Friends,* though there are those who claim that they used it themselves well before that. Me? Many times in books I refer to "Friend with a capital F" versus "friend with a small f." I believe that while most of us have many of the latter, we're lucky to have even a few of the former.

What does it mean to be a Best Friend Forever? It often implies a shared past, though one friend I now consider a BFF is someone I met last year! BFFs may not see each other often, or text or e-mail or talk on the phone, but when they do get together, they pick up right where they left off and go on from there. BFFs respect each other enough to put their own needs aside if the other's immediate needs are greater, and trust each other enough to say *anything* with the confidence that it will be understood, accepted, and held private. BFFs know each other, warts and all, and love each other no matter what.

From the get-go, I knew that I wanted *Sweet Salt Air* to deal with friendship, and while it also revolves around other affairs of the heart, friendship is key. Nicole and Charlotte are childhood friends who haven't seen each other in ten years. Reuniting at the start of a pivotal summer, they do pick up where they left off—at least, until Charlotte confesses to having wronged Nicole in a totally reprehensible way. Nicole is devastated. "I thought you were my BFF," she cries. "A BFF is supposed to be loyal. She's supposed to be honest and considerate and generous. She's supposed to sacrifice something she wants if she knows that getting it will hurt the other." There's lots of repair work to do, on *both* sides, at a time when each desperately needs a friend.

I confess. I do have several former BFFs whose life needs evolved into such conflict with mine that we drifted apart and remain so. But the others—ah, the others—are vital to my psyche. I'm busy, they're busy. But if I needed them, they'd be there in a heartbeat. In this, I consider myself blessed.

Recommended Reading

Dear Reader,

I've been in the same book group for twenty-six years. A dozen women, give or take, we meet monthly, pick our list in June for the following year, and rotate leaders and hosts. This is not a reading group for writers; our occupations cover the spectrum. When we first formed, though, many of us were home with young children and little time to read, but we were hungry for a night out, some wine and cheese, and a meaty discussion. Over the years, certain books have been especially memorable. Here are a few, with a brief explanation why.

John Irving's *A Prayer for Owen Meany* was an early winner. The imagery worked for us, as did the New England setting, vivid characters such as Owen and his voice, and the element of the Vietnam War, through which we all lived.

The Awakening, by Kate Chopin, astoundingly first published in 1899, tapped into our evolving thoughts on feminism and motherhood, and our awe that this book could be written at that time.

Die-hard northerners, we loved glimpsing the American South in novels such as *Charms for the Easy Life* by Kaye Gibbons and *Fried Green Tomatoes at the Whistle Stop Cafe* by Fannie Flagg.

Each year, we try to pick a classic that we may have read in school but will now see with adult eyes. We've had great discussions on *My Ántonia* by Willa Cather, *To Kill a Mockingbird* by Harper Lee, and *Lady Chatterley's Lover* by D. H. Lawrence.

We loved Wallace Stegner's *Crossing to Safety* for its insight into relationships, and were amazed that this man wrote so successfully in a female voice. We had a similar discussion, with differing opinions this time, on *Memoirs of a Geisha* by Arthur Golden.

More on differing opinions: Some of our most interesting—and raucously memorable—evenings have involved books some of us adored and others hated. These included *Eat, Pray, Love* by Elizabeth Gilbert, *The Interestings* by Meg Wolitzer, and *Atonement* by Ian McEwan. Funny, but in none of these instances did any of our members switch sides. Not so with *Unbroken* by Laura Hillenbrand. After an emotional discussion of the price of war—on our own families, as well as on the characters in this book—many of us who began on the thumbs-down side had changed our minds. That's what a book group discussion can do. Then there was *Exit the Rainmaker* by Jonathan Coleman. A fictionalized account of a community college president who, of his own volition, simply vanished one

day, the book was our springboard to a discussion of where we would go and what we would do if we chose to disappear. That discussion turned out to be utterly fun.

In case you're wondering: No, we have not discussed *Sweet Salt Air*—but not because we wouldn't have a field day discussing friendship, family troubles, and marital stress. We would, but I suffer discussing any book of my own. Think about it. Would the discussion really be an honest one, with me sitting there and my friends wanting, above all, to be supportive and polite? I fear not, but I love this group to bits for that.

Yours,
Barbara

*Keep
on
Reading*

1. Quinnipeague is a fictional island, but based very closely on the many islands that dot Maine's coast and are popular with summer visitors. Have you been to a seasonal island or beach community on vacation? How was Quinnipeague similar to these places you've visited? What characteristics make Quinnipeague unique? What interesting dynamics play out in the story because of the seasonal nature of Quinnipeague? What differences did you find between the characters who are "locals" and those who are "summer people?"

2. One of the main plotlines in *Sweet Salt Air* revolves around Charlotte's and Nicole's efforts to write a cookbook. What is the significance of food—how it's prepared, served, and appreciated—in *Sweet Salt Air*? What makes the island's food special to the two women? Do they view food, and the process of collecting recipes and the stories behind them, differently?

3. Talk about the characters' lives off the island of Quinnipeague—Charlotte, who lives in Brooklyn but travels constantly, and Nicole who is firmly rooted to her home in Philadelphia. What does each woman's lifestyle reveal about her personality? Do their lifestyle choices seem in keeping with what the novel reveals about them?

4. If you were Nicole, could you forgive Charlotte for what she did? Do you think

there are some things in friendship that are unforgiveable? Do you think Charlotte has forgiven herself? If yes, what happened on the island that allowed her to forgive herself? If not, what do you think she still needs to do?

5. Nicole and Julian face challenges, but every marriage is tested at one time or another. What do you think is the hardest test? Illness? Infidelity? Money? Are we stronger for the suffering? In what ways?

6. Cecily Cole is a presence throughout the book, despite her death several years earlier. How do the locals see Cecily and her garden? How does Cecily's spirit affect each character in the novel? How do Leo's descriptions of Cecily as a mother affect your view of her? Do you believe in the kind of lingering legacy that the women discover in the herbs and food of Quinnipeague?

7. Discuss the role of *Salt* to the story in *Sweet Salt Air*. Do you and your friends have the same taste in books? How do Charlotte's and Nicole's differing reactions to the book reflect their natures? How did you enjoy the experience of hearing about a book you could not read? Were you surprised when you learned who had written *Salt*?

8. Nicole is upset over Angie's relationship with Tom. Do you feel that she's justified? Have you ever witnessed a parent's romantic involvement with a nonparent of yours? What emotions were involved for you? For your parent?

9. Leo has a "bad boy" edge. Does this make him more attractive to Charlotte? Do you think a little rebellion is attractive? Leo has committed some crimes in his life, crimes for which he's served time in jail. What is your sense of how Leo's time in jail affected him? Has he changed? Does doing bad things make us bad people? And what about Charlotte, who's committed no crimes, and yet, she's done some terrible things? Would you characterize Charlotte as "bad?"

10. If you could ask the author anything about *Sweet Salt Air*—clarification of a plot point, a detail about a particular character, scenes from the cutting-room floor—what would it be? (You may choose to contact Barbara Delinsky, via her Web site or Facebook, and ask her!)

Coming soon…

Home is where the heart is…but what happens when a mother and daughter find themselves on opposite sides of the picket fence?

Don't miss the next novel from beloved bestselling author Barbara Delinsky, who "combines her understanding of human nature with absorbing, unpredictable storytelling" (*Publishers Weekly*) in ways that no reader will soon forget.

Available in June 2015, in hardcover, from St. Martin's Press

Download These Books from *New York Times* Bestselling Author Barbara Delinsky!

Crosslyn Rise E-Trilogy

Matchmaker E-Trilogy

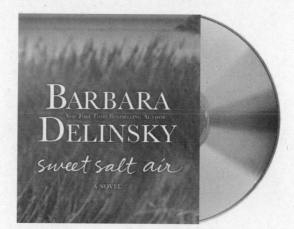